THE LAST CONCUBINE

An epic evocation of a country in revolution...

It is 1861. Growing up in rural Japan, Sachi has always felt different, with her pale skin and fine features. Then, when she is just eleven, an imperial princess passes through her village and sweeps her off to the women's palace in the great city of Edo, where she is chosen as the concubine of the young shogun. But Japan is changing. As civil war erupts, Sachi flees for her life. Rescued by a rebel warrior, she must unravel the mystery of her own origins – a mystery that encompasses a wrong so terrible that it threatens to destroy her.

THE LAST CONCUBINE

THE LAST CONCUBINE

by

Lesley Downer

Magna Large Print Books
Long Preston, North Yorkshire,
BD23 4ND, England.

British Library Cataloguing in Publication Data.

Downer, Lesley
    The last concubine.

    A catalogue record of this book is
    available from the British Library

    ISBN   978-0-7505-2995-2

First published in Great Britain in 2008 by Bantam Press
a division of Transworld Publishers

Copyright © Lesley Downer 2008

Cover illustration © Larry Rostant

Lesley Downer has asserted her right under the Copyright, Designs
and Patents Act, 1988 to be identified as the author of this work

Published in Large Print 2009 by arrangement with
Transworld Publishers

C460846041

Magna Large Print is an imprint of Library Magna Books Ltd.

Printed and bound in Great Britain by
T.J. (International) Ltd., Cornwall, PL28 8RW

To Arthur

If not to you,
To whom can I show
The plum tree's flower?
For, when it comes to colour and to scent,
Only he knows who truly knows

Ki no Tomonori

Contents

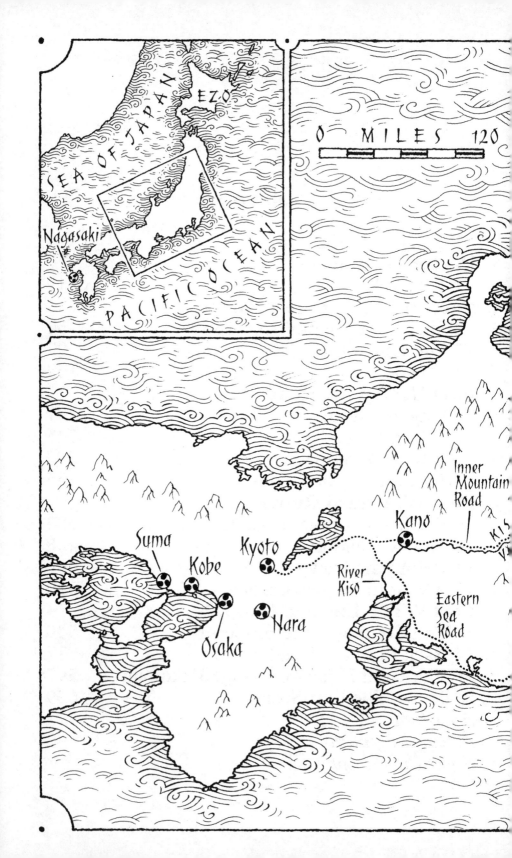

EZO

SEA OF JAPAN

PACIFIC OCEAN

Nagasaki

0 MILES 120

Inner Mountain Road

Kano

KIS

Suma

Kobe

Kyoto

River Kiso

Osaka

Nara

Eastern Sea Road

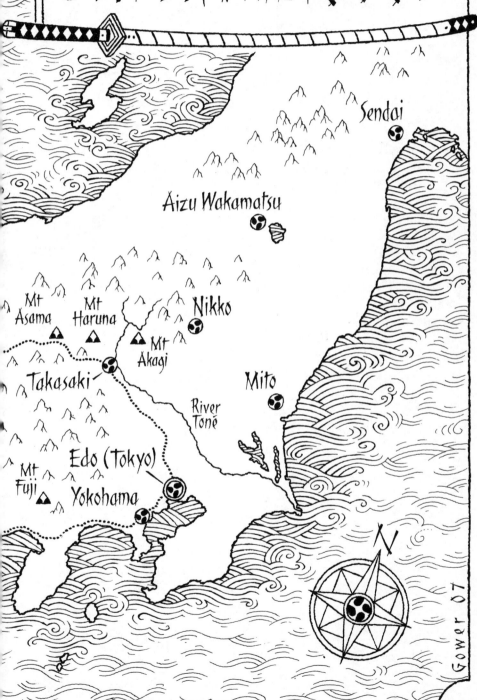

Part I
The Village

1

Kiso Valley, 1861

Oshikaraji   Without regret,
kimi to tami to no   If it is for you, my lord,
tame naraba   And your people,
mi wa Musashino no   I will vanish with the dew
tsuyu to kiyu tomo   On the plain of Musashi

Princess Kazu, 1861

I

'Shita ni iyo! Shita ni iyo! Shita ni... Shita ni... On your knees! On your knees! Get down... Get down...'

The shout came drifting across the valley, so faint it might have been the rustle of leaves carried on the wind. At the head of the pass, where the road dipped towards the village, four tousle-haired children bundled in faded, patched kimonos stood listening for all they were worth. It was one of those late autumn days when everything seems transfixed, as if waiting. The pine trees that fringed the highway were uncannily still and the lightest of breezes barely lifted the mouldering red and gold leaves that lay swept into tidy piles well away from the verges. A hawk circled lazily and for a moment a flock of wild

19

geese filled the sky. From around a corner in the road the familiar smell of woodsmoke mixed with horse dung, human waste and miso soup wafted up. From time to time a cockerel crowed and the village dogs replied with a chorus of baying. But apart from that, the valley was silent. Normally the highway would have been crammed with people, palanquins and horses, as far as the eye could see. That day it was completely empty.

That was how Sachi always remembered the day, when she thought back to it years later – the pine trees so tall and dark, soaring endlessly upwards, the bowl of the sky so blue that it seemed close enough to touch, far closer than the pale mountains that shimmered on the horizon.

Sachi was eleven, but small and slight. In summer she was as tawny as one of the famous Kiso horse chestnuts but now her skin was startlingly translucent and pale, almost as white as her breath in the frosty air. Often she wished she was brown and sturdy like the other children, though they didn't seem to care. Even her eyes were different. While theirs were brown or black, hers were dark green, as green as the pine trees in summer or the moss on the forest floor. But secretly, though she knew it was wrong, she rather liked her white skin. Sometimes she would kneel in front of her mother's tarnished mirror and look at her pale face glimmering there. Then she would take out the comb that she kept tucked in her sleeve. It was her talisman, her good luck charm, beautiful, shiny and sparkly. It had always been hers, ever since she could remember, and no one else had a comb like it. Slowly, pensively, she would comb her hair until it was shining, then tie it neatly back with a piece of bright red crepe.

A couple of summers earlier some travelling players had arrived in the village. For a few days they performed ghost stories on a makeshift stage, sending shivers down everyone's back. The children squatted together, frozen with fear, watching a drama about a deserted wife who dies from grief. At the end of the play the dead woman suddenly appeared floating in the air before her faithless husband, her face ghastly white. As she combed her long black hair, it fell out in clumps. The children screamed so much that no one could hear the actors' words. Now when the others wanted to tease Sachi they told her that she must be a ghost too.

'Sickly' was what her grandmother called her. Sometimes she heard her berating her mother. 'That child of yours, that Sa,' she would grumble. 'You spoil her! How do you expect her to get a husband, so pale and sickly as she is? And so vain, always combing that hair of hers. No one wants a wife who spends all her time in front of the mirror. You need a daughter with big child-bearing hips who knows how to work, that's what. Otherwise you'll be stuck with her.'

'She's delicate,' her mother would say mildly, smiling her tired, patient smile. 'She's not like the other children. But at least she's pretty.' She always took her side.

'"Pretty",' her grandmother would reply. 'That's all very well. What good is "pretty" for a farmer's wife?'

Rubbing her hands and blowing on them, Sachi

shifted from foot to foot. Despite the layers of rough cotton, the thick wadded jacket her mother had managed to find for her and the scarves wound around her head, she was still cold. The only thing that provided a little warmth was the baby tied in a sling on her back. She was fast asleep, her head flopping like a rag doll. Huddled next to Sachi was her friend Mitsu. The two had been inseparable since they were tiny. In appearance she was almost the exact opposite of Sachi, so brown and squat she was almost like a monkey, with small eyes and a pug nose.

When she was born, her mother had told the midwife to kill her. 'She's so ugly, she'll never get a husband,' she had said. 'And then what will we do with her?' The midwife nodded. It was a sensible request. Many babies were killed at birth. She spat on a bit of paper, put it over the baby's mouth and nose, then wrapped her up tightly in rags. But just as they thought she was dead, she started to wriggle, then to howl and bawl. The gods, it seemed, had decided she was to live. 'And who were we to interfere with the gods?' her mother said, spreading her work-reddened hands expansively. She seemed to love her daughter all the more because of her miraculous escape. Mitsu, a cheerful, down-to-earth, motherly girl, was not at all worried by the story. Like Sachi, she carried one of her siblings on her back.

The sounds from the far side of the valley were growing louder. Listening hard, the children made out the crunch of feet, the muffled clatter of hooves shod with straw, the jangle of iron on iron and iron on stone. Above the hubbub rose a

22

chorus of voices, at first a babble, then clearer and clearer until they could hear every syllable, repeated again and again in sing-song tones: '*Shita ni iyo! Shita ni iyo! Shita ni... Shita ni...*' The marchers were still deep in the forest, hidden beneath the dense thatch of foliage that clothed the mountainside, yet the voices never stopped, not for a second. It was as if they expected everything – the tall trees with their thick cap of leaves, plants, wolves, foxes, deer, the lumbering black bears and ferocious mountain boars with their sharp tusks – to get down on their knees.

Genzaburo, the unchallenged leader of the children, scrambled up a tree and edged along a branch until he was swaying precariously above the road. A wiry, long-limbed boy with skin burned almost black by the sun and an impish grin, he was forever getting into scrapes, sneaking away to catch fish or swim in the river when he should have been working. He was adept at sneaking up behind a horse and snatching a few hairs from its tail then darting off with the groom chasing after him. Grey hairs made the best fishing lines because the fish could not see them, so it was always a particular challenge to grab a few when a grey horse came by. Genzaburo had also made a name for himself by wrestling a wild boar that had charged into the village one day, terrorizing everyone, when he was only ten. He had punched it and kicked it again and again until the beast turned tail and ran back into the woods. He sometimes showed off the scar where the tusker had gored his arm. It was his badge of honour.

Only Chobei, the youngest of the children,

Sachi's brother, a grubby little boy with spiky hair, swathed in a thick brown kimono, paid no attention to the approaching commotion. He crouched by the road, examining a lizard that had crawled out of the undergrowth.

Genzaburo worked his way further along the branch, screwing up his eyes and peering into the distance.

'They're coming! They're coming!' he shouted.

In a minute everyone could see the first banners poking above the trees, red, purple and gold, fluttering like petals. Shards of light glanced off the steel tips of standards and lances. The children watched intently, their hearts thumping. They all knew exactly what *'Shita ni iyo!'* meant. It was the first lesson they had ever learned. They had all felt their fathers' big rough hands on their heads, pushing them down on to their knees until their faces were in the dirt, and could almost hear their fathers' voices barking, 'Get down, right now! You'll get yourself killed.'

No one had forgotten the dreadful fate of Sohei the drunkard. A few years earlier, after a few too many sakes he had gone staggering out into the path of a procession. Before anyone could pull him back, a couple of samurai whipped their swords out of their scabbards and cut him down, right there in the street. The villagers lugged his body out of the way in numb silence. It just went to show how cheap life was. The samurai were their masters; they had power of life or death over them. That was how it had always been and how it would always be.

But the banners were still far away. The children

gazed and gazed, mesmerized by the thrill of doing something so forbidden and so dangerous.

In the distance tiny figures in blue and black were swarming out of the woods. Shading their eyes, the children made out battalions of soldiers tramping along in close formation, warriors on horseback with the horns on their helmets glinting and long lines of porters humping gleaming lacquered trunks. The figures grew larger as the column of marchers drew nearer. The jangle of the metal rings on the guards' staffs, the shuffle of feet, the crunch of hooves and the ominous chorus – '*Shita ni iyo! Shita ni iyo! Shita ni… Shita ni…*' – grew louder and louder.

Suddenly the spell was broken. Grabbing each other's hands, tripping over in their panic, the children turned and raced helter-skelter down the slope, the babies on the girls' backs bobbing and bouncing.

The mountain that shadowed the village was so high and steep that the first shafts of sunlight had only just begun to pierce the icy air, although it was the hour of the horse and the sun was almost at its height. As they reached the beginning of the street, the children paused for breath. They had never seen it so crowded with people. The rickety inns that lined each side seemed to teeter under the crush. The innkeepers had thrust the slatted doors right back and clouds of woodsmoke swirled out of the cavernous interiors. Gangs of bow-legged porters in wadded cotton jackets and leggings hustled in and out, slurping bowls of barley gruel. Grooms grappled with bad-tempered horses no bigger than ponies, strapping saddles on to them and tying straw horseshoes on to their hooves. Other men bobbed through the throng in straw cloaks, like moving haystacks. Many just stood waiting, fondling their long-stemmed pipes. Some were from villages round about and always turned up when porters or grooms were needed, but most were strangers, gnarled men from villages deep in the hollows of the mountains, who had hiked for an entire day to get there.

Standing in the middle of the mob was a tall man with a broad, calm face and a thatch of thick hair tied back like a horse's tail. He was bellowing orders, waving his arms, sending people running here and there. Sachi and the others burrowed through the crowd, ducking under arms, and grabbed his sleeves.

'The princess is coming! The princess is coming!' they chorused.

He grinned down at them and slapped their heads approvingly. 'Good, good,' he barked. 'Now get back inside to your mothers, right now!'

II

Jiroemon was Sachi's father and the village headman. He was responsible for everything that went on in the village, as his family had been for as long as anyone could remember. He had taken over the job ten years earlier, when his father became old and infirm. In the past the family had worn the two swords that marked them as samurai but the privilege had been revoked centuries ago, though Jiroemon still carried a short ceremonial sword to

26

mark his superior status.

He was a big man, big at least compared to the other villagers, who were squat and brawny, true Kiso 'mountain monkeys'. He was probably less than forty years old – few adults in the village kept track of their exact age – but his face was already furrowed from years of mediating between the villagers and the authorities. All the Kiso land belonged to the local lord and the villagers were allowed to cut only one small section of forest for their own use. Every year people desperate for firewood chopped down trees. Officially the penalty was 'one tree, one head', though Jiroemon always pleaded as hard as he could for leniency. The villagers were never allowed to forget for one moment that, in the eyes of their overlords, they were no better than animals.

Jiroemon's main job was to ensure that traffic flowed smoothly on the section of the great Kiso highway – the Nakasendo, the Inner Mountain Road – that passed through the village. In normal times the highway was clogged with travellers, spangled with the exotic air of faraway places. Groups of pilgrims in their white robes came ambling through, ringing their bells, on their way to distant shrines, though most of them seemed more interested in having a rollicking time and seeing the world than in prayer and devotions. Some were wealthy merchants accompanied by a retinue of wives, concubines and servants, all dressed in the height of fashion. Some were poor peasants and others were begging their way, dependent on alms. Convoys of samurai rode on horseback or in palanquins, and merchants supervised consignments of freight packed into chests and carried by cavalcades of porters. Wandering poets stayed for days to lead poetry-writing evenings and scholars and priests relayed the choicest news, controversy and gossip from the three great cities, Osaka, Kyoto and Edo. Then there were mail couriers, stopping just long enough to change horses, and shifty-eyed characters everyone knew were spies or police agents, who kept an eye on all the other travellers.

Add to them renegade samurai, tinkers, peddlers, gangsters, gamblers, travelling players, magicians, rogues and sellers of toad oil – guaranteed to cure every ailment under the sun – and there was plenty to keep the villagers in business. Every evening the geishas were out in force, dragging in passing men. The sounds of music, merriment and dancing spilt from the lamp-lit inns into the dark street.

Jiroemon too kept an inn, but his was a very splendid and exclusive one, designated for the use of the daimyo lords who travelled the Inner Mountain Road every year. In the off-season, officials and other important or very wealthy personages were allowed to stay there too.

The daimyos were provincial rulers. Each was the lord of his own small domain and kept his own army. They collected taxes and had power of life or death over their subjects. But they all owed allegiance to the shogun in Edo and were obliged to travel there every year to pay homage, show their faces at court and stay for several months. Each had two or three palaces in the city where their womenfolk lived permanently, prisoners in golden cages.

There were thirty-four greater or lesser daimyos who used the Inner Mountain Road. Some would be going one way, some the other, east to Edo or west towards Kyoto, the holy city and official capital of the country, where the emperor lived in seclusion. They were always accompanied by a magnificent entourage, with hundreds of attendants and guards. It was a breathtaking spectacle. The peasants were supposed to keep away from the road when they passed or at least to stay on their hands and knees with their heads bowed; but they all did their best to see as much of the procession as they dared.

All, except the palanquin bearers, would be smartly turned out in black silk. Some would be on horseback but most marched on foot, in close formation. The lower ranks, the pikemen and the bearers of sunhats, parasols and trunks, always put on a grand display for the benefit of the cowering villagers, swaggering along with their robes hitched right up at the back, their bare buttocks glinting in the sun with only a loincloth to cover the gap. With every step they kicked one heel up nearly to the buttock and thrust the opposite arm forward as if they were swimming through the air. The pike-bearers twirled their pikes, the hat-bearers their hats and the parasol-bearers their parasols, all in precisely the same rhythm.

The processions always stopped in Jiroemon's village to rest and change horses and porters. While the underlings were busy the palanquins carrying the daimyo and his retainers would proceed to Jiroemon's inn, where they took tea or stayed overnight. Most of the daimyos had been visiting for many years and had got to know the well-educated and rather entertaining innkeeper. When they had consumed a little sake and the time came to call in their favourite geishas, some even relaxed enough to summon him for a chat, though no one ever forgot the huge discrepancy in rank. Jiroemon knew very well that, as far as they were concerned, he was a mere rustic, though a clever one.

A couple of times Jiroemon himself had been up to Edo, that fabled metropolis in the Musashi plain, a fourteen-day tramp through the mountains. He brought back startling news. Some eight years earlier, four Black Ships, iron-clad monsters bristling with cannons and spouting smoke and steam, had appeared on the horizon and dropped anchor on the coast near Shimoda. Soon afterwards a succession of disasters had occurred – violent earthquakes and tidal waves – and a comet had appeared in the sky, clearly presaging doom.

The ships had disgorged a delegation of barbarians. Jiroemon had not seen any himself but he had been told they had huge noses and coarse pallid skin covered in red fur and stank of the dead animals they ate. They had not only placed their impure feet on Japan's sacred soil but insisted that they intended to stay and set up trading stations.

The travellers who passed through Jiroemon's inn had made it frighteningly clear that the country was in crisis. Only the previous spring, rumours had come winging down the valley that

30

Lord Ii Naosuké, the Great Counsellor and iron-handed ruler of the country, had been cut down right outside the gates of Edo Castle, the shogun's residence. Some of the assassins were samurai from Mito, the domain of one of the most powerful and high-ranking princes in the country, a blood relation of the shogun. Others were from the wild southern domain of Satsuma, one of the shogun's traditional enemies. Life for the villagers had always been hard, cruel and unfair; but at least they knew where they stood. Now they could not be sure of anything. They dreaded what might happen next. Old men muttered darkly that the world was mired in the Age of Mappo, the last age described in Buddhist scriptures. Perhaps the end was approaching.

III

The first year of Bunkyu – the year that would go down in history books as 1861 – was unusually cold. It was nearly barley-planting time but icicles still hung from the eaves, and only the most determined travellers came tramping along the snow-encrusted highway. Then one day the mail courier arrived, urging his horse through the mud and slush. He had a letter for Jiroemon from the district commissioners in charge of transport.

Jiroemon broke the seal with trepidation, opened the box and unscrolled the letter. What new demands could they possibly have dreamed up now? He read it, scratched his head, then studied it until he could decipher the convoluted official language. The commissioners wished to notify him, as headman of the village, that Her Highness Princess Kazu, the emperor's younger sister, would be passing along the Inner Mountain Road and through the village in the tenth month of that same year. He was to start preparations immediately.

An imperial princess of the highest rank, the daughter of the late emperor and younger sister of the Son of Heaven, passing through their village! Such a thing had never occurred before. Slipping and sliding on the icy paths, Jiroemon rushed back to the cramped quarters where the family lived, in a distant corner of the splendid inn where the daimyos stayed. Smoke swirled out as he slid open the door. Everyone was huddled around the hearth, waiting for him to come back.

'I've never known such times, Mother, in all my years,' he grunted as he burst into the room. He always called his wife, Otama, '*Kaachan*', the affectionate rural term for 'Mother'. His usually calm face was crumpled with worry, the furrows in his forehead deeper than ever and his black hair stuck out in tufts.

The children's grandmother ladled out a helping of gruel for him, then a second one. Her face was as brown and shrivelled as a walnut and her back bent double after a lifetime of hard work.

'The road always overburdened, the outside villages refusing to supply porters – and now this!' he said. 'How many travellers do we get a day, do you think? A thousand? And even that's far more than we can cope with. It says here there'll be ten thousand in Her Highness's party, without even counting the porters. It will take – what? – four, five days for the whole lot to pass. And we're supposed to find two or three thousand porters. Two or three thousand! And five hundred horses each day that it passes. Six thousand pillows. Rice. Charcoal. Dishes. And we're supposed to feed all the lower ranks. How can we possibly do that? It can't be done!'

Otama was a thin, worn woman, her face crisscrossed with thin lines and her hair twisted into a rough bun. Her hands were swollen, cracked and ingrained with dirt from cleaning, cooking, digging and weeding and her back was beginning to bend from years of planting out rice shoots. Her parents had sent her to marry Jiroemon when she was very young, not much older than Sachi. She bore him child after child but after each one died they had eventually adopted a frail, pale-faced baby girl. They named her Sachi, 'Happiness', hoping this one at least would survive.

This much Sachi knew. She had never enquired further. Her young life was far too full ever to think of asking where she had come from or who her parents had been. Half the children in the village were adopted or passed around, depending on which family had a sickly child or needed a son to continue the line, until some people had no idea who their real parents were. No one much cared. You belonged to whichever family you had been adopted into.

A few years later Otama bore Jiroemon a boy, little Chobei. He survived and other babies followed. She was strong, healthy, hard-working, quiet – everything a man like Jiroemon could want in a wife – and he was devoted to her. Now that Granny had become old and infirm, she was the power in the house.

She had been watching him closely as he spoke. Silently she laid her bowl and chopsticks beside the hearth, knelt behind him and began to knead his shoulders with her thumbs. He grimaced as she worked on a particularly stubborn knot.

Finally she spoke. 'I suppose they told you what a great honour and privilege it is,' she said. 'I doubt we'll see a single copper penny or a grain of rice. They know very well we only have a couple of hundred men at most and fifty-odd horses. Even if we go to all the villages round about we still can't round up that many.'

'The letter said there might be some sort of financial recompense. But of course they're not guaranteeing anything.'

'You'll find a way,' she said soothingly, pressing her thumbs into his shoulders. 'You always do.'

Usually Sachi barely listened to adult talk. It was always jobs that needed to be done, plans, worries, money, gossip, the day's routine. She let it all flow by and drifted off into her own thoughts. But today was different. Her parents had always been reassuring presences who protected her, admonished her and solved her problems. She had taken for granted that they were not affected by worries and fears, as she was. Now she saw that they were as weak and helpless as her. It made her feel frightened and alone.

Yet at the same time she was strangely entranced. A princess, passing through their village... Princesses had never entered her mind before.

Sometimes she saw wealthy merchants travelling with women, some of whom had skin nearly as pale as hers. Perhaps the princess too had white skin.

She fingered the comb in her kimono sleeve, as she always did when anything was on her mind. She was nearly an adult, and she knew she would be sent away in a year or two. She had seen the older girls disappear. One had gone off to a cousin's house to enlarge her knowledge of the world and make her a more useful bride, a couple had been taken into service in a samurai household, and the rest had been sent to be married. Soon it would be her turn. What else could there be? Her grandmother's words echoed in her mind: 'How do you expect her to get a husband, so pale and sickly as she is? What good is "pretty" for a farmer's wife?' Supposing she was too small and whey-faced to be accepted by another family as a bride? Maybe when all the other girls left home she would still be living with her parents, a shame and a burden to them, pitied by everyone in the village.

To make things worse, the village geishas teased her that she ought to become one of them. They covered their brown country faces in thick white paint, they told her, giggling coyly in that way geishas had. But her face was already as white as the full moon, as white as a mountain cherry blossom, and without any makeup at all. And she was pretty, too, and getting prettier. To hear them say such things only made her feel more of an oddity. When her mother heard them, she would smile her tired smile and lead her firmly away.

The morning after the villagers heard that the princess was to pass through, Sachi took up her usual place beside the work-stained loom, spooling cotton on to bobbins and passing them to her mother, while her grandmother sat in the corner, bent so close to the spinning wheel that her nose brushed against it. For a while the only sound was the rhythmic clack of the bobbin flying to and fro, the banging of the loom and the creaking and clattering of the wheel. Finally Sachi took a deep breath.

'*Kaachan*,' she said tentatively. 'Mother. The princess... Can you tell me...? What kind of...?'

Otama had stopped throwing the bobbin back and forth to wind on a newly woven length of fabric. She thought for a moment.

'Well, Little Sa,' she replied. 'I don't know. Your father says she's going to Edo to be the shogun's bride.'

To be the shogun's bride! It was like one of those fairy tales her grandmother sometimes told. Was the shogun old and ugly, she wondered, wizened and dried up like the village priest? Or was he young and full of life? The image of Genzaburo's lean young body darting about in the river came to her mind.

In the days that followed, travellers brought rumour after rumour. Every night the oil lamps in the meeting house smoked and guttered until late and the family waited longer and longer for Jiroemon to come home for dinner. He would rush in exhausted and swallow a few bowls of barley, then towel down over a pan of steaming water and throw himself on to the rough straw sleeping mats next to the children. The villagers were to pave the road with flat white rocks throughout the village and for one or two *ri* on each side. The road had to be twelve *shaku* wide, even if that meant knocking down the walls in front of people's houses.

The day after the last of the snow disappeared, Sachi slipped on a pair of clog-like *geta*, checked the old wooden pail to see if it was still watertight and skipped down to join the line at the well. As usual, the group of women there were chatting excitedly. Fetching water was a young woman's job. It was the perfect excuse to escape from their shrewish mothers-in-law and gossip among themselves.

'You know she's only fifteen?' twittered Shigé from the inn across the road. 'My father-in-law says so.' She was fifteen herself, plump and girlish with sunburned cheeks and a mouth jostling with crooked teeth. She was the bride of the eldest son of the house and the mother of his son and heir, and brimming with her own importance. Genza-buro was her husband's younger brother. Sachi was in awe of her. She could not imagine ever being so grown-up and confident.

'Is that right?' squealed Kumé, the child bride of the clog-maker's son. She had been born with one leg shorter than the other and walked with a limp, but could spin as fine a thread as the oldest woman in the village. 'But you know what I heard? They say she didn't want–'

'That's right,' Shigé butted in. 'She refused several times. Imagine that – a woman refusing to go as a bride!'

There was a chorus of high-pitched whinnies of disbelief.

'She was already betrothed,' Shigé persisted. 'To an imperial prince. She had been promised to him when she was six. She said she'd rather become a nun than marry the shogun.'

'My father-in-law says it's a scandal to send such a young girl so far away!' said Kumé, finally managing to interject. 'Edo's a soldiers' city. Not a place for someone who's been brought up so delicately.'

'How beautiful she must be,' whispered Oman from the inn next door to Sachi's. She had only recently arrived as a bride from a nearby village and was still subdued and prone to tears. 'I heard they are bringing spring water for her bath all the way from Kyoto.'

'That can't be!' gasped the others, tilting their heads in disbelief.

'It's true,' sighed Oman. 'She is too delicate for our Kiso water. What would I give to see her, just for one second!'

There were shocked giggles at the audacity of the thought. 'That's right,' said the young women, nodding. 'Too bad none of us will ever see a princess. No one ever gets to see a great lady like that!'

Sachi listened in silence. So the princess was not much older than herself. How sad she must feel, plucked from her home and sent on a long journey to a place she did not know, to marry someone she did not know and did not want to marry. In that respect her life was no different from that of the poorest villager. Only in her case she had dared to refuse; though in the end she had been overruled. She was one of the greatest ladies in the land yet she too had no say over her own life.

'She probably has white skin, even whiter than yours, Little Sa,' said Oman.

'Perhaps she looks like you, Little Sa,' said Kumé. 'With that long face of yours and that high nose.'

'Don't be silly,' sneered Shigé, with the air of a woman of the world. 'The princess is beautiful. She doesn't look anything like any of us.'

The year went by in a flurry of festivals, lucky days and unlucky days. In the spring Sachi was up before dawn every morning, scrambling around the lower slopes of the mountain harvesting fiddlehead ferns, horsetail shoots, burdock root and all the other edible roots and shoots that grew there. Then came the spring festival, followed by the girls' festival, then the planting out of the rice shoots. In the summer the children were busy working on the road and in the fields, but whenever they could they sneaked down to the river. There they would tear off their clothes and plunge in, joyfully splashing around in the cool water. Genzaburo led expeditions into the woods to climb trees, play games and chase the rabbits, foxes and badgers that lived there. In the seventh month, when it was so hot it was hard to move and everyone was soaked with sweat, came the Bon festival when the ancestors returned from the dead and the villagers danced until late at night. Then in the autumn Sachi was up in the hills again, collecting mushrooms.

Otama cleaned, polished, swept and cooked,

making sure the inn was always pristine for each of the grand guests who passed through. The loom clattered and Granny's spinning wheel whirred. Yet as the women went about their everyday tasks, they were all too aware of Jiroemon's frantic efforts to prepare for the great procession. He negotiated endlessly with the headmen of more and more distant villages to ensure there would be enough porters and horses. It was not a question of whether: it had to be done.

When the ninth month came round, a huge procession of officials, guards, soldiers and local daimyos with their entourages suddenly appeared, heading for Kyoto to escort the princess back. Day after day the highway was choked with traffic. The porters, bearers and foot soldiers were pressed so close together that they were treading on each other's heels. Jiroemon had organized more than a thousand extra porters but they were vastly overworked; there were still far from enough.

One day a line of palanquins appeared that were more ornate and gorgeous than any that anyone had ever seen. Rumours quickly spread and soon crowds of villagers were squatting along the sides of the road, craning their necks to get a peep inside before the guards shoved them out of the way.

'Ladies from the Great Interior!' Sachi heard Jiroemon telling Otama. 'They're stopping here for the night. What am I supposed to do? Do I go out and greet them? I've had no instructions at all!'

'The Great Interior?' queried Otama.

'The women's palace in Edo Castle,' said

Jiroemon impatiently.

'Grand ladies like that on the road?' said Otama, shaking her head. 'That's something special! You never see that!'

It was true. The only women Sachi saw were peasants or townsfolk on pilgrimage and sometimes the elegant wives of merchants, who usually bargained harder than their husbands. Occasionally a woman poet came by, but never anyone of higher rank. The daimyos' entourages consisted only of men. The guards at the village barrier post were well aware that their most important job was to ensure that no great ladies crept through in disguise, trying to escape from Edo to their home province. Any other failure on the part of the guards was excusable, but for that one they paid with their heads.

For nine days the traffic continued. Then there was a lull. The villagers totted up the damage. The meeting room had been smashed up and many of the paper doors in the inns had been ripped when drunken samurai started fights. Some porters had been beaten and two who tried to run away had been shot. People started to find bodies along the verges of the highway, unceremoniously kicked out of the way of the processions. Some twenty or thirty porters had collapsed under their burdens and died. That was the way of things: there was nothing to be done. The villagers set about making repairs as quickly as possible, before the princess's cavalcade came through.

Then the transport commissioners arrived in person, jogging into the village in a line of palanquins escorted by servants, attendants and

41

guards. They strutted up and down in their starched *hakama* trousers with their two swords swinging importantly at their sides. They stayed the night at Jiroemon's luxurious inn, though they had their own cooks to boil up their tea and cook their dinner; they were far too grand to eat even the best food that Otama could offer.

Tapping their fans, they drew up plans and measured the road. When the princess's cavalcade passed through, they told Jiroemon, women and children were to remain inside with the shutters closed, on their knees, in silence; anyone outside should prostrate themselves, face to the ground. Dogs and cats should be tied up, there were to be no fires lit and the heavy stones that kept the roof tiles in place should be securely fastened to make sure there were no accidents. All traffic on the road was to stop for three days on either side of the princess's passage. Suddenly the highway became eerily quiet.

The first contingent of the princess's convoy arrived on the twenty-fourth day of the tenth month. For two days there was a non-stop procession of porters staggering under the weight of baskets and boxes covered in rich brocade and lacquered trunks gleaming with gold. Jiroemon had managed to round up a total of 2,277 men from thirty-three neighbouring villages. They relayed the baggage to the next village along the road, then came back to pick up another batch.

On the third day the princess herself was to pass through. Sachi was up well before dawn to help her mother make sure that everything was perfect. Otama arranged branches of maple leaves in a vase in the elegant way the daimyos liked, while Sachi scuttled up and down the silent rooms like a crab, pushing a damp cloth, until the pale tatami matting gleamed and the silken edges were spotless. They polished the wooden floors in the corridors and entranceway one last time until there was not a speck of dust anywhere. Then Sachi ran to the edge of the village with the other children to watch for the procession.

By the time they reported back to Jiroemon, everyone could hear the jangle of the iron rings on top of the guards' staffs, the crunch of approaching feet, the clatter of hooves and the never-ending cry – *'Shita ni iyo! Shita ni iyo!* On your knees! On your knees!'

'I'm going to hide under the eaves and watch the procession go by,' hissed Genzaburo. 'Why don't you come, Sa? It'll be fun. Nobody will know!'

But Sachi had a more pressing duty. Whenever a procession passed through, Jiroemon had to go to the entrance to the village to greet the daimyo. Then he would run back to the inn to welcome him again at the porch where the palanquins drew up. But the princess presented a problem. For a start, she was a woman. Not only that, she was the highest, most important woman in the land. It was unthinkable for any man, let alone a lowly innkeeper like himself, even to cast eyes on a woman of such high station. But it was equally unthinkable not to welcome her to the inn. As the day approached, Jiroemon grew more and more worried. The transport commissioners had not deigned to give him any advice. Finally he made

43

up his mind: he would greet her palanquin in the usual way, but accompanied by his wife and daughter. His family had, after all, once been samurai; they were a cut above the other villagers.

Sachi put on the new indigo-blue kimono which Otama had been saving for her for New Year's Day. Granny had spun the yarn and Otama had woven the fabric in a design of lighter and darker checks and stitched a charm bag containing Sachi's protective amulet into a corner of the sleeve. Sachi tucked her special comb into the same sleeve and wrapped a red crepe obi around her waist. Then she took her place on her knees next to her mother, beside the entrance reserved for important guests.

Jiroemon's inn was in the middle of the village but set back from the road, well away from all the noise and rowdy bustle, hidden behind a high wall. There was a second wall inside the entrance to shield his high-ranking guests from the vulgar gaze of villagers and travellers. Sachi could hear feet tramping along the road outside, making the ground shudder, and could see the tops of lances, banners and great red parasols bobbing along in stately procession above the wall. Apart from the thunder of feet and hooves and the insistent shout of *'Shita ni iyo! Shita ni iyo! Shita ni... Shita ni...'*, there was utter silence. No one said a word.

Suddenly some men appeared around the inner wall. Sachi twisted around a little and lifted her head just enough to peep at what was going on. There was a line of bare-buttocked porters, their faces shiny with sweat, lugging buckets of water, baskets of food, shiny lacquered trunks and an ornate gold and black chest, big enough to hold a bathtub, around to the back entrance. Burly men in multi-layered short kimonos and leggings, with conical straw hats and wearing the two swords of samurai, took up positions around the porch, along with bearers carrying shiny black benches.

Then a palanquin drew up at the entrance porch. A woman stepped out, slipping one tiny foot, then the other, into a pair of clogs that had been set on the bench. More and more palanquins began to pull up. Women emerged from each, greeting each other in high-pitched coos. To Sachi their voices sounded no different from the trilling and warbling of birds and they were every bit as impossible to understand. The porch was awash with fabrics as fine and soft as flower petals and as colourful as a meadow in spring. Scents filled the air, so sweet and powerful that she felt herself growing dizzy. She grew bolder, peeping again and again. She had never before seen such exquisite creatures. It was another world, more gorgeous than anything she could ever have imagined.

Twisting her head even more, she caught a glimpse of a magnificent palanquin like a tiny mobile palace, gleaming with reddish-tinted gold, with fat red tassels swinging over the window blinds and a red banner draped across the roof. Even the carrying pole and window frets were encrusted with gold leaf. The walls were covered in ornate designs and embossed with a chrysan-themum, surely the imperial crest. There were six porters to carry it, three at the front and three at the back. Guards marched alongside and liveried retainers shaded it with large red umbrellas. As the porters lowered it gingerly on to the palanquin stand the women fell to their knees in a graceful flurry of silks. Jiroemon and Otama kept their faces pressed to the polished wooden floor, but Sachi was burning with curiosity. For a second she glanced up. Surely this was the princess! She had to see her.

Attendants slid open the door of the palanquin and a woman emerged from the shadowy gold interior. The many layers of her kimonos, in subtle shades of orange, gold and green, were visible at throat and wrist. She was wearing a travelling hat with a thick veil that fell to her shoulders, but as she stepped down she raised a white hand and pushed it aside. Sachi saw her face before the veil fell back into place.

Quickly Sachi lowered her head. She did not know what she had been expecting or, indeed, how she had dared expect anything. She had been thinking about the princess so much. She had expected to see something wonderful, but instead she felt puzzled and confused. The face she had seen did not belong to a princess – certainly not to the princess of her imaginings. The woman was certainly painted like a great lady, with a whitened face, tiny blood-red lips and eyebrows brushed in high on her forehead; but she seemed to shrivel inside her lavish kimonos. Strangest of all was the expression that had flickered across her face – a look of naked fear, such as Sachi had seen in the eyes of chickens about to be killed. She felt a sense of unease. Something was wrong.

Even a child like Sachi knew that great lords

and ladies had lookalikes. There were always enemies lurking, hoping to kidnap or even kill a lady. So perhaps that was what she was. Or perhaps she really was the princess. Perhaps princesses were just ordinary people after all.

Swishing their bell-like kimono skirts the women ushered the princess into the inn, gliding past Jiroemon, Otama and Sachi, who were still on their knees, as if they did not exist.

Palanquins continued to pull up, disgorging yet more women. Now only a few lingered in the porch. Jiroemon and Otama seemed frozen, still with their faces to the ground. Then a rather undistinguished palanquin with plain wooden walls and bamboo blinds drew up. Sachi was in a dream, half stupefied by the drama of the day and the obscure feeling that all was not as it should be. She lifted her head and watched as a woman stepped out. This one, dressed more plainly than the others, looked like a maid. For a moment her eyes met Sachi's.

The woman was a mere girl, not much older than Sachi, no older than the young wives who gathered at the well. She was not beautiful but there was something about the way she carried herself that held everyone's attention. Her face was oval and childishly plump, with large sad black eyes, a straight nose, a pointed chin and a small mouth pursed in an expression of dazed resignation. Her skin was so white it was almost tinged with blue. She stepped awkwardly from the palanquin and stood uncertainly, as if she did not know what to do next. The other women flocked around her, hastily throwing a veil over her head. They seemed to be trying to play-act indifference, looking away from her and talking loudly to each other. But they could not hide the deference in their gestures and the way they held their bodies, instinctively dipping and bowing so that their heads were always lower than hers.

Sachi was mesmerized. There was something familiar about the girl. Somewhere – surely in a dream – she had seen this face before. The girl in her turn had seen Sachi. Something sparked in her eyes as if she too felt a sense of recognition. As the other women arranged the veil over her face, she whispered to one of them. Suddenly everyone turned to look at the child kneeling in the entranceway, daring to stare at them. The women began to move towards her and the guards stationed around the porch put their hands on their sword hilts. Hearing the commotion, Jiroemon looked up, horrified.

Instinctively Sachi felt for her comb, tucked safely in her sleeve. The fate of Sohei the drunkard and the porters left dead along the roadside flashed through her mind. For a moment her young life passed before her eyes and she thought of Genzaburo, hidden in the eaves just across the road, not far away. But one thought overwhelmed all the others: I have seen the princess.

It had begun to dawn on her why the girl's face looked familiar. It could almost have been the face she saw glimmering in her mother's tarnished mirror – a slightly more grown-up version of her own.

Part II

The Women's Palace

2

Shells of Forgetfulness, 1865

I

Sachi was playing the shell-matching game with Princess Kazu. Kneeling opposite her with her hands folded in her lap, eyes modestly lowered, she heard the whisper of silk as the princess languidly drew back the long sleeve of her robe and dipped her hand into the lacquered gold-embossed shell box. There was a faint clatter as she ran her fingers across the small dry shells. She took one out and laid it face up on the tatami matting. Sachi leaned forward. Inside was a painted world of miniature noblemen and ladies on a background of gold leaf.

More shells lay in neat rows face down between the two women. The princess took one and glanced inside it.

'Why is my luck always so bad?' she sighed, tossing it down pettishly. 'If only these were forgetting shells. Then maybe I could forget.' She murmured a poem:

'Wasuregai	I shall not gather
Hiroi shi mo seji	Shells of forgetfulness,
Shiratama o	But pearls,
Kouru o dani mo	Mementoes of

51

Katami to omowan The jewel-like one I loved.'

Sachi peeked up at her. She thought of the stories she had heard of how the princess had been forced to come to Edo and marry the shogun against her will, and how she had once been betrothed to an imperial prince. But that was all long ago. If only Her Highness could stop dwelling on the past, if only Her Highness was not always so sad...

The princess was looking at her expectantly. Sachi let her hand hover above the shells which lay face down. She picked one up, glanced inside and gave a little shriek, then snatched up the shell which the princess had taken from the box. They were a perfect match. She shouted with joyous laughter, then, remembering where she was, flushed bright red and clapped both hands over her mouth.

'Such a child,' said Lady Tsuguko, the princess's chief lady-in-waiting, smiling indulgently. Lady Tsuguko was the most powerful person in the princess's entourage and the authority on the all-important matter of protocol. She was a tall, aristocratic woman whose floor-length hair was streaked with grey. Most of the junior ladies were terrified of her, but to those whom the princess favoured she was kindness itself.

The princess too gave a wan smile. 'She could charm anyone with those green eyes of hers,' she murmured. 'She takes such delight in life. I wish all days were as peaceful as this...' She glanced at Lady Tsuguko. 'There is so little time left to us,' she added, her voice dying away.

'Human life is always uncertain, ma'am. But perhaps the gods will favour us just this once.'

'Not if the Retired One has her way. I know she has His Majesty's ear...'

It was the fifteenth day of the fifth month of the first year of Keio, and the rains were late in starting. Every day was hotter, stickier and more oppressive than the last. Dark clouds hid the sky. The paper doors that divided the rooms and the wooden doors that formed the outer walls of the buildings had been taken out, turning the whole vast palace into a labyrinth of interconnected pavilions. But there was not even the tiniest breeze to rattle the bamboo blinds.

That morning Sachi had been given a few minutes off from her duties. She dashed to the veranda and gazed out at the palace gardens. The lawns, neatly clipped bushes and spiky-needled pine trees spread before her in a dazzling patchwork of greens. The elegant lake with its half-moon bridges was as still as a picture. Bamboo shoots thrust out of the soil and gnarled branches groaned under fat new buds and leaves. She breathed the moist air, drinking in the warm scent of earth, leaves and grass.

A cicada shrilled, shattering the silence. The sudden noise took her away, and for a moment she was on a hillside among thick trees. A cluster of slate roofs weighted with stones huddled in the valley below her. She could almost smell the woodsmoke and the aroma of miso soup. The village. The memory was so clear and sharp it brought tears to her eyes.

As she did every day, she thought back to that

53

fateful autumn morning when the princess had passed through. Sachi was back in the entrance hall of the great inn, feeling the wooden floor cold and hard against her knees. Women crowded around her and voices twittered. Her parents were bowing, her mother brushing away tears. Then her father had said, 'You are to go with them. You're a lucky girl. Never forget that. Whatever you do, don't cry. Be sure and make us proud of you.'

The next thing she knew, she had been walking along the road with a lady-in-waiting firmly holding her by the hand. She remembered fighting back tears, twisting around again and again, trying to keep her eyes on the village until it disappeared from sight. Many days later they had reached the great city of Edo and finally she saw the white ramparts of Edo Castle filling the sky in front of her. They had gone inside and the gates had swung shut behind them.

How lonely she had been to begin with! She had never imagined it was possible to be so sad. She hadn't even been able to understand what anyone said. There had been so much to learn – how to walk and talk like a lady, how to read and write. Since then four winters and three summers had passed. But every day she thought of her mother and father still and wondered how they were and what they were doing.

Now she took her usual place beside the princess and began to fan her, trying to keep the air around her as cool and fresh as possible. A thread of fragrant smoke coiled from the incense burner in the corner. On the other side of the ornate gold screens that enclosed the princess's private section of the room, groups of ladies-in-waiting reclined, chattering and laughing, their robes billowing around them like leaves on a lily pond. Only a chosen few were allowed behind the screens. If Sachi had not been so young she might have felt it strange that she of all people should have been there. But for some reason the princess cared about her. She found her company soothing, she said.

Sachi glanced at the princess. She knew she was supposed to keep her eyes modestly lowered at all times, and especially in the princess's presence. But there were so many rules, so much to remember. And besides, sometimes she felt that she was the only person who really cared about Princess Kazu. To Sachi she was perfection. Her handwriting was more elegant than that of any of her ladies, her poems more poignant, and when she played the koto, listeners were moved to tears. When she performed the tea ceremony, her movements were pure poetry. Yet there was something about her that was like a wild creature, trapped within the net of ceremony and deference that surrounded her. Sometimes Sachi thought she saw a flash of panic in her black eyes, like that of a frightened deer. Young and powerless though she was, she yearned to protect her.

From far off came the pad of footsteps, hurrying along the corridor towards them. Sachi heard the door to the outer chamber sliding in its grooves and the boards creaking as the visitor knelt. There was a flurry of voices, the rustle of silk, then a lady-in-waiting appeared, bowing at the edge of the screen. Lady Tsuguko leaned towards her in her lofty way, then turned to the princess and whispered in her ear.

Sachi caught the words: 'The time of the morning visit approaches.'

The princess froze. Then, for some strange reason, she looked straight at Sachi. Sachi quickly looked down.

The princess took a breath, as if remembering what and who she was. Then she turned to Lady Tsuguko and said with studied calm, 'Tell my ladies to make preparations.'

Quickly Sachi gathered up the shells and put them back in their boxes, carefully tying the tasselled cords that bound them. When she had first arrived at the palace, everything had been so new that she had barely noticed where she was or been aware of the immense luxury that surrounded her. Now, almost four years later, she handled the tiny painted shells and the lacquered eight-sided boxes with reverence.

Only ladies of the highest rank ever entered the presence of the shogun. The life of the palace revolved around him. When he was absent it was as if darkness had fallen. All the women who pattered about the women's palace from the highest in the hierarchy to the lowest – grand ladies, lesser ladies, old, young, maids, maids' maids, halberd-wielding guards, bath girls, cleaning girls, carriers of charcoal and water, even the lowest-ranking errand girls whom everyone called the 'honourable whelps' – were silent and afraid. When he returned it was as if the sun had come out. But most of the women who devoted their lives to serving this godlike being never expected to see him.

Indeed, it was extraordinary, as Sachi heard the older women saying to each other, for the shogun ever to have been away. The third shogun, Lord Iemitsu, had visited Kyoto in the Kan'ei era, more than 200 years ago, but since then no shogun had ever left Edo and few had left the castle. The previous shogun, poor Lord Iesada, like all his predecessors, had been born, lived and died there.

For why would anyone ever want to leave? The castle was a world in itself. Besides the inner palace, with its offices, guard rooms, great kitchens, dining rooms and baths, its sub-palaces for the great ladies and labyrinths of rooms where the women lived, all set in exquisite gardens with lakes and streams and waterfalls and stages for plays and dances, there was also the middle palace, the shogun's residence when he was not in the inner palace, and the outer palace, where official business took place and the government had its offices.

The women, of course, never went there and in theory did not know what went on, though in practice news and gossip seemed to flow like air into the inner palace so that even though the women never left, they knew exactly what was happening in the world outside. All this – the inner, middle and outer palaces – made up the main citadel. But there was also the second citadel, where the heir – when there was one – and his mother had their court, and the west citadel, where the widows – the wives, consorts and concubines – of the late shoguns were supposed to live, having taken holy vows. Each was a smaller version of the main citadel, complete with its own outer, middle and inner palaces. Within the great moat and the soaring walls, there was also the wooded expanse of the Fukiage pleasure gardens and Momiji Hill, where the women could stroll to enjoy the changing seasons, and the palaces of the Tayasu and Shimizu families, blood relations of the Tokugawa family.

Everything, in fact, that anyone could ever want was there. Once the women entered the castle they knew that, unless they were unhappy or behaved badly, they would be there for the rest of their lives. Of course they were permitted to visit their families from time to time. Sachi knew that soon she too would be allowed a few days to visit her family, though her old life seemed so far away she could barely remember the little girl she had been when she lived in the village.

In the past when the princess made the daily journey to greet the shogun, Sachi had stayed behind in the royal apartments. But today something had changed. Perhaps, Sachi thought, it was to do with her age. Now in her fifteenth year, she had come of age and her monthly defilement had begun. Her hair was knotted in a more adult hairstyle and she wore a style of kimono that marked her as a junior handmaiden. She even had a new name.

Instead of Sachi, 'Happiness', she was now officially Yuri, 'Lily'. She liked the new name. It made her feel delicate and feminine and rather grand, part of a more splendid world than before.

Her body too was changing, sprouting nearly as fast as a bamboo shoot in the rainy season. Her arms and legs had grown long and slender and her small round breasts had to be squashed into place inside her kimono. Even her face seemed different almost every time she looked at herself in the mirror.

Perhaps that was the reason why, that morning, Lady Tsuguko had told her to prepare to attend the welcoming for the shogun. But it was not her place to ask questions. As the older women reminded her again and again, she herself and her feelings counted for nothing. No matter what happened, no matter what she felt, she must strive to maintain a placid, unruffled surface, like a pond becoming still again after a stone has been thrown in. The key was to remember her place, to be obedient and never to bring shame on herself or others.

At mid-morning, as the hour of the horse approached, the women prepared to leave. The princess rose to her feet and, holding her ceremonial cypresswood fan at her waist, glided out of her apartments. She moved so softly that the smoke coiling from the censer barely quivered. Her wide red trousers rippled and the quilted hem of her brocade coat spread like a fan behind her. A subtle perfume enveloped her, wafting from her scented robes. Her ladies followed, like an endless procession of huge flowers in their thin white summer kimonos and bulky vermilion skirts. Usually Lady Tsuguko would have been at the head of the line, as befitted her rank of chief lady-in-waiting. But today she stayed at the back, shepherding Sachi at her side.

Outside, the passageway was full of women on their knees. Bowing again and again, the ushers greeted the princess. Sachi scurried along with tiny steps, wary of the swathes of fabric that eddied around her feet. Being shorter than everyone else, she almost had to run to keep up. Once she stumbled over her train. 'Smaller steps,' Lady Tsuguko cautioned, tucking an elegant finger under her elbow. 'Toes turned in. Hands on your thighs, fingers straight, thumbs tucked in. Head down. Look at the ground.'

Preceded by the ushers, the princess and her ladies glided infinitely slowly, with measured steps, along one corridor after another, their robes swishing gently like waves lapping at the edge of a river. The palace was a maze. Pattering along, eyes fixed firmly on the tatami mats, Sachi wondered how she would ever have found her way back again if she had been on her own. Glancing up, she caught a glimpse of the long corridor disappearing into the distance, lined with rows of closed wooden doors. Behind them, she knew, would be the crowded rooms where some of the hundreds of ladies-in-waiting and their maids lived.

When she peeked again they were skirting a vast audience chamber. Most of it was swallowed up in darkness. On one set of doors, dimly visible in the gloom, painted cranes soared and turtles swam; on another were mountains and waterfalls that reminded her for a moment of home. Leopards and tigers lurked in the shadows, their eyes glinting. Dragons coiled along the lintels and friezes and the ceiling glimmered with gold. Even the nail heads were of gold, intricately moulded. To one side of the hall was a courtyard with a small pond and a tiny square of grey sky. White flowers sparkled on the rocks. The heat was so intense it was difficult to move. The air was steamy, dense with moisture.

'Head down!' barked Lady Tsuguko.

They came to a walkway which led to the shogun's private wing, rising like a pavilion amid lawns, willows, sparkling streams and beds of purple irises. A crowd of women were waiting on their knees there. They shuffled back as the princess approached. At the front were seven shrivelled women with parchment faces and elaborate wigs of glossy black hair – the elders, who ruled over every detail of life in the women's palace. They had, so people said, once been beauties, among the hundreds of concubines of Lord Ienari, the present shogun's grandfather. But as far as Sachi was concerned they were fire-breathing dragons. She lived in fear of their sharp tongues and hard knuckles. What might they say or do, seeing a lowly creature like her daring to climb so high above her station? She raised her eyes just enough to see their faces as Lady Tsuguko ushered her past and was startled to see that they were looking at her kindly. One even smiled and nodded encouragingly.

She barely had time to register the strangeness of it before the princess and her entourage had swept on into a long, gloomy passageway. Reed blinds decorated with huge red tassels formed one wall. At the far end was a hefty wooden door.

This was the famous Upper Bell Corridor, the point of entry into the women's palace from the middle and outer palaces which were the domain of the men. Only the shogun used it; he was the only man who ever came into the women's quarters. There were a few men who worked in the women's quarters – desiccated priests, a couple of smooth-faced doctors, the brawny guards at the outer gates – but they did not count. As far as the women were concerned, they didn't exist.

Beside the door hung a ball of copper bells that sounded when the shogun was about to pass through; to ring them at any other time was a terrible crime. A lady-in-waiting was kneeling on each side, together with a couple of the lady priests, gnarled old women with shiny shaven pates who dressed like men in priests' robes. When Sachi had first seen them she had stared in surprise but now they just seemed part of the palace population.

The princess and her entourage wore the white robes, scarlet trousers and vermilion brocade coats which were the formal costume of the imperial court at Kyoto. But the noblewomen who filled the passageway were dressed in robes more lavish than any Sachi had ever seen. Some were embroidered with designs of wisteria and irises, others with cypresswood fans and oxcarts. On some, miniature landscapes in shades of blue scrolled across the ladies' curved backs. The princess and her ladies wore their hair long and straight, cascading to the floor. But the heads bent to the ground were adorned with heavy loops and coils of oiled hair bristling with combs, hairpins and ribbons.

The Dowager Lady Jitsusei-in, the shogun's real mother, was kneeling in the place of honour nearest the closed door. She had a pinched, sallow face. As a widow, she wore the short hair, plain robes and cowl of a nun. Sachi thought of her as the Old Crow. Every day she swooped into the princess's apartments in her black robes, finding fault here and there. No matter how hard everyone tried to please her, she always unearthed something to complain about.

The princess took her place on the cushion opposite her. But just as she was tucking her skirts tidily under her knees, a bevy of women in richly embroidered robes advanced slowly, grandly, into the passageway. At the front was a tall, imperious woman. She was dressed, like the Old Crow, in a nun's habit but her robes were of the finest silk, grey verging on purple, and her mantle was cunningly draped to reveal a glimpse of the soft skin of her snowy-white throat. Her bearing made it clear that, no matter what her costume, she was a princess.

Glancing up from her place at the end of the line, Sachi quailed. It was the Retired One, the fearsome Dowager Lady Tensho-in. Everyone was in awe of her. She was said to have a fierce temper and to be as strong as a man. Everyone knew how she had once picked up the late shogun, her husband, in her arms and carried him out of the palace during an earthquake. She was also, the women whispered, a superb horsewoman who could wield the halberd as skilfully as any soldier, and an expert at performing the chanting and dancing of the Noh theatre. Not yet thirty, she was in the full bloom of her beauty. A knowing smile lurked on her jewel-bright lips and her eyes burned with a fiery energy.

But all heads had swivelled to stare at the young woman who flitted behind her. She was no older than Sachi, with the snub nose and olive complexion of an Edo girl, quite different from the aristocratic pallor of the Kyoto women. Her childishly plump face was expertly painted in the Edo way, her full lips shiny with the greenish gloss known as 'fresh bamboo red'. She teetered along with tiny in-turned steps, one foot carefully placed in front of the other, her eyes demurely cast down. But the set of her shoulders showed that she knew every eye was on her.

Sachi gasped when she saw her. Beneath the make-up was Fuyu, the acknowledged star among the junior ladies. Sachi yearned to be as poised and self-confident as she. In Fuyu's presence she felt terribly conscious of her humble background and lack of breeding. As for Fuyu, she did not bother to speak to Sachi, except on the rare occasions during halberd practice when Sachi managed to get in a strike with her stick. Then Fuyu would raise her chin, look down her dainty nose and say with a sniff, 'Not bad, I suppose ... for a peasant!' She was the daughter of one of the captains of the guard and, like Sachi, a junior handmaiden. For all her airs, she was no more entitled to enter the presence of the shogun than Sachi was.

But what sent a murmur of admiration through the crowd was her spectacular over-garment. On

64

it was embroidered a breathtaking depiction of the city of Edo. Curving around the padded hem was the River Sumida lined with storehouses, with Nihonbashi Bridge arching across it. Edo Bay was a sinuous curve of blue at the hip. Spread across the back and sleeves were houses, temples, a pagoda, streets dotted with tiny embroidered figures, clouds of foliage, even a glimpse of the turrets of Edo Castle picked out in gold thread. It was a work of art, unimaginably costly, designed to draw every eye.

While her ladies took up their places along one side of the corridor, the Retired One swept up to the Old Crow and the princess and bowed deeply.

'Greetings, Your Imperial Highness,' she said, addressing the princess. She spoke quietly but her voice – unusually deep and sonorous – carried right to the end of the corridor. 'You are most welcome. What an honour it is to have you amongst us. I do hope you are taking good care of your health in this hot weather.'

The corridor was silent but for the flutter of fans. The heat was more intense than ever. Sachi wriggled uncomfortably, feeling her heavy garments clinging to her damp skin. She bowed her head, listening fearfully for the princess's reply.

As one who 'lived above the clouds' – she was, after all, the daughter of the late Son of Heaven and sister of the reigning one – Princess Kazu expected the deference due to her superior status. She never forgot for a moment that she had given up the gracious life she had enjoyed at the imperial court in Kyoto to descend to the level of these low-class commoners. Yet, far from behaving with proper respect and showing her appreciation for the princess's sacrifice, the Retired One took every opportunity to assert her own pre-eminence. As the widow of the previous shogun and adoptive mother of the present one, the Retired One had been the undisputed power in the palace before the princess arrived and was determined to maintain her authority.

In the privacy of the princess's apartments the aristocratic ladies who had accompanied Princess Kazu from the capital had nothing but contempt for the Retired One and her handwomen. They were unpolished, not to say downright vulgar, they whispered. How dared they treat the princess with such disrespect? And as for their samurai way of dressing and speaking and comporting themselves – well, it would be pitiable if it wasn't so laughable. When the princess's ladies met the Retired One's in the corridors, they would sweep past, barely bothering with a disdainful nod of the head. But among their maids there was frequent bickering. Voices were raised and they had even been known to start scratching, pinching, biting and tearing at each other's hair and clothes.

The two great ladies did their best to steer clear of each other. Nevertheless sometimes matters came to a head. The princess was far too proud and gently bred to stand up for herself, but Sachi knew what pain these encounters caused her.

When she had first arrived at the castle, the princess had insisted on speaking the archaic dialect of the imperial court. That was the idiom that Sachi had first been taught. Indeed, the princess had expected that everyone in the women's palace would adopt the Kyoto language and customs; that had been one of the conditions of her marriage. But in that as in much else she had been disappointed.

Now, instead of saying 'I thank thee for thy kindness' in her Kyoto drawl, as she would once have done, she whispered, 'I am indebted to you, Honourable Retired One.' She had a high-pitched, breathy little voice, like a bird.

For several minutes they traded compliments, each outdoing the other in the floweriness of their language and the extravagance of their flattery. Then the Retired One drew herself up.

'Once again I offer you my most sincere thanks, Your Imperial Highness, for taking such good care of His Majesty, my adopted son,' she said, looking straight at the princess and drawing her lips back in the sweetest, most poisonous of smiles. 'But I am embarrassed to see that the ushers have made their usual mistake. As always they have erroneously seated you in my position. You appreciate that, as your mother-in-law and the first lady of this household, I must be the first to welcome my son into his home. I'm sure you will be eager to join me in rectifying the error.'

There was silence. Everyone held their breath. Princess Kazu kept her eyes on the ground, chewing her lip.

'On the contrary, I should express my gratitude to you, My Lady Tensho-in,' she murmured with icy politeness. 'I am delighted to see you. But you know rather well that as the representative of the Son of Heaven and His Majesty's humble consort, I am obliged, unworthy though I am, to take precedence. I hope you would be so kind as to allow me to remain in my proper place, at least this one time.'

'We have had this discussion many times before, Daughter-in-Law,' said the Retired One smoothly, her black eyes sparking fire. 'You speak of tradition and of established ways of doing things. But you forget that we are in Edo Castle. Here in Edo we have our own traditions and our own ways of doing things, which were established by the first shogun, His Revered Majesty Lord Ieyasu, and which have held good for centuries. You know very well that I am the widow of His Majesty the thirteenth shogun, Lord Iesada. As your mother-in-law I am aghast that you could even think of going against my will. You insist on retaining your quaint title and provincial hair-style and way of dressing. That is all very well. But when we are forced to meet, you must behave with appropriate respect.'

Sachi quivered with horror, feeling the princess's humiliation as if it were her own. Princess Kazu said no more but shuffled back and knelt on the floor, while the Retired One took her place on the cushion.

II

The bells at the end of the corridor jangled. The thin, tinny sound was still reverberating when four drumbeats echoed one after the other from the ramparts of the castle, marking the hour. The elders and ushers, the ladies-in-waiting and grizzled lady priests prostrated themselves on each side of the door.

Sachi too was on her knees, staring at the tatami. She heard the screech of iron bolts being drawn through their hafts and the groan of the great door sliding open. There was a long silence followed by the muffled clank of steel. Among the babble of voices was the unfamiliar timbre of a male voice, the first Sachi had heard for nearly four years. Along with the patter of female feet and the swish of silk came the sound of soft-shod feet moving across the tatami mats with a jaunty male tread and the scent of an exotic and complex perfume. Time passed with painful slowness. The voice and the scent grew nearer. The chatter of compliments, of talking and laughter grew closer. Little by little the firm male footsteps advanced. Then they stopped, right in front of her.

'And this is she?' enquired the voice. The words sounded strange and archaic. Sachi had never before heard the formal terminology that only the shogun could use and it was with an effort that she worked out what he had said.

'Look up, child,' hissed Lady Tsuguko, the princess's chief lady-in-waiting, who was kneeling right behind her. 'Greet His Majesty!'

Sachi raised her head just enough to see a pair of white silk stockings. Then for a second she glanced up. She found herself looking straight into a pair of inquisitive brown eyes. Quickly she lowered her face, so hot with confusion that the tips of her ears were burning.

There was a long silence.

'What is her name?' asked the voice.

A murmur like the wind rustling a field of summer grasses rippled along the corridor. Lady Tsuguko laughed, a silvery tinkle of laughter.

'Sire, this humble child is Yuri, of the house of Sugi, bannermen to the daimyo of Ogaki,' she said, using Sachi's official name. 'She is under my protection.'

Sachi was still trembling long after the footsteps and the scent had faded away and she had heard the doors to the shogun's private apartments slide open and shut again.

In silence she followed the ladies-in-waiting back to the princess's suite, her thoughts whirling. She had broken the cardinal rule. She had raised her face to a being even higher than the elders, or Lady Tsuguko or the Retired One – to His Majesty the shogun, who was closer to a god than a man. Princess Kazu, of course, was of a higher rank even than he. But that was different. Sachi belonged to the princess. The princess had chosen her and kept her close to her. Had she misunderstood? Surely Lady Tsuguko had not intended her to commit such a breach of protocol?

Stranger still, His Majesty was young. She had always assumed that someone so powerful and all-knowing that he could never be seen by ordinary mortals must be old, gruff and fearsome.

And then there was Fuyu. Why had she been there, and in such showy finery? It was all too confusing. Padding along one corridor after another with bird-like steps, her shoulders modestly rounded as she had been taught, Sachi felt suffocated by all the rules and protocol. If only she could throw off the swathes of fabric and run,

70

skip and jump as she used to. She had to talk to Taki, her friend. She understood everything; she would know the answers.

Lady Tsuguko too kept silence until they reached the princess's apartments. There she swept Sachi behind the screens and made her kneel, facing her.

'Well, my dear,' she said. 'What a lucky girl you are!' She was positively beaming with delight. Sachi had never before seen her behave with anything other than grandeur and haughty condescension.

'You have done very, very well. Your parents will be proud of you.'

Quite forgetting her training, Sachi stared at her, dumbfounded.

'It seems His Majesty has accepted Her Highness's offer. Of course the arrangements must be made in the proper way. His Majesty has made his wish known, as you heard, and Her Highness has given her permission. The letter will be drafted and sent to His Majesty's emissary immediately. Come to me this evening when the sun begins to set and I will instruct you and prepare you.'

'Prepare me? For what?'

'The innocence of the child,' said Lady Tsuguko, laughing softly. 'You have been promoted to a maid of middle rank. At His Majesty's request Her Highness is presenting you to him as her farewell gift, as a concubine for him.'

A concubine! Sachi bowed her face to the tatami.

'I am not worthy of such an honour,' she stammered. Then, as she began to grasp the full

71

meaning of the words, she gasped with shock.

'Madam... Your ladyship... This is too great an honour. Her Highness has always been far kinder to me than I deserve. I have no greater ambition than to serve Her Highness.' The words came tumbling out. 'Please choose someone else. Not me, your ladyship. Please don't make me. I'm sure I won't do it right. I won't know what to do. I'm not ready. I know nothing, your ladyship. I know nothing at all.'

'Child! Do not presume to question our decision,' said Lady Tsuguko sharply. Then her voice softened. 'I know you are young still and know nothing of the world. But even you must understand that this is the greatest honour and the greatest opportunity any girl could ever have, particularly a girl of your background. Everything has happened very fast. I have not had time to teach you everything you need to know. But that is good. Your innocence is your charm. His Majesty leaves for Osaka tomorrow, so we will postpone the formal ceremonies of union until his return. If only you can please His Majesty, your foot will be firmly set on the lintel of the jewelled palanquin. Believe me, you will never have a chance like this again.

'We are depending on you,' she added, her voice stern. 'You will go to His Majesty tonight.'

Sachi was still kneeling in a daze when there was a commotion at the door. It was the Retired One. She had never before come anywhere near the princess's apartments. There was a flurry of silk as the ladies-in-waiting fell to their knees. The next moment she had appeared behind the screens. Her beautiful face was frozen except for a vein that throbbed in her temple. She faced Lady Tsuguko.

'Well,' she said, drawing herself up imperiously. 'You must be proud of yourself. You have done very well, you and that mistress of yours, foisting this creature – this foundling – on my son!'

Lady Tsuguko was on her knees. Looking up, she lifted her eyebrows and wrinkled her forehead in an expression of mock humility.

'What a surprise!' she said. 'We are most honoured, my lady, that you grace our humble quarters with your esteemed presence. Thank you so much for your congratulations. I have no need to remind you, of course, that Lady Yuri is the adopted daughter of the house of Sugi, bannermen to the daimyo of Ogaki.'

'Jumped up she may be but we all know where she comes from,' snapped the Retired One, the colour rising in her cheeks. 'She is an animal, an illiterate bumpkin. We saw her when you brought her here. She could not even speak like a human being.'

'Calm yourself, my lady. Your ladyship knows very well that we have been desperately searching for a concubine to provide His Majesty with a son. You too have been concerned about that. It would be the worse for all of us if the regent, Lord Yoshinobu, were in a position to take power. Several times we have set the selection process under way, but His Majesty has rejected every lady-in-waiting we have assigned him. Nevertheless,' Lady Tsuguko continued smoothly, 'for some reason this humble girl has taken his fancy.

73

We should thank the gods.'

'You bring disgrace on the House of Tokugawa,' spat the Retired One.

'I'm sure you have not forgotten, my lady, that the Lady Tama, the mother of the fifth shogun and the beloved consort of the third shogun, Lord Iemitsu, began life as a grocer's daughter, too lowly even to enter His Majesty's presence.' Lady Tsuguko's voice was sugary. 'She was, you will remember, an attendant delegated to assist with His Majesty's bath when she caught his august fancy. The sixth shogun, Lord Ienobu, was the child of a commoner so lowly that she could not even be granted the status of an official concubine. His Majesty, if I may take the liberty of reminding you, had to be reared in secret by a retainer. Then there was the Lady Raku, the mother of the fourth shogun. Let me think now. Was her father not a seller of second-hand clothes?'

'Enough, enough!'

'In any case it is nothing to do with us, my lady. You were present when His Majesty himself chose not your candidate but ours.'

'He is a boy,' hissed the Retired One. 'He knows nothing. You have bewitched him.'

'You know very well too that it is Her Highness's prerogative to offer His Majesty a concubine as a gift. You see, you have no reason at all to complain.' She placed her hands on the fragrant rice-straw matting, fingers together, the tips of her forefingers touching.

'Thank you so much for deigning to visit us,' she said with an air of finality, touching her fore-

74

head to her hands.

'And you have trained her, have you, in the arts of the bedchamber? I think not. The creature is a yokel. She will not last long!' With that the Retired One flung out of the room.

When the door had closed and the swish of her footsteps had faded away, Lady Tsuguko turned to Sachi, her aristocratic features crumpling with concern.

'Such cruel and unconsidered words!' she said. Sachi had never heard her speak with such feeling before. 'We are all expected to show deference to Lady Tensho-in but she takes her due too far. This one time she has lost the battle. Don't be sad, my dear. Put her mean-spirited envy out of your mind. The first time Her Highness saw you, she knew you did not belong there, in that rustic place. She knew your destiny was different, that you belonged with us. His Majesty is young and gently bred, not interested in playing with women. Lady Tensho-in and the elders assigned him many beautiful ladies of noble blood, well coached in the arts of coquetry, but he rejected them all. Her Highness knows him well. She knew that you, with your lovely face and pure heart, would be to his taste. Don't be afraid. Her Highness and I have full faith in you.

'But beware. Until tonight, stay here in the royal chambers. Who knows what jealousy may drive a woman to do?'

Sachi was still on her knees. She had been the target of barbs as savage as the Retired One's many times before. The women's palace, she had learned, was a slippery place where women would smile, then utter words that cut like a dagger twisted in your belly. No matter that she had been officially adopted by a samurai family, everyone knew where she came from. Many of the princess's ladies and the ladies from the women's palace too had been there when Her Highness had seen her and taken a fancy to her. To them she was a wild thing, an animal that the princess had inexplicably adopted as a pet. Even though she had learned their language, their walk and their manners, even though she moved among them every day, their world would always be closed to her. They were kind to her as one is kind to a dog.

She was still too numb to take the slurs to heart. The words that echoed in her mind were not the Retired One's but Lady Tsuguko's. 'Your lovely face and pure heart...' That was not how she saw herself at all.

If only she could see Her Highness. Was this why she had taken her from the village and lifted her to these heights? Was it to perform this service for her? She was sure there must be one last thing she needed to know that would make it all clear. But the princess did not return.

Nevertheless, she understood her duty. No matter what happened, she would serve Her Highness to the best of her ability. She was ready for whatever the gods might have in store for her.

III

Sachi went to the room where she slept with the

other maids and took off her formal kimono, laying it carefully over a kimono rack. Numbly she put on her maid's robes, took up her sewing and settled on her knees in a corner. She sat staring blankly in front of her, her needlework untouched in her lap. Then footsteps came skidding along the wooden corridor outside. The door flew open and a girl burst in, her face wreathed in smiles. It was Taki.

'Did you see him?' she demanded. She had a voice like a mouse's squeak.

Taki was from Kyoto, the daughter of an impoverished samurai who was a retainer of one of the princess's ladies-in-waiting, Lady Kin. Lady Kin had taken her into service when she was twelve and brought her to Edo. She and Sachi had entered the castle at the same time.

Taki was not beautiful – in fact she was rather plain. She had a thin, pale face, scarred with smallpox, and protruding teeth that made her look a little like a rabbit. When Sachi arrived, the junior maids, especially the Edo girls who had lived in the castle for some time, had bullied her mercilessly, imitating her accent and sneering when she made mistakes of etiquette. Taki always took her side, defended her fiercely and helped her learn the proper way to speak and behave. They had become firm friends even though Taki was of much higher birth.

Taki was jumping up and down, clapping her hands.

'Everyone's talking about it,' she cried. 'Everyone's jealous. You're to be the new concubine! But tell me, did you take a peep? What does he look like? Is he young? Is he old? Is he handsome? I've heard he's young and handsome.'

She threw herself down next to Sachi and put her arms around her, beaming up at her, waiting for an answer.

'Well,' Sachi mumbled uncomfortably, 'I hardly saw him. He looked quite young. He might have been handsome.'

'And you're to be a middle-rank maid. You must have done something very good in your last life to have such good fortune! You've jumped aboard the jewelled palanquin! I knew the gods couldn't have given you a face like yours for nothing.'

'But what does a concubine have to do?'

'Well, as far as I know the middle-rank maids have three shifts. There's the morning shift, the afternoon shift and the night shift. There have to be maids ready to serve Her Imperial Highness at any time of night or day.'

'Stop teasing. You know what I mean. What about His Majesty?'

'Well ... I don't know exactly. You'll be his number-two wife, the queen of this whole palace – if you have a baby, that is; but of course you will. Your family will be rich. They'll never have to worry again. It's the greatest thing that could ever happen to a girl. You will need maids. Let me be your maid. Please, Sachi, please. Please ask Lady Kin.'

'But ... I have to go to him tonight.'

'Don't worry about it. You must have seen pillow books and those strange pictures some of the ladies have, those "laughing pictures". Just shut

78

your eyes and bear it. It probably won't last long. It might even be fun. I've heard people say it's fun. Come on, don't hide here. Let's go and join the ladies.'

They had barely returned to the main chamber when Haru, Sachi's teacher, appeared, bowing at the door. Sachi was overjoyed to see her. She ran to greet her, tripping over her skirts in her haste. The ladies-in-waiting and their maids, filling the room like a flock of colourful birds, avoided looking at her. Only one cast a glance in her direction as she dashed by – whether of pity, envy or something else, she couldn't tell.

Haru greeted her with a deep bow, pressing her face to the ground. 'Profound congratulations,' she said solemnly.

She sat back on her heels and looked at her, then put her hand over her mouth and smiled hugely.

'The whole palace is abuzz,' she said, with a giggle of delight. Sachi gave her a wobbly smile in return.

Haru had a round face that might once have been pretty though she had long since become rather plump. Her cheeks were full and pink and her cat-like eyes nearly disappeared when she smiled, which was often. Sachi called her Big Sister though she was close to her thirtieth year. Usually she was full of laughter and merry stories, but in unguarded moments her face crinkled into sadness. She had lived most of her life in the women's quarters of Edo Castle, the most opulent palace in the land, she was accustomed to luxury unimaginable to those outside the precincts, yet she still wore the plain kimono of a lower-level maid and twisted her hair into a simple knot. While other women climbed through the ranks, she had remained a teacher. Perhaps because of her many accomplishments, or perhaps because she came from a part of the country not far from Sachi's area and could make sense of the barbarous dialect the child had spoken when she arrived, Haru had been assigned to turn Sachi into a lady.

They retired to their usual corner of the great room. For a while they made an effort to work at their lessons but Sachi's mind was far away. There was so much she needed to learn; and the only person she dared ask was Haru. Eventually she plucked up courage.

'Have you ever known a man?' she murmured in the softest of whispers.

Haru leaned forward. When she caught the words, she pressed her hands over her mouth, rocked back on her heels and exploded with laughter. The ladies who crowded the room glanced around, startled.

'Everyone envies you,' Haru said, smiling rather sadly. 'It is an experience most of us will never have, certainly not me.'

Even Sachi knew that very few of the three thousand palace women were ever likely to be chosen as concubines, yet they all had to remain pure throughout their lives.

'That happiness is denied us,' said Haru. 'Though I knew one lady once who grabbed at it.'

'What happened to her?'

'She disappeared. Women are not permitted to

80

make choices like that for themselves, particularly when they belong to the shogun. She was very beautiful. She looked a lot like you.'

Sachi could think of only one thing.

'What's going to happen? What do I have to do?'

'How on earth should I know?' said Haru with another burst of laughter. 'Be sure to shout out in pain so they know you have never been with a man. His Majesty is leaving tomorrow but he will be back soon, and then you can begin your career as his concubine in earnest. I can teach you the theory of what gives a man pleasure. I've studied plenty of pillow books. You are very young and you have a good chance of bearing a healthy son. The main thing is to ask no questions and do exactly as you are told. Never forget that you are a noblewoman now. Maintain your dignity at all costs. No matter what happens, never reveal your feelings, not for a moment.'

'But will it hurt?'

'Don't ever let anyone hear you say such a thing! This is the greatest honour anyone could ever aspire to! You are in your fifteenth year, Little Sister. Most girls your age are married. It's time you discovered what it means to sleep with a man.

'It is not my place to say such things,' Haru added, lowering her voice, 'but you are lucky. His Majesty is gentle and kind-hearted. His predecessors have not all been so. And he's young.'

Nervously Sachi ran her fingers along the tines of her comb, hidden in her waistband.

'What do you have there?' asked Haru.

81

'Nothing...'

But it seemed wrong to conceal anything from Haru, so Sachi brought out the comb and showed it to her. Haru's face changed.

'Where did you get this?' she snapped.

Ever since Sachi came to the palace the comb had been tucked away in the folds of her garments. Now she looked at it properly. It was beautiful, tortoiseshell embossed with gold, with what looked like the crest of some noble family inlaid in gold on the edge. It caught the light and lit up the dark corner of the room where they sat.

'I brought it with me from the village,' she said, bewildered. 'It's my lucky comb. I've had it ever since I was little.'

'Let me see it,' said Haru. She took it in her hand and turned it this way and that. Sachi peeked at her questioningly. Haru was staring at her as if she was trying to find something in her face. Her usual sunny smile had entirely disappeared. Then she blinked and seemed to come back to the present with a start. Sachi snatched the comb and tucked it into her waistband again.

'It's a magnificent comb,' said Haru, shaking her head as if to dislodge some private memory. 'A very fine piece of work. I didn't know they had such things in the countryside.'

IV

Long before evening Sachi was back behind the screens in the princess's private section of the room, waiting for Lady Tsuguko to give her her instructions. Still the princess was not there. Sachi had never known her to be absent for so long. She knew she belonged to Princess Kazu and that Her Highness had chosen to give her to His Majesty. If only Sachi could be sure that whatever she did now would lighten the princess's sadness, not increase it.

'The time is approaching.'

Sachi followed Lady Tsuguko into the principal dressing room. Oil lamps and tall candles lit up the darkest corners, casting flickering pools of light on the birds, trees and flowers exquisitely painted on the gold screens. Even the humblest items – the round mirrors on their stands, the towel racks, the make-up chests with brushes, combs, tweezers and tubs of cosmetics laid in neat rows on the floor in front of them, the round basins and long-spouted ewers – were lacquered in gold and marked with the imperial crest. Kimonos embroidered with summer flowers hung over kimono stands.

Sachi knelt. The maid in charge of the dressing room opened the small iron kettle containing the mixture of sumac-leaf gall, sake and iron used to blacken the princess's teeth. The bitter odour filled the air. Painstakingly the maid began to paint Sachi's teeth. Sachi watched in the mirror as the white teeth she had known since childhood – as shiny as those of a savage or an animal – disappeared. When she smiled she saw the cavernous mouth of an adult woman, one who has known a man.

The maid shaved Sachi's eyebrows, tweezing away every last hair. She massaged wax into her

83

face, then brushed on a layer of white make-up and puffed powder on top. Then she dipped her thumbs into charcoal powder and carefully pressed them precisely a finger's breadth above the place where Sachi's eyebrows had been. Two smudged ovals like the tips of a moth's antennae appeared on her forehead. The maid outlined her eyes in black, rouged her cheeks and painted a tiny petal of red safflower paste on each of her lips, turning her mouth into a small puckered rosebud.

From the mirror a flawless white mask gazed back at her. Sachi had become a doll, like the dolls that they set on tiers for Girls' Day.

Other maids kneeling around her divided her hair into strands, tugging and easing it until it lay spread on the floor like a fan. They oiled and combed each section, then swept it up and back, away from her face. It flowed down her back in a ponytail, as black and shiny as lacquer, bound with ribbons. Sachi stood motionless as the maids wrapped her in a ceremonial kimono of white silk like a wedding kimono – or a shroud.

The corridor outside was full of shadows and dark corners. It was the first time Sachi had ever left the princess's apartments after nightfall. The women lining the corridor stared at her curiously and whispered as she passed. The tapers that the attendants carried gave off a flickering light and the lanterns which burned along the passageways crackled. The smoke prickled her nostrils. Shadows danced along the wooden walls. The polished floorboards creaked under the light tread of many soft-shod feet.

When they reached the Upper Bell Corridor, Lady Tsuguko knelt outside the door to the shogun's apartments. She bowed her forehead to the ground and announced, 'I bring the lowly lady of the side room. I beg your favour.

'Do your best, child,' she whispered.

Inside her robe, Sachi felt a bead of sweat trickle from her armpit and run down her side. Silently she prayed that the crisp silk gauze was not stained or crumpled. She felt terribly alone. It was difficult to believe all this was not a punishment for some dreadful crime she had committed.

She found herself in an antechamber lit by lanterns and huge smoking candles set in tall gold candlesticks. The chief of the seven elders, Lady Nakaoka, tiny and elegant under her gleaming black wig, was there on her knees. Her attendants hovered respectfully around her.

'Come here, child,' she said, not unkindly. In the dim light her yellow flesh and sunken cheeks gave her the unearthly look of a demon mask.

In a dream Sachi stood stock still while the attendants removed her clothes.

'Legs apart,' said Lady Nakaoka briskly, gesturing at the futon spread in front of her. Sachi lay down, feeling small and vulnerable. The old woman leaned forward, tugging and probing. The examination seemed to go on for ever. Finally she pushed a knobbly finger deep inside her. Sachi stared at the ceiling, studying the intricate weave of the bamboo.

Haru's words echoed in her ears. Somehow she must retain her dignity. She must never show

85

what she was feeling, no matter how great the pain and humiliation. Sachi fixed her mind on a happier memory, as her old life came flooding back to her. She thought of the big wooden house with the tiled roof, the shrilling of the cicadas and the cool waters of the River Kiso. She tried to recall the little girl who had lived in the village, deep in the mountains, but there was only a breath of a memory left. Life had been so care-free then. Now she was utterly changed. She could never go back.

Lady Nakaoka nodded. 'Good,' she said.

Sachi knelt and the women untied her hair. Lady Nakaoka riffled through it strand by strand as if searching for something hidden.

'Good,' she said again.

Naked, Sachi was escorted into a dressing room. Maids bustled around her, tying her hair back loosely, securing it with a comb and helping her into a loose sleeping robe of fine white damask. Lady Nakaoka ordered her to kneel opposite her.

'This is your first time, child, so I will explain your duties. Pay full attention. Lady Chiyo and one of the lady priests will be keeping watch nearby. I myself and Lady Tsuguko will be in an adjoining room. We will all be alert and wakeful all night. It is our responsibility to listen to every word that passes between His Majesty and your-self. In the morning you will report your convers-ation to me. Remember it with care. Lady Chiyo and the lady priest will also report. All three accounts must tally. Beware of asking any favours from His Majesty. And remember – make sure you sleep facing His Majesty.'

V

As four drumbeats marked the hour, the bells in the Upper Bell Corridor sounded with a tinny jangle. Footsteps came sauntering along the corridor, accompanied by a peal of boyish laughter. The door slid open and the room was suffused with a musky scent. The ladies prostrated themselves.

Time seemed to stand still. Sachi kept her face pressed to the floor. Perfumed garments brushed past her. She heard the tinkle of sake being poured, the dull click of wooden cups, the sound of voices and laughter. The sweet smell of tobacco smoke mingled with the scent of perfume and the sound of small pipes being lit, puffed and tapped out.

'Come, my lady.'

The maids led her into the shogun's bedchamber. She was faintly aware of the splendid furnishings, the luxurious layers of bedding, the glimmer of red and gold and the sheen of the white silk coverlet. An arm's length away, to the right of the dais where the shogun's bedding was laid out, was a smaller, thinner futon with a lacquered pillow, cosmetics boxes and a day kimono beside it. That was where she would sleep once her duties were over. A little distance away were two more futons, one on each side. The futon next to the shogun's was for Lady Chiyo, the one next to her own for the lady priest.

Sachi knelt, eyes cast down. The maids were

fussing around the shogun. She heard the muffled clinks as with great care they laid his swords in the sword rest at the head of the bed and the rustle of silk as they removed his clothes and helped him into a sleeping robe.

Finally he lay down. There was a padded wooden pillow covered in red-tasselled silk for his head. Still not daring to look at him, Sachi pulled her robe tightly around her and took her place beside him. The futon was so soft and downy she felt as if she were floating. The maids snuffed out the lamps, leaving just one glowing. She heard the rustle of Lady Chiyo and the lady priest taking up their positions on each side of them.

In the gloom she lay with her eyes squeezed shut, hardly daring to breathe. She could feel the heat of the shogun's body like a burning ember right next to her. The smell of his sweat mingled with his scent was so strong she thought she would suffocate. Then a hand reached over and pulled her sleeping robe open.

'Beautiful,' murmured a boyish voice. For a while there was silence. She could feel his eyes roaming across her. Then a hand, soft as a woman's, brushed her stomach. She shivered at his touch. Light as a feather, the hand stroked her chest and circled her breast, cupping it for a moment.

'Beautiful,' whispered the voice again.

Gently he brushed her nipple with his fingers then ran his hand between her breasts to her belly button, very slowly as if exploring. Then he pushed her legs apart. She felt the heat of his hand as he stroked the inside of one thigh, then the other. Her body was prickling with strange sensations. But she was too afraid to pay much attention – afraid of what might happen next. Whatever he did, she knew she would have to endure it.

There was a gentle but firm shove. Dutifully she allowed herself to be pushed over on to her stomach. Fear swept over her, obliterating all thoughts from her mind. The hand pushed her legs wider apart. The moment had come: a heavy body was on top of her. Crushed beneath him, slippery with his sweat, she felt as if she was being ripped apart.

In shock and pain she shouted out. The heaving and panting seemed to go on for ever. Her face pressed against the pillow, she wondered how much longer she could endure it. But then something strange happened. An unknown sensation began to suffuse her body. First it tingled in her belly, then it crept up her spine. Her limbs seemed to have turned to water. The feeling rose to her throat. It was not at all unpleasant. In fact, it was quite delicious.

Then everything disappeared. She forgot her fear and pain. Drowning in the sensation, lost in his scent, a groan slipped from her lips. The shogun too grunted and lay heavily on top of her.

For a while they lay in silence. Coming to herself, Sachi felt a great wave of relief. It was over, she had survived. But she had done nothing, she had not known what to do. Supposing he was disgusted with her, suppose he no longer wished her to be his concubine?

He reached out. A bell rang.

'Oi!' he shouted. A maid scooted in on her knees. She lit a long-stemmed pipe, gave it to him and slipped out again.

Sachi turned and peeped at him. In the flickering lamplight his smooth chest seemed to glow with the pallor of someone who has never worked in the fields or even walked in the sun, who has lived his life entirely protected from the elements.

As her eyes crept up she made out an unassertive chin, then a delicate mouth shaped like a bow, curving at the ends. Then came a nose, slightly turned up, set in an oval face, then a pair of narrow brown eyes under fine eyebrows. The whiteness of his skin continued to the top of his head, which was shaved in the samurai manner. His neat topknot had become tousled and strands of his oiled hair hung loose around his face.

He was unlike any man she had ever seen. Indeed, he was not a man but virtually a god. This was the shogun, the ruler of the whole great land of the rising sun. This was also the first man she had gazed on since she had entered the women's palace. To her dazzled eyes he seemed to embody every noble quality she could ever imagine. And here he was, lying right next to her, his silken robe flung carelessly open.

He was gazing at her seriously. He seemed to be studying every curve of her face. He ran his fingers across her cheek and chin and around the nape of her neck.

'*O-yuri-no-kata...*' he said, as if trying out the

syllables. He had a clear, slightly high-pitched voice. 'Lady Yuri?' He drew on his pipe. Then he tapped it out, added a plug of tobacco, took the tongs, picked up a piece of charcoal and sucked at the pipe again.

'Shall we be friends?' he asked, almost plaintively.

Sachi gasped, shocked and frightened that this grand personage was speaking to her directly, and in such everyday language. She could feel the wakeful ears beside them straining to pick up every word. Dared she, she wondered, reply to him? She took a deep breath.

'Sire?' she whispered.

'Call me Kiku,' he said. 'That's what my women call me. Kikuchiyo is the name I had when I was little.'

She knew she had to obey, even though what he was ordering her to do was against all the rules of protocol.

'Sire ... I mean, Kiku-*sama*,' she whispered nervously, stumbling over the intimate syllables. There was the faintest of rustles from the shadows. 'You must know ... their ladyships...'

She gestured helplessly towards the bundles of bedclothes to each side of them.

'Don't worry about them,' he said, grinning at her. 'There are watchers and listeners everywhere. I won't say anything to harm you.

'The first time I saw you, you were in the gardens,' he added mischievously. 'You didn't know that, did you! You were running here and there, laughing, kicking up cherry blossoms with your feet, your hair flying. You looked so sweet,

91

like a little girl.'

Sachi could feel her face burning. She dared not say a word. He looked at her and laughed, not a polite artificial laugh like the court ladies uttered when they were embarrassed but an open, merry laugh.

'I had never seen anyone like you,' he went on, growing serious. 'You were like a deer, so free and so graceful. Your face is quite perfect. Your skin is so white, so smooth, so dewy. Like a lotus flower. Your lips.' He ran his fingers across them. 'And your eyes are green, dark green. Like a forest of pine trees in the mountains. My women are all chosen for their beauty, but none of them is like you – except, of course, Princess Kazu, your mistress. You are like matching shells. She told me about you. And once I'd seen you I noticed you again and again. I'm sure our destinies are entwined.'

Sachi lay in silence. She tried not to look at him, but every now and then she could not resist letting her eyes flicker shyly to his face.

He paused to refill his pipe and continued as if thinking aloud. 'In this world everything is in the hands of the gods and our karma. None of us can choose our destiny. I am a prisoner, like you. I have been called upon to be shogun. My predecessors – Lord Ieyoshi, Lord Iesada – spent their lives here in the palace with their page boys and concubines. They played music and wrote poetry, they hosted the deer hunt and went falconing. I thought my life was going to be like that too.

'But it has turned out quite differently. I've been out of the castle. I've travelled the Eastern

Sea Road and seen the fifty-three famous sights. I've been to the capital and negotiated with the Son of Heaven, more than once. I have seen my people, too, thousands of them. I'd never seen people like those before. They're not like samurai, they don't keep their feelings hidden. You can see their lives in their faces. You're like that. You bring sunshine to this gloomy place.'

'Sire!' said Sachi, horrified. A man should not reveal so much of himself, even to a worthless girl like her; and this was not just any man but the shogun. To have taken the remotest interest in the inferior beings who lined the road might hint at weakness to the listeners in the shadows; and to compare her to them might even be taken as criticism of their efforts to make her more polished. Unperturbed, he continued.

'Now my responsibilities grow heavier still. I'm supposed to be a true Barbarian-Quelling Generalissimo, not just bear the title. Tomorrow I leave for Osaka, to lead my troops to quell the Choshu rebels.'

He said the last words with a grunt, twisting his mouth into a samurai scowl as if trying on the face for size. Then he laughed disarmingly.

'Let's enjoy my last night here,' he said. 'There's so much I want to talk to you about. When I come back, we'll get to know each other properly. Now... Let me look at you.'

He lifted her hair, running the smooth heavy strands through his fingers. Then he shoved her sleeping robe aside. She closed her eyes as she felt the touch of his hand on her belly. She could feel the heat of his skin, breathe his scent. Gently he stroked, then began to move his hand lower.

'So fine, so soft... Like a flower,' he murmured.

VI

That night the rains broke, crashing on the tiled roofs like an army of galloping hooves. In the morning every leaf, petal and blade of grass in the gardens sparkled with moisture. Deep inside the palace the shogun and his concubine could feel that the humidity had lifted and the air had cleared.

The maids who came to wake them found the small futon beside the shogun's larger one undisturbed. The shogun had gone, slipping away before daylight broke. Only his scent lingered.

The four women who had watched over Sachi during the night – the venerable Lady Nakaoka, Lady Tsuguko, Lady Chiyo and the shaven-headed lady priest – were waiting for her in the antechamber. Sachi knelt before them. The morning air poured in. Feeling four sets of eyes fixed on her like hawks eyeing a field mouse, she tried to straighten her tousled hair and smooth her make-up. She knew she would have to repeat every conversation she had had with the shogun, but His Majesty's words were so precious that she wanted to keep them to herself, not recite them like a lesson. Timidly she glanced at Lady Nakaoka. To her surprise she was smiling at her.

'Well, well, my dear,' she said, stifling a yawn. 'You did very well. We heard all we needed to hear.'

A bevy of maids tidied Sachi's hair and make-up and helped her into her day kimono then swept her back along the corridors to the princess's apartments. She walked in a daze, hardly seeing where they led her. Everything had changed. She had awoken into a new world but she did not yet understand what that meant or what she had become.

Lady Tsuguko ushered her into the princess's presence. Princess Kazu was at her writing desk. She put down her brush.

'You must be tired,' she said, using the formal phrases with which a mistress thanks a servant. 'You have served me well.'

It was the first time she had ever spoken to Sachi directly. Sachi peeped up at her. For a moment their eyes met. Princess Kazu smiled a little sadly.

'You have done me great service,' she added. 'We must pray to the gods that you will succeed in bearing a son for me. Lady Tsuguko will see that you are properly rewarded.'

She turned back to her writing, and Sachi bowed silently and withdrew. She realized too late that in obeying the princess's orders she had jeopardized her affection; but she had had no choice. There was nothing else she could have done.

She was still pondering the princess's words when the shogun's emissary arrived attended by a train of maids carrying gifts. The shogun had sent a kimono chest to the princess, exquisitely lacquered in black and gold with a design of irises and swirling water. There was a cosmetics box for Lady Tsuguko and combs and fans for other ladies-in-waiting. For Sachi there was an amulet in a silken bag.

The princess accepted the gifts graciously and set them aside. Then she took up a brush and in her graceful hand wrote a note on a scroll.

After the emissary had gone Lady Tsuguko leaned forward.

'Madam, the time is approaching...'

'Today I am a little unwell. I have sent word to His Majesty that I will be unable to see him off. There is no need to trouble my ladies.'

Her face was a mask.

Sachi had never before found it so difficult to maintain a façade of decorous calm. It was so unfair. Her feelings had just been awakened; and now the shogun was leaving. Then there was the princess – her beloved princess. Why should she spurn her own husband, refusing to make her farewells when he was departing perhaps for several months? Sachi had hoped that, as one of the princess's ladies, she might have seen him one last time.

Slowly she opened the amulet bag. It was beautiful, of white silk with a silken cord. She had hoped he might compose a poem for her to mark their night together. But this was something even more precious – an amulet to ensure the birth of a son. She tucked it into her waistband along with her dagger.

She dared not shame herself by weeping in public. Careless of what anyone might think, she rushed out into the gardens and began to run blindly, splashing through the puddles in her wooden sandals. She ran and ran until the palace buildings were like dolls' houses in the distance. Then she turned her face to the sky and let her tears mingle with the rain.

Taki caught up with her, panting. She unfurled an umbrella and held it over her solicitously.

'Don't worry,' she said. There was something comforting about her familiar mouse-like squeak. 'He'll be back soon.'

3

The Lady of the Side Chamber

I

Deep inside the women's palace Sachi listened as shouts and barked orders drifted across the walls, echoing from the far reaches of the castle. Ominous rumblings set the windows and doors rattling in their wooden frames. She tried to imagine what the bangs and crashes might be – the creaking of great gates opening and closing; the sound of massive cannons, perhaps, being dragged out. There was the patter of running feet, the echo of distant gunfire. She made out the booming of war drums, the melancholy wail of conch-shell trumpets, the pounding of hooves, the whinny of horses. Then she heard the thunder of thousands of feet tramping away, fading further and further into the distance until there was no more than a murmur. She listened until every last sound had ended.

Silence fell, blanketing the castle. The shogun was gone, along with half his court and advisers and most of the regiments that were garrisoned there.

In the princess's apartments the women chattered quietly, trying to pretend that nothing had changed. The princess herself remained hidden behind her gold-encrusted screens. In the past Sachi had always been at her side. But today the princess did not summon her. Quietly Sachi went to help Taki and the other maids who were busy teasing out and combing the ladies' floor-length hair. Taki smiled at her.

'Lady Oyuri is the honourable lady of the side chamber,' she whispered. 'She is no longer a maid. Come and sit over here.'

So Sachi knelt while the maids massaged her shoulders. They renewed the dye on her teeth and manicured her small pink nails. Then they combed and oiled her long silky hair, lifting the tresses strand by strand and waving an incense burner under them to scent them. They painted her face and helped her into a fine silk-gauze kimono of plain white with red overskirts.

The lady of the side chamber! Just the previous day, she would never have aspired even to look on such a grand personage as the shogun. Now it was over, that experience she had dreaded so much. She could hardly believe it had really happened. As the maids fussed around her, she sat in a dream. She tried to picture His Majesty's – Kiku-*sama*'s – smile, his sparkling eyes, his

98

white skin, his hands. But already the image was fading. The more she tried to hold on to it, the more it slipped away.

All day long the ladies of the castle swept in and out. At midday the seven elders swirled in with a swish of silk and disappeared into the princess's audience chamber. The heavy scent of their robes lingered, perfuming the air. Puffs of smoke came wafting out from their tiny long-stemmed pipes. The shadows were gathering and the sultry heat had become bearable by the time Lady Tsuguko emerged. The ladies-in-waiting clustered round. She addressed Sachi directly.

'You will sleep in my chamber now,' she announced in her grandest tones, 'not with the maids. Of course, if you have a child you will receive your own room, with a staff of four maids and three dressers. You will be given a monthly salary in rice and gold *ryo* sufficient to feed and pay them. You will also receive a clothing allowance and grants of lamp oil, soy bean paste, salt and firewood for heating the bathwater. If you have a child, your family too will be given honours. Your father will be promoted and will be awarded a good stipend. I will personally make sure that all this comes to pass. His Majesty too will protect you and ensure that your family is suitably honoured.'

After the evening meal, while the maids were clearing away the trays of small dishes, sweeping the rooms and laying out bedding for the night, Sachi sat down and began a letter to her mother and father. Ever since she had arrived at the palace, she had not had time to write to them at

99

all, neither had they written to her. Her father, she knew, prided himself on his writing skills. After all, he was the village headman. And although her mother couldn't write, she could always call on him or on the village priest, the local scribe, to write for her. Perhaps they thought themselves too humble now that she had become a great lady; or perhaps they were not even sure what had become of her.

Sachi picked up a brush, chose a plain paper of mulberry bark, sat down with a candle at her elbow and began to write as simply as possible, forming the letters carefully in her childish hand-writing.

'Greetings,' she wrote. 'I trust you are taking good care of yourselves in this humid weather. Here in the palace gardens the irises are in full bloom. I am well. I have been working hard, pursuing my studies. I try my best not to bring shame on you. Don't worry about me. They are taking good care of me here. I have recently been promoted. I am now a maid of the middle rank.'

As she thought of the tiled roofs of the village and the sun rising over the mountain, tears welled in her eyes and trickled down her painted cheeks. She could not bring herself to say more. She ended with conventional greetings then gave the letter to Taki. She had already requested that she be her personal maid, the official maid of honour to the new concubine.

Sachi took up her sewing but her thoughts were far away. In her mind she went over and over everything that had happened in the course of the night, trying to recall the shogun's words, his

100

gestures and his touch. Taki sat next to her in companionable silence, busy with her needle. After a while she turned her small pointed face towards Sachi, looked at her with her big eyes and asked in the tiniest, softest of whispers, 'Was it terrible? Did it hurt? Was he ... handsome?'

Sachi glanced around. The ladies-in-waiting were chatting loudly, busy with their sewing. They were doing their best to remain distant and aloof but every now and then one or other of them shot a glance at her. She knew they too were bristling with curiosity. She thought of the shogun, of his soft white hands running across her body, and for a moment a ripple of those sensations he had awakened quivered in her stomach. She felt a surge of happiness at the memory of the night before and the knowledge that this youth – the greatest man in the realm – cared about her. Then she remembered that he was gone, she didn't know for how long, and she was overwhelmed with sadness.

She met Taki's eye and gave her a shaky smile. Taki smiled back. She understood everything Sachi wanted to tell her.

The maids had moved Sachi's belongings into Lady Tsuguko's chamber and laid out two sets of bedding on the dais. Compared to the cramped quarters where she had slept before, the room seemed frighteningly huge, full of lurking shadows and dark impenetrable corners. Sachi lay on her futon feeling small and lonely, listening to Lady Tsuguko's regular breathing and the occasional rustle of Taki and the other maids turning in their sleep.

101

Then she felt a tug at the corner of her quilt. It was Taki. She crept quietly under the cover and curled up next to her. The two girls fell asleep with their thin white arms wrapped around each other.

The next day was the official naming ceremony. Afterwards Lady Tsuguko smiled at Sachi and said, 'Come. We must conduct the ceremonial visits.'

Sachi bowed in silence. She had been thinking of nothing but that night with the shogun. But now she realized her new life as the lady of the side chamber was just beginning.

'First we will pay our respects to the Retired One,' Lady Tsuguko told her. 'Remember that yesterday was yesterday and today is today. There is no need to be apprehensive.'

This time Sachi was at the front of the group that swished with slow deliberate steps along the shadowy corridors, escorted by a bevy of maids. Rain clattered on the tiled roof of the walkway as they crossed to a section of the palace she had never seen before. The oppressive heat had lifted a little and it was possible to breathe again. More corridors led to the Retired One's apartments, where maids scuttled before them, sliding open one set of doors after another. In each room a crowd of ladies-in-waiting knelt, bowing gracefully, manicured hands pressed to the rice-straw tatami. Sachi's plain robes in the imperial style seemed sadly impoverished compared to their gorgeously dyed and embroidered garments.

As for the rooms, she had never before seen

such opulence. The Retired One's chambers made Princess Kazu's seem quite threadbare. Even the tatami mats with their gold bindings were finer and softer than those in the princess's apartments. Cabinets and shelves laden with writing boxes, tea ceremony utensils, mirror stands and cosmetic sets of the finest lacquerware were crammed along the walls. Embroidered kimonos, among them the magnificent one Fuyu had worn the previous day, hung over kimono racks. The folding screens that partitioned the rooms were painted with landscapes and designs of birds and flowers on a background of lustrous gold leaf and the alcoves were furnished with elegant flower arrangements, paintings and calligraphy. Even the handles and sheaths of the guards' halberds were adorned with gold or mother-of-pearl.

Everything was almost too luxurious, too splendid. Even the incense which suffused the air was a little too heavy.

The Retired One was awaiting them in the innermost room, surrounded by attendants. Fuyu was among them, kneeling close beside the great lady. Beneath her cowl the Retired One was wearing a pale silk kimono with a design of wisteria, quite unbecoming for one who had taken holy orders. Her perfectly proportioned face was carefully arranged into the blandest, most innocent of smiles, as if there was nothing she could dream of that could give her greater pleasure than to see Sachi. Sachi bowed to the ground. She was trembling with nervousness.

'So this is the new concubine,' said the Retired One in her deep, vibrant tones, inclining her head

103

graciously. 'Welcome, my dear. The gods have smiled on you. You have found favour with my son. We all pray that you will bear him an heir.'

Sachi had thought the all-powerful Retired One would ignore her and address her remarks to Lady Tsuguko or at the very least communicate through her chief lady-in-waiting. She had certainly not expected her to speak to her directly. She prostrated in silence. The Retired One's smile was even more terrifying than her scowl and there was a distinct hint of malice in those unfathomable black eyes.

'But I am afraid, Lady Tsuguko, that your protégée may not be comfortable here,' the great lady went on smoothly. 'Our life is rather poor. She is used to the far greater luxury of Her Imperial Highness's quarters. I am sorry that I will have to deprive her of the comforts she enjoys there.'

With a shock Sachi realized what she meant. As the shogun's concubine, she was now officially the Retired One's daughter-in-law. It was a harsh enough fate to be the daughter-in-law of a peasant, let alone the daughter-in-law of such a woman. Not only that, she was a daughter-in-law of far lower status than the shogun's wife, Princess Kazu. Would she really be required to live in the Retired One's quarters and obey her every whim? She quailed. The attendants tittered sycophantically. Amongst the laughter she could pick out Fuyu's mocking tones. The Retired One was playing with her like a cat plays with a mouse.

'This unworthy creature is very sensible of your kindness in recognizing her new status,' said

Lady Tsuguko dryly, 'but she is, as you know, the property of Her Imperial Highness. I will not impose upon your generosity by forcing her upon you. We are unendingly grateful for your condescension.'

Sachi did not relax until they had backed out of the last of the Retired One's chambers, bowing profusely with every step.

'Lady Tensho-in's apartments are magnificent, are they not?' said Lady Tsuguko with a curl of her aristocratic lip, once they were safely in the corridors again. 'Almost excessively so, one might say. When Her Imperial Highness came as His Majesty's bride, Lady Tensho-in refused to move to the widows' quarters in the west citadel. She insisted on remaining in the apartments designated for His Majesty's consort. Thanks to her machinations Her Highness was allocated servants' quarters in which to live. Servants' quarters! The shame of it! Can you imagine? That is why our rooms are so humiliatingly crowded and dark. Her Highness has two hundred and eighty ladies-in-waiting and each of us has staff and we are all expected to fit into one small wing. Now perhaps you begin to understand the bad blood between Lady Tensho-in and Her Highness.'

Sachi had never heard her speak so fiercely before. They padded along in silence for a while.

'If you have a child you will find the Retired One shows quite a different face,' said Lady Tsuguko after some time. 'But now we will visit the Dowager Lady Honju-in. She will wish to be your friend.'

Lady Honju-in's apartments were deep inside the palace where only the occasional ray of sunlight ever penetrated. When Sachi's eyes became used to the gloom, she saw that they were passing through a labyrinth of rooms even more sumptuous than the Retired One's. An army of aged ladies-in-waiting knelt in greeting. Finally they reached the innermost room where, in the midst of heaps of treasures, a tiny imperious figure knelt very upright on a dais with her elbow on an armrest. Her small white face peered out of the shadowy folds of her cowl, illuminated by the flicker of the lantern which burned beside her. Sachi had never seen anyone so old.

'What a pretty face!' Lady Honju-in wheezed, stretching out a small finger to brush Sachi's cheek. Her skin was as fragile as a moth's wing, like a membrane stretched across the bone. 'Such a relief for us all that my grandson has taken a fancy to you. Such a difficult boy. We all hope and pray you will bear him a son.'

At the mention of the shogun Sachi felt her face blazing as hot as if Lady Honju-in had discovered some terrible secret she had been keeping hidden. Horrified, she kept her head bowed. Why were these great ladies speaking to her directly and even deigning to touch her? If only all the politeness and ceremonial could be over. The old woman chuckled.

'When I came to this palace I was a young girl, as young as you, my dear,' she went on. Her voice crackled like autumn leaves crunching underfoot. 'Do you know what I used to do? I used to help out in the altar room and the kitchens. I was

106

pretty then. At that time Lord Ieyoshi – Toshi-*sama*, I used to call him – was the heir to the throne. His father, Lord Ienari, was shogun still – now that was a man! He knew how to make children. Fifty-three he had. Let me see now. There was Princess Toshi – that was long before my time; then a daughter – she lived three days...'

She listed all fifty-three, one by one, counting them off on her fingers.

'Then there was Princess Yasu. She was the last one. That was when the old man was nearly sixty. What a man! Women, men – even dogs, I heard. He bestowed his seed far and wide.

'Anyway, one day Lord Ieyoshi saw me. The old man had his eye on me too, but he let Lord Ieyoshi have me. And that was it. The next thing I knew, I was a concubine. In those days there were plenty of us. Some had babies, some didn't. But mostly the babies died. I was young and vigorous, like you. They tell me you're a peasant, so you must be more vigorous even than I was!'

She gave a wheezing cackle like ancient bellows opening and closing. Then she peered at Sachi, her black eyes glittering. Sachi started as the old woman clamped a withered hand on her arm.

'It's very hard to be a concubine, my dear,' she said. 'Look at you, so young, so glowing, those pretty eyes shining. Try and remember that you are only one of many – if not now, then soon enough. You are only a womb for hire. Never forget that. That is woman's lot.'

Sachi felt a shiver run down her spine.

'You will never be a samurai but you can at least try to live like one. You must learn to hide your feelings, your happiness as well as your sadness – even from yourself. Learn to be strong. Few people in the great interior will ever have any idea how you feel. But I do. Come and see me when you feel sad.

'The gods favoured me,' she went on dreamily. 'My boy, my first son, Masanosuké, lived. I was in my fifteenth year. My other sons died, everyone else's sons died – but he lived. He was a darling boy, like a child his whole life. Everyone died and died, so many people died. Then Lord Ieyoshi died and Masa became shogun. Just think! My boy, my little son, became Lord Iesada, the thirteenth shogun! Then even darling Masa died. How I wept! It's a terrible thing to attend the funeral of your own child.

'I have been blessed. But now I'm tired. Too many terrible things have happened. Now I leave it to my daughter-in-law. She runs everything. She's a strong woman. You can come to me if she makes you miserable. I haven't forgotten what it's like to be a daughter-in-law.'

'Lady Honju-in is still a power in the palace,' said Lady Tsuguko gravely when they were once more gliding along the corridor. 'It's good that you have her approval. If the gods are with you and you tread with care, your life may turn out like Lady Honju-in's. To be the mother of the shogun's heir and later of the young shogun himself – there is no position more powerful than that. I will make sure that everyone knows you are under her protection. You must be very careful. There are many people who will be jealous of you.'

There were many more visits still to make. Swishing grandly from room to room, Lady Tsuguko led the way to the apartments of Dowager Lady Jitsusei-in, the shogun's mother. But instead of her usual frown the Old Crow's sallow face, framed in its black cowl, was wreathed in smiles.

Then they paid their respects to the three ladies – the chief elder, Lady Nakaoka, Lady Chiyo and the lady priest – who had watched over Sachi throughout her night with His Majesty. They thanked each of them for their help and kindness and presented them with lavish gifts. They also had to visit the other six elders, the lady priests and all the ladies of high enough rank to enter the presence of the shogun.

The day was coming to an end by the time they turned wearily back towards the princess's chambers. The last visits had been a blur – the warrens of rooms, the doors sweeping open, the bowing, the smiling faces, the choruses of greetings, the polite exchanges. Sachi's legs were as heavy as if she had climbed several mountains. She had seen corners of the palace she had never even imagined existed. Her face was aching from smiling so much.

'In days to come you will find that the most unlikely people want to be your friends,' Lady Tsuguko told her. 'Beware of those who conceal enmity behind a mask of kindness. Her Highness has always protected you, but now your fortunes have changed she may no longer be able to do so. If you are to survive you will have to understand the workings of the women's palace. It is time for your education to begin in earnest.'

Sachi had been hoping that the princess might summon her when they returned to her apartments. But Princess Kazu remained invisible behind her screens. Perhaps she was writing poetry or just looking blankly into the darkness as she sometimes did. Sachi wondered what she thought about at those times. Did she wish her life had turned out other than it had? She had given up everything to marry the shogun and now he was not even there. If only Sachi could bear a son for her, that might make her happier.

Then Sachi remembered what old Lady Honju-in had said: 'You are only a womb for hire.' The words made her shudder.

II

Early next morning Haru's round smiling face appeared at the door of the princess's chambers.

'Congratulations, my lady,' she said to Sachi, bowing deeply. 'How does it feel to be the new concubine?' They retired to the usual corner where they had their lessons.

'Oh, Big Sister,' whispered Sachi, 'it's so hard to keep silent. My thoughts are not my own. Ever since that night with His Majesty, I have been floating about like a bit of pondweed. I'm counting the days till he comes back.'

Haru covered her mouth with her sleeve and laughed until her eyes crinkled up and disappeared in the folds of her cheeks.

'Sounds like someone gave you powder of dried

110

lizard,' she said. 'Did you ever hear of that? They find two lizards, let them copulate, and just as their yin yang essences are about to spill they pull them apart. Then they put them in separate ovens and bake them. Their desire for each other is so strong that the smoke from one seeks out the smoke from the other, no matter how far apart the ovens are. Then they grind them into powder. It's said to be unbeatable.'

'Poor things,' said Sachi, putting her hands over her mouth and giggling helplessly. It was a relief to be able to be herself, even if just for a moment. The ladies-in-waiting and their maids who filled the room, chattering and sewing, nudged each other and chuckled.

'In my village there was an old man who sold baked vipers for that purpose,' gasped Sachi, dabbing her eyes with her sleeve. 'We called him Grandpa Viper. I can see him now. People said that if a woman nibbled even a small piece no man would be safe!'

'These stories are all very well,' said Haru, looking stern. 'But don't ever forget that that's all these feelings are – just so much nonsense, exactly the same as if someone had given you lizard powder or dried viper. They'll pass soon enough. You're now His Majesty's number-one concubine and his number-two wife. You're bound to His Majesty by ties of fealty and obligation. That's what's important. You can enjoy these foolish feelings but don't be taken in by them. Don't let them take over your life.'

Haru's advice was always wise. But Sachi couldn't help thinking that, as Haru had never

111

even been with a man, how could she possibly know? It was best to change the subject. Besides, there was something else on Sachi's mind.

'Big Sister,' she said, 'supposing I am not with child. What will happen then?'

'We will pray and make offerings,' said Haru. 'There is nothing more we can do. The gods will decide. Be careful,' she added. 'There are women here who may wish you ill.'

'Big Sister, there's so much I need to know,' said Sachi. 'Why...?'

She stopped. Even she knew better than to ask why anyone would want to harm her. She would have to be patient, to wait and watch.

'Make sure you are never alone,' said Haru, frowning and looking very serious. 'Not for a moment. You must always be surrounded by your women. Never touch your food till it's been tasted, and stay away from wells and high places. Too many concubines lose their lives. We all care for you and will help you, but there are others who may be eaten up by jealousy.'

Sachi stared in disbelief. She'd never seen Haru so serious. Her words sent a shudder down her spine, but it was too soon for her to worry about herself. All she could think of was the gentle young shogun.

'Many dreadful things have happened here, ever since the barbarians came and even before that,' said Haru sternly. 'People outside the palace know nothing about what goes on here. I'll tell you a story. It took place right at the beginning of poor Lord Iesada's reign, it must be ten or eleven years ago now.'

112

Sachi leaned forward with her chin in her hands, resting her elbows on the low table between them, and tried her hardest to banish all thoughts of the shogun from her mind.

'It was the year after Lord Ieyoshi died,' said Haru. 'He had twenty-seven children but only one son survived. That was Lord Iesada, the son of Lady Honju-in, that sweet old lady you visited yesterday; she was not so sweet then, that's for sure. As for him, he was... How can I say?'

She glanced around at the princess's ladies. They were all busy at their sewing, chattering in their high-pitched Kyoto accents. She moved a little closer to Sachi and lowered her voice.

'He was ... how can I put it? Anyway, he was not interested in women, probably not in men either. He was like a little boy. His first two wives passed away before he even became shogun. The first was Lady Nobuko. She was the daughter of a court noble from Kyoto. She was twenty-five when she came down with smallpox and died. I remember her well. I was a little girl when she died. I had just arrived in the palace. She was a sweet lady and she played the hand drum beautifully. He used to sit and listen while she practised. He may even have been fond of her, though everyone knew they would never have children.

'The next wife arrived the following year. She was a daughter of the Minister of the Left at the imperial palace in Kyoto. She was a shrunken little thing. When she climbed out of the imperial palanquin, she stood no higher than it did. One of her legs was shorter than the other. She used to

113

hobble around the corridors. Behind our hands we all said she'd hopped aboard the jewelled palanquin. Not that Iesada cared. He carried on playing his games and paid no attention to her. She lasted a year, then she died too. People started to worry that there was a curse on His Highness. "If you want to die, marry Iesada," that was what they said. And there was still no chance of an heir.

'That didn't matter so long as his father, Lord Ieyoshi, was still shogun. But then His Majesty passed away. It was very strange and sudden – a terrible thing. He didn't die a natural death, we all knew that.'

She stopped for a minute, then dabbed her eyes fiercely with her sleeve and went on.

'So Lord Iesada became shogun. He had no wife, no concubines and no heir. When he came to the women's palace, it was to see his mother, Lady Honju-in. He was a sickly boy – not a boy, he was a man then, he must have been in his thirtieth year; but he still seemed like a child. He was always ill. He had this thin pale face like a hungry ghost and big unfocused eyes. What he loved most of all was roasting beans, stirring them about in the pan with bamboo chopsticks. He had a gun a Dutch merchant had given him. He used to chase after his courtiers with it. It made him laugh to see them run. Or he would just sit and stare around him blankly.

'So, you see, Lady Honju-in was the most powerful person in the inner palace – you could say the most powerful person in the realm. Whenever the chamberlains had a new law that needed to be signed, it was Honju-in who told His Majesty whether to put his stamp on it or not. Everyone was wooing her. There were bolts of brocaded silk, vases, tea bowls, lacquerware, sugar cakes, all sorts of beautiful things pouring into the castle. Gifts to her, gifts to her ladies... What a life she had!

'One day the guards were making their morning rounds. They were checking the garages when they noticed blood dripping from one of the palanquins and an arm and a leg dangling out. The door had been shoved back and a woman stuffed inside, bundled up in a hanging. When they unrolled it she was stark naked and quite dead. We all rushed to look and ran away screaming. Everyone was in the most terrible panic.

'It turned out to be a Lady Hitsu, one of the higher-ranking officers in the catering department. Of course, you can't know everyone in a place like this. She had been stabbed. We all thought it must be jealousy. She had had relationships with several of the ladies. One, a Lady Shiga, had been mad about her apparently, so suspicion fell on her.

'But then it came out that Lady Hitsu had become rather close to Lord Iesada. She had had access to the kitchens and used to bring him beans and sit with him, chatting to him while he stirred. There was a particular sort of dried fish he really liked and she used to bring that to him. Maybe she was planning to seduce him. If she had become the mother of his child, she would have ousted Lady Honju-in. She would have become the power behind the throne.

'There was no investigation, of course. No one ever found out who had hated Lady Hitsu enough to kill her, whether it was jealousy or because she tried to reach above her station. No one dared suggest it was anything to do with Lady Honju-in; and even if it was, she was far too powerful for anyone to do anything about it.'

Sachi shuddered with horror. Her hands were clasped so tight her palms were clammy with sweat. She glanced around at the ladies-in-waiting, imagining she saw them exchanging glances, plotting against her. She knew very well that beneath its placid surface the women's palace was seething with rivalries and hatreds. But she had always assumed such enmities would never affect a lowly person like herself. Now her position had changed. Everyone must be waiting to see if she would be the mother of the shogun's heir. She would have to be very careful indeed.

Suddenly she thought of the Retired One. She must have been still in her teens – not much older than Sachi was now – when she entered the palace to be Lord Iesada's third bride. And she had won. She had outlived him and taken old Lady Honju-in's place. But all the same, to have shared a bed with such a lord... In this world no man could choose the path his life took and women even less so, even someone as brilliant, fiery and beautiful as the Retired One. And then, at the end of it all, to be a widow, washed up on the shore of life not long after her twentieth year. Sachi tried to imagine what sadness and disappointment lurked behind her steely exterior. It was something that previously would never have entered her mind. But now, with the memory of His Majesty still so fresh, the world looked different.

'What happened to Lord Ieyoshi?' she asked uneasily. 'And to Lord Iesada?'

Haru scowled and shook her head. 'Another day,' she said grimly.

III

Sachi was so distracted she was sure she would not be able to concentrate on her studies. But as she copied out poems, trying to make her brush dance across the paper with the same fluidity and grace as Haru's, she felt her mind becoming calm like the surface of a pond after the wind has died down. She was way behind the other junior ladies in practically everything – calligraphy, poetry writing, tea ceremony, incense guessing and all the other courtly arts that women had to know – but she was determined to catch up as quickly as she could.

In the afternoon she went to the training hall. Her maids followed behind her, bearing her costume. Taki carried her halberd.

Several junior women were already there, dressed in the uniform of palace guards. Sachi too changed into stiff black divided skirts and a black jacket of coarsely woven silk with the crest of the House of Tokugawa – three hollyhock leaves – appliquéd on the back. The fabric felt rough against her skin. She put on a stiff black cap and tied it firmly in place with a white band

117

wrapped tightly around her head.

It was the first time she had seen the others since her promotion. They gazed at her curiously. They were still children, with thick black eyebrows and white teeth. She alone had the shaved eyebrows and blackened teeth of a married woman, one who has known a man. She kept her face lowered. Her cheeks were blazing with self-consciousness but she also felt a quiet sense of pride.

Her fellow pupils gathered around her, bowing and chorusing 'Congratulations.' Fuyu was among them, as pretty and pert as ever, her make-up perfect, her hair glossy with oil. She even managed an icy smile as she spat out the word 'Congratulations.'

The first job was to clean the mats. As the students scuttled up and down, sliding damp cloths across the tatami, Fuyu pushed in between Taki and Sachi, close to Sachi's shoulder.

'Well,' she hissed, 'what a surprise. I suppose Her Highness forced His Majesty to choose one of her women, and the only one the right age was you. What an ordeal for His Majesty, having to touch a creature like you!'

Sachi was taken aback. Fuyu must have forgotten herself completely to reveal her feelings like this, in such a crude, direct way. She started to run faster but Fuyu sped up too.

'If you need anything, let me know, anything at all,' Fuyu panted, her voice growing louder. 'You must have trouble eating white rice. I'll get you some barley, or millet. Or some animal feed from the stables. You should sleep there too. You'd feel at home.'

Sachi said nothing. Perhaps Fuyu was hoping she would make a fool of herself by getting angry. But she would not succeed in provoking her.

When the mats were spotless, the students knelt at the side of the hall and slid their halberds from their bags. With an effort Sachi focused her attention on her weapon. Just to hold it made her feel calm. She drew it from its scabbard and studied the blade. It was beautiful, of the finest steel, elegantly curved. The convex edge was sharp enough to cut a man in half with a single sweep and there was a channel along the blunt side to let the blood drain away. Like a sword, it was strong enough to slice through armour twice as thick as a man's finger but flexible enough not to shatter, made by a swordsmith whose family had specialized in the art for many generations. The long wooden shaft was lacquered with a design of flowers and inlaid in gold with the Tokugawa crest. With the blunt side towards her Sachi powdered the blade, cleaned and oiled it. She ran a cloth along the handle, then returned the blade to its scabbard and put the weapon back in its bag.

Then she took a practice stick from the side of the hall. When she held it upright it was nearly twice as long as she was tall. It was of white oak, light and smooth, tapering at one end.

'Do your best,' shouted the teacher, Lady Masa, a sinewy, grey-haired woman. She was nearly as tall and slender as a halberd herself and had a reputation as a dazzling swordswoman. 'These are dangerous times. Now that His

119

Majesty is absent, we must be ready to defend the castle. Focus your minds. Train hard.'

The students practised the different moves – striking, slashing, thrusting, parrying and blocking. Then they put on helmets and protective clothing and began to spar. The hall was filled with the deafening smack of wood on wood.

Growing up in samurai households, Sachi's companions had begun learning the halberd when they were little girls so that they would be ready to defend their houses when the menfolk were away. Among the samurai, halberds – *naginata*, 'long-handled swords' – were part of a bride's trousseau. They were long and light – light enough for a woman to wield and long enough to enable her to take a good swipe at her assailant's legs before he could get close enough to grab at her or strike with his sword. For many years – throughout the reigns of twelve generations of shoguns, longer than anyone could remember – Japan had been at peace. Apart from driving off the occasional brigand or thief, women had never expected that they would have to use a halberd for defence. Halberd practice had become largely a form of martial art, a discipline of mind and body.

But in the women's palace halberd practice was deadly serious. The palace was the shogun's home. He went to the outer palace, where the men gathered, to deal with matters of state, but the women's palace was where he relaxed and spent his nights. And of course there were no male guards there. All the palace women were required to be adept with the halberd so that they could defend the shogun if an enemy ever attacked. Everyone knew that the women of the shogun's palace were formidable warriors, and to reach such a level of expertise required strict training and daily practice.

Sachi had missed years of training, but today she felt invincible. Her body seemed light as a flame. She darted forward, scything at her opponent, then skipped out of reach before letting fly with a barrage of sweeping cuts and thrusts. She could feel the lightness of the stick in her hand and the tingling vibration of the tip as it swept through the air.

But compared to Fuyu she was clumsy. Fuyu was the best fighter in the class. She and her stick seemed to become one, flowing gracefully from one crisp movement to the next. She was beautiful to watch.

They hadn't been practising for long when Fuyu broke away from her sparring partner. Out of the corner of her eye Sachi saw Fuyu coming towards her. She planted herself firmly in front of her and stared at Sachi, her eyelids twitching and her eyes narrowed to slits. It seemed she had totally lost control of herself.

'Such pretty white skin,' she sneered, her voice shaking. 'So proud of yourself with your shaved eyebrows and black teeth. Think you fool us, do you? We know what you are. Well, peasant girl, let's see you fight.'

Her lips drew back. Sachi remembered both Lady Tsuguko's and Haru's warnings. She knew Fuyu was a much better fighter. There would be no quarter. She was in for a beating, that was sure, but nothing would stop her accepting Fuyu's challenge. Nothing could be worse than to be seen as a coward. She drew herself up, trying to match Fuyu's disdain. She thought of the shogun's steady eyes and cool touch. She would prove to everyone that she was worthy to be his concubine.

She bowed. Then she braced herself, feet wide apart, holding her staff loosely in both hands, and took a deep breath. Focus, she told herself. Hold your centre.

The next moment Fuyu was bearing down on her, her eyes glaring and her forehead beaded with sweat. Sachi quailed like a field mouse watching as a hawk swoops down, unable to move, unable to escape. Flailing her stick and shouting at the top of her voice, Fuyu took a swipe at her chest.

Sachi felt the rush of air as the stick swung towards her. She was braced, staff poised. She parried the blow, though the force of the stroke sent her staggering back. Her staff was still quivering when Fuyu spun round and aimed another, then another, launching blows at her chest, her head, her shins. Sachi leaped and danced, blocking and parrying. It was all she could do just to fend off the attack. She tried to get a blow in for herself but there was no chance.

Then Fuyu paused, panting, just long enough for Sachi to get her balance. When Fuyu hurled herself at her again, Sachi was ready. Sachi caught the blow on the handle of her staff, spun round on her toes and lashed out with the blade end. Fuyu drove her back, striking at her chest and shins, battering at her wrists, trying to force

122

her to drop her staff.

Sachi was gasping for breath. For a moment she lost concentration and let down her guard. A mighty whack in her ribs sent her staggering back. Fuyu charged in, walloping her with her staff, battering her with blows. Then she dropped to her knees and stabbed at her stomach. Sachi doubled up, gasping. The room spun. She could hear the blood ringing in her ears. Fuyu loomed over her, her face purple, her stick raised.

An image swam into Sachi's mind of the gentle shogun and of the baby that might be growing inside her. Suddenly she was perfectly focused. Panting, she straightened up. The two women circled around and around, holding each other with their eyes, staves pointed. Sachi could see nothing but Fuyu's hate-filled face and the walls of the training hall revolving behind her.

Then Fuyu stepped back and raised her staff. It curved through the air and came swinging down in a blur. Sachi parried the blow. The two staffs came together with a thwack.

Sachi leaped back, spun round on her toes and lashed out, driving Fuyu back. She struck out with one end of the staff then spun round and struck with the other before Fuyu had time to recover her balance. A look of disbelief flashed across Fuyu's face. Sachi had her on the defensive. She skipped to and fro, poised like a dancer. She was air, she was flame. The staff was part of her body, an extension of her arm. Sachi danced forward and back, putting her weight behind every blow, striking here, thrusting there, trying to get under Fuyu's defences.

Fuyu's face was puffy. She looked as if she wanted to cry. She lost concentration. At that moment Sachi brought her staff down on Fuyu's arm. Fuyu yelled, her face twisted in fury. Sachi dropped to her knees and swung at Fuyu's legs.

Fuyu returned to the attack. Her face was flushed dark red. She struck at Sachi's stomach. Sachi tried to parry the blow but her stick flew from her hand. Thrown off balance, she staggered and fell. Before she could get up Fuyu started to rain blows on her, whacking her back, her legs, her arms. Then she tossed away her stick and jumped on her, pummelling with her fists.

Sachi twisted, wriggled and got in a punch wherever she could but Fuyu had her firmly pinioned. They rolled over and over, punching, kicking and scratching. Sachi felt Fuyu's hands close around her throat. She grabbed Fuyu's hair and felt a triumphant thrill as a clump came out in her hand. Fuyu let out a shriek and relaxed her grip. Sachi sat up sharply, threw her on to her face and knelt on top of her. Fuyu was wriggling and shrieking. Sachi took hold of her arm and twisted it up her back until Fuyu thumped the floor with her free hand in submission.

Apart from their gasps, the hall was totally silent. A long shadow fell across them. Lady Masa was standing over them.

'Enough!' she yelled. 'Never bring your private feelings into this hall. You're breaking the prime rule of the samurai code. Training is to be done with humility, you hear?'

Gingerly Sachi took off her helmet. She was bruised all over, but she didn't care. She threw

Fuyu a triumphant glance. But she now knew for sure she had an enemy.

The women clustered at the entrance to the hall, slipping their feet into wooden sandals. Fuyu glared at Sachi. Her round snub-nosed face was stained with tears, her lips pressed together in a scowl. She bent down and picked up a mud-encrusted sandal. Before anyone could stop her she drew her arm back and hit Sachi full on the side of the head with it.

Reeling from the blow, Sachi put her hand to her head. Earth-soiled footwear: it was the ultimate insult. The pain meant nothing, but the humiliation was not to be borne. In the old days a samurai woman, she knew, would have committed suicide in the face of such an affront. She certainly would not do that. She was not a samurai and never would be. She would practise and practise until she could beat Fuyu with ease every time. And one day she would repay the insult.

'After all,' Taki said in a triumphant whisper, putting a skinny arm round her, 'His Majesty chose you, not Fuyu.'

IV

A few days after the shogun left, letters arrived for Princess Kazu, for the Old Crow, his mother, and for the Retired One, his stepmother. There was also a letter for Sachi. She took it off to the room she shared with Lady Tsuguko and held it for a long time then very slowly unscrolled it. It was written on lightly scented mulberry paper. The calligraphy, she could see, was exquisite – gentle but passionate, like His Majesty. She pictured him sitting in his palanquin or at a small table at one of the rest stops, his brush dipping and swooping like a plover in flight. While most women of the samurai class knew only the *hiragana* syllabary, growing up in the women's palace she had also begun learning the *kanji* Chinese characters in which classical literature was written. She did not yet know enough to decipher every word in the shogun's letter, but she could tell that he was describing his travels. He concluded with a poem in which he referred to some beautiful flowers he had seen which, he wrote, filled him with yearning for her lovely face.

The problem was, she would have to reply. Sachi had learned enough to develop an eye for a fine hand. But her handwriting was so childish it would surely give him a bad impression of her, and her poetry composition was still elementary.

There was also a letter from her mother. The village priest had written it for her in plain round script. As she unrolled it Sachi was overwhelmed with homesickness.

'We are so happy to hear from you and grateful to you for being such a devoted daughter,' Otama said. 'We did not know what had become of you. We dared not write to you at the castle. We were sure if you were living there you would be ashamed of us. Please take care of your health in this humid weather. We are happy to hear that you are working hard. Please be sure not to make yourself a burden on the good people who have adopted you. We are proud you are now a maid of the middle rank. As you know there is great disorder on the road, but don't worry about us. We're all fine.'

Disorder on the road? Sachi had never heard of such a thing. Even when there had been famines and rioting, the road had always been clear and orderly. Her father had seen to that. It sounded strange and disturbing. But there were more immediate things to think about. Sachi read on.

'Little Omasa who you used to carry on your back got ill in her stomach when she was in her third year and died. We have another daughter now called Ofuki. So far with the blessing of the gods she is healthy. Your little brother Chobei is in his ninth year. He has become a strong boy. He is doing well with his studies and helping your father at the inn. You remember little ugly Mitsu from the inn along the road? She went as a bride to her cousins on the other side of the hill. Her first baby died but she has a healthy child now.'

Sachi sat in silence for a while. In her mind she was back at the top of the hill with her baby sister on her back and her friend and little brother beside her, on a cold autumn day with clouds scudding across the sky. She could see the line of porters emerging from the woods on the far side of the valley, as small as insects, pouring out in an endless swarm. So many things had changed since then. She thought of her sister and tears ran down her cheeks.

But there had been someone else there too. What of Genzaburo, their leader, with his gangly brown legs, whooping laugh and talent for mischief? He had been an older brother to her, her comrade in arms. She remembered the madcap adventures he had led them on, the forays into the woods to climb trees or root out badgers, the secret jaunts down to the river to swim. What had become of him?

She ground some ink and started to compose an answer. The weather, she wrote, was improving. The rains had come at last and the humidity had lifted. The hydrangeas were in full bloom in the palace gardens. She enquired after her grandmother, the innkeeper across the road and the women who used to gather at the well. Then she added, 'And by the way, how is the innkeeper next door and his family?' She rolled the letter up, sealed it and gave it to one of her maids.

Then she sat down to think about the poem she would send to His Majesty.

Sachi was having to learn how to be a great lady, carving out a niche for herself in the palace hierarchy and discovering how to behave towards the lower ranks. Until recently she had been almost as lowly as they. Now she was expected to treat them as if they did not exist.

Exasperated, Lady Tsuguko told her, 'When you call the honourable whelps, you don't say, "Excuse me." You shout, "You! Come here!" You don't ask them to do something, you command them. They're not people. They don't count.'

Morning to night, Sachi busied herself with her studies, while Taki learned the shogun's schedule off by heart, down to the last detail – where he would be having lunch that day, where he would rest and where he would stop to admire a famous view or to worship at an important shrine.

Every morning, when Sachi woke up, Taki announced, 'His Majesty will be on the road by now.' When the drums sounded the hour she said solemnly, 'The fourth hour. He'll be at Chigasaki, having lunch,' or 'He'll be in Yumoto at Sounji Temple, viewing the hydrangeas; they're said to be lovely right now,' or 'The sixth hour. He'll be at the great inn in Mishima, dining on eel.' Then she would smile and glance at Sachi to check that she was properly impressed with the extent of her knowledge.

Sachi smiled back at her. It was a comfort to know that in this vast palace full of women whispering and plotting behind her back, there was one person she could trust completely. It made her feel she was not alone.

The place names meant little to her. She only knew that with each day that passed the shogun was moving further away. This was his third journey to the west in little more than two years. Before, she had been too young and too involved in her own concerns to know anything about the shogun and his activities. Now that she was his concubine she waited impatiently for reports to arrive. Messengers galloped back and forth bringing dispatches to the government offices in the outer palace, and from there news quickly seeped into the women's palace.

But it seemed an oddly reluctant progress. On the previous occasions, the shogun had reached the capital, Kyoto, a couple of weeks after leaving Edo. This time the journey was to take a month, with plenty of stops for rest and sightseeing along the route. It seemed a strange way to go to war.

Indeed it was hard to imagine him fighting at all. Sachi could picture him stepping out of his palanquin to gaze at a famous sight, composing a poem, joking with his courtiers or dining at some country inn like the one her father ran. She could even picture him on horseback, looking splendid in a suit of armour and a helmet with a ferociously moustachioed face mask such as she had seen on the samurai who had passed through the village. His surely would be far more magnificent and awe-inspiring than theirs. But leading his troops into battle? She could not begin to imagine what that might mean.

The following morning Sachi awoke with a dull pain like a sword turning slowly in her belly.

'Taki, Taki,' she whispered, shaking Taki awake.

'What is it?' asked Taki, frightened.

'I don't know what to do. My monthly bleeding. It's started.'

'So you're not with child,' said Taki.

Sachi began to sob, wiping her eyes with her sleeves. She had failed the shogun, failed the princess, failed to provide the House of Tokugawa with an heir. She thought back to the battle she had had with Fuyu and wondered if it was the blow to the belly that had brought it about. She had never known before what it meant to have enemies.

Confined to her chamber, she spent the days alone with only Taki and her maids for company. Sometimes she paced up and down, sometimes she toyed with her sewing, unable to think of

130

anything except her failure in this all-important task. She hardly dared look at the amulet the shogun had given her, supposedly to ensure that she would have a child. She hid it deep inside a drawer.

'There's no point upsetting yourself so,' said Taki on the second day. 'There's nothing to be done. You're still His Majesty's concubine and you are both very young. Our destinies are in the hands of the gods. There will be plenty of opportunity when he returns.'

Sachi nodded. She was beginning to feel a strange relief. She had been under such pressure, but now she knew where she stood. She looked at herself in the mirror. Her oval face glimmered palely back at her. She gazed at the smooth contours, at her green eyes slanting upwards, at her small rosy lips. It was all she had in the world, that face. It was that face that had brought her to the palace and taken her into the shogun's bed. How was it possible that she, a mere peasant girl, had been born with a face like that? It was almost as if the princess was there, hidden behind the mirror, but a younger, more childish, carefree version.

She smiled at her reflection. She must learn everything that was necessary to make His Majesty happy – to sing, to dance the elegant court dances, to play the koto, to write a beautiful script and turn a witty poem, to perform the many varieties of tea ceremony and play the games that sophisticated women played, like the incense-guessing game and the shell-matching game. She would make herself the perfect concubine.

By the time her confinement ended, the rains had finished and summer had begun in earnest. In the princess's chambers the ladies-in-waiting lounged, fanning themselves languidly, too exhausted to sew. By day even the insects and birds were silent. In the evening mosquitoes buzzed maddeningly in the twilight. Cicadas shrilled and the bullfrogs in the palace ponds brayed like a stableful of ancient horses.

Not long after Sachi had re-emerged, Lady Tsuguko swept grandly into the room that they shared.

'Her Highness requires you to attend upon her,' she said, smiling.

Many days had passed since Sachi had last seen Princess Kazu. Overjoyed, she followed Lady Tsuguko through the princess's apartments. Shyly she slid on her hands and knees to the edge of the folding screens and peeked around. The gold walls of the inner chamber shimmered in the light of lamps and candles.

Princess Kazu was kneeling at a low writing desk, her brush poised above a scroll of paper. Her hair cascaded down her back in a glossy black waterfall and coiled around her on the floor. She had grown thin and wan. Beneath her white make-up her skin was translucent. Her long, melancholy face, aquiline nose and small mouth puckered like a rosebud seemed to embody everything that was noble. To Sachi the pallor of her skin made her look all the more regal, as if she really did live above the clouds.

When she looked at Sachi her face brightened.

She spoke softly to Lady Tsuguko.

'Her Highness is glad to see you,' Lady Tsuguko told Sachi. 'She is sorry to hear that you are not with child, but she begs you not to distress yourself. In the future you will have plenty of opportunity. His Majesty frequently writes to Her Highness of his regard for you. You are sisters now. She would like you to attend upon her regularly, as you used to.'

Thrilled and grateful, full of the love and awe she had always felt for the princess, Sachi took her place beside her. She picked up a fan and began to fan her. This part of her life at least was returning to normal.

But why had the princess kept away from her when she had been such a favourite before? Sachi waited until she was alone with Taki in a corridor, far from even the sharpest ears. Then, in the softest of whispers, she asked her.

'If she was an ordinary person and not Her Imperial Highness, I might wonder if she wasn't jealous,' Taki replied firmly.

'You mustn't say such things!' exclaimed Sachi, horrified at the suggestion that the princess could have anything other than the most exalted feelings.

'If you had had a child, you would have taken precedence over her. It would have given you power in the palace. Now everyone can relax, at least until His Majesty returns.'

'It is not for us to speculate on Her Highness's feelings,' said Sachi sternly. 'But maybe...' She glanced around to check there was no one within earshot. 'Maybe she was sad because she did not bid farewell to His Majesty. Maybe seeing me reminded her of that.'

'Don't you think sometimes she might become tired of living above the clouds? She might wish she could run and jump and laugh, like you do. Maybe seeing you makes her more aware of how dull her life is. Maybe that's why she didn't want to see you.'

Sachi took Taki's thin hand and curled their fingers together.

'That's a terrible thing to say,' she said, smiling at her fondly. 'Her Highness is not like you and me. Anyway, I'm trying to improve my behaviour. I'm a grown-up now.' But in her heart of hearts she wondered if Taki might be right. 'I couldn't help noticing,' she went on softly. 'The Retired One and Lady Honju-in – they were surrounded by their ladies. They were not hidden away behind screens.'

'Of course not,' said Taki impatiently. 'They are great ladies but they are not royalty. The princess is of the blood. That's the way things are done at the imperial court. Only those of the very highest rank can enter her presence, or those she specially favours – like you. I know I shall never see her.'

'I'd hate to be as grand as that,' whispered Sachi. 'I'm glad I have you as my friend.'

A few days later another letter arrived from Sachi's village, much longer than the last. Everyone in the family was fine, Otama wrote. 'We all miss you very much but we are happy that you have become a fine lady. Thank you for

134

remembering us.

'Times are hard here,' she added. 'We hear talk of chaos in the capital. The fighting has not reached us yet, but the policing of the road has declined. A lot has happened that I can't tell you about in writing. Do you remember Genzaburo, the younger son from the inn across the road? He had become a fine young man. His father had high hopes for him. But when the rebel force from Mito came through, all that talk of politics turned his head. He told his father he had heard that even peasants could join the militia. He asked permission to go and defend his lord and master. His father said no. Then one day he disappeared. At least it was him, not his older brother Ichiro. At least Ichiro is a dutiful son. He is still here, taking care of his family.'

The words merged together in a blur. So Genzaburo had gone to fight. Sachi dared not even wonder what might have become of him. And all this talk of fighting...

When she first arrived in the palace, Sachi remembered, she had heard a strange unearthly wailing. It had been so unlike a human noise that she had thought it must be the ghost of some long-dead concubine who had shrivelled away, old and unloved. Taki had told her it was one of the princess's ladies-in-waiting whose brother had been killed in fighting in the capital. After that from time to time she heard crying, sometimes from the princess's chambers, sometimes floating down the corridors from some distant part of the palace.

Once she remembered the princess herself in

135

tears, quietly weeping behind her screens. It had been the previous summer, when the heat was at its height. A flurry of messengers had arrived. Distracted, the princess had ordered Lady Tsuguko to send the messengers in to her directly they arrived and to call in priests to arrange prayers and ceremonies to avert ill fortune.

If only she had a better idea of what was going on, Sachi thought. Sometimes the clang of alarm bells floated across the castle walls and she heard shouting and the rattle of gunfire, like pebbles tumbling down a hillside. Once, after the shogun left, she had heard baying in the distance like a pack of wolves. Later the older women told her they had heard there was rioting in the city, but there was no need to worry, it was under control. The previous autumn there had been thunderous crashes from just beyond the moat. The flimsy walls of the women's palace shook so violently that everyone had thought it was an earthquake. It turned out that the palace of the lord of Choshu was being torn down beam by beam.

When was His Majesty going to move against the lord of Choshu? And when was he coming back? Those were the questions on everyone's minds. But the days went by and nothing seemed to happen.

V

Autumn had arrived. The trees in the palace gardens were blazing red, orange and yellow. Every morning Sachi's maids laid out five unpadded

136

raw silk kimonos for her to wear, one on top of the other, in shades of maroon and green. The nights had grown long. Dusk came so quickly that the attendants had to start lighting the lamps in mid-afternoon.

On the surface at least, life in the palace continued as it always had. From time to time letters came from the shogun, brushed in his beautiful calligraphy. He was now in Osaka Castle. The maple leaves in the gardens, he wrote to Sachi, were particularly lovely this year. He told her in conventional phrases that he missed her, but there was no hint of what was going on and he never mentioned when he was coming back.

She was thrilled when his letters came and happy to know that she was his. She did her best to keep her memories of him alive. But the intensity of her initial feelings had faded. Until he returned – whenever that might be – she would concentrate on learning as much as she could about this strange new life of hers.

In some ways it was a bit like a prison, though an opulent one. Now that Sachi was a great lady, she was expected to remain closeted in her rooms. Taki had become her mediator just as Lady Tsuguko was the princess's. Sometimes she played the shell-matching game or the card-matching game with her maids. From time to time one of the ladies-in-waiting invited her for a tea ceremony or an incense-guessing party. And she often went to sit with the princess, who was helping her with poetry composition.

There were the usual festivals to mark the passing of the seasons. But when the palace women

137

celebrated the Festival of the Dead in the seventh month Sachi discovered that she was now too grand to participate in the dancing. She had to sit primly, peeking from behind her fan, as the lower-ranking ladies and maids undulated in and out of the verandas and around the palace gardens in their summer kimonos, waving their fans and clapping their hands to the tootle of flutes and the roll of drums. It was the price she had to pay for having risen to such heights.

But despite everything she was contented. The only person who might have disturbed her peace was Fuyu, but ever since their battle in the training hall Sachi had done her best to avoid her. Sometimes their paths crossed in music lessons or dancing class or during a tea ceremony or an incense-ceremony practice, but when this happened Sachi always bowed with scrupulous politeness and quickly moved on. She attended halberd class at a different time. And she never saw the Retired One at all.

It was early morning. Footsteps came scooting along the corridor outside the rooms that Sachi shared with Lady Tsuguko. The door flew open and Taki's thin face came peeking round.

'Mushroom hunt today!' she announced in her mouse-squeak of a voice, beaming with excitement.

Sachi loved the mushroom hunt. She waited impatiently for the maids to finish combing and scenting her hair. Then they did her make-up and swaddled her in kimonos, tugging the layers into place so that the different colours flared at the neck and wrist. On top of it all they put an over-

138

kimono, a thick padded coat with a quilted hem embroidered with autumn leaves in red and gold. Swathed in her layers of clothing she was like a huge multi-petalled flower.

Taki led the way outside. Holding baskets of woven bamboo, the two girls slipped away from Sachi's other maids and ran off, giggling. The landscaped section of the gardens was a perfect place to play hide-and-seek. Entirely forgetting that she was supposed to be a grand lady, Sachi crouched behind a towering rock tufted with moss and lichen and waited for Taki to find her. They skipped along the paths that meandered from rock to pond to bridge to teahouse, kicking through the red, brown and gold maple leaves.

Taki, who had grown up among the beautiful gardens of Kyoto, had taught Sachi the names of all the rocks, ponds, bridges and teahouses and what they were meant to represent.

'This is Eight-Fold Bridge,' she said solemnly as they clambered up a curving bridge that arched across a stream lined with small white pebbles. Her black eyes were sparkling and her pale, rather plain face was flushed. Her thick hair hung to the ground in a long black ponytail, tied here and there with ribbons. She had tucked her kimono skirts up. A skinny white leg peeked out some-what unbecomingly.

'No, it isn't,' laughed Sachi. 'It's Half-Moon Bridge. And over there we have Lotus Pond,' she said, gesturing towards the green-tinged lake in front of them, where turtles huddled on the rocks and red-lacquered pleasure barges were moored. She caught a glimpse of her reflection in the water – a court lady in voluminous robes, with hair immaculately coiffed. Framed in the glossy hair was the same oval face that used to glimmer back at her from her mother's mirror in Kiso. There were her eyes slanting upwards, sparkling green. There were her small lips and arched nose. It was a shock to see herself there, like seeing a ghost.

'No, it's West Lake, like West Lake in China,' shouted Taki. 'That's the stone causeway, those are Crane and Tortoise rocks and that's White Thread Waterfall.'

They ambled around the lake, skirted Moon-Viewing Pavilion and sat on the veranda at Lapis Teahouse, swinging their legs inside the bell-like skirts of their robes. Then they crossed a bridge to another section of the gardens where great rocks and silvery streams made them imagine they were strolling among soaring peaks, rushing gorges and dark rock-strewn gullies.

'And this?' asked Taki, glancing sideways at Sachi.

'Kiso...' said Sachi under her breath, shivering a little in the autumn air. It was uncanny how much it reminded her of home.

Women were pattering around in their outdoor clogs, clutching their bamboo baskets and peering at the ground. As a child Sachi had spent happy days every autumn searching for mushrooms in the hills around the village. Here, she could see mushrooms poking out of the pine needles that carpeted the ground and places where the needles had been disturbed, indicating that there was a mushroom underneath. To her it was obvious that the mushrooms had been carefully placed for the ladies to find; they could not possibly be growing there naturally.

'I can't see any,' said Taki, getting bored.

'Here are some,' said Sachi, picking a couple and slipping them into her basket. The important thing was not to be too successful but to leave plenty for the other ladies to find.

Haru came bustling over, bundled in so many layers that she looked like a big round dumpling. Her cheeks were even pinker than usual and her eyes were screwed up against the cold. She turned the large brown flat-topped matsutaké mushroom that she was holding upside down so that the fat stem stood straight up.

'Look what I found,' she said. She peeked into Sachi's empty basket. 'You'll have to do better than that at pulling up mushrooms.' She covered her mouth and shook with laughter. 'You never heard the verse about the bride who didn't know how to pull up a mushroom stem? This is the closest any of us will ever get to being a bride – apart from you, of course, my dear Lady of the Side Chamber! You can tell us all about mushroom stems!'

Sachi and Taki looked at each other. Every year Haru made the same joke, but this year for the first time Sachi understood it. Hot with embarrassment, the two girls put their hands over their faces and giggled.

Then Sachi heard the crackle of pine needles. Footsteps were approaching through the trees. A young woman dressed as a junior handmaiden was stumbling towards them, staring at the

141

ground, chewing her lip. Her pretty pert-nosed face was pale and drawn, her eyes puffy. Her make-up was smudged, her hair roughly twisted into a knot. Her kimonos had been carelessly thrown on. Strangest of all, she was alone.

It was Fuyu.

Sachi looked around hastily, wondering how they could escape. But Fuyu had already reached them. Her eyes flickered downwards then up at Sachi, as if she had been overcome by an uncharacteristic bout of shyness.

'So it's you,' she said in a dull voice.

Sachi could not bear to look at her. She had not forgotten Fuyu's savage attack in the training hall, nor the blow with the sandal.

'You've done well, peasant girl,' said Fuyu. Her words came out in a rush. 'Your star's gone up and mine's gone down. There must be some destiny that joins us.'

Sachi frowned. Was this a game? Was Fuyu playing with her? She didn't know how to reply. Taki had grabbed her sleeve and was trying to pull her away.

'I know you hate me... I wanted to see you,' Fuyu mumbled, brushing her eyes with her sleeve. 'There are things I understand now. No matter what you hear about me... I wish we could have talked.'

For a moment she looked straight at Sachi. In her eyes Sachi caught a glimpse of the same wild fear she sometimes saw in the princess's eyes, like that of a deer caught in a trap. Then Fuyu turned and rushed away distractedly as if she hardly knew where she was.

Taki and Sachi looked at each other and laughed uneasily. It was a laugh of perplexity, not amusement. The day seemed suddenly to have grown colder and darker.

A couple of days later, Taki came bursting into the room where Sachi sat sewing.

'Have you heard?' she gasped.

'Of course not,' said Sachi, pretending to be cross. 'I don't hear anything these days unless you tell me.'

'Let's go for a walk,' said Taki. They pulled on extra kimonos and went into the gardens. It was a chilly autumn morning and the sun cast a pale light on the rocks, ponds and pine trees. They hurried along until they came to Lapis Teahouse, as far as possible from curious ears, and huddled together on a sheltered corner of the veranda.

'What's happened?' Sachi asked, smiling in anticipation of exciting news.

'It's Fuyu,' said Taki. 'She's run away. The palace is full of it.'

Sachi wanted to laugh with relief. Could it really be true? Was her rival really gone? Could she walk in the gardens and go to halberd class freely, without worrying about meeting her? Yet somehow she was not surprised. Fuyu had looked almost haunted the other day, as if she barely belonged to this world any longer.

'It was yesterday, when Lady Onkyo-in went out to pray at the shogunal tombs,' said Taki. 'Fuyu was in her retinue. When it was time to leave they found she was missing. In the end they had to come back without her.'

143

'Lady Onkyo-in...?'

'The one everyone calls Lady Shiga. The late Lord Iesada's concubine – you know, old Lady Honju-in's son, the one who... She was Lady Shiga before she took the veil.'

Sachi drew her breath through her teeth and pulled her padded outer kimono tighter around her. The wind rattled the thin walls of the teahouse. A heron rose, startled, from the far side of the pond and flapped away, its white wings flashing. Somewhere, somehow she had heard of Lady Shiga, but she could not remember why or what she had done. She had a feeling that whatever it was, it had not been good.

'Maybe Fuyu wandered off,' she said slowly. 'She was acting so strangely. It's dangerous out there in the city. Maybe she was abducted.'

'She told Yano, one of the Retired One's maids, she was going to try to escape. She sometimes got letters in a man's handwriting. When she failed to be chosen as lady of the side chamber, she went a bit crazy. Some of the maids say she might have got herself with child.'

'Never!'

'She often went out with Lady Onkyo-in. You can always find opportunities if you want something badly enough and don't care what happens. Maybe that was how she felt. She might have smuggled someone in, in one of those big luggage trunks. That's what some of the women do sometimes.'

'So they're out searching for her?'

'She'll probably go home. Or the palace police will find her and take her home. I have a feeling

144

we'll hear she's suddenly been taken ill and died. That's what happened with a lady-in-waiting who ran off a few years ago.'

Sachi gasped in horror. She hoped this was not her doing. She had wished for it so hard, maybe she had made it happen. But she had only wished for Fuyu to go away, not to die. Even Fuyu did not deserve such a fate.

'Won't they just bring her back?' she asked, aghast.

Taki shook her head.

'I keep forgetting you're not a samurai. Of course not. Women can't just do as they please. We samurai know that. And she's shogunal property, like us. Her whole family will be in terrible trouble. Her father will have to deal with her immediately.'

Sachi nodded numbly. She remembered now why she had heard of Lady Shiga. Haru had mentioned her when she had told the story of the body in the palanquin. Lady Shiga had been Lady Hitsu's lover – and perhaps her betrayer or even her murderer.

It should have been a relief that Fuyu had gone. It meant Sachi could walk around freely without bumping into her or having to think about her any more. But in fact she thought about her more than ever. There was an unbearable mystery around her disappearance, as dark and sinister as Haru's story of Lady Shiga and Lady Hitsu.

Sachi was becoming aware that something was terribly wrong. Everyone seemed to know something she didn't, and no one would tell her what

145

it was. They seemed to think she was just a child and wouldn't understand – or were they trying to hide something from her? She heard footsteps in the corridor, not gliding in a slow and dignified way but running, panic-stricken footsteps pattering to and fro. Shrill voices were raised, then, when they realized she was around, fell silent. It was as if she had awoken from the innocence of childhood. Suddenly she could see the flicker of fear in every eye. Perhaps it had been there all along but she had never noticed before.

Then news arrived that the shogun was finally massing his troops and preparing to march on Choshu. One day Lady Tsuguko flung open the door to Sachi's rooms. Sachi had never seen her so agitated.

'Her Highness urgently requires your presence,' she said breathlessly. 'There is no need for your attendants. Only your maid of honour need accompany you.'

She rushed Sachi and Taki along the corridors, moving so rapidly that they almost had to run to keep up, and ushered them into the princess's private audience chamber. Princess Kazu was in her usual place on the dais with her screens arranged in front of her. Her ladies-in-waiting would normally have filled the room, but today the great chamber was empty.

Lady Tsuguko showed Sachi to a place in the shadows at the back of the dais where her face could not be seen.

'You need not speak,' she told her, 'but the princess wishes you to be present.'

Sachi was still adjusting her skirts when the

doors at the far end of the chamber opened. Two men were waiting there on their hands and knees. They were in formal dress, in layered black kimonos and wide pleated *hakama* trousers, and without their swords. They bowed in unison then slid forward until they reached the dais. Each laid a small fan on the floor in front of him, then they prostrated again and remained on their knees with their foreheads on their hands.

Utterly astonished, Sachi stared at the gleaming pates and pomaded samurai topknots. Apart from His Majesty, they were the first men she had seen since she had come to the women's palace. Even their smell – the sweat of their bodies, their perfume, their pomade – was unfamiliar.

'Her Imperial Highness has proclaimed that the Honourable Lady of the Side Chamber should attend this meeting,' Lady Tsuguko announced.

After a respectful pause, one of the men raised his head and spoke, keeping his eyes respectfully on the floor.

'Tadamasa Oguri, Lord of Bungo, city magistrate, treasury commissioner and commissioner of the army and navy, at your service,' he said in soft but clear tones. 'I am glad that Your Imperial Highness is in good health. I beg your clemency for having intruded in this unseemly way into your private quarters. I beg forgiveness too that I am obliged to attend on you without the regular quota of retainers. As Your Highness knows, I have come in secret.'

He bowed again.

At first Sachi too kept her eyes cast modestly downwards. But then, remembering that the men could not see her face, she peeked at them curiously.

The one who was speaking had skin the colour of vellum and the pursed lips and refined expression of a courtier. The hands pressed to the tatami matting were as small and soft as a woman's, the nails carefully manicured. He reminded her of the village priest, a pale, scholarly man who spent his days in the shadowy depths of the temple, bent over sutras, reading, writing and chanting.

The other man had broad muscular shoulders and powerful wrists. The top of his head was tanned and leathery. When he looked up she caught a glimpse of a swarthy, heavy-jowled face scarred with the marks of smallpox and a mouth which creased naturally into a scowl. While the first man was like a fox, this one was a hawk.

'Tadanaka Mizuno, governor of Tosa, master of Tankaku Castle in the domain of Shingu and son of Tadahira Mizuno, chamberlain to the House of Kii. I am honoured to serve you, Your Highness,' he growled. 'As Your Highness knows, my family has had the privilege of serving His Majesty and his ancestors for many generations.'

He pressed his face to the ground.

The first man spoke again. Sachi tried to concentrate but soon gave up. When she first came to the palace she had learned the lisping Kyoto dialect of the princess and her ladies and the more earthy Edo speech that the Retired One and the other ladies used. But that was women's language. She had never met samurai, let alone heard them speak. The man's talk was full of rough, guttural sounds and impossibly convoluted, garnished with

148

honorifics and complicated words and phrases.

The other man was looking at the floor, his topknot bobbing as he grunted agreement. He seemed to have a nervous tic. Every now and then his right arm would jerk back as if to draw an imaginary sword. He would place it firmly back on the floor.

Then the princess whispered urgently to Lady Tsuguko. Lady Tsuguko moved to the edge of the screen and addressed the two men.

'How long has he been ill?' she asked, her voice harsh with fear. Sachi started. Suddenly she was paying full attention.

Lord Oguri slid closer to the screen and leaned forward. 'Madam,' he said in confidential tones, 'we are very concerned.'

'Is he being properly cared for?'

It was the princess's own voice, a gentle high-pitched warble like the song of a bird. At the sound of the imperial tones, a tremor of shock rippled through the room. Everyone hastily prostrated.

'Highness, I am here because I wanted to make sure you heard the truth before any rumours reach you. Pay no attention to what others say. Eminent doctors, the best there are, specialists both in western medicine and in Chinese medicine, are in attendance day and night. We are praying for his survival. But his illness is severe. He suffers cramps in his stomach and severe swelling of the legs and groin. He vomits frequently. He has great difficulty passing urine. He has been given boiled sarsaparilla and steam vapour treatments. He–'

149

Sachi put her hands over her ears. She could not bear to hear any more. It could not be true.

'Oguri, I want to know.' The princess was speaking again, her voice shaking. 'His illness. Is it natural?'

Lord Oguri sucked his breath through his teeth. The hiss was loud in the silent room. Lord Mizuno's sword arm twitched.

'Well...' said Lord Oguri slowly.

'I see. There's no hope then. We must all... We must all...' Behind the screens the princess had slumped forward with her hands on her face. Tears were trickling through her fingers, spreading in a damp stain across the tatami.

Lord Tsuguko finished her sentence. 'We must all pray and make offerings.'

By the next day the news had spread through the palace, and soon everyone was engaged in prayers for the shogun's rapid recovery. Candles burned before every shrine and clouds of incense spiralled to the heavens. Priests chanted sutras and rang bells before altars heaped with offerings. Messengers galloped to the Edo branches of the Kurume Suitengu Shrine and the Kompira Daigongen Shrine, the shrines of the two great gods of healing, to order prayers and purchase charms which were sent post haste to Osaka. Women whispered prayers as they went about their work. The faces that passed in the corridors were puffy with weeping and smudged with tears.

Sachi sat in her room, holding her sewing, trying to concentrate. Every other hour she sent Taki out to see if there was any news. Surely by

150

now the shogun must be recovering. She thought of the handsome, healthy young man with whom she had lain. She pictured his pearly skin, his mischievous smile, his bright eyes. It was inconceivable that he would not soon shake off whatever ailment afflicted him.

She tried her hardest not to think about what she had heard in the princess's chamber but it was impossible to forget. His illness not natural? She had heard so many hints of what had happened to previous shoguns that this was too fearful to contemplate. She dared not even let the thought cross her mind that something bad might happen to His Majesty. She was afraid that if she did it might bring it about. She told herself again and again that he would soon recover.

When the days passed and the news was no better, she prayed to Amida Buddha, begging him not to take His Majesty to the Western Paradise but to leave him here with her. She offered three years of her own life if only he might have three extra years added to his. She prayed to the gods of the trees and mountains who had watched over her in the village. She wrapped up the amulet the shogun had given her in paper blessed by a priest and threw it away, hoping that the shogun's bad luck might go with it.

The princess often called for her. She had never seen her so distraught.

'If only I had wished him farewell,' she whispered again and again, wringing her hands.

Then one day a letter came. It was brushed in an unfamiliar hand. The signature was so shaky it was almost impossible to decipher. It looked as if it had been written by an old, old man. With a shudder that was like an icy finger running down her back, Sachi recognized it as His Majesty's.

'It seems Lord Amida summons me,' he wrote. 'I will not see you again. I think of you with great fondness. You are young and innocent. Your life is before you. Do not weep for me. Life is harsh. Learn to be strong and resilient like bamboo that bends but never breaks, no matter how fierce the wind. Pray that we may meet again in the Western Paradise.'

Sachi struggled to grasp the meaning of his words. She thought of the delicate, courtly young man she had known, relived every moment of their time together. She wanted to cry out that she wouldn't accept it, that it couldn't be true, that it was too much to bear. Then little by little the full impact of the letter swept over her. She rushed away into the gardens where no one would see or hear her and wept at the unfairness of it. They were both so young. What would become of her without him? What would become of everyone? Without him they were all doomed. She was on the edge of an abyss, hanging on for all she was worth. She dared not look down or she would fall for ever.

Later that day Haru arrived as usual with a poem for Sachi to copy.

'I have a poem already,' said Sachi. She read it aloud:

'*Yugure wa*   Twilight
Kumo no hatate ni With the clouds stretched out
                 like banners

152

Mono zo omou	I think, indeed, of that:
Amatsu sora naru	That is how it is to love
Hito wo kou to te	One who lives beyond my world.'

'Do you remember?' she asked. 'You told me that "one who lives beyond my world" means "one who is impossibly high in rank". But maybe it means "one who does not live in this world at all".'

Kneeling at her small table, she wrote it out, taking care to make her brushstrokes so eloquent that when she next wrote to His Majesty, he would be seduced by the passion and maturity of her writing.

Then light footsteps came dashing along the corridor. It was Taki. Two women's palanquins had arrived at the gate, she announced breathlessly. Lord Oguri and Lord Mizuno had alighted, entering by stealth on a secret mission. Sachi was to go to the princess at once.

Sachi closed her eyes and sat very still. She could sense a tidal wave rushing towards her.

Carefully she cleaned her ink stone and washed her brushes. She put the ink stick back in its box and set paperweights on the paper so the ink could dry. A single thought was battering on the edge of her mind.

'Of course,' she said. 'I'll come immediately. Thank you for telling me.'

She did not need to ask. She already knew. The shogun was dead.

4

Escape, 1867

I

Sachi scuffed her feet along the earthen path, staring listlessly at her small wooden clogs peeking out, one then the other, from the skirts of her bulky winter kimonos. Leafless trees sighed in the chilly wind and gnarled branches swayed like skeletal arms against the cold blue of the sky.

Taki scurried behind her, the quilted hem of her thick outer robe sending the dry leaves swirling as she walked. They reached Half-Moon Bridge and clambered to the top. The water of Lotus Pond was murky. The lustrous red lacquer of the pleasure barges had grown faded and dull.

'Look at those turtles,' said Taki brightly, pointing to a rock where three or four stone-coloured shapes huddled motionless. 'Poor things! The lake will be completely frozen over soon.'

Sachi raised her head and tried to smile. She wished she could stop the thoughts and memories endlessly revolving in her mind. Tears came to her eyes and spilled down her cheeks. Ever since the shogun had died nothing good had happened, nothing at all. It was as if a spell had fallen over the palace. The gardeners still tended the grounds, the lower-ranking maids cooked and swept and dusted, the ladies-in-waiting combed their hair and did their make-up and sewed and practised the halberd. But the life had gone out of it. The shogun had been the heart and soul of the palace. Without him it was like a dried-out husk, a chrysalis left behind after the butterfly has flown away. There was no gaiety any more. No one felt like staging plays or dances or masques without him to see them.

Women had begun making excuses, saying there was illness in the family. They left the palace and did not return.

More than a year had gone by since the shogun's death. Sachi was in her seventeenth year now, taller and willowy, though when she looked in the mirror she still saw the softly rounded face of a child. Her skin was as white as ever – as white as a mountain cherry blossom, as white as the moon, even whiter than that of the proud noblewomen who surrounded her. Her small nose arched delicately, her lips were full and rosy. Her eyes were dark green still, like the pine forests of Kiso. But there was sadness in them. Sometimes when she looked in the mirror she thought she saw the princess there, as she had been when she first caught a glimpse of her at the inn.

Like the princess's, Sachi's glossy black hair no longer cascaded to the floor but swung at her shoulders. They had both taken the veil, as widows of great lords did. Sachi now had a Buddhist name: she was the Retired Lady Shoko-in. But how could she be a 'Retired Lady' already when she had barely tasted life?

Every moment of every day Sachi thought of the shogun. Sometimes she saw his face so clearly it was as if he were there. She pictured his smile, the soft skin of his hands, his smooth pale chest, and felt the warmth of his body. Then she remembered he was dead and a great shuddering sob would pass through her. When she left her rooms she covered her head with a cowl. She dressed in plain robes and, in theory at least, spent her time in prayers and devotions. Her world had shrunk so much there was almost nothing left.

When she closed her eyes and tried to sleep, she saw his embalmed face as he lay in state, painted chalky white with his eyebrows brushed in and his cheeks and lips rouged. He had looked so small and shrivelled, nothing like the noble youth she remembered. Again and again in her memory she was back in the great hall, kneeling at his bier surrounded by hundreds of ladies-in-waiting, all in white. She heard the drone of priests mumbling prayers and smelt the incense and the dusty scent of thousands of white chrysanthemums. He had been so young. And to have died in such a way!

'Why, Taki, why?' she groaned.

'If you'd been brought up as a samurai you'd know it's not our place to ask questions,' said Taki, taking her arm and squeezing it. 'You just have to endure.'

There were footsteps in the distance, the clatter of wooden clogs coming along the path. They caught a whiff of a musky scent and swung round.

Lady Tsuguko was hurrying towards them. Her hair, tinged with grey, was tied back in a long tail which swung behind her. They ran down the bridge to meet her.

'I was hoping to find you here,' she said.

Sachi could tell from the agitated way Lady Tsuguko fingered her fan that something terrible had happened. Whatever her news, it was surely extremely urgent for such a grand lady to be rushing through the gardens.

'His Majesty the shogun...' said Lady Tsuguko. She stopped for a moment, as if she couldn't bear to continue. A frown creased her forehead.

His Majesty the shogun... Not Lord Iemochi, of course, not the much-lamented young shogun, but the new shogun: Lord Yoshinobu, His late Majesty's cousin. Just to think of him made Sachi feel as if icy fingers were closing round her heart. Along with all the women in the palace, she had the gravest suspicions about Lord Yoshinobu. She had never met him – none of them had, for he had never even visited the palace. He had been in Osaka since long before Lord Iemochi's death. As the prince regent, he had effectively ruled the country during Lord Iemochi's reign because His Majesty had been so young. And he had taken over the reins of power completely after His Majesty's death: he was now the head of the House of Tokugawa and thus the shogun. There had been no other candidate. Lord Iemochi had had no heir. Even now, to think of that caused Sachi a stab of pain. If only she had not failed in that, if only she had borne him an heir, who knew what might have happened?

157

She glanced at Lady Tsuguko's stony face. Gusts of wind rippled the women's sleeves, sending clouds of perfume wafting through the air and blowing strands of Sachi's short hair around her pale cheeks. Clouds scudded across the sky. Yellow leaves fluttered down.

'Lord Yoshinobu...' said Lady Tsuguko, 'has abdicated. There is no shogun.'

Sachi and Taki looked at her aghast, their eyes wide, trying to take in the enormity of what she had said.

'But... But ... he only just became shogun,' Sachi stammered.

Sachi had never said a word of what she had heard in the princess's chamber – the details of the shogun's illness, the horror of the way he had died. Nevertheless all the women assumed he had been poisoned. Most probably poison had been applied to his writing brush: everyone knew his habit of licking the tip as he wrote. The official report on his death had said His Majesty had passed away of a heart attack following a bout of beriberi. The women had sneered in disbelief. Beriberi! It had been beriberi when the last shogun died and the shogun before that. No one believed it for an instant. Besides, it was all too obvious who stood to gain from his death. But that would mean...

'You mean he took the title ... only to give it up? But ... but why?'

'For fourteen generations the House of Tokugawa has governed this country and given it peace and prosperity,' said Lady Tsuguko in measured tones. Only the gruffness of her voice gave a hint of her disgust. 'Now Lord Yoshinobu

158

is throwing it all away. He's offered to return power to the emperor.'

Just as there was a new shogun, there was a new emperor too. The previous emperor had died very suddenly at the beginning of that year. Sachi glanced fearfully at Lady Tsuguko, then at Taki. She knew nothing of the emperor except that he had been Princess Kazu's brother. Lady Tsuguko and Taki were both from Kyoto, where the emperor had his court. They had come to Edo with the princess. Along with the princess they had wept and mourned for months after he died.

The emperor: *Tenno-sama*, the Son of Heaven. Until Sachi came to the women's palace she hadn't even known there was an emperor. He lived in seclusion in his palace in Kyoto and never left it. He was said to be sacred and pure, a divine being who had a special connection to the gods and conducted rites to ensure that crops succeeded and humankind was prosperous.

The new emperor, his son, was only fifteen. It seemed unlikely that such a being could be interested in wielding power.

Lady Tsuguko's shoulders slumped as if the whole weight of the world had descended on them.

'Here in the castle we lead an enchanted life,' she sighed, 'untouched by the world outside. But even you, young though you are, will soon know the truth. There has been terrible fighting in Kyoto for years now, practically ever since the princess left. Everyone there lives in fear of their life. No one knows what will happen next. There are skirmishes daily, murders, assassinations, sometimes pitched battles. Much of the city has burned down and the imperial palace itself was attacked.'

'By *ronin*,' snapped Taki, scowling. 'Southern *ronin*.'

Sachi gasped. *Ronin*. She knew what that meant – masterless samurai, two-sworded men who had left their clan and belonged nowhere. They had no lord to answer to, no one to take responsibility for their deeds. They were nameless, faceless men, wild men who operated outside the law, knowing their actions would not bring shame or censure on their clan. Far from being an organized army, they committed acts of random violence, raping, looting and murdering. They wielded their two swords without reserve. For them the only constraint was death.

'His Majesty spoke to me of ... of the Choshu rebels,' she whispered. 'He was going to put down their uprising.'

Lady Tsuguko nodded. 'It's true,' she said. 'The cause of all the trouble in Kyoto is clansmen of the southern domains – Choshu, Satsuma, Tosa and the other great domains of the south-west. Their lords have risen against the Tokugawas and are trying to wrest power from them. The northern lords are loyal and are trying to hold them back and keep the peace, but the southerners are rich and powerful and armed by the English barbarians.'

'But why does the shogun, Lord Yoshinobu, want to give power to the emperor?' asked Sachi.

'The southerners have clever thinkers who've put about the idea that the shogun derives his power from the emperor – that generations back the emperor delegated the shogun to rule as his representative,' said Lady Tsuguko.

'Well,' muttered Taki, 'I grew up in Kyoto and I never heard anything about that.'

'Now, they say, the time has come for the shogun to give that power back,' said Lady Tsuguko dryly. 'It's all a pretext, of course. The late emperor, Her Highness's brother, would have nothing of it. Perhaps that's why ... anyway, he passed away. His son is very young and easy to manipulate. He is a pawn, a puppet. It's a question of who is going to work the strings. There are powerful men in the emperor's court who are in league with the southerners.

'But Lord Yoshinobu is very clever too. He's engaged in some complicated game. And even though he has abdicated as shogun, he is still head of the House of Tokugawa. Nothing can change that. The northern clans are firmly behind the Tokugawas and will fight to the death for them. And everyone still reveres Lord Yoshinobu, no matter what he does. It's what he stands for that counts, not what he is.

'The most fearful thing of all is that the enemy is closing in. There are gangs of southern *ronin* right here in Edo now. They rove around causing havoc in our streets, looting, setting fires and killing anyone they suspect of being a supporter of the shogun. The townsfolk dare not go out.

'Even here in the palace you must have heard the fighting. We're safe here, but maybe not for much longer. We don't know what will happen, or how much longer this life of ours can go on.

161

Sooner or later the southerners will try to take the castle. They're bound to. It's the last stronghold of the Tokugawas. They may also try to capture the princess and the Retired One and hold them as hostages. We must be prepared.'

Sachi felt as if she had been turned to stone, like one of the rocks in the gardens. She had spent so many years learning the rules and traditions of the women's palace, doing her best to become part of this ancient way of life. She had thought nothing could ever change it. But now it was rushing towards a terrible end. Darkness surrounded their frail world, threatening to swallow it up at any moment.

'I will willingly give my life for the princess,' she said quietly. 'You know that.'

'Be ready,' said Lady Tsuguko. 'The time may come sooner than we think.'

II

Somewhere in the distance Sachi heard the jangling of fire bells. There seemed to be many, ringing faintly at first, then louder and louder. Someone was shaking her.

'Wake up! Wake up!' It was Taki's voice.

The fire bells really were clanging – not far away in the city but right there in the castle. Suddenly she was wide awake. She pushed her covers aside, shivering as the icy air pierced her sleeping robes. All around her women were stumbling to their feet. Heavy garments swished against the closed door and voices whispered urgently. It was night

162

time still. There were lanterns lit around the room. With no time to wait for Taki to help her dress, she grabbed the nearest robes she could find and threw them on, then tugged her cowl over her head. She slid her dagger into her obi and slipped her comb, mirror, amulets and handkerchief into her sleeves.

Taki was rolling up a few of the most valuable embroidered kimonos, bundling them together with Sachi's favourite poetry books. Even in the castle, with its massive stone ramparts, thick plastered walls and sturdy wooden beams and pillars, fire was a real danger. A few years earlier the second of the three fortified palaces that occupied the grounds had gone up in flames. Many people had been killed and large sections of the palace had been gutted.

Looking around hurriedly for things to take with her, Sachi noticed a dusty bundle shoved away in a corner. It was the one she had brought with her from the village. For some reason the tattered old fabric suddenly seemed far more precious than all the gold and brocades she had accumulated in her years in the palace. She tucked it under one arm and took her halberd in its silk bag from its rack on the wall.

There was a sudden silence. The footsteps dashing up and down outside stopped, as if the crowd of women jostling past had turned to stone. Then there was a whisper like the wind rippling a field of long grass – the sound of many women drawing in their breath. The door to Sachi's room slid open. Standing in the shadows outside was a tiny figure. A pale face glimmered in the darkness, half hidden in the folds of the cowl draped around it.

It was the princess. Without waiting to be announced, she burst in and stood very still in the centre of the room. The subtle scent of a musky winter perfume swirled in with her. She was panting, her fists clenched so tightly that her knuckles were white. Lady Tsuguko and a bevy of ladies crowded in after her. Shocked, Sachi and her maids dropped their bundles, threw themselves on their hands and knees and pressed their heads to the matting.

'My Lady Shoko-in,' said the princess, addressing Sachi by her formal name.

Sachi glanced up. It was the first time she had ever seen the princess without make-up. With her wide eyes and uncombed hair she looked like a child. Her skin was so translucent she seemed scarcely human, as if she could not possibly be a creature of this world. But there was something else. There was a spark in her eye, a grim determination about her that Sachi had not seen before.

'Lady Shoko-in,' said the princess, drawing a deep breath. 'Child. They're here. They've broken in. Southern *ronin* have set the palace afire. Now they're out to find me and kidnap me in the confusion.'

'Here in the palace? Southerners?' stuttered Sachi in horror, trying to grasp what the princess was saying. 'But ... how can that be? How could they possibly break in?'

Southerners inside the castle? It was unthinkable. The castle was supposed to be impregnable

164

and the women's palace was deep inside the castle grounds. The southerners would have had to cross moats, scale massive ramparts, cross drawbridges and evade squads of guards. If it was true, then the last stronghold had been penetrated. This was what the women had been training for all their lives – to defend their world against their enemies no matter what it took.

'I have my spies,' hissed the princess. 'We have to move quickly.'

Lady Tsuguko was a couple of steps behind the princess. Her black eyes shone. She seemed to have grown in stature. She was full of quiet excitement, eager to take command. She raised a hand, signalling to Sachi to listen.

'Your time has come,' said Princess Kazu. 'I have a service to ask of you, the greatest service anyone could ask. Take my palanquin and leave the castle. I have sent orders to my guards. You must lure my enemies away from the palace.'

'You are the only one who can do this,' Lady Tsuguko chimed in. 'You know that. This is your chance to repay your debt to Her Highness.'

The bells were clanging urgently. Feet raced past the closed door. Smoke was beginning to waft into the room. The princess's ladies glanced around nervously.

Sachi knew very well that this was a desperate mission. If she was to be bait for the enemy she was very probably going to her death. But she was bound to the princess. She had every reason to sacrifice herself for her. It was the princess who had taken her from the village and installed her in a position of luxury and privilege and given her to the shogun as his concubine. She had always known the time might come when she would be called upon to repay that debt.

There were practical reasons too to choose her. The southerners could have no idea what Princess Kazu looked like. No one apart from her closest ladies-in-waiting and her family in Kyoto had ever seen her. But everyone knew that she was a high-nosed aristocrat with the whitest of skin and, as His Majesty's widow, that she must be a nun. Sachi looked just like Her Highness and she too was a nun; she wore her hair cut short and covered it with a cowl. She was a perfect copy. She could have been born to be her lookalike.

But to set off in a single palanquin without guards or attendants... No one would ever believe a princess would travel in such a way. It was a crazy scheme, thought up in the panic of the moment. Nevertheless Sachi had been given a mission and she had to carry it out as well as possible. If a spark of fear flared in her heart she must stamp it out.

She took a deep breath.

'My debt to Her Highness is endless,' she said quietly but firmly. 'I can never repay it. Whatever Her Highness requires I will do. I am grateful to have the chance to prove my devotion.'

'The world has fallen into darkness,' said the princess. 'Our friends have become our enemies and our enemies our friends. Lord Yoshinobu has betrayed us, as you know, and abdicated. There is no longer a shogun. The southern lords control my poor nephew, the emperor. Our lives are of no account. We are already dead. No matter what happens, our duty is to the House of Tokugawa. As the aunt of the Son of Heaven and the widow of His late Majesty, I may be a valuable hostage. It is vital that I remain here in the palace.'

Sachi was struggling to grasp what was going on. The only thing she fully understood was the depth of the princess's pain. Princess Kazu had been forced to give up everything she cared about for a marriage she did not want, and now the imperial family and the Tokugawas were on opposite sides. It seemed that all that was left to her was to do her duty. She was a member of the Tokugawa family now and would be till the bitter end.

'I am ready to die whenever I am called upon to do so,' Sachi said. 'I am honoured to take your place in the imperial palanquin. I will not fail you.'

The princess had tears in her eyes.

'You have been like a sister to me,' she said softly. 'My life will be sadder without you. May the gods protect you. I pray we may meet again in better times.'

She inclined her head.

'Do your best,' she said.

Lady Tsuguko waited until she and her ladies-in-waiting had gone, then turned to Sachi.

'Hurry,' she said. 'There's no time to waste.' She slid open the door.

Sachi snatched up her bundle and halberd. Her heart was beating strangely. It did not feel like fear at all, but excitement. It was as if she had awakened from a long sleep. She had almost forgotten what it felt like to be alive.

The corridor was jammed with women, clutching bundles and carrying candles and paper lanterns. In the flickering light they were like an army of drifting ghosts, pale and gaunt, in strange outfits thrown together with no thought of what went with what. Their hair was wild, their eyes wide with fear. Some pushed and shoved, sobbing in panic. But mostly they stumbled along in eerie silence.

When Lady Tsuguko and Sachi appeared they stopped and drew back respectfully.

'Make way!' barked Lady Tsuguko. She began to push through the crowd, away from the gardens, towards the section of the palace where the smoke was coming from. But there were too many people, so she turned aside into one of the great audience chambers. Sachi followed, wiping her eyes. Smoke was billowing around them. When she stopped to catch her breath, she saw Taki's small pale face, pointed chin and large eyes close behind her.

'Go back, Taki,' she hissed. 'You don't have to come.'

Lady Tsuguko swung round sharply.

'Leave us,' she barked. 'Now. Only the lady of the side chamber need come. Go to the gardens with the other maids.'

Taki said nothing but stuck doggedly behind them.

'Go back,' shrieked Lady Tsuguko in a frenzy of rage. 'How dare you disobey my orders!'

There was no time for talk. They ran on. When they reached the wing where the kitchens and

168

offices were, the smoke was so thick they could barely see. They stumbled along blindly, holding their sleeves over their faces. Finally they burst into the great entrance hall. The doors stood open. They stopped, gasping, feeling the icy dawn air flood into their lungs.

III

The moon glimmered on the horizon like a huge round mirror, reflecting a watery light. Hordes of men were dashing past, their breath white in the frosty air. Most were in the uniform of guards from the middle and outer palaces. Some were firemen from the town, wiry fellows in brown leather coats and thick hoods pulled well down over their heads and shoulders. They scuttled along like an invasion of giant cockroaches. Some carried water pumps and tubs of water on wooden poles on their shoulders, others bamboo ladders and long-poled hooks. Officials in brocade robes were waving batons, directing operations.

'Pull your cowl close around your face,' Lady Tsuguko muttered to Sachi. 'And say nothing.'

Sachi tugged on a pair of straw boots and followed Lady Tsuguko along the covered walk-way, pulling her robes tight around her. Taki was still there, panting along behind.

The fire seemed to be everywhere. The white-plastered walls and sweeping grey-tiled roofs glowed with an eerie light as flames exploded from the windows and leaped from roof to roof with a tremendous roar and crackle so fierce that it was impossible to hear anything else. Firemen scrambled up bamboo ladders and swarmed across the rooftops, ripping off tiles and spraying pitifully thin jets of water. Beneath them women were still running out of the burning palace.

For a moment Sachi stood in silence, gazing at this building that had been her home for so many years. If only this too might be a dream. But the freezing cold told her all too clearly that it was not. She shivered. Even the layers of padded silk were not enough to protect her.

Groups of ladies-in-waiting huddled at the doors to the palanquin sheds. They stared at Sachi with wide, envious eyes as the guards bowed and escorted her into the imperial garages.

The princess's palanquin stood open. Sachi looked at it with a shock of recognition. It was the same one she had seen years before when Princess Kazu and her entourage had arrived in the village. Everything was just as she remembered – the lacquered red walls fretted with gold and marked with the imperial chrysanthemum, the ornate gold roof and the bamboo window blinds hung with fat red tassels. It seemed all too obvious that if the princess was really trying to escape, she would never travel in such a showy conveyance.

An image flashed into Sachi's mind of the woman who had stepped from this splendid vehicle when she had seen it as a child, back in the village. She remembered her wide terrified eyes. Even then she had guessed that the woman was a decoy for the princess, which was why she had been so afraid. It was Sachi's turn now. She was a samurai, a warrior. She would not be afraid – or, if she was, no one would ever see it.

She scrambled into the palanquin, folded her legs under her and tucked her skirts under her knees. There was a commotion outside.

'Let me through!' It was Taki's thin bat-squeak of a voice. 'Let go of me!'

'Foolish child, you'll ruin everything!' came Lady Tsuguko's imperious bark.

Suddenly Taki's small head bounced into sight. In her large, slightly protuberant eyes there was a look of fierce determination. Her bony arms grabbed at the door of the palanquin as if she was trying to scramble inside. Sachi gasped. For a moment she was so overcome with amazement and joy she couldn't move. Then, her heart thudding, she took hold of an arm and hauled. Lady Tsuguko gave a squawk of rage. Brawny arms encircled Taki and yanked her away.

Tears of disappointment and frustration sprang to Sachi's eyes. She swallowed hard. If only Taki had come too she could have borne anything. Now there was nothing for it but to endure alone.

The door slammed shut. The carrying pole was already in its hafts. With a grunt the bearers heaved the palanquin on to their shoulders.

In the sudden darkness, Sachi felt the little box swing into the air. Taken by surprise, she lost her balance and fell against the wall. She had never been in a palanquin before and was breathless with the suddenness and strangeness of it. It was like being in a small boat on very choppy water, like the boats she'd been in on the River Kiso and the ferries she'd taken when she travelled in the princess's procession towards Edo. Even an hour before, who would have guessed she would end up in such an extraordinary place?

She could hear the clatter of hooves and the crunch of straw-clad feet. She pushed apart the slats of the bamboo blind. Pale dawn light threaded through the darkness, burnishing the gold leaf of the inner walls and etching the contours of her small white hand. She was in a tiny mobile palace, painted with ornamental rocks, a winding stream and blossom-covered plum trees.

Outside she could make out the enormous silhouettes of warriors on horseback and guards jogging along. They were in a convoy of palanquins, skirting the inner wall of the women's quarters, moving at a fast clip towards the great gate. In all the years she had been immured in the palace, she had never once passed beyond it. Behind her the flames roared and there were booms and crashes like falling masonry. She could not bear to think of the princess and the other women. And Taki... What had become of her?

Then they were deep in the shadows of the gate. They passed between towering wooden doors bound with iron bars and huge bolts. On the other side the grounds continued. They skirted landscaped gardens, ornamental ponds, lonely pavilions and groves of cryptomeria trees. The pines were all trussed for winter, the branches tightly bound with ropes.

After a long while they came to another gate, heavily fortified, with massive sloping walls of granite blocks, each taller than a man, piled one

172

on top of the other, and tiled roofs topped with golden dolphins. The guards posted at each side bowed as they passed through. Beyond was a long bridge. The first rays of the sun sparkled on the green waters of a wide, still moat. A couple of ducks were swimming there. Sachi twisted around, hoping for a last look, but the castle was invisible behind clouds of pine trees and the gargantuan granite blocks of the ramparts. A tongue of flame licked the sky where the women's palace should have been.

They were in a broad avenue lined with forbidding walls with sweeping tiled roofs looming behind. The street was full of men, walking, running or passing in sedan chairs. They were curious-looking creatures, like the crowds she had seen tramping the road through the village all those years ago. Some were bent and gnarled, others burly and muscular. Some swaggered like samurai, others slunk like townsmen. Even inside the palanquin she could smell the odour of their bodies. It was strange to imagine that such creatures could be human.

But why were they not on their knees? Some seemed to be staring insolently, bending down, trying to peek inside. Sachi was acutely aware of how conspicuous the palanquin was – a moving target, declaring to anyone who cared to notice that a rich, aristocratic lady was travelling inside. Her heart beat faster. Was it her imagination or was there hostility in their eyes? Even the palanquin bearers seemed to be tossing her from side to side, as if they knew they were not carrying anyone really important.

Bouncing along in her little box, she felt like one of the prisoners she used to see being transported in wicker cages through the village. She snapped the window blind shut. The lurching of the palanquin made her drowsy and nauseous but she dared not close her eyes. If the southerners had penetrated deep enough inside the castle grounds to set fire to the women's palace, they could not be far away. She needed to stay alert. If something was to happen, it would be now that they were outside the castle walls. She straightened up, smoothed her kimono skirts and tried to gather her thoughts.

Could it really all be gone – the treasures, the priceless kimonos and exquisite lacquerware? What had become of the women – the Retired One, with her two hundred and eighty maids of honour, each with their retinues of servants, and old Lady Honju-in and her household of creaky ladies-in-waiting? Sachi had always thought of the village as her home. But she had been wrong. The palace was her home and all these women – some kind, some stern – had become her family.

Ever since the shogun died her days had been without meaning. Now she had a mission – to be a decoy, to lure the southerners away from the castle so that they would pursue her, not the princess. Her own life, she knew, was of no importance. Women were in this world to obey without questioning or thinking. That was what she had to do – stop thinking. She murmured the death poem which the poet Narihira had composed back in the Heian era:

Tsui ni yuku	That it is a road
Michi to wa kanete	Which some day we all travel
Kikishikado	I had heard before,
Kino kyo to wa	But I never thought that today
Omowazarishi o	Would bring that far tomorrow.

She felt for the hilt of her dagger, tucked firmly into her obi, and caressed the silken threads of the binding. In her years at the palace she had been taught to be ready at any moment to use the dagger to protect her lord or, if need be, to kill herself rather than be taken by an enemy. But the privilege of suicide was not for her. If she killed herself she would have failed in her mission. The princess would have no lookalike.

Her mind was calm but her body was afraid. Her heart was beating so fiercely she could hardly breathe. A pain like a knife twisted in her guts, consuming her from the inside. She hated the shame and ignominy of the feeling. She had to stamp out her fear. No matter how high she rose in the palace hierarchy, the snobbish aristocrats always whispered that she was just a peasant. Now was her chance to prove herself: when the time came, she would show them all what Lord Iemochi's concubine could do.

She tried to slow her breathing. She needed to think, concentrate, prepare. Would she be taken as a hostage? What must it be like to die? Hers was a story without an ending.

Her thoughts turned, as they always did, to His Majesty. She remembered the days and months of

175

sadness – the thirty days of mourning, the months of ritual restrictions, chanting before his memorial tablet on the seventh, fourteenth, twenty-first, thirty-fifth, forty-ninth and hundredth day after his funeral. Day and night she had prayed that he might be safely reborn in the Western Paradise. And here she was, in her seventeenth year, a widow and a nun, imprisoned in this tiny box, rushing headlong towards some unimaginable fate.

She was utterly alone, with no one to help her or tell her what to do. If there were big decisions to make, she would have to make them on her own.

IV

Sachi had no idea how long they had been travelling when there was a commotion. She heard the scuffle of feet, then shouts and yells. She edged the slats of the blind apart a fraction and peeked out cautiously.

They were in a narrow alley between high walls. She caught a glimpse of a menacing figure lurking in the shadows, then another and another. They were clad in thick layers of wadded clothing. She could see two swords, one long and one short, poking from under their garments. Two swords – so they were of the samurai class. But they were not dressed like samurai. Their faces were swathed in scarves, hiding everything except the glitter of their eyes. They were *ronin*, probably from the south. The alley was full of them.

One leaped forward. There was an ear-piercing guttural wail, a blue flash, then what sounded very much like a blade slicing through flesh.

Sachi gasped and lurched forward as the palanquin came to an abrupt halt. She heard the screech of swords ripping from their scabbards and the clang of blade striking blade. The swishing of swords, the clash and clink of steel on steel, the yells and shouts grew closer and closer until they were deafeningly loud, right outside the palanquin wall. Clutching her dagger, Sachi sat helplessly in her frail conveyance, willing herself not to think, only to be ready. The blood was thudding so loudly in her ears she could hardly hear. The palanquin rocked, jolted crazily, tilted to one side then crashed to the ground. She ended up winded and bruised, sprawled on the floor. Feet pounded away into the distance.

Gruff voices shouted in a sing-song dialect. Sachi could not make out the words but she recognized the accent. It was a rough male version of the lilting southern burr she heard when the Retired One's ladies spoke among themselves. So she was right: they were southerners.

Panting, Sachi picked herself up. She sat up very straight, brushed her skirts off, adjusted her collar and pulled her cowl into place, then gripped the hilt of her dagger. This was it. The moment had come. She would have to submit to the humiliation of capture. But she would fight before she was taken; at least no one could stop her doing that.

She sat utterly still, trying not to move or

breathe. In the silence a hand rattled the door of the palanquin.

Then she heard something unexpected – the thunder of hooves, approaching from behind. It could only be more of the southern hoodlums. There was an explosion so loud her ears were ringing with it. She knew the sound. She had heard it reverberating outside the castle walls, but never so close before – musket fire. There was another volley, then another. She heard grunts and yells, the screech of steel biting into bone and thuds like bodies hitting the ground. An unearthly silence followed. A lone bird twittered and a chill wind blew.

She took a deep breath. Her heart was beating so hard she couldn't believe the men outside could not hear it. She drew herself up proudly, hand on her dagger. She would show them that a seventeen-year-old girl – and a peasant, did they but know it – could be as brave as any samurai, or braver.

There was a man's voice. He was very close, just outside the thin wooden walls of the palanquin. It was an educated voice with only a slight rural burr. He spoke so clearly and politely that she could understand most of what he was saying. He gave his name – Toranosuké of the Matsunobé family – and his domain, Kano. He seemed to be asking her to make herself known.

Kano! Sachi froze. Kano was near Kyoto and her village. But she had no idea of its allegiance, whether these men were with the north or the south. No matter what, she had to convince them that she was the princess. What would the princess do in this situation? Would she speak? Would she open the door of the palanquin? Surely not. She would never make herself known to any man.

The silence stretched interminably. Then she heard a voice – a woman's voice, thin and high-pitched, like a mouse's squeak.

'Step away, sir!'

Sachi nearly shrieked with shock and disbelief. Taki! What on earth was she doing here? But her relief was quickly replaced by horror. Even if it meant breaking her word to the princess she would jump out of the palanquin and fight along-side her. She would do anything at all, whatever it took, to make sure Taki was not hurt.

'I am Lady Takiko of the imperial household, handmaiden to the shogun and escort to the lady who travels in this palanquin,' squeaked the voice in loud clear tones. 'If you wish to address her, you may do so through me.'

The next minute Taki's big eyes appeared on the other side of the blind.

'Are you all right?' she whispered.

'Taki, I'm so glad to see you. How did you get here?'

'I'll tell you later. We were attacked by south-erners. These other fellows turned up and beat them off. The southerners must have gone for reinforcements.'

'But who are they? Who are these men?'

'I'm not sure. I'm going to speak to them.'

Sachi heard Taki's clear tones and the male voice speaking in reply. Then Taki was back at the window.

'They're from Kano. They say they're with us. They say we have to go with them – for our safety.'

'So they're kidnapping us.'

'They say they can't risk the princess falling into southern hands, and if they leave us here that's what will happen. Anyway, you can't abandon your mission and go back to the palace.'

'But how do we know they are what they say they are?'

'We have to trust them. We have no choice. Our guards have been killed and our bearers and attendants have run away.'

'Run away!' snorted Sachi in disgust.

'There was a plot of some sort and we were betrayed. There are southern hoodlums all over the place. We have to carry on with the pretence. If the southerners think the princess is fleeing for the mountains, they'll follow us instead of heading for the palace. That's our duty. These men have a baggage train, they have bearers.'

'But who are these men?' Sachi persisted.

'*Ronin.*'

Ronin. Sachi had never before come face to face with such creatures. Men like that were reckless, dangerous characters, not answerable to anyone. They probably changed sides depending on which way the wind was blowing. But Sachi and Taki were in their hands. They had no choice but to accept their word.

'They want to see you,' said Taki. 'They want to make sure there isn't a man in there. I'm going to open the door. Don't say anything. Just bow. Then I'll close it again.'

Sachi hastily tossed her cowl around her face as the door slid back. Daylight flooded in, dazzlingly bright. Drawing herself up with as much dignity as she could muster, she nodded curtly, as she had seen the princess doing. Silhouetted outside were three figures. Two were on horseback, the other on foot, holding the reins. The tops of their heads were bristly and unshaven. They did not even have topknots. One had hair sticking out like a bush and the other two had rough ponytails. She had never before seen such wild-looking men.

Beyond them she could see palanquins collapsed on their sides. Bodies were heaped here and there, blood still gushing from their torsos. Some twitched and writhed. The soil was so wet it looked as if it had been raining; but the puddles were an ugly shade of dark red, already congealing at the edges. There were strange rock-like objects lying around. Sachi stifled a gasp as she realized they had hair and ears and faces. A foul odour filled the air, the mingled stench of blood and flesh and human excrement. As it swirled into the palanquin, she retched and pulled her cowl tighter about her face.

Then the door slid shut.

Sachi tried not to think about what she had witnessed but the image was imprinted on her mind. Again and again she pictured that hideous scene and the noises she had heard, the dreadful groans and gasps. She shuddered with the horror of it. Those men had died like samurai – some trying to seize her, others to protect her. Some must have been the guards and bearers who had ridden alongside. Yet in death they were all the same.

But at least Taki was there. Knowing that she was close by, Sachi was no longer prepared to die. Next time she was called upon to give her life she would fight, and fight hard.

Maybe they could escape. But where could they go? The women's palace was gone, reduced to ashes. There was only one safe place – the village. For a moment Sachi imagined herself back in the tile-roofed house with the river rushing below and the mountain soaring overhead. It was something to hang on to, something real in the middle of all this madness. If she survived, if she got out of this box alive, she would find some way to get there.

Somewhere in the distance there was a hubbub. Suddenly all Sachi's senses were alert. She was listening with all her might. The southerners... But the noise was in front of them, not behind. Besides, if the southerners attacked, they would creep up on them silently.

Chimes and gongs were jangling, whistles tootled and drums pounded feverishly. She peeked through the slats of the bamboo blind. They had left the broad avenues of daimyo mansions and were threading their way through alleys lined with ramshackle houses and shops. A stream of people hurried in the same direction, stooped under huge bundles tied on their backs.

The noise grew louder. At first she could not catch the words. Then she began to pick them up. The singers were chanting, *'Ee ja nai ka? Ee ja nai*

182

ka? Who gives a damn? Who gives a damn?'

Then came some verses that made no sense at all, something about 'butterflies flying from the west'. The tune was so catchy she found herself humming along. Despite everything she had to smile. She had not heard language like that since she left the village.

The convoy came to a halt. The street ahead of them was overflowing with people, crammed so tightly it was impossible to pass. The mob drew back for a moment as if startled by the intrusion of the imperial palanquin, then closed in around it. There were people dressed in flaming red with red lanterns on their heads, men capering about in women's kimonos and women in *happi* coats and leggings like men. Some of the men, and women, too, had thrown off their clothes and were cavorting half naked, their leathery skin shiny with sweat. They barged up against Sachi's palanquin, squinting through the blind.

'Hey, lady! Come and dance,' they bawled. 'Come and dance! Who gives a damn? Who gives a damn?'

Some had bowls of sake and pieces of fish and rice cakes and thrust them up against the blind. Sachi shrank away, wrinkling her nose at the stench of sweat and food and sake and the staring eyes. There had been plenty of festivals in the village, and in the palace, too, they had performed the summer dances to welcome the spirits of the dead. But there was a crazed desperation to this dancing she had never seen before. Scraps of paper, like the lucky charms that temples sold, blew about in the wind. People chased after them, grabbing at them.

'Hurry up, get a move on,' barked the *ronin* riding alongside.

'Clear the way,' yelled the guards, shoving their way through. The crowd danced on, waving their arms in the air and swaying in unison, singing at the tops of their voices.

When the convoy reached the border post that marked the edge of the city, the gates were wide open. The guards let them pass without even bothering to bow. The whole world seemed to have gone mad.

Gradually the smells and uproar of the city faded behind them. The sky arched overhead, dazzlingly blue. Clumps of trees cast long shadows. Parched brown fields stretched to the horizon, merging into the mountains that shimmered in the pale light of the winter sun. Sachi was beginning to relax. Out here among the fields there was nowhere to hide. If the southerners came after them they would see them. She breathed the air, savouring the coldness and freshness.

'Who gives a damn? Who gives a damn?' she hummed to herself. It was oddly comforting.

It was not until they were well away from the city that the palanquin stopped. Taki was at the door to help Sachi out. Sachi gazed at her small, thin, determined face, her pointed chin and large fierce eyes. There was something new about her, as if she too had come alive, as if she was enjoying being outside in the great world. Taki had saved her life. If it hadn't been for her Sachi might be dead. Impulsively she threw her arms round her.

'I can't tell you how happy I am to see you!' she

184

said, tears springing to her eyes. 'You risked everything to come with me.'

Taki hugged her back.

'I'm your maid,' she laughed, shrugging. 'I was just doing my duty.'

They were at a small roadside inn, not at all the kind of place a princess would visit. There was no sign of the *ronin* or anyone else, so it seemed that at least they had some respect for her position.

A small bent woman with a round, smiling face ushered them, bowing profusely, into a shabby room. It was years since Sachi had been in such a place. She glanced at the rough walls, the worn matting spread on the bare wooden floor and the patches on the paper of the doors. The smells of woodsmoke and tobacco and food cooking reminded her of home – of the village. She sat with Taki while the woman served them steaming bowls of buckwheat noodles. A few hours back, Sachi had thought she would never eat again. Now she was starving.

'How could you bear it, Taki?' she said. 'You saw all that. You were in the middle of it. Weren't you afraid?'

Taki looked puzzled. Then she smiled proudly.

'You're teasing,' she said. 'They were our enemies. I was pleased they were dead. I'd love to see their heads nailed to the castle gates.'

Sachi drained the last mouthfuls of soup. It was strange to hear Taki say such things. But she was a samurai. Sachi had to learn to be like her, calm and composed even when battle was raging. Now they were on their own, away from the castle, it was all the more urgent.

185

'Well,' she said finally, 'at least we're safe, so far.'

'Not quite,' said Taki.

'That's true,' said Sachi. 'Anyway, we've outrun the southerners, for the time being. Trouble is, we don't know what's ahead. And these men – who are they? How do we know they're on our side? They don't even have a lord to answer to. How do we know they're not taking us as hostages?'

'Careful what you say,' said Taki. 'There are spies everywhere. There's nothing we can do. We just have to obey.'

'Obey what?' said Sachi. 'We were supposed to lead the southerners away from the castle – or I was rather. You already disobeyed! You were told not to come along.'

She smiled at her friend. Taki was picking at her noodles. She'd probably never had plain peasant fare before. The voluminous skirts of her court robes half filled the bare little room. She was such a samurai, such a court lady. 'But I'm glad you did, Taki. I'm very glad.'

'Lady Tsuguko realized you needed a chaperone,' said Taki in her matter-of-fact way. 'Even the most ignorant southerner would never believe a princess would travel without one, no matter how many attendants she had.'

'It's a long way to Kano,' murmured Sachi.

'It's madness to go all that way,' grumbled Taki. 'I can't imagine what these fellows are thinking of.'

They looked at each other.

'But we have no choice,' said Sachi. 'I can't reveal that I'm not the princess till I know she's

186

safe. And I can't go back to the castle. I've been given a mission and I have to fulfil it. Perhaps the southerners saw the imperial palanquin leaving the city. They could be on our tail right now.'

There was a rumble as the heavy wooden door creaked in its grooves. The women started and glanced at each other. Sachi quickly pulled her cowl across her face as the door opened. It was the man she had seen holding the reins of the horse. He slid on his knees into the room.

He was holding two halberds in elaborately embroidered silk bags. Keeping his eyes on the coarse straw matting, he pushed them towards the women.

'Here,' he croaked. His voice had barely broken.

Dumbfounded, Sachi stared at the exquisite silk. Quite forgetting she was supposed to be the princess, she let her cowl fall aside and stretched out her small white hand to touch the hard steel inside the delicate case.

She glanced at the man. He was barely a man at all. He still had the long forelock of a child, though it was loose and shaggy instead of neatly oiled. Beneath the uncombed hair and dusty travelling clothes, he was just a boy. His face was so pretty, his cheeks so round and smooth, he might almost have been a girl were it not for the straggly hairs sprouting above his lips. The tips of his ears were scarlet.

'You have taken good care of us,' she said. She felt a smile crossing her face. With her halberd to hand she could take on any enemy.

The youth grew redder still. He took a deep breath.

187

'Domain of Kano. House of Sato,' he gabbled. His voice was shaking. 'Name of Tatsuemon. At your service.'

A board creaked outside the room.

'My masters,' he stuttered. 'If your honours... If your honourable ladyships... If you permit...'

Sachi realized with a shock that this child-man, who had just wielded his sword in a ferocious battle, was more afraid of her than she was of him. Then she remembered how they must look, she and Taki, with their white skin and fine-boned faces, in their magnificent brocade kimonos, wafting perfume wherever they moved. Even her nun's robes must seem unimaginably lavish. If this boy thought she was an imperial princess, he must think her way above the clouds. These men risked execution for daring even to breathe the same air as beings so high above their station.

Taki nodded haughtily to the boy as Sachi rearranged her cowl over her face. The door slid open again and two men came in. One shuffled forward while the other remained on his knees by the door.

So these were men. Not children like young Tatsuemon but real men. Sachi felt a moment of blind panic. It was years since she had been in the presence of such exotic and dangerous creatures. They carried with them a faintly salty odour mingled with the smell of tobacco smoke. And Taki? Had she ever spoken to a man other than when playing with her brothers as a child?

Taki broke the silence.

'How dare you enter our presence without

asking our permission?' she demanded, using the language with which court ladies addressed commoners. 'We could have you executed like common criminals, without the privilege of suicide, for actions unbecoming your station.'

'Our offence is neverending,' muttered the first man, brushing his head on the worn matting. It was the voice Sachi had heard outside the palanquin, soft and cultured despite the rough samurai intonation. 'We are sorry for inconveniencing you. Toranosuké of the Matsunobé, at your service,' he added, with a formal bow.

'Shinzaemon of the Nakayama, domain of Kano,' growled the second.

'Where are you taking us?' barked Taki.

'We are sorry,' said the first man. 'We had to make a rapid decision. Her Highness's safety is paramount. There are rumours that the southerners are searching for her and determined to capture her. We can't allow that to happen. We have urgent business in Kano and we are taking you there. We will arrange a safe place for you to stay until the danger is passed. We undertake to be responsible for your safety and well-being. We will protect you with our lives.'

'And suppose we don't want to go with you? Kano is near Kyoto, isn't it? I have heard it's a hornet's nest there.'

'You are our responsibility,' said the man. 'Our fates have been thrown together.'

Sachi peeked at him from behind her cowl. He was bundled like a samurai in layers of thick winter clothing. But his hair was long and unoiled, tugged back into a glossy black tail and

189

bound with a thick purple cord. It was strange to see hair on top of his head where samurai were supposed to be clean-shaven. The hands on the rough straw mats were soft, too soft for a soldier's. He did not seem the kind of person who could create the mayhem she had glimpsed outside the palanquin.

The second man was squatting silently behind. He looked up suddenly and for a moment their eyes met. Sachi had never seen such a face before – lean with jutting cheekbones and piercing eyes that slanted upwards like a cat's. A scar cut across the dark skin of his cheek. He had a shock of hair, bushy as a fox's tail, and large, powerful hands – swordsman's hands. She felt a tingle of something like fear and quickly looked away.

'We are at war,' he barked. 'We all have to suffer. Time is short. If you ladies don't want to come with us, we'll leave you here.'

'Don't be hasty, Shin,' muttered the first man. It was strange – rather touching – to be in the company of men after all this time, to hear them talking among themselves in their gruff way. 'We can't do that. It's our duty to protect the princess.'

'We have other duties too. All this talking wastes time. Quickly. Tell them.'

The first man turned to the women again.

'I am afraid your ladyships must suffer yet greater inconvenience,' he said. 'We are attracting too much attention. You must leave your palanquins behind. These people will store them for you. You can trust them.'

'What?' snapped Taki. 'So how do we travel? You don't mean...?'

Her voice trailed off. The man bowed. Taki looked outraged. She glanced at Sachi, who nodded. There was nothing they could do. In any case, luxurious though it was, she was beginning to hate the imperial palanquin. The man drew in his breath apologetically.

'And... Excuse our rudeness... Your garments. We have spoken to the lady of the inn. She will provide you with clothes. Your garments will be carefully transported.'

Wafting in from the road outside came a familiar refrain. *'Ee ja nai ka? Ee ja nai ka?* Who gives a damn? Who gives a damn?'

V

Sachi's hair was already short and could easily be twisted into the kind of knot that townswomen wore. But Taki's swept the ground. With great ingenuity, exclaiming at the beauty of it, the lady of the inn combed and coiled and oiled and twisted it until her hairstyle at least was just like that of an ordinary townswoman. Taki carefully rolled up their priceless silk kimonos and wrapped them in bundles to be loaded on to the packhorses. A peasant turned concubine pretending to be a princess disguised as a townswoman, Sachi thought. She could be anything. All it took was a change of clothes.

On the battlefield surrounded by heaps of corpses, addressing wild men who threatened to take them captive, Taki had been fearless. Yet now she seemed discomfited – horrified, indeed – by her abrupt decline in status. Here she was, of gentle birth, a different species from these rough soldiers and common townsfolk. Admittedly she was a lady's maid, but that was in the greatest palace in the land. She had never in her life worn anything except the finest silks. She was used to having a fresh kimono and new white *tabi* socks every day. She fingered her coarse cotton garments with dismay.

'The southerners will never find us dressed like this,' said Sachi. 'They'll never even notice us. Think of your favourite, Zeami,' she added, trying to console her. Taki loved to chant the great playwright's verses. '"If kept hidden, it is a flower. If not hidden, it is no flower." You're like a flower, a single flower. Or a Korean tea bowl. Or a tea room. Yes, you're like a tea room – very plain and simple, no splendour or luxury, and all the more beautiful for it.'

'Yes, but the tea room is in a nobleman's garden and very expensive, not out on the road brushing up against the common people,' sighed Taki. 'The smell is so dreadful! And this gown scratches my skin.'

Sachi glanced at her friend and smiled. They certainly made extraordinary townswomen, the pair of them. Taki's pale face with her pointed chin, large eyes and supercilious eyebrows looked quite incongruous framed by a townswoman's hairstyle decorated with combs and hairpins. Her thin body, which was usually concealed within the bell-like skirts of her court robes, looked rather gawky and awkward in the skimpier townswoman's kimonos.

Sachi twirled around, enjoying the feel of the heavy quilted hem of her outer kimono swirling at her feet. The black of her teeth was beginning to fade and there was a faint smudge of darkness above her eyes where her eyebrows were growing back. Her melon seed-shaped face, small arched nose and rosy lips looked even prettier now that she was no longer wearing thick make-up. Without the layers of heavy silks she was no longer like a great flower, sweeping slowly along. She could pull up her kimono skirts and skip and jump and run. And her delicate neck, of which she was rather proud, was set off far more fetchingly by the collars that swept low at the back.

Nevertheless it was lucky it was winter. They would both have to keep their heads and faces well wrapped up, otherwise it would be obvious they weren't really townswomen at all.

When the little party set out again, Toranosuké – the handsome, well-spoken one of the two *ronin* – was riding in front with smooth-cheeked young Tatsuemon leading his horse. The two women walked some distance behind with the men's retainers on each side, armed with swords and staves, guarding them. Then came porters and grooms leading the packhorses, as many as they had been able to hire. The second man brought up the rear, his swords clanking as he rode.

The road snaked across the plain between lonely paddy fields. They seemed to be avoiding the main highway and travelling by small back roads. Dotted along the way were hillocks crowned with scrawny fir trees marking the distance from Edo.

Every time they passed one they knew they had travelled another few *ri*. What was happening back home in the castle? The whole country was falling into chaos and here they were, in the middle of nowhere, heading for a place they knew nothing about, with no way of escaping and nowhere to go if they did. No one knew where they were. No one would rescue them. The only consolation was that their guards were their protectors, not their enemies – or so it seemed.

For the moment the roads were flat and well paved though there were hills rising in the distance. But the women were already getting tired. Taki had never in her life walked anywhere before and Sachi had forgotten how it felt to be on the road from morning to night. They longed to stop and rest but they kept silent.

Bitter winds blew across the flat plains. They pressed doggedly on, heads bent against the gale. Flocks of geese flew overhead. From time to time they came to small open stalls, offering tea and snacks. The stallholders would rush out, begging them to stop and buy.

The convoy kept up a brisk pace. Occasionally a village poked up like an island in a dreary brown sea, breaking the monotony. Smoke swirled around the thatched roofs hidden behind clumps of trees and groves of withered bamboo. The wind soughed through the dry rice stalks. They passed groups of farmers tugging carts and bow-legged old women so bent their noses seemed to brush the ground. Even though Edo was in upheaval, in the country life seemed to go on as usual. Among the travellers were parties of

194

refugees from Edo, plodding along, dragging carts heaped with belongings. From time to time the distant refrain, 'Who gives a damn?' wafted across the fields.

'I can't believe it,' groaned Taki. 'Out here in public where anyone can see us, without a single attendant, dressed in townswomen's clothes... If my mother saw me now she would weep.'

'No one's even looking at us,' said Sachi wonderingly. 'We've disappeared.' She rather liked being invisible.

After a while Taki brightened up.

'For lordless samurai these fellows are quite civilized,' she said carelessly. 'The one at the front seems rather cultured. And that innkeeper, that peasant. She was almost human!'

'Hush,' said Sachi.

She felt a strange fascination for these unfamiliar creatures with their odd, slightly repellent odour. Men though they were, they were of much lower status, so much so that the fact she was a woman and they men was barely relevant. To Taki, a high-ranking samurai and a court lady, she knew they must seem far beneath her, beings of no account. In her life Taki had hardly ever met men, other than family members and the odd merchant with silks to sell. And these were not just men but *ronin*, utterly outside the bounds of civilized society. As far as she was concerned, they probably barely existed. The two of them – she and Sachi – were walking along in a kind of dream, a nightmare from which hopefully they would soon awake and find themselves comfortably back in the women's palace.

But Sachi could not see things the same way. She was not a samurai. Dressed in these home-spun clothes, she felt her old life sweep over her more vividly than ever. The chafe of the rough cotton felt familiar. It took her back to those long-gone days when she had roamed in the woods with Genzaburo. Everything she knew was coming to an end, just as it had when she was snatched up and whisked away from the village. Perhaps that was just the way life was. Like the delicate pink cherry blossoms that flowered and fell on the same spring day, it could end at any moment. That was what gave it its poignancy and beauty.

It was becoming harder and harder to carry on the deception that she was the princess. Rocking along in the palanquin, she had not been called upon to play-act. But here on the road, in full view of everyone, it seemed an impossible task. Nevertheless she had to try.

At least they were all travellers together. Travel seemed to level the barriers, even if only temporarily. 'Travel is human life,' she murmured, remembering Basho's words. The old poet had spent his life roaming from place to place, exchanging poems with local poets as he went. She thought of the shogun and the letters he had sent her describing the places he had seen on his way to Osaka. Her whole life had been spent in the village or confined in the palace. True, the palace was a world in itself, but she was beginning to enjoy being away from it. She was not like Taki. She belonged here, among these fields, not in a luxurious dolls' house full of whispering women.

After a while the rosy-cheeked young Tatsuemon drew back.

'Master says please take his horse, eminent personage,' he said in a whisper, lowering his head and looking up at Sachi with big timid eyes.

'That's unthinkable. Ladies don't ride.'

'He said you'd say that but to ask you again. Nobody seems to care any more. Are you sure you won't ride?'

She smiled at him. He really was a pretty boy. He might have stepped straight out of one of those novels by Saikaku, about the beautiful page boys who inspired adoration in their fellow pages or their samurai masters.

'You serve Master Toranosuké?' she asked.

'Yes, eminent personage,' he said, flushing to the roots of his forelock.

'How long have you been in his service?'

'We've all three been on the road since the troubles began,' he said. His voice died away. He fixed his eyes on the ground and did not look up again but hung anxiously behind, careful not to walk alongside them. Sachi had never imagined that, as a woman, she would ever walk anything other than three steps behind a man.

'Tell your master we'd like to speak to him,' she said. Taki frowned at her. Sachi paid no attention.

Toranosuké joined the women, careful to keep a step or two behind.

'Master Toranosuké,' Sachi said after a while. 'That song – weren't they singing something about butterflies from the west?'

As she said the syllables she suddenly understood 'butterfly' – 'cho cho'. Of course. They were

197

singing about the southern domain of Choshu.

'Cho is Choshu, eminent personage,' he explained obligingly. 'Choshu is in the south-west. They mean the Choshu clansmen are on their way.'

'Is that true? Are they?'

'Have no fear, eminent personage. We will defeat them, of course. But they are fine warriors and they have foreign weapons. We encountered them many times in the streets of Kyoto. And now they are allied with the Satsuma clan...'

'In Kyoto? You were there?'

It was Taki, her voice brittle. Of course, Taki was from Kyoto. Her family was there. It was her home, and the princess's too. It was the imperial city, the emperor's city.

'Yes, my lady.'

'We were told there was a fire,' Taki gabbled breathlessly. 'I heard the city burned down. I heard the Choshu attacked the imperial palace.'

There was a grunt. It was the second man, the man at the back. Glancing around, Sachi caught his eye. He looked away, almost reluctantly. So he was watching her. Of course, he was guarding her. But... Was she imagining it or was there something strange in his look? Maybe he disapproved of having to take weak women like them along, slowing down their journey. Maybe it was the way she wore these unfamiliar clothes or the way she walked, mincing along like a court lady instead of waddling on bowed legs like a peasant. Surely a true princess would die rather than tread the same soil as a troop of samurai – and *ronin* at that.

As Sachi walked on, she could feel the prickle of his eyes on her back.

VI

That evening they stopped at an inn. Sachi and Taki were exhausted, their legs aching and their feet sore. After they had bathed and eaten, they tumbled into their downy futons. They could hear voices in the next room. The men were swapping poems: first one recited a few lines, then the other. Then came the notes of a flute, infinitely sad, and men's voices, singing softly. It was one of those melancholy ditties travellers sing, full of yearning for home.

The further they got from Edo, the more ragged and scruffy the paddy fields became. Hills pushed up like the humps of a long-buried dragon bursting out of the soil, smothered in a tangle of trees. The little group grew more relaxed, although they could never forget that the southerners might be on their tail.

In one village they managed to hire a sedan chair and bearers to take Sachi and Taki as far as the next. They took turns swinging along, wrapped up in as many layers as they could find. They no longer cared what they looked like. It was cramped – more cramped than a palanquin – and bitterly cold but it was better than walking. Their delicate feet were blistered and raw. Even Taki had abandoned her worries about propriety and rode on one of the horses from time to time. By now the black on Sachi's teeth had faded.

Like Taki, she had the white teeth of a child again. Her eyebrows too were growing back and she had long since stopped wearing her cowl.

But as they travelled, Taki became quieter and quieter. Sachi guessed she was desperate to find out what had happened in the capital where her family lived and where she had grown up, but was reluctant to speak to men such as these. Finally her curiosity got the better of her.

'My good man,' she said. It was hard to be dignified when you were bobbing along in a sedan chair, dressed like a commoner, but Taki managed.

Toranosuké had been waiting for her summons. Taki chatted half-heartedly about the weather and the famous temples they had passed along the way. Then she came to the point.

'What do they say in Kyoto about His Grace's...?'

At the beginning of that year, just five months after the death of the shogun, strange and terrible rumours had reached the women about the emperor, Princess Kazu's brother. It seemed a page boy had had smallpox. In the whole vast imperial palace, only the emperor had caught it, no one else. He was thirty-five and a robust, healthy man. The best doctors had treated him and he had seemed to be making a good recovery. Then he had taken an abrupt turn for the worse. The next day news came that he was dead. His son, the princess's nephew, Prince Mutsuhito, had been proclaimed the Son of Heaven. In public the princess had maintained a façade of stoical calm. But Sachi could not forget hearing her convulsive sobs as she wept behind her screens.

There was a long silence.

'My lady,' said Toranosuké, 'it is common knowledge that His Grace was murdered...'

The women shuddered. It was as they had thought.

'...by courtiers in league with the southern clans. His Grace was a man of stern principles and opinions. Now they can do as they please. The young Son of Heaven is only fifteen, easy to control.'

'I remember His Grace,' Taki whispered to Sachi, wiping her eyes. 'I was presented at court before we left Kyoto.'

A voice burst out from the back of the convoy.

'We are loyal servants of the Tokugawas. We've been fighting for years. We defended the imperial palace when the southerners attacked, trying to capture the Son of Heaven. We left our homes when we were children to fight. We gave our blood. Most of our comrades have died. And for what? Now the shogun has abdicated. Why? Just tell us. Why?'

Sachi and Taki spun round in amazement. It was the second man, Shinzaemon.

Everyone fell silent. They all felt they had said too much. When the men spoke again, it was to tell the women the names of the temples they were passing and the mountains that rimmed the horizon. Sometimes they sang or recited poems. But no one said another word about the emperor or the shogun or the war.

As the road climbed into the mountains, the

landscape grew more and more rugged. They toiled up hill after hill. Each time they arrived, panting, at the top of one they saw another, even higher, rising in front of them, buried in impenetrable forest. Sachi was exhausted but exhilarated too as she tramped along, breathing the country air. The wind whistled through the long grasses. They walked faster and faster, blowing on their fingers, crossing their arms and pressing their hands into their armpits to keep them warm.

The road climbed ever more steeply but they dared not slow down or rest. They needed to get to Kano. But what would they find when they got there? Sachi dared not even think about it.

Ten days of hard walking had passed when they emerged from a forest at the top of a hill. Before them, spread across a lea of land in the distance, were the layered grey roofs and meandering walls of Kano. As they plodded wearily towards it they could see the castle looming above the town with its battlements and tiled roofs with golden dolphins at the beam ends, glittering in the sun like a miniature Edo Castle, magnificent and awe-inspiring. The men walked faster. They started to talk excitedly, telling the women about the city's famous river, the Nagara, and the delicious trout that was caught there.

But as they passed the great gates and entered the narrow streets they found tumbledown samurai mansions with their doors closed and sealed, so dark and gloomy they might have been haunted. It was like a ghost city. The men grew silent. Something very strange and bad had happened while they were away.

Finally they arrived at a big decaying mansion. A woman bustled out, drying her hands on her apron. She had a broad, warm, open face with fleshy cheekbones and a generous smiling mouth. She was bowing again and again in welcome, beaming like a mother greeting travellers returned.

'You must be so tired. Please. My abode is very humble but please come inside and rest yourselves.'

Sachi and Taki had slipped off their straw sandals and *tabi* socks and were wiping their feet on the threshold when a courier came panting up, the gleaming black box on his shoulder swinging. Toranosuké took the box and opened it, read the message, then passed it to Shinzaemon.

'It's from our comrades in Edo,' said Toranosuké.

The women were silent. They were desperate to know more but dared not ask.

'They say there was a fire at the women's palace,' he said, 'and it was totally destroyed. The main mansion of the Satsuma clan was burned down the following day in retribution. The southerners who set the palace alight have been apprehended. They confessed their intention was to capture Princess Kazu, but they failed. Her Highness and the Retired One both escaped harm.'

'Thanks be to the gods,' Sachi whispered. The men looked at her. There was a long silence.

'You were very brave to take the princess's place,' Shinzaemon said. She had never heard him speak so softly before. 'You risked death. You have no need to hide your face now. Tell us, what is your name?'

Sachi was silent. What was her name? Was she the Retired Lady Shoko-in or Lady Yuriko or...

'Sachi,' she said tentatively. Then she said it again, firmly. 'My name is Sachi.' Again she felt Shinzaemon's eyes on her. Before she had only noticed the wild hair and fierce eyes. Now she could see the high forehead and full-lipped mouth. He was smiling.

Part III

On the Road

5

City of Ghosts

I

So the princess was safe.

Sachi had barely had time to take in the news when people came crowding out of the house to greet the returning wanderers. She and Taki were quite forgotten in the clamour.

'Is that really you, Shin, under all that hair?' the broad-faced woman asked. She prodded him in the ribs, laughing and weeping at the same time. Shinzaemon grinned and blushed furiously like a little boy before fixing his samurai scowl firmly back on his face.

Dazed with tiredness, Sachi had an uneasy feeling that all was not as it should be. In spite of the warm greetings, everyone seemed watchful and tense. Every now and then someone glanced around nervously. Was she imagining it, or did a look of fear cross the woman's face? Almost immediately it was gone and everyone was talking and chattering as before.

'Off you go, everyone,' said the woman. 'Inside, quickly.' Sachi thought she heard a note of urgency, almost panic, in her voice. She was just tired, she told herself. She was imagining things.

A maid hurried Sachi and Taki into the house.

Lighting the way with a taper, she led them through a labyrinth of shadowy rooms to a high-ceilinged chamber somewhere at the back. She bowed and slid the door shut. Her footsteps faded away into silence.

Sachi and Taki huddled together beside the dying embers in the hearth, small and lost in the huge room. The tatami mats were faded and worn, the paper doors patched and repatched. A single lantern cast a lonely light. They were alone, without even a servant or a maid to attend to them.

Sachi was thinking about the look she had seen on the woman's face.

'Taki,' she said, 'did you notice anything strange?'

'They seemed a little nervous,' said Taki. 'After all, those men are *ronin*. It's a crime to leave one's clan. It's treason. They'll be in trouble if they draw too much attention to themselves.'

Sachi nodded. They must have had good reason to come back, she thought.

'On our own again,' she murmured. 'I was getting used to them. They were beginning to seem like family – almost brothers. It feels lonely without them. Isn't that odd?'

She could still feel Shinzaemon's eyes burning into her. Was she imagining that too or had he turned to glance at her one last time as he was led away by his family?

'What could he have been thinking of, staring at you like that?' snorted Taki, as if she could read her mind. 'Did he imagine you were for sale, like a play-woman or a geisha? *Ronin* or not, you can't

208

go behaving like that towards a lady of the court. The insolence of it! Has he no manners? It's a good thing he's gone. I know he's loyal but that's all he has to recommend him.'

Sachi smiled at Taki's indignation. Taki was right. With that hair of his Shinzaemon was like a wild animal, a bear or a wolf. No one could be more different from the only man she had ever known or cared about – gentle, noble Kiku-*sama*.

Now that had been a man – so cultured, so delicate, so sensitive. If only he had lived! She would have passed her days as his concubine, the honoured number-two wife. What had he said? 'Be like bamboo. Bend in the wind but never break.' She would have to be strong. But the thought of him and of that whole beautiful, fragile world that was lost made her eyes fill with tears.

'We're exiles,' she sighed. 'Stranded.'

She thought of Prince Genji, the Shining One, in the old story, playing his flute forlornly while the waves beat on the shore in distant Suma, hundreds of *ri* from the court. '"His sleeves like the grey sea waves",' she murmured. She had almost forgotten how it had felt to be a pampered concubine with nothing to do all day but read poetry and practise singing and dancing, surrounded by a retinue of maids and retainers eager to serve her. It was as if that life had never been.

And here she was in Kano. It seemed a dreadful, desolate, windswept place. Even the room had a musty smell to it. The damp and cold gnawed into Sachi's bones. No matter how many layers of robes she piled on or how close she huddled to the fire, she could not get warm. Her teeth were chattering. Her feet in their thin cotton *tabi* socks were frozen.

'At least Her Highness is safe,' said Taki, holding her thin hands close to the fire, 'and you've completed your mission. You no longer have to pretend to be the princess. I suppose we should go back to Edo and report. They'll be expecting us.'

It was true. Sachi was free. She didn't have to stay in this dreadful city a moment longer. But Edo was swarming with southern hoodlums, as Lady Tsuguko had told them. And the roads were dangerous; they couldn't go on their own. Besides, she was tired. She could sense that Taki too was reluctant to turn around and go straight back again. Now she was outside the palace everything looked different.

'Her Highness doesn't even know I'm alive,' whispered Sachi. 'She sent me away. There's no one else I owe allegiance to, only her. Those bonds are broken now. My destiny is in my own hands.'

She paused for breath, shocked at her own rebellious words. At the palace she had learned always to say the proper thing. She knew what she was expected to say and even to feel at every moment of the day. But things were different now.

Taki looked at her with her big eyes.

'Don't say that,' she said sternly. Sachi could hear her samurai training in her squeaky voice. 'You're forgetting your duty. There's nothing for us in this terrible place. It's the end of the world here. We can't be beholden to people like these.

210

We must get back to Edo, to our own people.'

'But when the princess sent me away she cut the cord,' Sachi protested. 'You too, you disobeyed orders when you came after me. Those men promised to protect us and now they've disappeared. I hope we're not separated from them for too long.'

Sachi had never before seen Taki look worried but now she did. Her face was pinched and drawn.

'We can't stay here,' Taki muttered, staring at the worn tatami. 'We're too conspicuous – the way we look, the way we talk, everything. But we can't just set off by ourselves. We're women and it's nearly New Year. The weather will be closing in. All the inns will be shut. And even if we make it back to Edo, what do we do then? We saw what it was like on the streets.'

'We need to wait and find out what's going on there,' said Sachi firmly.

Someone had brought in their bundles and stacked them neatly in the corridor along one side of the room. Even the lowest-ranking court lady would have had a trunk at least, and most probably a retinue of soldiers, maids, retainers, cooks, shoe-bearers, bath-carriers and endless amounts of luggage. But all they had was a forlorn pile of things tied up in rough silk squares.

'We'll need to sell a gown to pay for our keep,' said Taki gloomily. 'I can't even remember what I packed.'

Rummaging through the heap, Sachi came across the tattered bundle she had brought from the village. It was cold and clammy. She held it to her nose and shut her eyes, breathing in the faint earthy odours of woodsmoke and miso and dung – smells of the village, of home. It took her back to the day when the princess arrived there. She remembered her mother turning away and the tears running down her face as she dashed them angrily away with her hand. But there was another scent mingled with the familiar village smells, a mysterious silky odour like the elegant perfume of some great lady or nobleman.

She picked at the knot. The fabric was half rotten and the bundle fell open as she tugged at it.

Inside was a thick roll of brocade. Sachi looked at it, dumbfounded. It was not hers at all. She had never seen it before. She gave it a shake. Perhaps there was something wrapped up inside it. Slowly, like a great log rolling down the River Kiso, the brocade unrolled across the tatami.

It was the colour of the sky on a bright winter's day, embroidered with tiny leaves and flowers – delicate purple plum blossoms, clusters of spiky bamboo leaves, bristly sprigs of pine. It lit up the dreary room like sunshine.

'Pine, bamboo, plum,' exclaimed Taki. 'A New Year's gown!'

A rag doll came tumbling out of the folds.

'Little Bean!' cried Sachi. She snatched it up. It was a faded, shabby thing made of two red crepe bags stuffed with beans and stitched together, the smaller one making the head, the bigger one the fat round body. It was worn where she had cuddled it. It had been her dearest plaything. She cradled it, feeling the soft weight in her hands.

There were also a few strings of copper coins, tied with strands of hemp. To someone who had lived in the palace they were practically worthless; yet she knew how much her mother must have sacrificed to give them to her.

Taki was examining the brocade.

'Glossed silk,' she said, running her thin fingers over the fabric. 'Looks like palace style. It's a noblewoman's robe! Must be brittle after all these years.'

She spread it on the threadbare tatami. The clusters of leaves and flowers formed a landscape. On one shoulder the verandas of an embroidered pavilion peeked from behind the leaves. At the hip was a brushwood fence with a rustic gate and below that a rope curtain rippled in an imaginary breeze. A silver stream tumbled across the back of the gown. Near the hem was a wheeled carriage such as a Heian-period nobleman would have used. The reins coiled picturesquely as if the oxen had wandered off while the owner was away, perhaps visiting the imaginary lady who lived in the garden.

'It's an overkimono,' murmured Sachi in hushed tones. 'A wraparound. It's a treasure! It's been in that bundle all along and we never opened it!'

She picked it up with care, afraid it might fall apart at her touch. She stood up, draped it over her shoulders and tied it in place at the waist with her worn cotton obi. Then she let the fabric fall. It cascaded around her hips in a double layer and formed a train that swirled at her feet.

She was transformed: no longer a wanderer in

213

a shabby townswoman's kimono but a lady of the finest court in the land. Spreading the skirts to show the lining, she glided around the room. Then she stretched out her arms and took a few measured steps. The heavy fabric swung and sparkled as it swished across the faded tatami mats.

"'It is an angel's cloak of feathers",' Taki sang softly.

It was true. It was just like the angel's cloak that the fisherman had found in the Noh play.

"'A cloak no mortal man may wear",' Sachi chanted, remembering the next line. How had the story gone? Wasn't it that without her robe of feathers the angel could not return to heaven? She had begged and pleaded and eventually the fisherman had conceded. But first he had insisted that she dance for him.

For a moment Sachi was back at the palace on a steamy summer evening. The air was heavy with incense and the fragrance of flowers. Cicadas kept up their ear-piercing shrill. Blazing torches crackled and spat, lighting up the gardens with their huge yellow flames. While the other ladies watched Sachi danced on and on into the night with movements so slow they were almost imperceptible, forgetting everything in the passion of the story and the feeling of her body moving with perfect control. The singers chanted and wailed and the drummers thwacked their drums. The memory was so sharp it brought tears to her eyes. It was a shock to come back to the dismal present.

What was this gown? Where did it come from?

214

There was something sinister about it. It was too beautiful, too seductive – as if it belonged to one of those women in the fairy tales who turned out not to be women at all but foxes, or to have been dead for hundreds of years.

'You try it,' said Sachi, hastily throwing it off.

'I can't,' said Taki. 'It's a concubine's robe. It's for you to wear.'

'But I don't understand. It's not mine. I don't know how it got into my bundle.'

She lifted the collar. Embroidered at the back of the neck was a crest with a pattern of three narrow leaves. There was another on each shoulder.

'That crest,' she said. 'Haven't you seen it somewhere before?' Taki tilted her head to one side.

'Yes,' she said. 'But I can't think where.'

'It's not mine,' said Sachi fiercely. 'We have to get rid of it. We must find out where it comes from and return it.'

But how could they? They were adrift, lost in a strange city about which they knew nothing. They looked at each other helplessly.

They had tidied the gowns away when footsteps came pattering towards the room. The door slid open. A smiling face appeared. It was the woman who had come out to meet them.

'How rude, leaving you all alone so long!' she cried, scrambling in on her knees. 'You must be frozen. Please, have some tea and try these pickles. I made them myself.'

She had a raspy voice like a crow's caw and spoke with the same Kano lilt as the three men.

She introduced herself as Shinzaemon's aunt, of the Sato family. Her high-cheekboned face and

215

direct gaze were very much like his. Sachi warmed to her immediately. She was brisk and down to earth, full of common sense. Although obviously a samurai and a woman of rank, she wore her hair in a simple knot and it was a little ruffled, as if she did it herself. It was a long time since Sachi had been in the presence of someone so reassuring and motherly. She radiated calm and competence as if nothing could surprise her, as if mysterious ladies travelling in disguise turned up every day to billet themselves in her guest chambers.

'Welcome, ladies. Please stay as long as you like,' Aunt Sato said, bowing and smiling. 'My nephew, Shinzaemon, has asked me to take care of you. I will do my best to keep you safe and comfortable.' She added quietly, 'Things are uncertain here at the moment. It would be best if you stay within the house and grounds. I'm sure you understand.'

Sachi glanced at Taki. She had been right. They would have to be careful.

II

All day long the house had been in upheaval. The women swept, polished and scoured feverishly as if they believed they could wash away all the bad luck of the previous year if they scrubbed hard enough. The air sparkled with dust as they heaved out the tatami mats and leaned them against the walls to air, then fitted them back into their frames again with a thump. The old year was ending – the third year of Keio – and a new year

216

beginning. But no one dared guess what it would bring.

Sachi and Taki retreated to their chamber and listened to the distant sounds. Sachi pushed back the wooden shutters so the gloomy room was flooded with sunlight. She stepped out on to the veranda.

'Come and see!' she called.

Outside was a small tea garden. It must once have been lovely. But the meandering stepping stones, pond, carefully placed rocks and small artificial hill had almost disappeared beneath a mantle of weeds and moss, and the crumbling stone lantern had toppled over and was lying on the ground. The whole garden was covered in a dusting of snow.

'Beautiful, isn't it?' said Sachi. '*Wabi*, wouldn't you say?'

'There never was such a perfect example at the palace,' Taki agreed.

Sachi's teachers had taught her about *wabi* – the beauty of poverty – and *sabi* – the patina of age that gave a tea bowl or an ancient iron kettle beauty. At first it had made no sense to her. In the village everything was old and poor but nobody thought it was beautiful. But now that she was used to the riches of the palace, she could see how soothing these simple things were. Here in this garden it was the work of nature and time, not of man. That made it all the more beautiful.

The two pulled quilts around them and huddled side by side in silence, drinking in the melancholy of the scene. It seemed to echo everything that had happened since they'd left

217

the women's palace.

A day had gone by and there was still no sign of the men. Sachi and Taki had begun to accept that they would be staying at the great house for a while. It was as gloomy and forbidding as ever but they were getting used to the creaking of the rafters and the icy winds that whistled through the shutters and rattled the paper doors in their frames. When they wandered the grounds, they were less shocked at the grass that sprouted between the roof tiles of the main gate and no longer jumped when a fox or a badger rustled through the undergrowth.

To Taki, who had only ever lived the life of a high-class samurai, Kano was horribly provincial. She felt banished, cut off from civilization. Like hungry ghosts, both of them were exiled from everything and everyone that mattered to them. They missed the castle – the grand rooms crowded with women, the constant chatter and bustle, the splendour of the gold-encrusted walls and coffered ceilings, the pleasure gardens, the moon-viewing pavilions. And the space. The women's palace had been as big as a small city.

Towards evening Aunt Sato's broad, homely face appeared. She was followed by a maid staggering under a pile of kimonos.

'Miserable gifts but please accept them,' she said in her croaky voice, covering her mouth as she smiled and bowed. 'New kimonos for the New Year.'

Taki fingered the fabric. The kimonos were of homespun cotton in shades of brown, indigo, grey and grey-blue. They were the plainest, dullest kimonos Sachi had ever seen. Even the rough townswomen's gowns she and Taki were wearing were more stylish.

'Tonight we're going out to pray,' said Aunt Sato. Her kindly race had changed. Her eyes were fierce, her jaw set in an expression of stubborn determination. 'We can't let New Year's Eve go by without that, no matter what. We can't hide here for ever. We must keep up our normal lives. You'd better dress like everyone else so that you blend in.'

She looked at them hard as if to make sure they understood. Sachi remembered the fear she had seen crossing her face the first time they had met. She had thought she must have imagined it but now she knew she hadn't.

She tried on a plain grey kimono. It was in the style prescribed for samurai, but not very different from what she had worn in the village except that it was new and crisp instead of old and ragged. She twirled around, enjoying the new-found freedom. She rather liked this modest new self. With her simple unadorned hairstyle, skin free of make-up and unblackened teeth, she was as fresh-faced as a child. She caught a glimpse of herself in the mirror – even in this drab kimono, no one would ever mistake her for an ordinary samurai wife.

Aunt Sato looked her up and down.

'I don't know what you used to do in Edo,' she said, 'but round here you can't go about with unblackened teeth at your age. Unmarried or not, it looks strange. I'll send the maid straight away.'

Later that evening, feeling rather self-conscious in their dowdy kimonos, Sachi and Taki emerged from their room. A fire burned in the hearth in the middle of the great hall. Smoke wafted like a low-lying mist, making their eyes water.

Men in *haori* jackets and pleated *hakama* trousers milled around the open hearth, blowing on their hands and rubbing them. They all had the shiny shaven pates and oiled topknots of samurai. There were no wild-haired *ronin* to be seen. The women were in drab browns, greys and indigos, so Sachi and Taki fitted in perfectly. Everyone seemed strangely subdued. They chatted quietly as if everything was normal, but every now and then eyes met and a sudden silence would fall. Only the children, in crisp holiday kimonos, dashed about yelling with excitement. Their shouts echoed from the blackened rafters.

In the palace such a crowd would have exuded perfume with every movement of their sleeves, each person wearing their own distinctive blend. But here there was only the smell of freshly washed cotton, the camellia scent of the pomade that held the men's hair in place and the all-pervasive bitter smell of smoke.

The previous New Year had been so different. Taki had laid out an exquisite new kimono for Sachi of white silk with plum blossom, bamboo and pine embroidered in silver thread and cranes and tortoises of long life across the back. They had spent the morning visiting the grand dowager ladies and in the afternoon had sat with the princess, writing poems and playing round after round of the poem card game. And now here they were in this grim city with this unknown threat hanging over everyone. Where was the princess? What was she doing? Sachi took a deep breath. It was better not to think of such things, better not to think at all.

At the hour of the rat, when the night was at its darkest, the first bell sounded, booming out from a nearby temple. The hall fell silent. The children began to count: 'One. Two. Three.' They had reached a hundred and eight when the bells finally stopped. Again the adults glanced at each other. There was a long pause. One by one people began to file towards the side entrance of the house. Sachi and Taki followed Aunt Sato. They put on quilted jackets and wrapped their heads and faces in scarves so that only their eyes were visible.

Outside, the narrow lane wound between sturdy earthen walls topped with clay tiles. People clattered on wooden clogs, all heading in the same direction. The smoke from their lanterns rose with their breath in the frosty air.

Here and there a pool of yellow light glowed, breaking the line of the wall, and a massive gate loomed out of the darkness, marking the entrance to a samurai mansion. Lanterns glowed outside. A sacred rope with a wreath of ferns and an orange hung across the eaves, and tubs of bamboo and pine stood on each side of the gateposts.

Then they came to a gate that was shut and bolted. There were no lanterns burning and no festive decorations. Dry leaves lay in rotting piles in the corners as if no one had passed through for months. The place was as still as the grave.

221

Everyone hurried by with their eyes lowered, as if to look on such a sight might bring down the same dreadful fate on them too.

A little girl with a plump round face, like the moon, and huge innocent eyes was trotting beside Sachi. She wore her hair tied into two loops which flopped on top of her head like butterfly wings. A slight, nervous woman shuffled behind her, her head bowed and her shoulders stooped. Sachi had seen her moving around the house like a ghost, as if she didn't belong there and didn't want anyone to notice her. She had thought she was the children's teacher.

Suddenly the child spoke, breaking the silence.

'*Haha-ue!* Mama!' she piped. 'Are we going home soon? I'd like to go home!'

She tugged at the sleeve of Sachi's jacket and said in matter-of-fact tones, 'That's our house. See, it says Miyabe on the gate. That's our name. We'll be home soon.'

'Yu-*chan*,' said the woman gently. It was years since Sachi had been around children or heard the affectionate term of address *chan*, used for little girls. 'Little Yu. Hush. Stop bothering the honourable guest.'

She straightened her back and raised her head, revealing a refined, rather beautiful face with thin cheeks and large sad eyes. 'It's true,' she added softly but clearly, her voice proud and defiant. 'Everyone knows it. It's our house. That is...' She paused. 'It was our house.'

'Nonsense, Cousin,' said Aunt Sato hastily, glancing around and taking her arm. 'Don't say such things.'

Further on they passed another sealed, unlit gate. Some of the roof tiles lay on the road outside and there were holes in the clay and straw of the walls. Where the side buildings should have been were gaping spaces. Beyond them was the dark silhouette of a mansion, silent and still, like a house of the dead. They came to another, then another and another. Half the houses on the street were dark and bolted. They were like blind eyes, like missing teeth in a healthy mouth. Sachi stared around in dread, wondering what terrible cataclysm had happened here.

The grounds of the shrine to Hachiman, the god of war, were jostling with people. Smoke and succulent smells coiled from tiny stalls where burly men with tattooed shoulders and scarves knotted around their heads were cooking up year-end noodles and grilling rice balls, octopus and squid, yelling out their wares at the tops of their voices. Merrymakers laughed, shouted, pushed and shoved, welcoming in the new year in innumerable cups of steaming sake. Skeletal dogs slunk around, sniffing for food.

'They make me nervous, all these people,' said Taki, wrinkling her nose and drawing back with distaste as a crowd of townsmen staggered drunkenly by. 'I know they're countryfolk, but still, for samurai to be mixing with commoners like these – even samurai women! I've never come across such a thing. Have they no sense of propriety?'

Sachi too was looking among the merrymakers, wondering if she might see a wild-haired *ronin*. She needed news of Edo, she told herself. But the three men were not there. She was not surprised.

It would have been madness for outlaws like them to be seen in public.

The children had gathered around Aunt Sato. They tugged at her hand, her skirts, whatever part of her they could reach.

'Granny, granny. Give us money,' they clamoured. 'We want to go and pray for victory.'

They scampered up the steep stone steps that led to the shrine and disappeared through the huge wooden gateway into the darkness at the top. In a while they returned, each holding an arrow tipped with white feathers.

'For good luck,' said a plump-faced boy solemnly, waving his arrow above his head.

'And victory,' piped Yuki, her two loops of hair flapping.

'It's not victory we need, it's peace,' muttered Aunt Sato, shaking her head. She glanced around the crowds, her face tense and strained. Yuki's mother gave the ghost of a nod.

III

The next morning, the first of the new year, Sachi and Taki joined the others in the great hall. Men, women, adults and children mingled there. For these few days all the usual boundaries were set aside.

The men lounged around as if they were in their own homes, their hairy legs poking from thick indigo gowns, smoking pipe after pipe of tobacco. They had left their long swords at the door, but they kept their short swords thrust into

224

their waistbands. They were relaxed but watchful.

Someone brought out a pack of poem cards. Aunt Sato put them aside, frowning.

'Cousin,' she said, 'didn't you tell me you had a fine pack of cards?'

Yuki's mother was kneeling in a corner. She jumped up like a startled rabbit and scurried off, then returned with two sets of cards. Aunt Sato dealt out one set face up on the tatami while the maid stood tall candles in the middle. Everyone clustered around to look. The cards were of beautifully grained, thick, stiff paper. On each were two lines of verse in a strikingly assured, graceful hand.

'A master calligrapher!' murmured Sachi.

'It's Papa's writing,' piped little Yuki proudly, looking up at Sachi with her big innocent eyes. In her brightly coloured kimono with long flapping sleeves, she looked more like a butterfly than ever.

'Yu-*chan*'s father is a very famous calligrapher,' said Aunt Sato. There was a long silence. Looking at the bowed heads and grim faces, Sachi dared not ask why he was missing from the gathering. Yuki snuggled up against her.

'Do you know "One hundred poems by one hundred poets"?' she whispered. 'It's my favourite game.'

Uncle Sato, Aunt Sato's husband, sat cross-legged, his great belly hanging so far over his waistband it all but obscured it. He had a round head and shiny pate and half-closed eyes that peered out watchfully from heavy folds of flesh.

225

Smiling down at little Yuki, he took the second pack of cards and shuffled them then picked one out. The card was small in his big hand. In a deep rumble he chanted the first lines of a poem:

'If but for the dream,
Of a night of spring
I make your arm my pillow...'

Everyone leaned forward, making a great play of studying the cards that lay in neat rows on the tatami. Yuki stretched out her small arm and snatched one up.

'Lady Suo!' she squealed. 'It's Lady Suo!'

She read out the last two lines in her fluting voice:

'How I would regret my name
Coming blamelessly to shame.'

As the last syllables rang out, the room fell silent again. The words hung in the air. The adults all looked uncomfortably at the tatami. Sachi glanced around, wondering if there was some connection here with what had happened to Yuki's family.

Then everyone started chattering again, a little too urgently. As if to conceal the awkwardness, Uncle Sato pushed the card he was holding into Yuki's small hand. She held it out to Sachi.

Beneath the poem was a tiny portrait of the poet, Lady Suo. It showed a doll-like lady of the Heian period reclining languidly, her small head peeking from her brilliantly coloured twelve-layered robe. Her face was a white blob with dots for eyes and mouth. But the eyebrows painted high on her forehead gave her a distinctly disdainful look. The lavish robes, the air of melancholy resignation, reminded Sachi forcibly of the princess. The princess and her ladies – and Sachi too – had dressed just that way. Sachi remembered the arguments they had had with the Retired One and her ladies, who dressed in the florid Edo style. At the time the whole matter of whether one dressed this way or that had seemed so important. But now it was all over. The palace had burned down. Sachi yearned to know where the princess was and what she was doing this New Year's Day.

Yuki was gazing up at her.

'Is this how you used to dress in Edo?' she asked.

'No,' Sachi lied, swallowing hard. Her voice was wobbling. She tried to smile at the little girl. 'Much the same as here.'

No one must ever know about the palace or the life they had led there. It was their secret, to be treasured for ever.

Uncle Sato picked another card and sang the first half of a poem in his deep voice. Before he had even finished Yuki had shrieked and snatched up the card which contained the second half. She read it out triumphantly. Taki too was poised over the cards, hand stretched out. She took the game every bit as seriously as Yuki did. Soon there was a heap of cards beside each of them.

Only a few matches were left to find when there was a commotion at the side entrance. The heavy wooden door juddered open and a cold wind swirled in, setting the candles guttering. The servants rushed around taking the new arrivals' mantles and swords.

Then the great hall was full of people. Everyone was on their hands and knees, bowing.

'My brother and his family,' said Aunt Sato. She was smiling, playing the gracious hostess, but Sachi couldn't help noticing the tension in her voice. 'You know Shinzaemon, of course.'

Sachi raised her fan to cover her face and peeked curiously from behind it. She remembered that smile he had given her. Shinzaemon looked tidier now. His bushy hair was knotted into a ponytail and his sun-darkened cheeks clean-shaven. Without his horse and long sword, he looked uncomfortable and out of place. He stood around awkwardly, scowling, as if he wished he were somewhere else.

Aunt Sato introduced Sachi and Taki to Shinzaemon's stern, heavy-set father and small, soft-spoken mother and his bespectacled elder brother and his wife. Sachi had never imagined that a rebellious character like him would have a respectable, well-spoken family. But of course he did.

Shinzaemon was next in line. Sachi knelt beside Taki, keeping her eyes to the ground. She wanted to look up, to see those eyes which had stared at her so insolently, to see whether there was a spark in them, whether he was looking at her now. She wanted to say, 'You said you were going to protect us. But we never even see you.'

But of course she didn't. She kept her eyes lowered and murmured politely, 'Thank you for taking care of us.' Taki pressed her face to her hands in silence.

'I'm sorry,' he muttered. 'I wish I could do more.'

It was not like him to be so formal. There was uproar as Aunt Sato's sons clustered around him.

'Cousin Shin,' yelled a boisterous voice. It sounded like Gennosuké, the oldest. 'It's been a long time.'

'Where have you been?' demanded another. 'What happened to your hair? Is that the way they wear it in Edo?'

'Time you got it cut,' cried the first voice. 'We need you here. We're fighting here too, you know. What about that duel you promised me?'

'Any time.' It was Shinzaemon's gruff tones. 'You haven't got a chance.'

There was a roar of laughter.

'Haven't changed, have you?' said the second voice.

'This way,' said Uncle Sato, heaving himself to his feet and leading the menfolk off to his section of the house. While the maids prepared sake and food for the guests, the women gathered up the cards to play another round. The children were soon absorbed in the game.

Shinzaemon's small, plump mother asked polite questions of the newcomers. It was hard to see anything of Shinzaemon in her faded, pretty face. Like everyone in that strange city she had a haunted look in her eyes.

Aunt Sato knelt beside her.

'He's grown-up, that boy of yours,' she croaked in her raspy voice. Sachi bent over the cards,

229

pretending to be interested in the game, but she couldn't help listening. She was prickling with curiosity.

'He's not a boy any longer,' said Shinzaemon's mother, who spoke with a strong Kano lilt. She sounded sad and resigned. 'He's bloodied his sword.'

'How long has it been now? Three years? Four?'

'It was before the time of the troubles. We didn't think he'd ever come back. At least he didn't disgrace the family. His father gave him a scolding but there's no talking to him. He won't listen to anyone.'

'In this world there's no place for people who won't fit in,' said Aunt Sato, shaking her head. 'The nail that sticks up gets hammered down.'

Sachi had heard the proverb a thousand times before but that day the words gave her a feeling of foreboding. A *ronin* was undoubtedly a nail that stuck up.

'He was always a fighter, always practising with his sword instead of reading books,' said his mother with a sigh.

'He's a good swordsman,' said Aunt Sato firmly. 'One of the best.'

'We need that,' said his mother. 'If we survive, then's the time for scholarship. I dread to think what will happen now, now that his lordship's...'

Aunt Sato laid a warning hand on her knee. They both glanced at Yuki's mother who was kneeling in a corner, twisting her thin hands, gazing pensively at the poem cards, and fell silent.

Sachi was not the only one who had overheard the conversation. Taki had been listening too.

Sachi leaned towards her and whispered, 'I have to talk to Shinzaemon before he goes. I have to find out what's happening in Edo. They brought us here, those three, they have to help us get away. We can't stay here for ever.'

Taki raised her eyebrows and looked at her quizzically. There was disapproval in her big eyes. Sachi knew perfectly well that a lady like her was not supposed to speak to a man. If anyone addressed him, it should be Taki. But Sachi didn't care.

The maids were closing the shutters and lighting the lamps and the women had tired of playing the poem card game when they heard angry shouts.

'Insolent boy! Have you no sense of duty?' It was Uncle Sato. 'If you weren't my brother's son I'd take my sword to you.'

'I'll ride north when I see fit and not before,' came Shinzaemon's voice. 'I have a job to do here. I wish we could have got back sooner.'

Sachi leaped to her feet and ran to the entrance hall. Shinzaemon was thrusting his long sword angrily into his belt and throwing on an overmantle.

'Master Shinzaemon,' she said softly. He swung round, startled.

'Excuse me,' she said. 'I would be most grateful if you could pay us a visit when you have news. We need to know when things have settled down in Edo. That would be of great service to us.'

Shinzaemon stopped in his tracks. He looked straight at her, his eyes straying across her face, her hair. He seemed to take in every part of her –

231

her small nose, her rosy lips, her white skin, her green eyes.

With an effort Sachi broke the spell, lowering her gaze and biting her lips.

'Of course,' he said and bowed abruptly. 'I shall.'

Then the door slid open and he stepped out into the night.

IV

At first Sachi and Taki listened hopefully for Aunt Sato or the maid to come pattering through the house to announce that Shinzaemon or Tora-nosuké was in the entrance. Whenever the doors slid open they looked up expectantly. But it was always simply to bring in their meal, lay out their bedding or invite them to the great hall for a chat.

Little by little they were becoming accustomed to their new life. Their splendid kimonos – all that remained to remind them of their life in the palace – lay bundled up, gathering dust. Sachi tried not to think of that other strange robe she had brought with her from the village. But when out of the corner of her eye she glimpsed the silk scarf that wrapped it, she seemed to see it glowing inside like an ember. It really was like an angel's cloak. It was too beautiful. It frightened her, as if it was enchanted.

To fill her days, she taught Yuki poems from the *New Collection of Ancient and Modern Poems*. She taught in the way the princess had taught her, making the little girl recite each poem over and over again until she could do it without thinking. She was amazed at how quickly the child learned. Yuki particularly loved the poems of the monk Saigyo. 'They're so sad,' she said. 'They make me feel lonely.'

Sachi, also, as the princess had done, wrote out each poem in her best cursive-style calligraphy for the child to copy. In the palace she had learned not just *hiragana*, the syllabary that was all that women were supposed to need, but the Chinese characters that classical literature was written in. She started to teach Yuki these too, even though Aunt Sato protested that if the little girl was too highly educated no one would marry her.

'Where is your husband?' Yuki asked in her direct way as they sat together one day. 'Has he gone away, like Papa?'

'I don't have a husband,' said Sachi, taken by surprise.

'Is that why you don't have children?' Yuki persisted.

It was true. It was outlandish for a grown woman like Sachi to be childless, let alone still unmarried. She was now eighteen. Like everyone else, she had added a year to her age at New Year.

'I can't marry,' said Sachi gently. 'I'm too far from home. When I go back to my family, my father will find a marriage broker.'

'But you'll be too old then,' said Yuki. Sachi nodded. The words filled her with an indefinable unease.

For where was her home? In this world everyone belonged somewhere. But she and Taki were like weeds floating on a pond, cut off from their roots, or jealous ghosts, suspended between one world and the next. They needed to get back to the palace in Edo or, if not that, to their families. They couldn't go on hiding away, living a half-life for ever, no matter how kind their hosts.

Every day, sometimes with Taki, sometimes alone, Sachi took a quilt and went out to the veranda. She sat and contemplated the garden, brooding on the strange fate that had brought her and Taki there and trying to imagine what their future might be.

V

Not long after the end of the New Year holiday, when the festive decorations were being taken down to be burned, the sky became grey and heavy. Great white flakes began to waft down, at first slowly, then faster and faster. When Sachi went out on to the veranda that afternoon, the trees and rocks and toppled stone lantern had turned into a mysterious landscape of ghostly white shapes, muffled beneath a thick mantle of snow. She wrapped a quilt around her and absorbed herself in the stillness.

Suddenly there was a noise. Sachi started. Surely it was the crack of the bamboos, bending under the weight of snow? Or perhaps it was an animal or a spirit. No one ever came to this side of the grounds. This was her secret place, hers and Taki's.

'My lady,' hissed a voice. 'Don't be afraid.'

A figure emerged from the shadows at the side of the house, bundled so warmly that only the eyes were visible. He crunched across the snow towards her, leaving a trail of footprints marked with the weave of his straw boots. He followed along the wicker fence until he was so close she could see his breath like steam in the frosty air. She knew those piercing black eyes and that deep growl of a voice. It was Shinzaemon.

Sachi sat bolt upright, pulling her quilt tighter round her. 'Sir. This is quite improper.' She spoke in a low voice, looking hastily over her shoulder. Perhaps Taki was in the room behind her and could chaperone them. But the room was empty. She was not sure whether she was sorry or pleased that Taki was not there.

'I need to see you alone,' he muttered urgently. 'There are ears everywhere.'

For a moment he stood awkwardly shifting from foot to foot, staring at the ground, his hand on his sword hilt. With no one else around he seemed less sure of himself. It was extraordinary for them to be alone together – a man and a woman, just the two of them. It simply never happened. Even when Sachi had lain with the shogun there had been ladies-in-waiting hovering in the background.

'We are unendingly grateful to your family, sir,' said Sachi, fumbling for words.

'I'm sorry,' he muttered. 'It was wrong to bring you here. It was a mistake – a terrible mistake. I promised I would protect you but I've failed. I thought this place would be a haven. But I was wrong. It's not safe for you, not safe for any of us.

His lordship the daimyo...

'We're loyal retainers of the Tokugawas here. But the present daimyo...' He lowered his voice still further, glancing around as if even in this walled garden, with snow drifting down in huge flakes, there might be spies. Sachi leaned forward, listening hard. They were so close she could feel the warmth of his body and see his breath rippling the scarf which muffled his face. As she breathed she caught a faint whiff of sweat, mingled with tobacco smoke and dust. There was something about the smell – so raw, so natural – that sent a prickle up her spine.

'His present lordship is ... a man without honour. He refused to send troops when the shogun asked for them. He's been waiting to see which way the wind would blow. He wants to make sure he's on the winning side. My cousin was ... is one of his advisers. He's been doing his best to persuade him to do the right thing, to support the shogun, but there are powerful men among his lordship's counsellors who favour the south.'

His cousin... Could it be...

'So that's why you're here, to help your cousin?'

'It was stupid. We're *ronin*. There are men here who would hunt us down if they could. But all three of us, Toranosuké and Tatsuemon too, we all agreed we had to come back.'

'So that was where you were going...'

'...when we came across your palanquin.' He nodded. 'As servants of His Majesty it was our duty to protect you. But we also needed to get back here as fast as we could. We thought this would still be a safe haven for you. But...'

He stared at the ground, scowling. Beyond the overhanging eaves snow floated down.

'Your cousin...' gasped Sachi, feeling a sudden chill as the realization dawned. 'You mean ... Yuki's father?'

With a pang she thought of the little girl's bright hopeful face. She dared not ask any more.

Shinzaemon's dark eyes narrowed.

'We grew up together. He's like a brother to me. He's a good man, a man of honour.'

'And now...'

'He's in prison.' Sachi felt a jolt of horror. 'His lordship chose to side with the south. My cousin's been condemned to death. I've been trying to get him out. Every day I check the prison gates. As far as I know there's still a chance.'

'It was because of us,' said Sachi, wide-eyed with horror, 'because of us you had to travel slowly and couldn't get here in time.'

He shook his head.

'It would have been too late anyway,' he muttered. 'His lordship has given the southerners free rein. There's been a purge. Southern *ronin* have been cutting down anyone they suspect of supporting the north. A lot of people have been working out old grudges too. Many have been imprisoned or killed; whole families have been wiped out and their names struck off the register. So far my family have been left alone, but no one knows when the time will come.'

He paused as if to collect his thoughts.

'As ladies of His Majesty's court, you are in grave danger here. It was us that brought you and it's our responsibility to keep you safe. On no account go outside the house. We'll leave as soon as we can.'

Caught up in his words, Sachi stared at the only part of Shinzaemon she could see – his eyes. One burly hand rested on the hilt of his sword. Even here he was ready for anything. There was a dusting of snow on the back of his mantle. Behind him the garden glowed, white and eerie. The branches of the trees and the tall bamboos swayed and bent under the weight of snow.

There was a long silence.

'I know nothing of you,' he said. 'It is not my place to enquire. I know only that you are a lady of the shogun's household. When we were privileged to be of assistance to you, you were travelling in the imperial palanquin. As loyal servants of His Majesty it is our duty to protect you as best we can.'

Sachi nodded. She felt as if she were in a trance.

'Once we leave here our fate is in our own hands,' she said, remembering who and what she was. 'You are under no obligation to help us. But we would appreciate it if you could advise us as to conditions on the road.'

'I can't let you leave alone,' he said. 'It's too dangerous. We will escort you wherever you wish to go.'

His eyes had changed and Sachi could see that he was looking at her quite openly, smiling even. She should have been angry at his audacity, but instead she found herself melting under his gaze.

'Your eyes,' he murmured. 'They're narrow like

bamboo leaves and ... green. Dark green. Forgive me, I'm just a rough *ronin*. I never thought I would lay eyes on someone so... I never imagined I would meet anyone...' He stared at the ground and scuffed the snow with the toe of his straw boot.

'Forgive me,' he muttered again. 'It's not my place to speak to someone like you in such a way. But here we are. It must be destiny. Destiny brought us together. Karma binds us.'

He frowned as if he knew he'd gone too far.

'I have to go,' he grunted, turning abruptly as if something was tugging him away against his will. 'I will visit you here again.'

VI

It was nearing the bean-throwing festival, the celebration to mark the first day of spring, when Aunt Sato flung open the doors to their room. Sachi and Yuki were reading together and looked up, startled. Aunt Sato was out of breath and her hair was even more ruffled than usual.

'Shinzaemon and Master Toranosuké are here, my ladies,' she panted. 'They want to see you. They say it's urgent. I can take a message if you like, or be your chaperone.'

Sachi said firmly, 'We'll see them. Please chaperone us.'

The two men and young Tatsuemon were waiting in the entrance hall, their swords poking from under their thick winter mantles. Uncle Sato was with them. He was in crisp *hakama* trousers, with his round head immaculately shaved and his hair

239

oiled into a rigid topknot like the fine upstanding samurai he was. Compared to him, the three *ronin,* with their unshaved pates and glossy pony-tails tied with purple cord, looked like wild men.

They were frowning. But it was not just the usual samurai grimace. There was something flickering in their eyes that made Sachi uneasy.

Toranosuké stepped forward, bowing. Sachi had forgotten what a fine-featured, handsome man he was beneath the stubble.

'What have you heard?' she asked, cutting short the customary exchange of pleasantries. 'How are things in Edo?'

'Please excuse our rudeness,' said Toranosuké slowly. 'We have had reports but the news is con-fused. There may have been a battle south of Kyoto.'

'Kyoto?' repeated Sachi, catching her breath.

'Near the towns of Toba and Fushimi. We don't know much yet. We heard there was fighting for three days. Hundreds of men were killed and wounded. The northern battalions fought valiantly but... There may have been insubordination. Our men...'

Three days of fighting. And from his tone it sounded as if the northerners had been defeated.

Sachi glanced at Shinzaemon, fearful that he might make some gesture to betray their secret meeting. His scowl was growing deeper.

'You want to know what we heard?' he growled, butting in. He spoke in the rough language of men, in broad Kano dialect. It was strange – extraordinary – to have a glimpse into the world of men like this, to be present as they talked of

240

war and politics, matters women would never usually hear anything about. For a moment Sachi felt a secret thrill, like a little girl listening in to adults' talk.

'I'll tell you,' he snapped. 'On the third day our men retreated to Osaka Castle to regroup. They gathered in the great hall and begged Lord Yoshinobu to lead them personally into battle.' Sachi knew Lord Yoshinobu had abdicated as shogun and was no longer ruler of the entire country. But he was still head of the House of Tokugawa and liege lord of the northern clansmen who were fighting to hold back the southern advance. 'With him at the helm they knew they would be unbeatable,' Shinzaemon continued. 'Half of those clansmen were badly wounded. Some had had limbs hewn off. But they were all raring to get back on the battlefield and deal with the southern traitors once and for all.'

'Enough, Shin,' barked Toranosuké. 'Remember where you are!'

'Let me finish,' snarled Shinzaemon. 'Lord Yoshinobu swore he would be at the head of the army the next day. Then...' He paused, his lip curling in contempt. 'Then he sneaked off, him and some of his so-called advisers. Seems there was a secret passage to the harbour. They couldn't even find their ship when they got there, so they hid on a barbarian battleship.'

His face was dark as if he was going to burst with rage and anger.

'A barbarian ship?' quavered Sachi.

'An American ship. They sailed to Edo the next day.'

241

'He ran away!' said Sachi. It made a kind of dreadful sense. This was the man who had snatched the throne from her dear lord and master, who'd wanted it so badly he had not hesitated to have him poisoned. Was this what he had had in mind all along?

She thought she had said it to herself but in fact she had spoken aloud. Shinzaemon looked at her.

'He ran away,' he grunted, nodding. 'The shame of it!'

'Enough!' bellowed Uncle Sato. His hand was on the hilt of his sword. 'Have you no loyalty? This is all rumour. How dare you report it as fact!'

'There may be an explanation,' said Torano-suké, trying to calm them both. 'They say Lord Yoshinobu is planning a last stand in Edo.'

'He's in Edo right now,' said Shinzaemon with a sneer. 'You know that, you've seen the reports – you too, Uncle Sato. Everyone's laughing at him. "He came back in flight, afraid to fight, leaving his men behind."'

Uncle Sato looked as if he was about to explode. 'And you believe those commoners? You dare to guess at Lord Yoshinobu's intentions?'

'He's no friend to us either, Uncle Sato. You know that very well,' said Shinzaemon. 'But I will fight to the death for him. I know my duty.'

'So the north has been defeated...' said Sachi. She needed to be certain of it. Maybe if she said it enough times she would finally grasp what it meant.

'That means the southerners hold Kyoto. And the whole of the south-west,' said Shinzaemon.

There was a long silence.

'And Edo...?' said Sachi slowly.

'Total chaos,' said Toranosuké. 'There's no one keeping order. There are thieves and bandits everywhere.'

'Lord Yoshinobu's troops are coming in by the shipload from Osaka, on the rampage because they haven't been paid,' Shinzaemon added.

'The southerners have been distributing leaflets saying there's going to be war and people should leave the city,' said Toranosuké. 'The citizens are on the streets day and night carting their belongings to the countryside.'

'What of the castle?' asked Sachi and Taki, almost in unison. An image of the palace and the women and the princess – her dear princess – flashed before Sachi's eyes.

'As far as we know, the occupants are safe.'

'You have reports?'

'To tell the truth, we have no reports. But if things were otherwise we would have heard.'

'The southerners will be planning their advance,' said Shinzaemon. 'They've got good generals and English arms. If they take Edo they'll have the country by the throat.'

'And no one in Kano is going to prevent them,' snarled Uncle Saw. 'Not if his lordship has his way. The only thing for it is to ride north – try and hold back their advance.'

He glared at the women as if he had just realized they were there.

'I know we're only stupid women,' said Aunt Sato, 'but we can fight too. Don't forget that.'

'That Lord Yoshinobu is as slippery as a snake,'

243

growled Shinzaemon. 'No one knows who he really supports or what he will do next.'

After the men had left, Taki stayed to talk to Aunt Sato. Messengers were arriving. The great hall was full of raised voices and angry discussion.

Sachi went back to their room, took a quilt and went out on the veranda. Clumps of dark moss and the outlines of stepping stones peeked through the melting snow. Snow still lay on the fallen stone lantern, marked with tiny footprints where birds had hopped across it. A crow cawed and landed heavily on a tree, sending showers of snow tumbling through the branches and crashing to the ground. Sachi sat studying the ghostly silhouettes of the trees while the sky darkened and the evening drew in.

There was a faint noise. A figure bundled up, his head and face wrapped in a scarf, stepped boldly around the house. He crunched across the snow towards her, moving lightly like a cat. Two swords poked from under his mantle. He came close to the veranda. To Sachi's dismay she felt a quickening in her pulse and a rush of blood to her cheeks. She placed her fingertips on the polished wood and lowered her head.

'Master Shinzaemon,' she murmured sharply, vexed at her own confusion.

'Excuse me for intruding,' he said, keeping his voice low.

With relief she felt her cheeks cool.

'My lady, we must prepare to leave immediately,' he said. His dark eyes glinted above the folds of fabric bunched around his face, his eyebrows pushed together in a frown. 'This is war, my lady. Real war. The southerners are massing their armies. The people of Edo are preparing for a siege. Lord Yoshinobu... You are aware of his actions, my lady, and into what disarray this throws us and our cause. Pardon my directness, my lady. I know you're of His Majesty's court – but ... he's out to destroy us. He's doing everything he can to stop us defending ourselves against the southerners – his enemies. We're at a loss, my lady. No one can understand what he's playing at. But we are honour-bound to fight for the Tokugawas.'

Sachi nodded, frowning thoughtfully, although she barely heard the words. It was his voice, so gruff and fierce, so deep and vibrant, so different from a woman's. The sound of it filled her with secret pleasure and made her pulse quicken. Everyone else behaved as they were expected to behave and said what they were expected to say. But he didn't. He didn't seem to care what anyone thought.

'Tell me the truth,' she said, leaning towards him. 'What have you heard?'

'People say the southerners control the young emperor and issue edicts in his name. I heard that on the last day of battle they marched under the imperial banner, calling themselves the imperial army. They have branded Lord Yoshinobu a traitor and an enemy of the emperor. That was why he refused to fight. But it makes no difference to us what Lord Yoshinobu does. We are bound by oaths of duty and loyalty to the Tokugawas. We will fight for them no matter what.'

'Those southerners are greater villains than I had ever imagined,' whispered Sachi.

'When I was young I assumed I would serve my lord without question until I died,' said Shinzaemon. 'But now we don't even know who our leaders are. How can we be loyal servants?'

'What do you propose, sir?' she asked, lowering her eyes. Her heart was pounding. She tried to calm her voice, to speak steadily, imperiously, as a lady of her position should.

'For the time being the roads are quiet, my lady,' he said. 'Edo is no worse than anywhere else. The castle has been secured after the fire – doubly secured. It's impregnable, it's bristling with soldiers, it's the greatest fortress in the land. If anywhere is safe, Edo Castle is. My comrades and I have had enough of kicking our heels. We need to get back to the front. The quicker we can cut down a few southerners, the better. We're heading to Edo to join the resistance. If you wish to return too, we will escort you.

'When I lived here I was a child,' he went on, almost as if he was speaking to himself. 'I used to sneak into this garden to practise swordplay with my cousins. It's strange to be back.'

He ran his eyes across her face, caressing her with his gaze as if he wanted to capture her image for ever. She smiled. It was as if they were tramping across the hills again, like brother and sister. But no. It was not like that, not like brother and sister at all.

He was looking at the ground. He stooped down and thrust something towards her. Without thinking she reached out and took it. For a moment their hands brushed. She felt the touch of his rough swordsman's skin on hers. Then he turned and strode swiftly away.

In her hand there was a tiny white flower – a wild orchid.

6

Prison Gates

I

The snow was receding and spiky bamboo leaves and clumps of dark moss burst through. Here and there wild orchids shone like small white stars. On the plum trees buds were swelling and a few five-lobed blossoms, the colour of aubergines, glistened on the gnarled branches.

Ever since her conversation with Shinzaemon on the veranda, Sachi had been packed up, ready to leave. Taki had begged Aunt Sato to take the least valuable of her palace gowns to a merchant to sell or at least pawn. But Aunt Sato refused. She would lend them money, she said; after all, they were going with Shinzaemon and he was family. They could worry about repaying her when everything was back to normal. But there had been no further news from him. The silence became more and more ominous.

In the house, life went on as before. But something had changed. Was it that people walked a little more quickly or spoke more softly or started whenever the great main door slid open? Was it that everyone seemed to be listening as if something dreadful was about to happen? Even motherly Aunt Sato seemed ill at ease.

But something else filled Sachi's thoughts. Again and again she reached into her sleeve and took out the wild orchid Shinzaemon had given her. She had tucked it in there for safe keeping. She gazed at it, lying wilted in her hand. The way he had looked at her: surely he knew it was unacceptable to behave in such a manner towards a respectable woman, let alone a lady of rank like herself! She ought to feel outraged – yet she did not. Every word he had said reverberated in her mind like a bell ringing the hours. When she closed her eyes she saw his face.

To spend time alone in the company of a man was, she knew, unthinkable for any decent woman, let alone for her, bound as she was to the late shogun for the rest of her days. She had taken holy vows. Nothing could be more foolish than to imagine that she could disobey those above her or take any path other than the one laid out for her. That way lay only disaster.

Yet... It was wartime. Things were different. No one knew who or what she was. And who could tell whether any of them would live or die? Sachi sighed. If only she could see Shinzaemon alone again just one more time, to ask what he had meant.

It was approaching the hour of the snake and the maids had long since taken away their breakfast trays, yet Yuki had still not appeared for her poetry lesson. Ever since Sachi had woken up she had had a feeling something was terribly wrong. The distant hum of the house seemed different. Instead of the usual morning routine she heard agitated sounds of people rushing around, clattering and raised voices.

A melancholy wail echoed from the groves of cryptomeria trees that towered over the mansion. She started. It sounded like the moan of a conch shell summoning troops to war and for a moment she was back in Edo. But it was only the hoot of an owl.

Then the door slid open. Yuki skidded in and dropped to her knees. The butterfly loops on top of her head flopped forward as she bowed.

'I'm sorry,' she whispered.

'What is it?' gasped Sachi. The little girl's eyes were wide and staring. Her plump round face was as pale and haggard as a ghost's.

'Mama ... has disappeared. Gone home, I'm sure of it. They won't let me go and find her. Please help me!' She was struggling to maintain the composure proper for a samurai, biting her lips to stop them trembling. The last words burst out as a sob.

Sachi looked at her in horror. Gone home – what could that mean? Then she remembered the ruined house they had passed on New Year's Eve. She grasped the little girl's hand.

'Why do you think she's gone home, Yu-*chan*?' she asked urgently.

'I just know. This morning...'

Aunt Sato was close on her heels. Her face was frozen into a mask, as impenetrable as if it was carved out of stone.

'Enough, Yu-*chan*,' she snapped, her voice harsh. 'Just wait. She'll be back.'

Her lips were clamped tightly shut, her dark eyes opaque. She was no longer the sunny Aunt Sato whom Sachi knew.

'I have to find her,' said the child fiercely. 'I'll go alone, I don't care.'

Sachi looked at her. 'I'll go with you,' she said.

In silence Sachi and Yuki wrapped themselves in outdoor clothes and slipped their feet into clogs. It was the first time Sachi had been outside since New Year's Eve. The melting snow had turned the earthen road into slush. Snow lay piled in grimy mounds along the edges of the walls. The little girl dragged Sachi along, tugging at her hand. They passed a massive roofed gate with a couple of manservants standing guard outside, then another. Then they came to a gate with a wooden name plate reading 'Miyabe'. It was only a few doors away but the houses were so big and the walls so long it seemed like an eternity of walking.

On New Year's Eve the gate had been shut and bolted. Now it gaped open. The little girl shook off Sachi's hand and dashed through before she could stop her.

Sachi chased after her. Instead of a neat expanse of gravel, as at the Sato house, the grounds were a jungle of overgrown trees and bushes, half buried under snow. She could see the child pushing through the tangle of trees at the side of the house and followed as quickly as she could, trampling down twigs, beating through bushes and scrambling across rocks. Branches snatched at her clothes, as if trying to hold her back. Showers of snow tumbled from the trees, making her clothes sodden.

'Yu-*chan!*' she panted. 'Wait!'

But Yuki had already disappeared through the side entrance.

The door was half rotten and some of the boards had fallen out. Clenching her fists so tightly she could feel her nails digging into her palms, Sachi took a deep breath and followed.

The rain shutters were tightly closed. In the darkness Sachi could hear the little girl's foot-steps and her piping voice shrieking, '*Haha-ue Haha-ue.* Mama, Mama.' She stumbled after her, sending clouds of dust puffing from the moulder-ing tatami. Piles of leaves brushed against her feet and cobwebs stretched out tendrils to snag at her hands and face. There was an all-pervading musty smell of damp and mould.

She paused to listen. The child's voice and footsteps had stopped.

In the distance there was a glimmer of light. Sachi glanced about fearfully, half expecting to see a ghostly woman drifting like smoke, moan-ing and pulling out her long black hair in clumps. She was supposed to be a samurai, she reminded herself, unafraid of any mortal enemy – but it was not mortals that inhabited a place like this.

'Yu-*chan?*' She could hear her voice quavering in the silence.

On tiptoe she moved towards the furthest room. The shutters seemed to be open. Through the paper doors she could see that the room was bathed in light. Swathes of silk, as pure and white as new-fallen snow, rippled at the threshold.

She looked again. A dark red stain soaked most of the silk. Right in the middle was a white-clad figure. Yuki's mother was half kneeling, half lying face down. Her black hair was loose and fanned out on the floor. A stained dagger lay nearby.

Yuki had thrown herself down with her arms around her mother, clinging to her as if she intended never to let her go. There was a deathly silence. A sickly sweet odour filled the air.

Despite her samurai training, Sachi felt a shock of horror, like a bolt of lightning, go through her. She swallowed and turned her head away, closed her eyes and took a breath.

In her mind's eye she saw Yuki's mother sweeping the room until it was spotless, carefully cleaning the altar, spreading the silk across the tatami and praying for the last time. She would have stilled her mind, would have wrapped the handle of the dagger lovingly in paper, then knelt and tied her ankles together to ensure she would maintain her dignity even in death. She would have thrust the dagger into her throat with precision and economy of movement, modestly and quietly, without fuss, with a sort of calm joy. It was a textbook suicide, a death to be proud of.

Sachi was filled with admiration, almost envy. She knew, as a samurai, she should be prepared to die at any moment. She was well acquainted with the procedure. She hoped that when her time came, she too would be able to die in such a way.

Yet, seeing the lifeless body before her, she felt a horror that no amount of thinking would remove. What had been a gentle, lovely woman was now an inert mass. Sachi's heart was banging and she felt nausea rising in her throat.

Her eyes were drawn to a daguerreotype on the altar at the side of the room. There had been a few glass-plate portraits at the palace but she had not expected to see one in such a shabby out-of-the-way place as this. An image of two people, a man and a woman standing stiffly side by side, stared palely back at her. The woman was Yuki's mother. She glanced at the man. Surely not! Could it be ... Shinzaemon? His head was shaved in the conventional way and his hair oiled and folded into a samurai topknot but she knew the jutting cheekbones and fierce eyes and the stubborn set of the jaw. Startled, she looked more closely. It was not Shinzaemon after all, though the man looked uncannily like him.

Beside the picture were two scrolls, tied with ribbon. One was addressed to Uncle Sato, the other to Yuki. As Sachi picked them up, the note to Yuki fell open. It was very brief.

'My child,' her mother had written. 'You must be brave. When you are older you will understand. I cannot bear the shame of your father's death. My place is by his side. Be a true samurai and carry the Miyabe name with pride.'

Yuki had been lying so still that Sachi was afraid she too was dead. Then she started to sob convulsively.

Slowly, their legs dragging, they made their way back to the Sato mansion. They were covered in dust, cobwebs, blood and grime. Shinzaemon was in the entrance hall waiting for them. His

253

face was grim. He was staring at the earthen floor, his broad shoulders sagging, his eyes dull.

He straightened up when he saw them. He looked down at the little girl and said, 'I'm sorry.'

Yuki gazed up at him. Her chin was trembling and her eyes were full of tears but her face was like stone. Sachi could see she was trying her hardest not to show weakness or weep, no matter what.

Sachi had never before seen Shinzaemon so gentle. She longed to take his hand and say, 'It's not your fault. You did everything you could.'

Their eyes met. He was so brave, so strong. If anyone knew what to do, he did. She would have to put her faith in him.

'It's over,' he said. 'The southerners are on the move and his lordship the daimyo of Kano is determined to prove that his loyalties lie with them. As ladies of the shogun's court you are in grave danger. We too. We'll leave immediately.'

'I must prepare my mother's funeral,' said Yuki distractedly. They were the first words she had spoken since she ran into her family's house. 'I must take care of her ashes and pray to her spirit. I am the only survivor of the house of Miyabe.' She looked around as if there was something she had forgotten. Her small face was furrowed, her eyes red and swollen. Then her expression changed. Her face grew very calm. 'I must avenge my father,' she said firmly.

'They'll kill you if you stay here,' said Shinzaemon gently. 'There is no house of Miyabe. It was terminated when your father was arrested. There's no house, no stipend, nothing. You can carry on the Miyabe name better if you stay alive. I told your papa I would take care of you. You must come with us.'

II

They left as the first light was streaking the sky, melting away into the shadows of the walls. They had made their farewells and expressed their thanks the previous night and it was safest to slip away without ceremony. Everyone knew the chances of meeting again in this lifetime were slight.

As she closed the door for the last time Sachi felt a pang of sadness. Their room in Aunt Sato's house had been cramped and cold, yet it had been a kind of home.

A cold dawn breeze was blowing. The women pulled their garments tighter around them. They were dressed as inconspicuously as possible, in plain townswomen's clothes. They had pulled their flat straw travelling hats low down over their faces to conceal their pale skin and distinctive aristocratic features. They took with them just a few changes of clothing and a robe each to sell if they needed money. Sachi had also packed the mysterious brocade overkimono. They put their halberds into cases. The men rode along with their two swords tucked into their waistbands. But they wore no crest. There was nothing to indicate which clan they belonged to or where their loyalties lay.

The plan was to avoid the Eastern Sea Road,

the main highway to Edo. The southerners would be bound to send their armies that way and it would be crawling with soldiers. Instead the men decided to take quiet back roads until they were well away from Kano, then link up with the Inner Mountain Road. It was a much longer route and passed through rough mountain terrain, but there would be less chance of running into southern troops. Everyone in the party knew they would be travelling through hostile territory – into the dragon's mouth. Some of the domains they had to pass through were supposedly friendly but no one could be sure any more whose side anyone was on. Clans seemed to switch allegiance with every change of the weather.

They set off towards the north-east of the city, the direction from which evil spirits came, where the execution ground and the prison were. Shinzaemon and Toranosuké had arranged porters, bearers and packhorses for the first few *ri*, until they reached the next staging post, and a couple of closed litters – you could hardly call them palanquins – to carry the women. They were flimsy conveyances with thin walls of woven straw and stiff reed flaps to cover the square holes which served as windows. Sachi and little Yuki swayed and bounced along in silence, huddled together in one. Numbly they heard the creak of the wooden carrying pole and the squelch of the bearers' straw-sandalled feet tramping through the mud. The wind whistled through the straw walls and through the layers of padding of their cotton garments.

Yuki pushed up one of the blinds and stared at

the city going by. The sun had not yet risen but the streets were already buzzing. At first they threaded their way between the high earthen walls that lined the shadowy lanes of the samurai districts. Then pungent aromas of woodsmoke and cooking began to waft into the litter. Cocks crowed and dogs barked. There were sounds of knocking and tapping, of planing and chiselling, and the smell of lacquer heating as they passed through the craftsmen's neighbourhood.

Then a new odour came creeping up, slow but relentless, until it enveloped everything like a fog. It was so strange and unpleasant that Sachi recoiled. It was many years since she had smelled it last, yet she knew it immediately. For a moment she was a child again, back in the village, playing with the other children. Some, she remembered, had been smaller, stunted, undernourished, their skin permanently blackened with dirt and the sun. The same faint, rather nauseous smell clung to their ragged clothes and strange broad hats. Sachi could hear her mother's voice ringing in her ears: 'That smell – I can smell it on you. You've been playing with the outcastes again. How many times do I have to tell you? They're unclean. Their parents deal in death. Decent people stay well away.' She too had learned to shun those who performed the jobs decent people spurned – tanning leather, disposing of animal carcasses and carrying out executions.

Taki was jogging along in the second litter. Someone like her, who had led such a protected life, had surely never before come anywhere near people like these. Sachi knew she must be shrinking in horror, terrified of pollution.

Yuki was slumped against the wall of the litter. Suddenly she jerked upright and squealed, 'Stop! Stop!'

At the same instant Shinzaemon barked, 'Stop!' The bearers lowered the litter to the ground. Yuki was already scrambling out.

Sachi leaned forward then shrank back, pressing her veil to her face. The stench was unbearable. It was decaying flesh, the reek of the charnel house. Through the open door of the litter she could see a pair of huge wooden gates. Nailed on to boards set on posts was a row of strange round objects. Some had long, tangled hair, like ghosts. Others, though dishevelled, still had their hair knotted into samurai topknots. Their eyes were shut and their jaws slack. Where their bodies should have been was nothing but air. Dark liquid still dripped from some of the severed necks. They were human heads.

The faces were grey and immobile as if modelled in clay but even in death they looked noble. Beneath each was a wooden board inscribed with their name, age, birthplace and crime. Ignoring the revulsion rising in her throat, Sachi tried to make out which of them resembled the countenance she had seen in the daguerreotype. The ignominy! It was a terrible death for a samurai.

Yuki, in her small child's kimono with her hair tied into butterfly loops, and big brawny Shinzaemon, with his bushy hair pulled back in a ponytail, stood side by side, chins tilted, staring up at them.

Finally Yuki nodded. 'It doesn't look much like Papa,' she said. There was a long silence.

'One day I shall avenge you,' she added. Her piping voice was soft but fierce.

'You are a true daughter of a samurai,' Shinzaemon said to her. 'Your father would be proud.'

III

There was no time to lose. As they jogged along in silence, Yuki sat staring straight ahead, her face as stony as the ones outside the prison gates. Sachi put her arms around her. She was afraid she would never speak again.

Shinzaemon and Toranosuké rode together, conferring in low voices. Sachi caught their words drifting down the wind.

'Checkpoint coming up. Could be southerners.'

She pushed up the window flap and peeped out. They were swinging and swaying along a narrow street lined with high earthen walls. At the end was a pair of massive wooden gates. She dropped the blind and sat in silence, hardly daring to breathe. Uncle Sato, she knew, had arranged travel permits – a wooden tablet for each of them with the signature and burned-in seal of the Kano authorities. But would the checkpoint be manned by the old guard, who were loyal to the shogun, or had southerners taken their place? If the guards were from the south, it was all too likely they would be arrested and escorted straight back to Kano. Sachi realized with a lurch of fear that they might well end up next to Yuki's father on the

259

prison gates.

Feet crunched on the frozen snow-covered gravel and swords and rifles banged against each other as soldiers swarmed around the litters. She could hear Shinzaemon and Toranosuké dismounting. In the distance was the pounding of approaching hooves.

'Hey, Aoyama, is that you? Doing all right are you?'

So Shinzaemon knew the guards. They were comrades. Sachi heaved a sigh of relief.

'Well, if it isn't Shin and Tora. Where're you off to?'

'Upcountry,' said Toranosuké nonchalantly.

'Travelling with women? Smart move. No one will suspect you're *ronin* if you have women in tow. Not going to Aizu then?'

'You'll have to wait awhile,' grunted another voice. 'There's a militia coming through.'

A troop of horsemen came trotting between the great wooden gates. Several were in full armour, visible beneath their brightly coloured silk field jackets. The cold winter light glinted off their scabbards, pennons and lances. Some wore helmets with ferocious horns, their faces hidden behind iron masks fringed with whiskers. Their breath came puffing out in little clouds as if they were fire-breathing dragons, and locks of black and white hair dangled to their waists. They were like demons in a nightmare.

Soldiers – and on their way to war. But which side were they on? Sachi guessed they must be escorting some noble and powerful personage but there was no palanquin, only right in the middle a group of several horsemen gathered together. Bringing up the rear was a train of packhorses with huge bundles strapped to their backs and a troop of gawky young peasants with hard brown arms and leathery faces, armed with clumsy rifles that reminded her of the old matchlock her father had kept to protect the village from bandits.

'Shin, Tora,' bawled one warrior. Above his gleaming breastplate he had the eager face and smooth cheeks of a teenage boy. So they were friends too, Kano men, and on the northern side. 'Where're you off to? Not coming to Aizu?'

'There's a pacification force on its way out of Kyoto,' yelled another. 'If you take the Inner Mountain Road, you'd better move fast or they'll be on top of you. Come with us and join the resistance. We're gonna hole up in Aizu. There's gonna be a huge battle. We'll wipe out those southern traitors. It'll be glorious!'

It was only after the whole procession – warriors, retainers, bannermen, grooms, servants, porters and packhorses – had disappeared through the gates on the far side of the checkpoint that Shinzaemon and Toranosuké took in their travel permits to be checked. When they were finally cleared and ready to leave, Sachi handed fresh-faced young Tatsuemon, Toranosuké's page, some money to give as gratuities to the guards for their wives.

They were nearly through the second set of gates when a sharp-eyed guard barked, 'Townswomen, you said? With skin like that? Don't look much like townswomen to me!'

261

He must have seen the small white hand pushing aside the flimsy wall of the litter. Quietly
Sachi felt for her dagger, tucked securely in her
sash.

'There've been spies from Edo around, on the
lookout for some of the shogun's ladies. Gone
missing, they say,' drawled the guard.

'Don't know anything about that,' muttered
Toranosuké. 'These are our cousins from the
Kano estate in Edo.'

'Our permits are in order,' growled Shinzaemon. 'Look to your own business. Things are
changing fast round here. See you on the battlefield in Aizu!'

IV

For a long time Yuki sat in silence, her small
round face pale and rigid, her butterfly loops
unmoving on top of her head. But then she
seemed to realize that she was leaving her home
for ever. She peered steadfastly under the blind
as the city of Kano grew small behind them.
Sachi, too full of relief that they were leaving that
city of ghosts, could not bring herself to look.

The roads were a lot wilder than they had been
even a few weeks earlier, when they had arrived
in Kano. They were full of ruts and craters,
littered with broken straw sandals. No one had
even bothered to collect horse droppings, which
lay in heaps on the ground. Swathes of plume
grass burst across the verges and there were
broken branches on the trees that marked the

distance. Many of the villages were surrounded by makeshift stockades and groups of farmers stood guard, wielding guns, bamboo lances and clubs.

At first they jogged through paddies and vegetable fields dotted with mounds of frozen brown earth. Shrivelled rice stalks punctured the grimy snow. Ragged haystacks canopied in snow straggled along the edges of the fields. Trees lined the road and from time to time they came to a village or a thatched-roof stall offering tea and snacks. On the horizon mountains poked up like jagged teeth.

At noon they stopped at an inn for a rest. The innkeeper looked them up and down.

'Well, you look mightily like a bunch of ruffians but I guess as you're travelling with women...' he said, before letting them in.

It seemed it was as convenient for the men as it was for them to travel together. Perhaps this was why Shinzaemon had sought her out. For some reason the thought made Sachi feel desolate. In any case there was no chance now for them to exchange words, surrounded by their companions and with the women hidden away in litters.

At first Toranosuké and Tatsuemon rode at the front while Shinzaemon brought up the rear, but once they were well away from the city Toranosuké dropped back. From time to time Sachi caught snatches of conversation. It was vital to know what was going on, she told herself. But there was also a certain sweetness in hearing Shinzaemon's deep tones, though she hardly

263

dared confess it even to herself.

'That prison governor is a fool,' Shinzaemon said. 'I should have had his head. But it's too late now. Reason or bribes – nothing would sway him. There must have been some way. I should have broken in there and fetched him out myself.' She guessed it was Yuki's father he was talking about.

'You did all you could, Shin,' said Toranosuké. 'There'll be plenty of killing to be done. These are bloody times. Let's just do our best to make sure we die honourably in battle.'

There was a long silence. The clanking of swords, the crunch of the horses' straw-shod hooves on the frozen ground and the rhythmic thud of the bearers' feet rang out eerily loud in the icy air.

'Did you catch what they were talking about at the checkpoint?' Toranosuké asked suddenly.

'Couldn't help it. So now he's fled Edo Castle.'

Sachi had been half dozing, huddled up against the cold as the miserable litter swung and jogged along. But she jerked awake when she heard the mention of Edo Castle.

'Sought sanctuary in Kanei-ji Temple. Taken holy orders.'

She could hear the bitterness and contempt in Shinzaemon's voice. They could only be talking about Lord Yoshinobu.

'Holy orders, is it? Hiding out, more like. He's heard the southern army is on the march, heading for Edo. He's surrendering before they even arrive! And he calls himself a samurai? That's the man we're gonna give our lives for?'

'We've no choice,' snapped Toranosuké. 'We've

264

been servants of the Tokugawa family for generations. We're not fighting for him; we're fighting for the Tokugawas and the northern cause. We have our honour to think of, Shin. We have to fight, it's our duty. To the death. It doesn't matter who the shogun is or what he does, we have to stand up against the southern clans. They're greedy for power. They'll murder and burn and reduce the whole country to ashes if they think that's the way to get it. They claim they want to drive the foreigners out and then they fight with English weapons. They have to be stopped.'

The conversation grew indistinct. They seemed to have ridden on ahead. Then voices came wafting down the wind again.

'You know the southerners are calling themselves the imperial army?' came Shinzaemon's deep growl. 'Now they tell us the emperor is our true lord and anyone who opposes him is a traitor.'

'A lot of daimyos are waiting to see which way the wind's blowing. One by one they're going over to the south. No one wants to be called a traitor.'

'We can't win. If we do the honourable thing and stand by our lord, we end up getting branded as traitors!'

'That's if the Tokugawas lose. We'll just have to make good and sure they don't. If the Tokugawa family falls, the government falls. The whole place collapses. Then those accursed foreigners will move their armies in and take over. They're like flies around a corpse.'

Sachi struggled to make sense of it all. If Lord

265

Yoshinobu had fled the castle and the southerners were closing in, what could have happened to the princess and the Retired One? They would never flee, or allow themselves to be taken alive. No doubt they were waiting, polishing their daggers. And what had the guard at the checkpoint meant when he said there were spies out looking for the shogun's ladies? It could only be that they were in search of her – His late Majesty's concubine. She trembled to think of it. Then she reminded herself of her training. She made her mind still, felt for the steel core inside herself. She must never forget that she was a warrior, a woman of ice and fire, a consort of the Tokugawas.

'And this crazy expedition of yours, Shin.' Toranosuké had lowered his voice but she could just catch what he was saying. 'It's certainly a good subterfuge to travel with women. But straight into the jaws of the southerners, just the three of us? On the whim of some idle court ladies? What makes you so interested in women all of a sudden? You're losing your muscle. Hang around women and children too much and you'll turn into a woman yourself. We need to get rid of them before we all go soft!'

That night they stopped at a ramshackle inn on the edge of a village. By the time the women had climbed out of the litters, the men had disappeared along with the porters.

Slowly Sachi straightened her back and stretched her legs, then brushed off her kimono skirts. She was aching and sore from the long day jolting in the litter. She wiped her face with her sleeve and glanced in a mirror. Her porcelain skin was grimy. Her smooth cheeks were specked with dirt and her black hair was ruffled and grey with dust.

Taki was rubbing her thin neck and stretching.

'I'm so stiff,' she grumbled. With her big eyes, pointed chin and patrician features, she looked even more out of place in this remote backwater than she had been in Kano. Sachi smiled at her. She took a comb from her sleeve and began to smooth Taki's hair, tucking the unruly ends into place. No matter where she went, no matter how distant or wretched the place, she knew Taki would go with her. It was a comfort to know she had such a loyal friend.

The room was dark and dank and dirty and much smaller than their room in Kano had been. A wizened innkeeper served them thrushes roasted on skewers, preserved mountain vegetables and wild boar meat.

'We call it whale – mountain whale,' the woman mumbled as she served the boar. 'So we can eat it and still be good Buddhists.'

But the women had little appetite, especially for such outlandish food.

'I wonder what's happening in Kano,' said Yuki after the innkeeper had gone. Her childish face was grave. There was a new look in her eyes, as if she'd suddenly had to grow up.

The women sat in silence, toying with their food. The same thought was on all their minds.

More to comfort herself than for any other reason, Sachi began to tell Yuki about her village

– the rushing river, the sun rising over the mountains, the tiled roofs, the woods where she had played as a child. She pictured her mother's gentle, tired face, her father's large capable hands, the big old house with its polished floorboards. She hadn't realized how much she yearned to see them again, those dear familiar faces.

Surely the village must be very close, she thought. It was on the Inner Mountain Road, somewhere in the Kiso mountains. They would have to pass straight through it!

Suddenly it became clear, as if a mist had lifted. She didn't want to go to Edo after all, not straight away, at least. They would go to the village, she and Taki and Yuki. They could hide there. It would be safe, far safer than Edo. The southerners would never bother with a little place like that. It would be a refuge for the three of them until things were more settled.

It was her only chance to go home. Once things had calmed down she would be back in the palace again, locked away for the rest of her life. She was the late shogun's concubine; she could never escape that.

It was a risk to go to the village, she knew. She had no idea what had happened while she had been away or if the village was even there any more. She wasn't even sure exactly where it was. She only knew she had to get there.

V

At the town of Mitake they joined the Inner

Mountain Road. Ahead of them they could see the hills beginning.

'We walk from here,' said Toranosuké. 'It'll be too steep for litters soon. And they draw too much attention.'

The road led straight into the mountains, winding steeply up between crumbling volcanic crags and pinnacles of rock that teetered towards the clouds. In the afternoon they reached the Hosokute checkpoint. There was a stockade around the town and guards posted at the gates, checking on travellers. Twenty soldiers armed with rifles came crunching across the gravel towards them. The women had made sure their faces were well wrapped up. They were allowed through without much fuss but the men were questioned at length.

Sachi was standing to one side of the compound, trying not to draw attention to herself.

'Kano, you say?' she heard an officer barking. 'We know all about you Kano men. We've had enough trouble from you. And these permits of yours – issued by the proper authorities, are they?'

'Beats me, all this political stuff,' grunted Shinzaemon in his coarsest Kano dialect. 'Gotta escort these women. They got relatives upcountry. Just following orders.'

'Is that so?" said the officer, raising an eyebrow. 'You'll do well to watch out for yourselves. The imperial troops are on their way. If they catch up with you you'd better be good and ready to convince them you're on their side.'

'Those guards – they bend whichever way the wind blows,' muttered Shinzaemon when they were safely through. 'I bet they were the shogun's men a few days back. And now they're all imperial loyalists. We'll keep going as best we can. Make sure we inflict some damage before anyone asks too many questions.'

Just beyond the ramshackle row of inns, the mountains rose in a line of crags that beetled into the sky. Taki and Yuki stared at them open-mouthed, but to Sachi they were no more formidable than the ridges that had over-shadowed the village. She had clambered around peaks like that as carelessly as a mountain monkey when she was a child.

The road climbed through forests of leafless trees along the side of the bluff. The flat stones that lined the path were covered in ice and snow. Taki and Yuki stumbled along, slipping and slid-ing, stopping more and more frequently, gasping, to catch their breath. At the post town they had bought straw boots specially woven to resist the snow, with spikes to help them keep a grip on the path, but even so the way was treacherous.

At first Sachi trudged as laboriously as they. When she stopped for breath she saw them sitting wearily on the road far below her. Tora-nosuké and Tatsuemon were with them, standing patiently, waiting for them to set off again.

Back in the mountains after all these years! The air tasted fresh and clean. She began to find her mountain legs again. She stepped out rhythmic-ally, feeling the cool air flow into her lungs.

Up ahead of her Shinzaemon was leading the group. Loping effortlessly along the steep path he was like a fox, with his bushy hair and black dangerous eyes, or a bear. He no longer seemed caged as he had in the trim, prim samurai world of Kano. He was back on the road and heading for action.

With a few quick steps Sachi caught up with him. He looked at her, startled, his slanted eyes glinting under his thick brows. His broad, open face with its great cheekbones had grown tawny from days outside in the wintry sun. Stubble sprouted on his chin, and his sweat was pungent and salty. He was not perfumed like a courtier.

Sachi was panting and hot from the climb. As she looked at him she felt the blood rise to her face and her cheeks grow hotter still.

'It's a long climb,' he said, frowning at her as if she was a naughty child. 'Four *ri*, they said at the post town. And steep the whole way. Slow down. Take it easy.'

Sachi looked away. She could feel the hairs on the back of her neck rising and something like panic deep in her stomach. Her heart was pounding, and not just from the thinness of the air.

They were alone together. She was aware of how wrong that was, even for a moment, but it was too late now to worry about propriety – too late for anything. This was the chance she had been yearning for. There was so much she wanted to ask him. That flower – had he given it to her simply because she was out of reach? Or was there more?

She peeped up at him. He was looking down at her as if he too had suddenly realized that a

271

moment had come that might never come again. They stood as the clouds swept by them and the shadows on the mountain changed.

He held out his hand to her. 'Let's walk together,' he said at last.

It was a hard steep climb but Sachi barely saw the road. She was conscious only of the closeness of his body, the sound of his breathing. She could almost hear the beating of his heart in the stillness.

The higher they climbed, the deeper the snow became. A bitter wind blew. Sachi's feet were like ice, but she hardly noticed. She stopped and looked around. The plain spread below them, bleak and brown, dotted with patches of snow. Here and there hills rose. Far in the distance, mountain peaks shimmered white above the clouds.

'Mount Hakusan,' said Shinzaemon. He stretched out his great hand and pointed. His skin was golden, his fingers firm and strong, scattered with black hairs. 'And Mount Ibuki. And there, do you see over there? The sea. And way over there in the distance, glittering? That's Kyoto.' Sachi shaded her eyes with her hand and looked as hard as she could.

Finally they reached the top of the pass. A few steps beyond the summit was a teahouse where they sheltered, warming their hands over the open hearth. The pungent smoke of burning pine filled their nostrils. The little hut was crowded with travellers. The fire spluttered and smoked, teacups clattered, voices chattered. But it all seemed far away. For a few precious moments

Sachi and Shinzaemon were free – free from their families, their duty, their obligations, even their social ranks. It was just the two of them at the top of this mountain with the clouds rolling beneath them.

'Where did you learn to walk like that?' Shinzaemon asked. His frown had disappeared and a smile spread across his face. His eyes flashed with a reckless look, as if nothing mattered any more. 'Not Edo Castle, that's for sure.'

'I had forgotten how alive I feel in the mountains,' Sachi said softly.

He reached out and took her small hand in his big rough one, holding it like a rare treasure. She sat in silence, feeling his skin on hers. So he too felt the same yearning for things to be different. And he too realized that they never could be.

What did the future hold for him? Death, a glorious death in battle. And if by chance he lived, no doubt his parents had already planned a marriage for him. He was one small ant in an ants' nest, a bee buzzing around a hive. His destiny was not for him to shape. He had taken on the mantle of a *ronin*, an outsider, but in the end he belonged to his family, his clan, his city.

And as for her – where were her family and clan and city? She could picture his life and the different paths it might take, but he knew nothing of her.

'Who are you, Lady Sachi?' he asked. He was looking at her with his slanted eyes that seemed to see deep inside her. A mischievous grin flitted across his face. He seemed to have brightened since they left Kano, as if the weight of the terrible events of the last few days was gradually lifting from his shoulders.

'Why should I tell you?' she said teasingly. She felt light-headed in the thin air. What difference would it make whether he knew her secret or not? He would find out anyway, and very soon.

'There's a village in the Kiso region, not far from here,' she went on quietly. 'It's where I grew up, where my parents live. It's on the Inner Mountain Road. We're going to pass straight through it. We want to stop and stay there, me and Taki and Yuki. It'll be safest for us there.'

Almost immediately she was afraid she had made a terrible mistake, but it was too late to take the words back. She looked at him, wondering how a proud samurai like him would react, knowing that she was nothing but a lowly peasant.

His eyes opened wide. 'A village?' he murmured in tones of disbelief.

'My parents are rural samurai – my adoptive parents, that is. But I spent years in service at Edo Castle.' She wanted to tell him that she was the adoptive daughter of the house of Sugi, banner-men to the daimyo of Ogaki, as indeed she was. But she was more than that, far more. She was the Retired Lady Shoko-in, the beloved concubine of His late Majesty. But that was far too dangerous a secret ever to reveal.

He looked at her as if he was seeing her for the first time. Then his lips curved into a smile that spread until his whole face was alight with it. He turned her hand over and gently ran his hard swordsman's fingers across her soft white palm.

'I thought you were above the clouds,' he said

softly. 'I thought you were a court lady, beyond my reach. I thought I would only ever be able to admire you from a distance. But you're not! You're a human being, like me.'

He leaned forward. 'You're like Momotaro,' he said.

Sachi smiled uncertainly. Momotaro – Little Peach Boy. Her grandmother had often told her the story of the old woodcutter and his wife who had prayed to the gods for a child. One day the old woman was washing clothes at the river when a giant peach came bobbing towards her. When she cut it open, a beautiful baby boy jumped out.

Maybe Shinzaemon was right, Sachi thought. Maybe she was a bit like Momotaro. She had always known she was different from everyone else. Like her, Momotaro hadn't stayed in his village. He had grown up and gone off to conquer ogres. But at the end of the story, after he had had his last adventure and the ogres were all dead, he had gone back and found the old woodcutter and his wife waiting for him, yearning to see him – as her parents must be yearning to see her.

For so many years she had thought of the village with longing and now she was beginning to recognize the countryside and knew she was nearly home. The evening before she had been so sure that that was what she wanted, but now she was not sure of anything. When she turned off to the village, Shinzaemon would go on his way to Edo and she would never see him again. Just as they were getting to know each other they would have to part.

The sun had gone in. An icy draught blew through the little hut. She shivered.

Shinzaemon brushed his finger across her cheek. 'Like a peach,' he murmured, as if to himself.

He gazed at her for what seemed like an age. Then he glanced around as if he had suddenly woken from a dream. His face darkened. He thrust her hand aside.

'What have you done to me?' he growled. 'You make life too precious. I have to be ready to die. How can I fight if I feel like this?'

Through the door of the teahouse Sachi could see their friends trudging up the snow-covered path towards them, followed by a line of porters with great bundles tied to their backs. Shinzaemon glared at her.

'I'm supposed to be a man and a soldier. Perhaps what Toranosuké says is true. Mixing with women too much turns you into a woman. This has to stop now, this mad behaviour. If my father caught me he'd kill himself for shame.'

Sachi swallowed hard. Her throat burned and hot tears started in her eyes. She did not deserve such cruel words. She took some breaths and tried to calm the beating of her heart. She needed to steady herself, to be ready to face Taki and Yuki.

Shinzaemon was right, of course, to thrust her away. It was foolish to think for a moment that their lives could be any different. And his harsh words would make their parting easier to bear. It was better this way, better to forget anything had ever happened.

The trek down from the pass was precipitous. Sachi walked with Taki and Yuki, taking their hands and helping them down the steepest parts of the track. She was ashamed to have left them, to have let her feelings run away with her. After all, she was not a child any more. She knew very well she was not free.

She was expecting Taki to scold her for allowing herself to be alone with a man. But Taki said nothing. She hardly seemed even to have noticed that Sachi had been away.

Sachi looked at her hard. She had been so caught up in her own thoughts and feelings she hadn't been paying attention to her. Taki seemed to be in a dream herself. Her face was bright, her big eyes glowing. Sachi had never seen her look so pretty and alive. The contours of her face seemed softer and more womanly.

Then she caught her peeking shyly at Toranosuké, flushing whenever he came near.

For the rest of the day they walked in silence, keeping off the main road as much as possible. Sachi took care never to catch up with Shinzaemon. Sometimes she stole a glance at his broad back disappearing. along the trail and wondered if he would look back at her. But he never did.

She was watching Taki now, noticing the way she glanced at Toranosuké and lowered her big eyes shyly when he was around. He was certainly very handsome, with his refined features and hair pulled back into a glossy horse's tail. For a man who had spent so much of his life at war his skin

277

was rather delicate, not sunburned like Shinzaemon's. He was a samurai through and through – muscular, well-bred and very polite. But he always kept an indefinable distance. There was something else too that made him the embodiment of the samurai ethos. Tatsuemon was constantly at his side. At night they always went off together.

Sachi had never paid much attention to them before. It was not her place to do so. But now she couldn't help noticing how Tatsuemon gazed adoringly at his master.

It was hardly surprising. Toranosuké's relationship with Tatsuemon was there for anyone who cared to look. It was so obvious it was not even worthy of note. As a samurai in the classic mould, Toranosuké lived his life among men, believing that contact with women would make him as soft as a woman himself. But surely Taki knew that? Perhaps her feelings had made her blind to what was clear to everyone else, Sachi thought. Toranosuké and Tatsuemon's was the sort of bond one would expect men to have with each other. It was sanctioned by society and did not threaten its norms. No matter how close they were, it would not interfere with their families' marriage plans for them.

It was Sachi and Shinzaemon who had to keep their meetings secret. It was their feelings that were beyond the pale, not Toranosuké's and Tatsuemon's.

VI

The next morning the raucous crowing of cocks at dawn broke into Sachi's dreams. Tramping through a village high on a plateau, she smelt woodsmoke on the breeze and heard the murmur of a stream tumbling along beside the road. She felt the wind in her hair, saw the sunlight speckling the rocks and realized she was nearly home.

But why did people look so poor and ragged? In one village people ran after them holding out straw hats upside down like baskets, begging them to throw in alms. They were as thin and bony as skeletons, their eyes staring and their cheeks blackened and sunken. From time to time she heard the sound of flutes and the rattle of drums. Voices hummed that strange subversive refrain: 'Who gives a damn? Who gives a damn?'

Wherever they went they heard rumours that the southerners were on their way. Shinzaemon, Toranosuké and Tatsuemon took the precaution of disguising themselves as servants. They stored their long swords in the trunks that the porters carried, along with the women's halberds, so that they had only their short swords with them to defend themselves.

They were resting in an inn late in the afternoon, warming their hands at the open hearth, when they overheard two men talking.

'Whenever I see the shogun's crest it brings tears to my eyes,' said one. Sachi glanced at him. He was a young man with a round ingenuous face, bulging eyes and an earnest manner. He looked a bit like a blowfish. Although he was dressed like a countryman he didn't talk like one; no one could be sure who anyone else was these days. There were notices posted in all the inns forbidding talk of politics, be it drinkers arguing over sake or women and children chattering. But who could enforce such a rule?

'Bit late for that kind of talk,' snapped the other, an older man with a fleshy face and small watchful eyes. He too was dressed like a country-man but his hands were far too plump and clean to fool anyone.

'You really think this new government is going to work?' demanded the first. 'At least we knew where we stood with the shoguns. The country was peaceful. We could get on with making a living. These southerners are pushing us all to the brink. What gives them the right to order us about? Their weaponry, that's all...'

He stopped and looked around quickly. The room had gone deathly silent.

'Whose side are you on then?' asked the older man in a tone of quiet menace, looking hard at the younger. Sachi glanced at him, wondering if he was a spy, watching out for traitors to the southern cause.

'The emperor's, of course,' said the younger man hastily. 'But I support the shogun too.'

'They're calling for Lord Yoshinobu's head,' said the older roughly. 'You know that. The southern lords are saying he's a traitor and should be ordered to cut his belly. You'd better be careful what you say. It's safest to have no opinion at all.'

Sachi felt a chill as sharp as if a blade of ice had entered her heart. If they were planning to

280

execute Lord Yoshinobu, they would be wanting to exterminate his whole family, root and branch, and everyone associated with him. What would become of the princess and the three thousand women at the castle? They were all servants, virtually family of the shogun. And what of Sachi herself? As the concubine of his predecessor, she was officially Lord Yoshinobu's mother-in-law even though she had never met him.

Thank the gods only Taki knew who she really was. Even the men knew no more than that she was a court lady and a lookalike for the princess. It was more important than ever to keep her secret safe.

Towards evening the little party stumbled wearily to the top of yet another pass. They stopped there, panting and wiping their brows. Ahead of them were mountain ranges, receding, paler and paler, until they faded to nothing on the horizon.

Sachi had noticed something glinting far below. Peering through the trees she looked and looked again. It was a river, snaking along the valley floor between jagged grey cliffs. Could it be ... the Kiso?

'Taki, Yu-*chan*,' she called. 'Look!'

She had been away so long she had begun to wonder if it really existed or if she had just imagined it. She stood listening, trying to hear the sound of the river as it came rushing down from the mountains, swollen with melted snow. She could almost feel the water on her skin. In her mind she was swimming, darting through the cold water like a fish with young Genzaburo, the ringleader in their adventures, and ugly little Mitsu. Genzaburo had gone off to fight and Mitsu had become a mother; they would not be at the village when she got there.

There was something else. Floating up from the valley behind them, clear as a bell in the mountain air, came a noise like distant thunder. It grew louder and louder. It was like the sound the daimyos and their processions used to make on their way to the village – the tramp of marching feet. There was another sound too, a discordant roar like a forest full of baying animals – voices, men's voices. If it was a song they were yelling out it was unlike anything she had ever heard before.

Then she saw them. From end to end and edge to edge, the valley they had just come from was filled with men. From the riverbank to the forest that bordered the road were men, marching. She had never seen so many, even when the princess's grand procession passed through. They swarmed along, as relentless as an invasion of cockroaches or a great tidal wave sweeping through the valley.

Soldiers. Southerners. She could even make out horses hauling cannons.

'Into the woods,' hissed Toranosuké. 'They'll be up here in no time. Better let them pass. They're animals. Women and boys don't stand a chance.'

The other travellers were already melting into the trees. In a moment the road was empty. Sachi, Taki, Yuki and the three men scrambled into the undergrowth, stumbling over stones, rocks and tracts of unmelted snow until they were a good distance from the road. Then they crouched down and waited. The sounds of marching and singing grew faint for a while as the soldiers entered the lea of the mountain, then louder and louder until the ground was shaking.

The tramp of feet and hooves, the wild whinnying of horses and the rumbling of cannon went on for hours. Through the trees they caught the occasional glimpse of banners and pennants fluttering in the breeze. A great drum boomed out a barbaric beat. The soldiers' song had a ferocious ring, utterly unlike the plangent melodies that women plucked out on the shamisen and the koto or the boisterous ditties that merrymakers danced to at festivals. After a while Sachi began to pick up the words:

'*Miya-sama, miya-sama...*
Majesty, majesty, before your august horse
What is it that flutters so proudly?
    Toko tonyare, tonyare na!

'Don't you know that it's the brocade banner
Signifying punishment for the enemies of the
    court?
    Toko ton yare, ton yare na!'

'Punishment for the enemies of the court...' How dared they threaten any such thing? Here were she and Taki, members of the true court, forced to hide in the bushes while these rough southern hoodlums strode along with the joyous tramp of conquerors, proclaiming themselves the masters. The humiliation was too much to bear.

Shinzaemon was quivering with rage and

283

hatred. 'Enough,' he muttered under his breath. There was such a commotion that no one could have heard him anyway. 'We're cowering like women. Just let me get at those southerners. I'll rip their throats out.'

'Don't be a fool, Shin,' hissed Toranosuké. 'You want to die in the road like a dog? We've got bigger battles to fight. Save your dying for Edo.'

The sun was low in the sky and the clouds were tinged the colour of blood before the road finally became quiet. One by one, travellers began to emerge from the trees. Sachi was hungry and dirty, scratched and stiff from crouching without moving for so long. Yet she knew that this could only be the vanguard. There would be more troops on their way soon.

At the checkpoint at Shinchaya they were told that the next detachment was due the following day. The little party scurried along, keeping their heads bowed and their eyes lowered. The road was trampled and rutted, the paving stones broken. The doors of some of the inns had been smashed. There was no food. The soldiers had taken everything. In the end they found one inn that still had some tea. They were grateful to drink that.

The next day they set out well before dawn. They wanted to cover as many *ri* as they could before the next division of soldiers came along. The women walked in front followed by the porters carrying the trunks. The men brought up the rear so that anyone they met would think they were servants.

They were on a deserted section of the highway, deep in the forest, when they saw a line of men straddling the road. Branches rustled and straw sandals crunched as more stepped out from the trees. There must have been twenty or thirty of them in grimy uniforms with wild bristly hair and broad, flat faces. Some had swords, some rifles. Others brandished staves and clubs.

Southerners! thought Sachi. *Ronin!*

Fear knotted in her belly and tingled up and down her spine. Her heart was thumping. Her breath came in shallow gasps. She groped for the dagger tucked in her sash and pulled her scarf close around her face. She knew that Shinzaemon and Toranosuké and probably even young Tatsuemon were expert swordsmen. She had seen how easily they had rescued her in her palanquin. But this time they had only short swords and they were hugely outnumbered.

The men closed ranks till they were blocking the road completely. One stepped towards Sachi, leering. He brought his face up to hers and grinned, revealing a mouthful of crooked teeth. He had a strange leathery odour, this southerner. She recoiled, staring at him in disgust. He was so close she could see his little close-set eyes, the tufts of coarse hair sprouting from his upper lip and the black pores on his flat nose. He said something in an accent so thick that she couldn't understand a word.

He moved closer still, breathing heavily. Five or six others gathered around her menacingly. She closed her hand on her dagger, feeling the cords that bound the hilt. She had never had to use a real blade before. She had only ever fought with women and with practice sticks. She tried to focus her mind and remember her training, but her blood was thundering in her ears so loudly she could hardly think.

The man clamped his hand on her arm. She felt his fingers tightening like a vice. Hardly aware of what she was doing, she ripped her dagger from her sash and plunged it into his chest as hard as she could. She was expecting to meet some resistance, but the blade glided in as easily as a knife through tofu. As she pulled it out, hot blood spurted on to her kimono. The man's grip relaxed. His jaw sagged. He gaped at her in an expression of astonishment. Blood foamed at the corners of his mouth and his eyes glazed. He made a noise like a sigh then staggered back. His knees folded and he crumpled to the ground.

Sachi was panting hard. It had all happened so quickly. She looked around. She was no longer panic-stricken but deadly calm, poised, ready for anything. The other soldiers were closing in on her.

The next moment Shinzaemon was beside her. There was a swish as he brought down two with a single sweep of his sword. He turned and looked hard at Sachi, as if to make sure she was unharmed. His eyes were blazing.

He had thrown off the right sleeve of his kimono to free his sword arm. He had a tattoo, a design of cherry blossom, covering his shoulder and the top of his arm. For a moment it caught Sachi's eye. Porters and litter bearers and gangsters had tattoos; but a samurai...? But there was no time to be puzzled. Toranosuké and Tatsuemon too had

286

thrown off the upper parts of their kimonos and were naked to the waist. They backed protectively around the women, holding their swords aloft in both hands, their muscles rippling.

Taki's eyes narrowed. She had her dagger out. Yuki looked up at Sachi calmly. She too was clutching her dagger in her small hand. Her big eyes were round with excitement.

With a roar like a pack of wild beasts, the soldiers hurled themselves on the group. Shinzaemon sprang forward, lashing out with his short sword. He swung it with lightning speed, far more quickly than the soldiers could react with their longer, more unwieldy weapons. There was a clang and the scrape of steel on steel as he parried a blow then caught his assailant's wrist and brought his sword down on the man's neck. The head flew off and the body crumpled. A sword descended behind him. He spun round, caught the blow on his blade and with a swift movement sliced open the soldier's throat. Toranosuké and Tatsuemon too were parrying, striking, thrusting and slicing. The noise was deafening. Dazzling shards of light flashed from the flying blades. One of the soldiers staggered back with half his jaw missing, his tongue hanging loose, pouring blood. Another's arm was dangling, half the sinews cut through. The injured southerners were screaming and yowling.

One of the soldiers raised his rifle. Sachi couldn't throw her dagger or she would be weaponless. Instead she pulled out her iron hairpin and, as her hair tumbled around her face, took aim and flung. It curved through the air. She felt a blaze of satisfaction as the soldier dropped his rifle and staggered back, clutching his face, blood oozing through his fingers.

There was a rush of wind as a soldier raced towards her, his sword raised. She pivoted around, caught the blow on her dagger and stabbed him in the neck.

The road was soaked with blood and strewn with broken bodies and ripped and torn limbs. The rest of the southerners turned and fled. Toranosuké raised his sword and flung it. It hit one of them in the back. The soldier seemed to hesitate then crashed forward with a thud. The three *ronin* raced after them, yelling, leaping on the slowest and slashing at them. They seized their swords and rifles. As Toranosuké wrenched his sword from the fallen man's back, blood gushed in a black fountain into the air. The three *ronin* went around methodically cutting the head off any bodies that were still twitching.

'The southern army will be here soon,' muttered Shinzaemon. 'Don't want to leave anyone alive to talk.'

Heads rolled about. A stubby finger lay on the ground. There was a vile odour, the reek of flesh and blood and sweat and human excrement: the smell of butchery.

Other travellers were cowering in the trees, watching in horror.

'Hot-headed idiots!' snarled one. 'We're in for it now.'

'You want to be ruled by those southern bastards?' demanded another. 'We're with you,' he shouted to the group.

Sachi wiped her dagger on her blood-soaked kimono. Her hands were shaking. Taki found a fresh overkimono in a bundle and helped her into it. The three men were cleaning their swords and slipping their kimonos back into place. As Sachi wiped her face and tried to tidy her hair, she felt Shinzaemon's eyes on her.

'I got one, Uncle Shin!' piped Yuki. 'Right in the stomach.'

'You did well. You avenged your father,' said Shinzaemon.

'I haven't finished yet,' said Yuki.

'So those are southerners,' said Sachi. 'They're a rabble.'

'Looked like peasants to me,' said Shinzaemon with a scornful curl of his lip. 'Barely trained. Violent thugs but not good swordsmen. Wait till the real army comes along, then we'll have some fun.'

His voice softened.

'You're a warrior woman,' he said quietly.

Sachi felt herself flush with pride. 'I've never killed anyone before,' she said. 'I didn't know I'd ever have to.'

She had proved herself, proved she could wield whatever weapon was to hand as skilfully and calmly as any samurai. She looked around at the scene of carnage. The first time she had seen corpses strewn about had been when Taki had opened the door of her palanquin, the first time she had met the three *ronin*. That time she had felt nauseated and horrified. Now she felt nothing but weariness and a quiet satisfaction. After all, they were the enemy. She glanced at Taki, who was

289

smoothing her hair as if nothing special had happened.

'We should move on fast,' said Toranosuké. 'We'll get you to the village and then we must go. We have a job to do.'

From then on they kept well off the main highway. They took paths through the woods and along the cliffs and scrambled up and down precipices on rickety iron ladders while the River Kiso rolled by far below. They never saw the southerners again but they heard the thunder of southern feet echoing along the valley and the rough strains of their victory song.

Taki and Yuki struggled along, their hands torn and bleeding. Even the men had trouble following the narrow paths and clambering across waterfalls. But to Sachi it felt natural to be roaming in the woods, finding small paths through what appeared to be impenetrable forest, making a noise to scare away wild boars and bears. The forest was full of sounds – the cracking of twigs and snapping of branches and roars and snarls that emerged from the darkness. But she was not afraid. The porters followed, as agile as monkeys with their heavy loads, at home among the mountains.

When night fell they found a hermit's hut in the woods. It was empty and crumbling but at least it was dry and safe and far from the marching soldiers. They brushed aside the mouldering yellow leaves, built a fire then curled up in their travelling clothes on the wooden floor. It was the lowest Sachi had sunk since she had left the palace. She woke up cramped, stiff and dirty, her muscles aching from the previous day's exertions.

They were following the edge of the river when it began to look familiar.

'I know where we are,' said Sachi. 'I used to play here when I was a child.'

She felt a wrench at her heart. The little party had become her family and she knew that once they separated they would never meet again.

Ever since the encounter with the soldiers something had changed. There was some unspoken understanding among them. Shinzaemon and she walked together, well ahead of the rest. Yet they spoke little.

Then they came to a small stream tumbling down between moss-covered rocks. Sachi hesitated, pretending to be afraid. Shinzaemon took her hand. After he had helped her across he did not remove it.

They sat together on the hillside. Below them the road wound into the shadow of the mountainside. Snow lay unmelted in heaps. Dogs were barking. Where the road turned a corner she glimpsed a few familiar roofs covered in rough grey shingles weighted down with stones. The smell of woodsmoke wafted up. It was her village.

Shinzaemon ran his fingers down her cheek and across her hair. His touch was light, the touch of a swordsman.

'I've been fighting ever since I was a child,' he said softly. 'That's all I've ever known. I used to practise every day, all day long. All I wanted was to be a great swordsman, to become one with my

291

sword. But now the world looks different. Larger. I was determined to die in the service of my lord, no matter what. You've made me want to live.'

He was looking at her. 'This face. I shall remember it for ever,' he said. 'When I fight you'll be there at my side, as you were yesterday. And when I die.'

'I shall pray with all my might for you to live,' she said. 'When the war is over, come and find me.'

He took her hands.

'What will you do?' he asked. 'Will you stay here with your family?'

She was shocked by his words. She realized she didn't know the answer herself. She shook her head.

'How can they be my family when we have been apart for so many years?' she whispered. 'I am not the person I was when I left. In the end I know I have to go back to Edo Castle. That's where I belong.'

He looked at her from under his thick brows. He was frowning a little.

'There's still a chance to make it to Edo,' he said. 'Why don't you come with us? The southern army will be here any day now. It's very dangerous for you to stay.'

'I'm so near,' she said, 'I have to see my parents. It's the only chance I'll ever have.'

It hurt to say the words, when he was about to leave and she would never see him again. But it was what she had to do. She held her sleeve to her eyes. It would never do for her – a warrior woman – to weep.

The rest of their party were approaching with the porters. He held her hands tight.

'You are a being from another realm,' he said. 'It's only because of the war that I've been able to meet a creature like you. I promised I'd protect you and I will. I won't let you stay here alone. Toranosuké and Tatsuemon can do as they like. I'll stay with you at least until the southern army has passed. I can catch up with them in Edo in a few days.'

She looked up at him in amazement.

'You mean...' She couldn't believe he had really said it. He was looking at her with his slanting eyes. She smiled shakily. There were tears running down her cheeks but she didn't care.

As Shinzaemon explained his decision to Toranosuké, Sachi was watching Taki's face. It was impassive as was proper for a woman of her station. Nevertheless her large eyes were on Toranosuké as if she was hoping he might stay too. But he raised his eyebrows uncomprehendingly, as if to show he was way above such foolish impulses.

'We're at war!' he said. 'Have you forgotten? You, of all people, Shin. You're the last person I ever thought would go soft like this. I was right. You've been hanging out with women for too long.'

'Give me two days,' said Shinzaemon. 'Maybe three. I'll see you in Edo.'

Toranosuké laughed and slapped Shinzaemon on the shoulder.

'Don't do anything rash, Shin!' he said. 'No single-handed heroics, right?'

Sachi realized sadly that he was entirely unaware of Taki or her interest in him. But even her sadness for Taki couldn't stop joy surging through her.

Then everyone was bowing and expressing formal thanks and wishing each other good luck. Sachi, Taki and Yuki watched, bowing again and again, as Toranosuké and Tatsuemon mounted horses and galloped away towards Edo. Shinzaemon was grinning and waving.

The three women linked hands and Sachi led the way down the slope towards the village.

7

A Wisp of Smoke

I

At the bend where the road dipped, Sachi turned for a moment and looked back. She gasped. The long highway stretching to the distant forest, fringed with pine trees, the mountains surrounding the valley like the walls of a fortress – it was the very place where she had stood with her friends, little Mitsu, long-limbed Genzaburo and her little brother, Chobei, watching for the princess's procession to appear. She remembered hearing the first shouts drifting across the valley, no more than a whisper in the wind – '*Shita ni iyo, shita ni iyo!* Down on your knees, down on your

294

knees!' – and seeing banners poking through the trees.

She was standing entranced when Taki raised a thin finger. There was a noise in the distance, a muffled roar not so different from the one she had heard all those years ago. It sounded like the Kiso rushing along in full flood, swollen with melted snow, but she knew it wasn't. A moment later the sounds became distinct – the boom of great drums, men's voices shouting out a barbaric victory song, the thud and thunder of feet, the crunching of hundreds of straw sandals. The dreaded pacification army. Yet more regiments of boorish southerners marching up from Kyoto, heading for the village.

There was no time to lose. They turned and hurried the last few steps, slipping and slithering on the icy road. They came to a wooden signboard listing the name of every family who lived in the village, each on its own wooden tablet. It marked the entrance to the village. Beside it was the water barrel with buckets piled on top, always kept full in case of fire. Snow mantled everything, making it look fresh and white.

All those years Sachi had clung to the memory of the cosy wooden houses with their roofs of grey shingles weighted down with rocks – so clean, so neat, with little stone walls outside. When life had seemed unbearable she had imagined herself back there. And now she really was.

But there was something wrong. The village had always been crowded with travellers, packed with women sweeping the road and children collecting horse droppings and discarded straw sandals. There had always been the tramp of feet, the chatter of voices, the clatter of looms and spinning wheels. The last time she had been there the street had been bustling with people, full of excitement because the princess was to pass through.

Now it was silent and empty. There were still the familiar smells of woodsmoke and miso soup, but even the cocks had stopped crowing. Every house was shuttered.

Sachi, Taki and Yuki tucked up their kimono skirts and ran, their porters scurrying after them. Sachi glanced around. Shinzaemon was strolling nonchalantly, his two swords firmly tucked in his sash, with that arrogant rolling gait the samurai affected, as if to say, 'Run? Me?' He was falling further and further behind. They passed the inn belonging to little Mitsu and her family and came to Genzaburo's inn. Across the road was the long wall that marked the splendid inn where the daimyos stayed. Her inn, where she and her family lived.

Panting, the women ducked through the gate, under the branches of the gnarled cherry tree that Sachi used to climb and around the sturdy whitewashed wall that hid the inn and the lords who stayed there from the eyes of the common folk outside. In front of them was the shadowy entrance hall and the wooden porch where Sachi had knelt when she first saw the princess. The inn was a little run-down and sad, but everything was there, just as she remembered it – the rambling grounds, the well, the palanquin shed, the stables. But what had happened to the ramp that

296

the bearers used to carry the palanquins up and down? It had been her job to keep it raked, trimmed and perfectly smooth. Now grass, weeds and stones poked through the snow.

Sachi led the way around the back of the building to the family quarters and shoved open the heavy wooden door. The creak it made as it slid in its grooves was heart-rendingly familiar. She hesitated, afraid of what she would find. Then she took a deep breath and stepped into the earthen-floored hall. Taki and Yuki lingered timidly outside. Shinzaemon had just appeared.

'Hurry, hurry,' Sachi said.

'But it's ... a peasants' house,' said Taki. 'I can't go into a peasants' house. It would... It would pollute me.'

Taki's eyes were wide with horror. Surrounded by *ronin* wielding naked swords she was fearless, but Sachi knew very well that, for Taki, mingling with peasants was like being surrounded by wild animals. Sachi smiled reassuringly.

'It's my house,' she said gently. 'Not peasants, country samurai. We're country samurai.'

Inside, smoke hung in the air. Pine needles crackled and hissed as they burned in the hearth, giving off a fragrant woody smell. The battered lid of the sooty iron kettle hanging over the fire jiggled and clattered.

'Anybody home?' Sachi piped. Her voice sounded thin and reedy in the high-raftered hall. She called again.

An old woman hobbled out, her face a blur in the darkness.

'Who is it?' she quavered.

She stood with her knees bent and one hand pressed to her hip. Her back was so curved her head was almost on a level with her knees. Her hair was speckled with grey and her face was lined and crumpled. But it was the same dear face that Sachi had kept in her mind for so long.

'Mother,' she said. 'It's me. Sa. I'm home.'

Otama stood with a hand on her back, rocking back and forth, peering at her through watery eyes.

'Sa,' she said, in tones of wonder. Painfully she got down on her knees and put her head on the faded straw matting.

'Don't bow to me, Mother,' said Sachi. Tears were running down her face.

'Look at you, how you've grown,' said Otama. 'My, how you talk! You've become a great lady. Come in quickly. The soldiers will be here any moment.'

Her Kiso lilt was so homely and familiar, like water tinkling over pebbles, that Sachi found herself smiling despite her tears. The four travellers untied their straw sandals, brushed the dust of the road off their clothes, wiped their feet and stepped up on to the mats. The porters hefted in their luggage and left it piled on the wooden floor of the corridor that ran alongside the rooms. On their journey it had always seemed a few pathetic bundles, but here in this house it was a massive amount. The place was over-flowing with it.

Otama seemed entirely unsurprised that she had arrived with friends. Sachi had forgotten how simple life in the countryside was. It was not wound about with rules as life in the court or even among the samurai had been. Among samurai it was unthinkable for a woman to be with a man but here nobody cared – life was much more free and easy. Men and women mixed together and there was nothing unusual about travelling in mixed company. Her parents had always been so good at taking life in their stride. Otama was not even surprised by Sachi's companions: the stick-thin, pale court lady, the samurai child, the bushy-haired *ronin*. All sorts of people travelled the road.

Two children pattered in and stood, heads bowed. The older looked up and stared at Sachi with big grave eyes. Sachi recognized the spiky hair and round inquisitive face.

'Chobei, you remember Big Sister?'

He had been a little boy when she saw him last. Now he was exactly the age Sachi had been when she had gone to the palace. She had often pictured him in his scratchy brown kimono, playing with a lizard on the road that last day when they had gone out to watch for the princess's procession. And the baby she used to carry on her back – little Omasa. She had died. This must be Ofuki, born after she had left.

Sachi knelt down and took the children in her arms, rubbing her nose on their rough brown skin, smelling the familiar country smells of woodsmoke and earth in their hair.

'Where did you go?' asked Chobei.

'A long way away.'

'Will you stay here now?'

'I hope so,' said Sachi, smiling at her mother.

'Please stay,' said the little girl.

Yuki was staring at Chobei. They were almost the same age. At last here was a playmate for her.

'I'm staying,' Yuki said firmly. Her hair, tied into two butterfly loops, flopped emphatically as she nodded her head. For the first time since they left Kano she was smiling.

Otama filled a teapot from the kettle and set cups of tea around the hearth. She gazed at Sachi longingly as if she wanted to keep her there for ever. She opened her mouth to say something. Then she sighed, shook her head and looked away.

Somewhere in the distance there were shouts and the tramping of feet. Otama started and went pale. She drew in her breath with a hiss and looked from one to the other, her eyes wide with fear.

'Off you go, children,' she said abruptly. She turned to Shinzaemon. He was sitting quietly, staring into the embers, cradling a tiny long-stemmed pipe in his great hand. 'You can't stay here,' she hissed. 'There'll be soldiers here any moment. They'll be on the lookout for people like you. It's very dirty but ... you'd better get upstairs into the attic.'

'I won't be much use to you up in the attic,' said Shinzaemon.

The shouts were growing closer.

'She's right,' said Sachi. 'They'll be after you. You can't take on a whole army. They'll leave us women alone.'

'They'll have passed straight through the place where we met those southern *ronin*,' said Taki,

300

nodding. 'They'll have found their comrades. If they find you here they'll take it out on us.'

'They'll massacre the whole village,' said Sachi pleadingly.

'I'm not leaving you on your own.'

'You can't protect us if you're dead,' said Sachi.

'The soldiers have been interrogating all the young men,' said Otama anxiously. 'They're looking for anyone they think is on the northern side.'

Shinzaemon sighed. 'Well, if you insist,' he said, scowling.

'Keep inside while the soldiers are here,' Otama said urgently, frowning at the women. 'Whatever you do, don't go out.'

Sachi took a candle and padded through the dark house to the staircase at the back. She gave Shinzaemon a lantern and a tinderbox and pushed up the trapdoor. His eyes, glinting like a cat's in the darkness, roamed across her face. Then he bent down and climbed through. She shut the trapdoor and rolled the stairs away. She could hear the floorboards creaking above her.

II

While Otama hurried off to prepare dinner for the soldiers, Sachi, Taki and Yuki stayed in the family quarters with the children.

In her mind Sachi was running over the events of the day. Shinzaemon's change of heart, the fact he was here in the village – she could never have dared imagine he would do such a rash and wonderful thing. Again and again she remembered his words: 'You are a being from another realm.' She glanced at herself in her mother's tarnished metal mirror. A pale face, oval with a pointed chin and a small full mouth; large wide-spaced eyes, dark green, slanted upwards at the corners. In the past she had always looked at her face to check her make-up, but now she looked at it as if she had never seen it before. She ran her finger down her smooth white cheek and across her small straight nose. So this was the face he saw – and liked.

Then she frowned and shook her head. She needed Taki to remind her that she was playing with fire, that any kind of alliance had to be sanctioned by one's family or, in her case, by the shogunal court. If she let herself get carried away, they would both end up without their heads. While they were on the road they had been able to flout society's laws; but here in the village they would have to be much more careful. In any case, all he had done was carve out a few extra days for them to be together. Once they left the village they would be on their way to Edo and there they would say goodbye, probably for ever. There was no point worrying about the future; they had no future. There was only the present.

'Well,' said Taki, 'on our own again.'

Now that there was no one but Sachi to see her, her thin face drooped. Her big eyes stared sadly into the distance. Sachi knelt behind her and kneaded her bony shoulders. Taki gave a grunt of appreciation as Sachi worked on a particularly stiff knot.

302

'We'll see them again in Edo,' Sachi said quietly, mindful that Taki hadn't confided in her. 'Shinzaemon's such an impulsive character,' she added. 'Toranosuké's much more steady. I expect he would have stayed too but he felt he had to get to Edo.'

'I don't know what's come over me,' said Taki ruefully. 'I'm not myself at all.' She sighed. 'I'll just have to wait for these foolish feelings to go away. After all, he's way below me in rank. What could I possibly hope for – to be his mistress? I'm a court lady, I'm going to spend the rest of my life in the women's palace, and that's an end of it.

'It's so smoky in here,' she muttered, dabbing her eyes with her sleeve.

Sachi knew it wasn't the smoke that was making her eyes water. She put her arms round Taki and they snuggled up together.

Sachi was half asleep when the door crashed open. A soldier burst in, then another, then another, till there were twenty or thirty of them crowding into the room. Some had red, swollen faces and their breath reeked of sake. They were brandishing naked swords. They didn't even bother to remove their straw sandals but stomped around the tatami fully shod. The stench of food and tobacco and stale sweat filled the room. Sachi and Taki sat up quickly. They pushed the children into a corner and crouched protectively in front of them, pulling their robes around their faces.

'Those outlaws. You got them in here somewhere. Just hand them over and you won't get hurt.'

The ugly southern syllables grated like the yapping of dogs. They looked like dogs too, these men from the deep south. They were short and brawny, their skin leathery and black from the sun, their eyes like slits. Instead of the dignified armour of warriors they wore outlandish black garments with tight-fitting sleeves and skinny trousers that made their legs look like sticks. Some had bands around their bristly heads with a square of iron to protect their foreheads as if they were engaged in a vendetta. They had the unshaved pates and long hair of *ronin*, tied back in horse's tails. Some had dog skins slung around their shoulders. They loomed over the women, staring down at them accusingly.

Sachi looked at them wide-eyed, composing her features into an expression of stunned innocence. She dared not even exchange glances with Taki. She knew all too well they couldn't defend themselves. The halberds were out of reach behind their luggage and there were too many soldiers to fight with hairpins and daggers. Besides, there were the children. Everyone knew the southerners were violent ruffians without conscience or human feeling. Rough of temper, rude of tongue, that was what people said; but also courageous to the point of recklessness. Only the gods knew what they would do if they were provoked.

'That troublemaker's been seen around this way,' barked one, a burly character with a swarthy bearded face and a squashed-down nose. 'Had enough of his sort in Kyoto. Fellow with a tattoo on his shoulder. Ugly brute.' He peered at them through narrow suspicious eyes. 'Some of our men were butchered by a mob of northerners – twenty at least, the survivors said. Their leader answered that description.'

Sachi couldn't help feeling a glimmer of satisfaction. Twenty at least? She was glad they had had such an impact.

'If you got any fugitives here, hand them over and we won't hurt you.'

Sachi was about to answer when one of the soldiers raised his rifle and rammed the butt into a cupboard door. The others joined in, ripping great holes in the paper doors. Then there was a splintering sound as one thrust his spear into the ceiling. The soldiers started jabbing the ceiling with bayonets and spears, roaring, 'We'll get the bastard. He's up there somewhere, for sure.' Dust fell in showers, making everyone choke. The women cowered, dazed by the noise and turmoil.

Sachi's heart was pounding so loudly she was afraid the soldiers would hear it. She peeped up, hardly daring to breathe, terrified that she might see blood glistening on the blade of a spear. Desperately she prayed to all the gods that Shinzaemon had stayed where she had left him, at the far end of the house, and had had the presence of mind to lie on one of the thick heavy beams.

The woven bamboo of the ceiling was dangling in shreds. Sachi pulled her scarf around her face, grateful that the room was too dark for them to see her clearly. She took a deep breath, rose to her feet and faced the crowd. Her mouth was dry. She told herself she was back in the training hall at the women's palace, facing her opponent. She tried to keep her voice steady.

'What do you think you're doing, barging into our house like this?' she demanded. The voice that came out was as clear and unwavering as if she was back in the women's palace, issuing orders to servants. She had been afraid she had forgotten her Kiso dialect but the words were perfectly accented. 'There's no one here,' she went on in a tone of quiet authority, gaining confidence as she spoke. 'You should be ashamed of yourselves. This is the house of Jiroemon, headman of this village. We are not peasants to be pushed around. How dare you destroy our house like this?'

The room fell silent. The soldiers gaped at her.

'There's no one here, only us women,' she said firmly. She was totally calm now and in control. 'We have nothing to hide. You don't believe me? I'll show you. Come.'

She led them from room to room, sliding open one set of doors, then the next, and opening the closets where the bedding was kept. She took care to steer them well away from the dark corner where the stairs that led to the attic were.

'You see?' she said, flinging open a final set of doors. 'There's no one here. Just us.'

'Woman's got guts,' muttered one soldier grudgingly.

'Certainly has,' nodded the others. 'May be a country wench but she's got the heart of a samurai. We should leave these women be.'

One by one the soldiers slid their swords into their scabbards. Some of them looked a little shame-faced. They were crowding towards the door when the bearded man swung round.

306

'Just one last look,' he growled, screwing up his eyes suspiciously and staring hard at Sachi. She was glad she had wrapped her face in her scarf. He stomped off with a couple of others, shining their lanterns into every dark corner. Sachi listened to their straw-sandalled feet crunching away across the tatami, fearing that at any moment they would find the stairs or look up and see the trapdoor in the ceiling. She thought she heard a faint creak from above and hoped that none of them had noticed.

Something had to be done. She let the scarf fall from her face, pretending to fumble clumsily before pulling it back into place again.

'Hey, look at this!' shouted a soldier, grabbing hold of the scarf and ripping it away from her face. 'What a beauty!'

The next moment he had grabbed her by the shoulders and shoved her against a wall. Sachi caught her breath. She had not thought even southerners could be as brutish as this. The man's face was pockmarked, his chin bristly, his eyes small like a pig's. She reeled from the foulness of his breath.

The others gathered round, leering. After all, she realized, as far as they were concerned she was just a peasant girl. They could do anything they liked with impunity.

'This one's mine,' chortled the pockmarked one, spraying her with spittle. 'Spoils of war. Come along with us, girl. We're the conquerors!'

Fiercely Sachi tried to push the soldier off, groping for her hairpin. For a moment she forgot everything except his vile sweaty body pinning

307

her to the wall. She would have his eyes out, even if the soldiers killed them all.

Then she stopped. With a shock of horror she remembered there was a whole army out there. She couldn't defend herself or she would bring down destruction on the village. Looking at these men with their brutish smell and sun-blackened skin, she had no doubt they would massacre them all.

The man was tearing at her clothes when Taki drew herself up and glared at the soldiers. Her big eyes were blazing and she didn't even try to conceal her posh Kyoto accent. In her squeaky voice she shrilled in tones of withering contempt, 'What are you – animals or men?' Her voice rang out across the hubbub. 'You should be ashamed of yourselves. We are loyal subjects of the emperor here, but we're not prepared to be ruled by wild beasts. So this is what southerners are! You burst in, frightening the children. I don't know who or what you're looking for but they're not here. Can't you see that? You've done enough damage. You southerners – you're no better than animals!'

The men fell silent. Some were shuffling their feet and staring at the ground. The bearded soldier had returned to see what the commotion was. He pushed through the mob of soldiers, grabbed the pockmarked man by the shoulders and shoved him away. The man stumbled and fell.

'You want your head chopped off?' barked the bearded man. 'You heard what the commander said. Leave these women alone. We're supposed

308

to be winning the locals over, not terrorizing them. There's no one here. Let's go.'

'I'll be back,' said the pockmarked soldier, leering at Sachi. Still peering round suspiciously and grumbling under their breath, they all trooped out.

The door closed and the room was quiet again. Sachi and Taki looked at each other, both trembling with shock. Sachi had only just come back and already she had brought danger and destruction on her family, she thought.

'We'd better make sure Shin stays up there,' said Taki. 'They're bound to return. I thought you told me this place would be safe? It's not safe at all.'

Much later Otama came in. 'Those officers,' she sighed. 'They call for sake, then more sake, then for food, then more food. And will they pay for it? No. But what can we do? Anyway, they're snoring now.'

She looked around enquiringly. Sachi and Taki had done their best to tidy up but there were gaping holes in the cupboard doors and the ceiling was shredded. Otama shook her head wearily and pursed her lips.

'And your friend?'

Sachi glanced upwards.

Otama went to the kitchen, lifted the trapdoor in the floor and brought out a bowl of buckwheat groats. 'This is all I have left,' she said.

She threw some wood under the great cooking pot, boiled up the buckwheat and made a brown porridge. She ladled some into a couple of bowls, chopped a pickled radish, put a few slices on to two dishes and laid it on a tray with a couple of pairs of chopsticks. Slowly she straightened up, one hand on her back.

Sachi was looking at her questioningly. She could understand two bowls – Shinzaemon could well be hungry. But two pairs of chopsticks...? Otama gave her a gentle smile but said nothing.

'Give it to me,' said Sachi.

She took the tray, picked up a lamp and padded through the dark house. She rolled the staircase into place, then knocked softly on the trapdoor in the ceiling and cautiously pushed it up a little.

'Shin!' she called.

She shoved the trapdoor back. Holding the lamp over her head she climbed a few more steps and peeked into the attic.

In the huge cluttered space with its sloping walls, she could see the underside of the roof slates neatly overlapping each other. She used to play hide and seek up there. Broken farm implements, piles of rope and ancient boxes loomed in the lamplight, casting huge shadows. It was icy cold. She held the lantern higher.

Shinzaemon was cross-legged in the middle of the dusty floor, wrapped up in a quilt. There was an unsheathed sword beside him. She blinked back tears as she saw him looking at her. His face was black with dust and grime.

'You're safe,' she said hoarsely. 'I was so frightened.'

'I heard those southerners barging around downstairs,' he said. 'You did well. If you'd yelled I would have smashed my way out of here and had their heads, the lot of them.'

'It's a good thing you didn't. If they'd known you were here they would have killed us all. I didn't know you were so famous, you and that tattoo of yours.'

There was a noise – a sound of shuffling. Another set of teeth gleamed in the darkness. There was someone else there too. Squatting next to Shinzaemon was a long-limbed gangly youth. Sachi looked at him and gasped. He was taller and more muscular than when she had seen him last, and coarse black hair sprouted on his upper lip. But there was no mistaking the impish grin and bristly hair that stuck out in unruly tufts. She could almost see him scrambling fearlessly along the shakiest of branches or darting about in the river like a fish.

'Genzaburo!' she cried. 'Gen! What are you doing here?'

'I'd know that white skin anywhere,' said Genzaburo. His voice was still slightly high-pitched, like a boy's. He grinned at her like a mischievous water sprite.

'Well, I'm not surprised,' she said, shaking her head in bemused delight. 'Not a bit. What on earth have you been up to?'

'Staying alive,' said Genzaburo. 'We had to do some creeping about up here. There were spears poking up all over the place. It was like being at the wrong end of a bayonet charge. Danced about until we found a couple of beams and squatted on them. Shin wanted to get down there and take them all on. I had to restrain him.'

Shinzaemon was looking at Sachi.

311

'You expect me to stay up here and leave you to deal with those brutes alone?' he grunted. In the lamplight the pair of them could almost have been brothers. They looked far too young to have required a squadron of southern soldiers to flush them out.

Later, when they had patched up the damage as best they could and spread out their futons, Otama whispered to Sachi, 'I heard those southerners talking about some gangster or other. Is that your friend?'

'It's all exaggeration. He came with us to protect us.'

'No need to explain. You're our Sa. That's all we need to know. And that Genzaburo,' she added, smiling quietly. 'Rampaging up and down the valley, having a one-man war with the southerners. I don't know how many he's cut down. Anyway, we have to protect our own.'

Sachi looked at her. Otama's hair was growing thin and sparse, her knuckles were swollen, her face was wrinkled, but she radiated calm and kindness and strength. It made Sachi angry that, after all her years of hard work, she now had to suffer these uncouth southerners strutting around destroying everything that she had built with such pain.

'So those southern officers are using our inn?'

'We've got no choice. Your father was notified they'd be on their way. We were ordered to arrange bedding and food. The place was falling down. We'd given up using it as an inn ever since the processions stopped coming through. When was it? Four years ago? Five? No one came to stay any more. Ordinary travellers couldn't afford it. No guests and twenty rooms to keep up. I've been sweeping and polishing, trying to tidy it up, but it's very shabby.

'You remember how we used to scrub the tatami together and arrange the flowers in the alcove when the lords were due to stay? You were so good at doing the flowers, Sa. You used to enjoy that. And Father sitting down there, chatting to their lordships? They were so noble, so dignified, those lords. They always came through on the same day, every year without fail. We knew exactly how many men they'd have with them, how much food to provide, how much bedding. Everything was set. Everything was organized and planned. And we got paid for it, enough to get by...'

There was a long silence. Finally she said, 'There's been famine, Sa. The crops have been bad every year since you left.'

There was another silence. Sachi had the feeling there was something Otama wasn't telling her.

Late that night the door slid open and a large figure appeared. He threw himself down on the tatami along with everyone else. Sachi knew it was her father but it was too late to talk. When she woke up in the morning he had gone, along with Shinzaemon and Genzaburo.

By daylight Sachi could see that the southerners had left the place a shambles. Burnt-out torches littered the road. The banks of the drainage channels had crumbled under the passage of so

313

many men and horses. The ground was a morass of trodden-down snow, churned and rutted from the wheels of the cannon carriages. Children rushed around sweeping up horse manure, straw sandals and straw horseshoes.

Sachi went out to help her mother tidy up. She kept a wary eye out for the pockmarked soldier. Standing in the morning sun, she couldn't help noticing how run-down and dingy the village had become. It was poorer and smaller than she remembered. The whole of it would have fitted into the compound of the Satos' house in Kano, and the whole city of Kano would fit easily inside the ramparts of Edo Castle.

Edo Castle. Sachi felt a pang of longing. She suddenly realized she no longer belonged in the village. She was no longer the innocent girl who had played so merrily, for whom the village was the whole world. With a sigh she forced herself back into the present and joined the villagers fixing up the road.

Everyone was chattering as they worked. It seemed the daughter of a local watchman had been raped while doing some washing in the stream. One of the southern soldiers had been unable to resist her pretty face. He had been apprehended and killed. Local men were bringing the head in a bucket. It was to be stuck on a bamboo stake and displayed at the edge of the village for three days, along with a notice describing the offence and the punishment. It was an extraordinarily severe punishment for something not usually even considered a crime. After all, the victim was only a woman, and a peasant at that.

314

No doubt the idea was to show the villagers that they would be protected under the new regime.

Sachi felt a certain grim satisfaction. Perhaps it was the pockmarked man.

Word had already spread of her return. Villagers came over to greet her and to have a good look at this child who had disappeared for more than six years and returned a great lady.

'Sa, how are you? Remember me?' It was a woman with a mouth that looked too big for her face, crowded with crooked teeth. She had a baby tied to her back and a couple of toddlers clinging to her shabby, patched work clothes. 'It's me, Shigé!'

Shigé – Genzaburo's brother's wife and the young bride of the inn across the road. Sachi remembered how much in awe of her she had been. She had been the queen of the village, so pretty and full of gaiety. Now her face had grown thick and fleshy, her cheeks were cracked and blackened from the sun, her forehead was furrowed and her back was already beginning to bend at the waist. How had she grown so old so fast?

Kumé, the crippled bride of the clog-maker's son, came limping over. She too had turned into an old woman. Only Oman from the inn next door to Sachi's retained a little of her youthful prettiness. Her face still had some of its soft roundness but she too looked tired and worn. Her hands were swollen and chapped and her cheeks criss-crossed with red veins.

Sachi looked at them all, standing around smiling and laughing. They did not need to say a word. She knew exactly how their lives had been in the six years since she saw them last. They had had children year after year. Some had died; they had reared the rest. They had taken care of the guests at their inns, cooked, cleaned, lugged water from the well, washed clothes in the river, dug their vegetable patches. And her life? They could not begin even to imagine it.

'Look at you,' exclaimed Shigé. 'So young, like a princess in a fairy tale!'

'When people passed through we always asked how things were in Edo. We wanted to make sure you were safe,' said Oman. 'We worried about you, hearing about the troubles up there. But we've had troubles of our own here too.'

They asked no more about what she had done or where she had been. Perhaps they too were afraid to look too deep into the chasm that divided them. Sachi thought of Urashima, the handsome young fisherman in the fairy tale, who was wooed by the dragon king's daughter. He had frittered away three years at her palace under the sea, dancing and feasting and love-making. When he returned to his village, everything had changed. Finally he met an old, old woman who remembered hearing, when she was a little child, of the man who had disappeared into the sea. Not three but three hundred years had passed.

Sachi had been away too long. Too much had happened in all their lives. They had moved too far apart ever to close the gap. She had wanted so badly to go back, just as Urashima had, but it was too late. The village had been like an anchor for her, the place she had thought of as home. But it was not the place she remembered. She really was Urashima.

The story had had a bad ending. The dragon king's daughter had given Urashima a box and told him on no account to open it, no matter what. Sitting disconsolate on the beach, it occurred to him that her gift was the only thing he had left. He decided to open it. A wisp of smoke curled out. It was those three hundred years. As he sat on the beach his hair grew white then his body crumbled away. In a moment there was nothing left but a pile of dust.

III

Sachi's father, Jiroemon, was sitting, legs crossed, by the hearth when she got back. Shinzaemon and Genzaburo were with him. Threads of smoke coiled from three small long-stemmed pipes. The faces that gazed at each other across the coals were very serious.

'Declared a traitor, huh?' said Jiroemon. 'They'll be asking for his head next.'

'They already have,' grunted Shinzaemon. Sachi lingered in the doorway. So they were talking about the retired shogun, Lord Yoshinobu, she thought. She stood motionless, listening to Shinzaemon's deep tones. She loved the sound of his voice when he thought there were no women around, the rough men's language he used, the way he growled out the syllables. 'They've got armies on all three highways, closing in on Edo,' Shinzaemon was saying. 'They're sweeping up

317

the domains as they go. The lords are all declaring for the south. They're afraid of being branded traitors if they don't.'

They stopped talking when they saw her.

'I'm back,' Sachi said simply.

Taki had been kneeling silently in a far corner of the room. Otama had given her some sewing to do; she only felt comfortable when she had a needle in her fingers, she said.

In the morning, after the last of the soldiers had left, Taki had gone to sit in the great inn for a while. She said she felt more at home in the big rooms with their gold-edged tatami, old and worn though it was. She had also been to gaze at the ornamental garden. But she wouldn't go out and mix with the people. Sachi wouldn't have expected her to. She was a court lady, used to living hidden away in shadowy interiors.

Now Taki slipped forward and joined them quietly. She made a pot of tea and poured out a cup for each of them, then sat down.

Jiroemon bowed as if he was slightly bemused at having a court lady make him a cup of tea. Then he turned to Sachi.

'It's good to see you, my girl,' he said. 'My little princess. You bring sunshine.'

He poked the coals and put another plug of tobacco into the small bowl of his pipe. He at least had not changed. He looked older, stiffer, slower. His thatch of hair, tugged back into a bristly horse's tail, was streaked with grey. But he was still the large, dependable father she remembered, his voice as deep and reassuring as ever. She looked at his huge hand, the nails blackened

318

and chipped, and remembered how safe it had made her feel when she held it as a child.

'These are dark times,' he said slowly. 'Very dark. I knew things were changing but I never thought they would change so much. We've all been hungry, some years worse than others. The price of rice has gone through the roof. And our taxes too. Half our young men have gone to fight. Most haven't come back. I do my best to keep order, but it's hard.'

He looked around at Shinzaemon and Genzaburo.

'Some of our young men come back and they're even more trouble when they get here,' he added with a chuckle. 'And other young men turn up bringing trouble in their wake. Genzaburo here, he's been gone for a long time, he has. The gods know what he's been up to!'

'I ran away,' said Genzaburo, grinning his impish grin. 'Joined the militia. Didn't fancy being an innkeeper for the rest of my days or chopping down trees either, just to hand it all over in taxes to this lordship or that lordship. Was a time you had to be a samurai to join up but they'll take anyone these days, even a peasant. I can fight better than a samurai now.'

'Is that so?' grunted Shinzaemon, giving him a sideways glance. 'We'll see about that.'

'I can ride a horse. I fought in Kyoto. I've seen the world.'

'And Shin,' said Jiroemon. 'Quite a legend round here. We never thought we'd meet you.'

'We knew each other in Kyoto,' said Shinzaemon, 'Gen and I. Fought shoulder to shoulder a few times. It was a big surprise to find him up there in the attic. But I'm afraid neither of us were much use last night.'

'And you, Sa?' said Genzaburo. 'The village was empty without you. Look at you – so beautiful. Who would have thought it? Our own little Sa. You're like a fairy creature.'

Sachi looked down, flushing, conscious of Shinzaemon's eyes on her face. There was a wistful note to Genzaburo's voice, as if he was aware she was no longer the person she had been.

'I've come home too,' she said.

Jiroemon looked at her gravely. 'We don't have much to offer you here, my girl.' He turned and stared at the fire as if he didn't want to meet her eyes. 'You're a fine lady now. You don't belong here any more. We're humble folk, we can't provide the things you're used to. Stay as long as you like, but when this war is over you must go to your father.'

The last words were like a sigh.

Sachi had been filling their teacups. She stopped and slowly lowered her arm. Surely she had misheard, she thought. She looked at him blankly.

'My father?' she said slowly.

'Didn't Mother tell you?' Jiroemon had a cup of tea halfway to his lips. He put it down on the edge of the hearth without tasting it.

Otama had just come in. Painfully she folded her legs and knelt. It brought tears to Sachi's eyes to see how bent her back was. She leaned forward till her head was very close to Sachi's.

'Your father passed through,' she whispered.

'Just a few days ago. I should have told you, but I couldn't bear to, not when we'd only just got you back.'

The words jolted through Sachi like a physical blow. The room seemed to shift around her. Shinzaemon sat staring at the embers, taking everything in. Genzaburo was drawing circles on the tatami with his thin brown finger. Sachi suddenly noticed how cold it was.

Smoke lingered in the air, drifting towards the blackened rafters. Tobacco smoke mingled with the woody scent of the pine cones burning in the hearth. The old house creaked.

'My father? But... But you're my father,' she stammered.

'Your real father,' said Jiroemon heavily.

Sachi stared at the coals. All those years that she had been at the palace, in the middle of chaos and despair, the threat of war, the horror of His Majesty's death, she'd always been able to think back to the village, to conjure up memories of her happy childhood. Maybe she had remembered it as more idyllic than it really had been but she had clung to the memory like a lucky charm, something solid and real in the midst of so much change.

Taki had put down her sewing. She was staring at her, her thin face tilted to one side as if she could see something Sachi couldn't see herself.

'What are you talking about?' Sachi said angrily, biting back tears. 'You're my father.' She glared at Jiroemon. 'I don't need any father except you!' She could hear her own voice shrill in the silence, echoing from the high rafters of the room.

It was not a big surprise to learn that she was adopted; so was half the village. Children got passed around to whoever needed a son or a daughter. But everyone else knew who their real parents were. They had filial obligations to them as well as to their adoptive parents. She was the only one who had never known her real parents. She had assumed they had died when she was a baby and had cleaved all the more closely to Jiroemon and Otama. They were all the parents she had ever had.

She put her hands over her ears. She didn't want to hear any more.

But at the back of her mind she couldn't stop those niggling thoughts that had been bothering her for so long. The way she looked – that white skin people made such a fuss about. And the brocade that she had brought back all the way from the burning palace, all the way from Kano. Maybe it was connected. The bundle containing it was piled carelessly in the corridor along with the rest of the luggage. She had not dared even unpack it. She could almost see it glowing, radiating heat as if it would burn a hole through the flimsy silk square that wrapped it.

'The brocade,' she breathed. 'That robe you gave me when I went off to the palace.'

'It's yours,' said Otama. 'You came wrapped up in it. Isn't that right, Father?'

Jiroemon took a puff of his pipe and tapped it out on the edge of the hearth, sending showers of sparks flying.

'Daisuké, he said his name was,' he said heavily.

322

'He was a distant relation. From a side branch of the family who'd moved to Edo a couple of generations back. We'd never heard a word of them since.'

'You were the tiniest, most perfect little thing,' said Otama, smiling wistfully. 'Like a fairy child we'd been given to take care of. And such skin, so white and soft, like silk. He'd come walking through the mountains, carrying you wrapped in brocade. Can you imagine! A man walking through the mountains with a baby. He'd found wet nurses along the way, he said.'

She stopped and poked the glowing embers in the hearth, wiping her eyes with her sleeve.

'But ... my mother,' said Sachi. 'My real mother. Where was she?' Her voice was breathless, shrill, like a lost child.

'He said, "This baby, I know she's only a worthless girl and of no account. The last thing you need is an extra mouth to feed, and a girl child at that. I should have killed her, I know. But I couldn't do it. She's very precious to me. She's all I have." Those were his words. I remember them exactly. "She's all I have. Please do me this favour. This baby. Please take care of her for me."'

'He was in quite a hurry, wasn't he, Mother?' said Jiroemon.

'He was a townsman, a real dandy. His clothes, so fancy. And so handsome, such a gentleman – we'd never seen anything like it in this village. And as for the brocade...'

'He said he was going to Osaka to look for work. He'd come back to fetch you when he had

323

found some. But weeks passed, then months, then years and he never came back.'

'We thought he was dead,' murmured Otama. 'It's a terrible thing to say but – we hoped he wouldn't come back. You were our little princess. We wanted to keep you. We still do.'

Sachi pressed her sleeve to her eyes. It touched her heart to know how much her parents cared about her. But there was still a question nagging at her.

'And my mother?' she whispered. 'So you don't know... So no one knows...'

Otama and Jiroemon looked at each other. 'That comb you have, the one you love so much,' said Otama softly. 'He gave us that too. It belongs to your mother. He said one day, if you wanted to find out who she was, you could show people the crest. Someone would know it.'

Sachi reached into her sleeve and found the comb, ran her fingers up and down the tines. She could feel the mysterious crest embossed there. She closed her small hand around it and held it so tightly she could feel the tines pressing into her palm. It was the only link she had to her mother.

Otama took a deep breath. 'And then, just a few days ago, he turned up again.'

A tear ran down her faded face. She was staring into the fire as if she knew that if she told Sachi this she would lose her. 'After all those years. Isn't that right, Father?'

'He stayed at our inn,' said Jiroemon, sighing heavily, nodding his head. 'Imagine that. Used to be lords we had staying here. Now it's Cousin

Daisuké, your father.'

'You should have seen him,' said Otama, shaking her head in wonder. 'The clothes he was wearing! The sort of things you hear that foreigners wear. And his hair. Not like any hairstyle I've ever seen. Cropped short. Still handsome. Bit older; had filled out a bit but still quite a man.'

'He was looking for you,' said Jiroemon. 'I told him the princess had taken you, that we hadn't seen you for years. He said he was going to Edo and would look for you there.'

There was a rustle as Shinzaemon sat back on his heels. He was staring at the tatami, frowning. Sachi looked at him, puzzled. There was something he had seen that she had yet to understand.

'I thought you said he was a townsman,' she whispered. 'How could he possibly have stayed at our inn?' Only daimyos ever stayed at their inn. No one else was allowed to – at least that was how it had always been when she was a child.

'Well, you know how things are these days,' said Jiroemon, avoiding her eyes. 'Everything's upside down. He's an important man now, your father.'

There was a long silence.

'He was with the southerners,' Jiroemon muttered finally, staring at the coals. 'With one of the generals. He's a powerful man these days.'

So that was it, that was what Shinzaemon had guessed. A southerner... If he had turned out to be a criminal, this father of hers, if he had turned out to be a gangster or a gambler – she could have lived with that. But marching to Edo with the conquering southerners...?

'You must have passed each other on the road,'

whispered Otama.

'If he's a southerner, he's no father of mine.' The words burst out before she could stop them.

'Don't talk like that!' said Otama. 'He's your real father. If he wants you back, we have to yield. He's family. He has no other child, no heir except you. It's your duty to go to him. It's nothing to do with what you want or don't want.'

'The southerners carry the brocade banner. They're calling themselves the imperial army now,' said Jiroemon heavily. 'They hold the south. Even a girl like you must know that. And they'll probably take Edo. They say the shogun has run away. His supporters are still fighting but they can't do much without a leader. Whether we like it or not, the war is almost over. That's how it looks to us villagers. It could well turn out to be good for you that your father is with the southerners. You'll see.'

'Give us a chance,' muttered Shinzaemon. 'The war isn't over yet, not if I have anything to do with it.' Genzaburo prodded him with his elbow.

'People of our sort can't afford to worry about politics,' said Otama firmly to Sachi. 'He'll find you a good husband. It'll be best for you to go to him.'

Sachi nodded silently. She knew, though they did not, that she had other ties that bound her far more tightly than any obligation to this unknown father who had abandoned her so many years ago. She was joined to His Majesty, the late shogun. She belonged to his family for ever. Whever was their fate was hers too.

IV

Sachi sat gazing into the fire long after everyone had left. Genzaburo and Shinzaemon had gone out on patrol, to see if there were any more southern troops on the way. Genzaburo wanted to show his brother-in-arms the village, he had said, and get in some sparring practice. Only Taki was still there, on her knees in a corner of the room, quietly sewing.

Sachi sat trying to absorb everything she had heard. She had thought she was coming home. Now, instead, she felt she had lost her parents – and as for the village, it seemed to have crumbled into dust, like Urashima. And what had she gained? Some swaggering southerner father and a mother who hardly existed.

The brocade, which had seemed to blaze with a supernatural light, was now just a miserable bundle, lying discarded in the corridor under a heap of belongings. She pulled it out, brought it into the room and began to fumble with the knot. Blinded with tears, she could hardly see. Perhaps it too would swirl away in a puff of smoke, taking her along with it. She almost hoped it would.

But the more she struggled with the knot, the tighter it got. Then suddenly the threads of the worn wrapper gave way and the brocade tumbled out.

It fell open, filling the room with its mysterious silky scent. It was as beautiful as ever, blue as the sky, embroidered with plum, bamboo and pine, the symbols of the New Year, and as soft and fine

327

as a flower petal. Impatiently she shook out the fabric. She turned it this way and that, hardly seeing the landscape which swirled across the hem. In her confusion she could scarcely distinguish top from bottom. Finally she found what she was looking for – the crest embroidered at the back of the neck and on the shoulders.

She reached into her sleeve and brought out her beautiful tortoiseshell comb embossed with gold. It sparkled in her hand. She looked at the crest inlaid in gold on the edge: it was the same as the crest on the brocade. So the brocade, like the comb, had been her mother's. She gazed and gazed at the crest as if it would yield up its secret if she stared long and hard enough. The most frustrating thing was that it seemed somehow familiar.

Taki came over, knelt beside her and gently put her thin arms round her.

'I know,' she said. 'I heard what your parents told you. I'm not surprised. I knew you didn't belong here. These are good people but they're not yours. It's only a distant blood connection you have with them.'

'This crest... It's my mother's. If only I can identify it, I might be able to find her family. And her too.'

Taki picked up the fabric and ran her fingers over it thoughtfully. She turned the comb over and shook her head.

'I've seen it before but I can't remember where,' she said.

They sat in silence, studying the brocade and the comb.

'Well,' Taki said at last, 'I can tell you one thing. This is a concubine's robe. It's a style that only concubines of the shogun's household are allowed to wear. I'd say it's from the court of the twelfth shogun, Lord Ieyoshi. That would make sense, wouldn't it? Wasn't that the time when you were born?'

'I don't know when I was born. It was the year of the dog, that's all I know.'

'You're in your eighteenth year, aren't you, same as me? That year of the dog was an iron dog year. His Majesty would still have been on the throne.'

'So this is a concubine's robe from when I was born...' said Sachi.

'It must be. That's why you were wrapped up in it.'

'But don't you see, Taki? Don't you see what that means? If this was my mother's robe, she ... must be a concubine. Or at least she must have been when I was born. She must have been one of Lord Ieyoshi's concubines!'

'That's not possible,' said Taki sharply. 'Didn't your parents say your real father was a townsman?'

They looked at each other. A concubine of the shogun could never have had an affair with anyone, let alone a low-class townsman. It was inconceivable. It would have been a terrible breach of duty – a shocking crime.

'Perhaps the man who brought you here was not your father,' said Taki. 'Maybe he was instructed to say he was. Maybe he was a courier, a servant...'

329

'Or maybe my mother was not a concubine. Maybe someone gave her the brocade...' whispered Sachi.

She picked up the robe and buried her face in it. It was a woman's scent. What did it tell her? There was musk in it, aloe, wormwood, frankincense, mingled with woodsmoke from the many nights her father had spent on the road.

She spread the brocade across her knees. It was exquisitely soft and fine. The gold and silver threads of the embroidery were stiff with age and crackled as she ran her fingers over them. At the hem, a nobleman's carriage with the harness coiled picturesquely on the ground as if the oxen that pulled it had wandered off; on the skirts, a thatch-roofed doorway with the ropes swinging as if someone had just rushed through and a rustic gate in a bamboo fence; and embroidered across the seam of the sleeve, the veranda of a secret pavilion overlooking a stream... Only a beautiful woman could have worn such a garment.

Supposing it were true, Sachi thought. Supposing her mother really had been a concubine and her father a townsman? That would explain why her mother had not been able to keep her, why she had been brought to the village. Perhaps she had had to be smuggled out to the countryside so that no one would know of her mother's crime. But what kind of a woman would dare do such a thing? Only someone who had let herself be caught up in a passion so consuming that she no longer cared about her duty. And what a secret she had had to keep.

Sachi gasped and sat up sharply. She felt the

blood rush to her face as she thought of Shinzaemon. She had been on the verge of committing that same crime herself. She had not given her body to another man but she had allowed him to enter her heart. Had she inherited her mother's reckless nature? she wondered. Did the same wild blood run in her veins?

For a moment the thought filled her with horror. Perhaps the brocade had revealed its secret as a warning to her. If only she could find her lost mother, then she might understand the wild impulses that drove her too.

She looked at Taki. Taki was staring at her, her big eyes wide. Sachi could see that the same thoughts were running through her mind.

'My mother could still be in the women's palace,' Sachi whispered. 'That could be why no one here knows anything about her.'

'After His Majesty died she would have moved to the Ninomaru, the Second Citadel, where the widows live,' said Taki thoughtfully. 'Like old Lady Honju-in.'

Sachi remembered the old lady, as dry and withered as an autumn leaf. She was the one who had told her, 'You are just a womb.' Sachi and Taki would never have met the other concubines of Lord Ieyoshi. Only Lady Honju-in had had the honour of bearing a son and only she had wielded power in the palace. The rest would have been left to their prayers.

'Taki, I have to find my mother,' said Sachi.

'In that case, we have to get back to Edo immediately,' said Taki. 'The southerners are heading for the city and they'll be determined to take

331

the castle. The women might have fled already and there'll be no chance at all of finding her.'

'But I have to try.'

But the moment Sachi got back to Edo was the moment she would have to say goodbye to Shinzaemon, she thought. The longer they stayed in the village, the more time they had together. Even though their feelings for each other had to be kept secret, she enjoyed knowing he was there, feeling his presence, being able to glance at him from time to time – his great hands, his rather delicate nose, the way his hair bushed out in that unruly way. From time to time she had the chance to pass a little closer to him than was strictly proper, to feel the heat of his body, smell his salty smell. Sometimes their hands brushed or she felt his eyes on her. But once they got to Edo it would be an end to all that. He would join the militia and would most likely be killed. That was what he expected himself.

But she knew she couldn't hold him back for much longer. He was far too wild a character to stay in a remote village or to let his life revolve around a woman for long – though she suspected that he too, knowing he was going to his death, wanted to squeeze all the pleasure he could out of these last moments.

They had packed away the brocade when the outer door creaked open. There was a blast of icy air as Shinzaemon and Genzaburo came in. They slid the door closed and stood in the entrance-way, their cheeks flushed as if they'd just been sparring.

'Well, luck was on his side today,' said Genzaburo, raising his eyebrows wryly as he slipped out of his shoes and wiped his feet before stepping up on to the tatami.

'But you put up a good fight,' said Sachi, smiling at him. He was like a brother, this person from her childhood, so rash and carefree. While she felt weighed down with cares, he was always buoyant, no matter what happened.

He nodded. 'Don't worry about this father nonsense,' he said abruptly. 'I was adopted three times. I've got four fathers and my real mother's probably that prune-faced old sow who runs the House of Orchids. It's the throw of the dice. Your parents care about you. You'll always have a home here.'

'I know,' she said. 'But I don't belong any more. I've been away too long.'

Her eyes were on Shinzaemon. He was putting his long sword in the sword rack. She could see there was something he wanted to say.

'There's been news,' he said quietly. 'Another detachment of southerners on its way out of Kyoto. It's time for me to move on, before they get here. The road should be quiet for the time being. It may be the last chance for quite a while.'

So the moment had come, the moment she had been dreading. But now she knew that she was ready to leave too. She needed to get back to Edo, to the palace, to the princess – and perhaps to her mother.

'I've spent enough time polishing my swords,' said Shinzaemon, staring at the ground, scuffing his feet. She recognized the stubborn set to his jaw. 'They're good and sharp now. I need to get back on the road – to help with the defence. If you want to stay longer, you can go with Gen. He'll be on his way in a few days. But I think you should come with me.'

He spoke carelessly, as if he didn't mind whether she travelled with Genzaburo or with him, but she knew she was being asked to make a choice.

'So ... you're going to Edo,' she said.

Into the hornets' nest. He nodded.

Taki's big eyes were shining. Her whole face had come alive. It was obvious where she wanted to be.

'What do you think, Taki?' Sachi said quietly. 'Perhaps it's time to go back to Edo. We'll take our halberds. Yuki will stay in the village, where she's safe. A child would be an encumbrance and we'll need to travel fast.'

'It's the right decision,' Taki said, beaming. 'But we'll have to take care. The road will be full of southerners – people like that awful pockmarked soldier.'

Sachi looked up at Shinzaemon and smiled.

'Taki and I are coming with you,' she said.

8

Into the Hornets' Nest

I

Jiroemon heaved a sigh when Sachi went to tell him she was leaving, then smiled resignedly, as if he knew it was inevitable, and nodded his great head.

'Edo, is it?' he said. 'If I didn't have an inn to keep and a village to watch over I'd be on the road with you. It's a long way,' he added, sucking slowly on his pipe. 'Eighty-one *ri*. It'll take seven to ten days, I'd say, maybe longer. Depends how much snow there is on the high passes. Let me give you some advice. People always rush at the beginning. Take it slow and steady and take care of your feet. That way they'll be in good shape still at the end. And make sure you get to an inn every evening well before nightfall. You don't want to be walking in the mountains after dark.

'That Shin. He's a good lad and a brave one. He'll take care of you. And remember, keep an eye out for your father when you get to Edo. He'll be keeping an eye out for you.'

Sachi nodded.

'I'll always know I have a father here,' she said, brushing her sleeve across her eyes.

They left the next day. Otama was up long

before dawn, clambering around the woods searching for ferns and horsetail shoots to cook for them. She wiped her eyes with her sleeve as she arranged food in lacquered wooden boxes – the last thing she would ever be able to do for her child. Sachi wept too. It seemed too cruel to have come home for such a short time and to be leaving again to search for a mother who might be no more than a ghost.

But now Sachi had decided to go she knew it was the right thing for all of them. She had to try to find her mother; Taki was totally out of place in the village and yearning to get back to Edo where, even if she couldn't see Toranosuké, at least she'd be a little closer to him; and as for Shinzaemon – she knew he had to be on his way. He had been planning to stay only a couple of days anyway. Heart-rending though it was, they had to move on.

Yuki nodded calmly when Sachi told her she must stay behind. She had found a new home here. She and Chobei had become playmates and Otama and Jiroemon were happy to replace the parents she had lost. Nevertheless Yuki was a warrior child. Sachi knew she would not be happy for long in the village and assured her that when things were more settled she would be back to fetch her if she wanted to leave.

Sachi took with her only the brocade. She left the rest of her belongings behind, with instructions to the family to pawn her robes if they needed money.

The three travellers had so little luggage they hired only a couple of packhorses. They put on mantles, leggings and broad straw travelling hats. Sachi and Taki carried their halberds like staffs. Jiroemon, Otama, Yuki and the children walked them as far as the edge of the village and waved and bowed until they were out of sight. Genzaburo was there too, grinning and shouting, 'See you in Edo!' The smells of woodsmoke and miso soup, the barking of dogs and crowing of cocks faded into the distance. As the village grew small behind them, Sachi could hear Otama's voice calling, fainter and fainter, 'Come back soon,' echoed by Jiroemon's gruff tones. With tears in her eyes she murmured the haiku Basho had written when he too was in Kiso, though in another season:

'*Okuraretsu*   Now being seen off,
Okuritsu hate wa   Now seeing off; and then –
Kiso no aki   Autumn in Kiso.'

Truly, life was nothing but a series of goodbyes, of meeting people and growing close to them, only to be torn apart again. And at the end of this journey there would be yet another goodbye, when Shinzaemon went to join the militia. With a sigh she pushed away the thought.

Even up here in the mountains where the snow was just beginning to melt, a few cherry trees were coming into bud. The previous spring Sachi had been at the castle. She remembered going into the gardens with her women to admire the fragile blossoms, dewy-eyed over the brevity of their beauty and the transience of life. Had it been only a year ago?

As they headed away from the village they heard water rushing and caught a glimpse of the River Kiso glinting far below them. The road wound up into the woods, through forests of cypresses and pine trees and glades of rustling bamboo. The path was paved with stones, cut into steps wherever it became steep. As Jiroemon had advised, they walked slowly and steadily. They had tied bells to their ankles to warn off the black bears that lived in the mountains. When they came across streams they stepped from stone to stone or leaped from rock to rock. Far off they heard the ringing of bells from trains of packhorses making their way along the valley floor and the plod of oxen dragging carts laden with rice or straw or salt.

It was good to be back on the road. Sometimes Shinzaemon loped in front, sometimes he brought up the rear, keeping an eye on the porters and the packhorses. Shyly Sachi ran her eyes across his broad back and unruly hair, and listened to the crunch of his straw sandals on the earthen road and his deep voice as he barked at the porters. She wished she could slow time down, turn every moment into an hour.

They were deep in the mountains, on an unfrequented stretch of highway, making their way through dense forest, when Sachi heard rough voices. There were tall trees all around them, enclosing the path with their great trunks. Her hand tightened on the handle of her halberd. Men burst out of the trees ahead of them, brandishing staffs and sickles. Bandits.

One charged straight up to Sachi, pressing his

338

face close to hers.

'Toll,' he growled, holding out a blackened hand, palm upwards. He spoke in Kiso dialect. 'Give us a thousand copper *mon*.'

The man had a thin pointed face like a rat. His mouth was a gaping cavern with a few yellow teeth surrounded by blackened stumps. His clothes were ragged and dirty, but his arms were sinewy and his little eyes glittered hungrily. His hair was tied in a greasy knot. She had heard of characters like these, low life who haunted the gambling dens in the poorest parts of town. In normal times their paths would never have crossed. What had happened to the officials who policed the highway? It seemed that the order everyone had always taken for granted had entirely broken down. She stepped back in disgust but the man came after her.

'Nah, tell you what,' he said, jerking his head towards the horses. 'We'll 'ave those. That'll do us.' Some of the men were already scrambling to grab the reins of the packhorses. They meant to take the brocade!

Sachi looked round desperately. There were ten, maybe twenty gangsters against her, Taki and Shinzaemon. She was about to slide off the sheath of her halberd when the man grabbed her wrists, gripping them hard in his bony hands. Scrawny though he was, he was very strong. She struggled fiercely, tears of frustration coming to her eyes.

Suddenly there was a hissing intake of breath. Rough voices gasped, *'Hora!'* followed by utter silence. The bandits had frozen in their tracks.

339

She looked at them in amazement. Their mouths were hanging open and their eyes popping.

She spun round. Shinzaemon had been bringing up the rear. He had thrown off the right sleeve of his kimono to free his sword arm, revealing his brawny shoulder and the cherry blossom tattoo. Some of the gangsters and the grooms who led the packhorses had tattoos that covered them from elbow to knee to neck like a second skin – scenes of warriors, geishas and kabuki actors, exquisitely pricked and coloured, as gorgeous as woodblock prints. Shinzaemon's was quite different. It was plain and unassuming.

His sword was in his hand. He looked at them and frowned slightly, then a glimmer of a grin crossed his face as if he was looking forward to some fun.

The next moment the bandits had crumpled to their knees on the stony path and were thumping their heads on the ground.

'Sorry, master, sorry,' they spluttered. 'Forgive us, forgive us. Have mercy.'

Shinzaemon's grin broadened. He took a long wistful look at his sword then slowly and deliberately slid it into its scabbard. He pulled his kimono back over his shoulder and gestured with his chin. The bandits turned tail and fled into the forest.

Sachi was watching in amazement. The tattoo had certainly not had that effect on the southern soldiers they had encountered. There was so much she didn't know about Shinzaemon – where he'd been, what he'd done in his life.

'Well,' said Taki in a low voice, once they were

well on their way again. 'That was lucky. So we don't have to worry about bandits with Shin around.'

That night at the post town they checked into a simple inn, the sort of place where ordinary travellers – such as they were supposed to be – would stay. Men and women slept together in the same room and even had to lay out their own bedding.

Once they had settled Taki in, Sachi and Shinzaemon sat on a bench in front of the inn. Stars glittered in the black sky. It was so dark they couldn't even see the silhouettes of the mountains. Water rushed through the drainage channels and every now and then animals rustled through the undergrowth in the woods behind them.

Sachi took a puff of her long-stemmed pipe. Like everyone in the women's palace, where she'd first taken up the practice, she enjoyed the occasional smoke. The embers glowed red and a spray of sparks lit up the darkness. They were sitting close together, not quite touching.

'I've never seen the stars so bright,' said Shinzaemon softly. 'I never expected to be somewhere like this with ... someone like you.'

They talked into the night. Sachi told him about her childhood in the village – about swimming in the river, about the time Genzaburo fought a wild boar, about the seasons in the mountains, the processions that went through and the daimyos who stayed at the inn. Finally she told him about the princess, how her procession had been so long it had taken four days to pass and how she had swept Sachi up and ordered that she be brought to Edo Castle. Then her story stopped. She didn't tell him about the palace or the shogun and he didn't ask.

'I spent a lot of time in the mountains too,' he said. 'I used to go out with bear hunters when I was a child. I got into a lot of fights. My parents were always angry at me. But then I found something useful to do with my sword.'

'What about your tattoo?' she asked shyly. 'Will you tell me about it?'

'I always wanted to improve my swordsmanship, especially once the troubles began. I spent a year at the Military Academy in Edo. Then I heard of a master swordsman who was the last proponent of the "hand of the Buddha" technique. He'd retired by then. I went and stayed with him in the snow country for a while. He was a great master. Once we'd been initiated, we disciples were allowed to have a cherry blossom tattoo like his pricked on our shoulders. The gangsters all over central Japan seem to know it. Ever since then I've had no trouble with them at all. It's my master, not me, that they're afraid of. Or maybe it's the hand of the Buddha. Maybe they'd rather not find out what the secret technique is all about.'

She could hear him chuckling quietly in the darkness.

They said nothing about the future. With each day that passed they were getting closer and closer to Edo and to the moment of their parting.

Day after day they walked, dwarfed by the towering crags like tiny figures in an ink painting. Sometimes the road was crowded, other times the little party walked alone. They toiled up snow-covered passes, gazing awestruck at the peaks soaring above them. They prayed at the shrines at the top, begging the gods to keep them safe. At times they climbed between trees that soared straight towards the sky, topped with foliage so dense that the road was as dark as night. They clambered across rocks, wobbled across flimsy bridges swaying above dizzying ravines, forded waterfalls and streams and picked their way across tracts of ice and snow. Sometimes, in places where the snow had melted, they had to wade through mud up to their knees.

They had become part of the endless procession that populated the highway. They plodded along, stopping every now and then to adjust the cords of their straw sandals and rub their sore legs and aching feet. They carried spare sandals dangling from their belts and threw away the old ones when they broke. When it rained or the weather turned cold they put on raincoats of straw and walked along like small moving haystacks. When the sun blazed they sheltered under straw hats. No one who saw them in their soiled travelling clothes would ever have guessed Sachi and Taki were court ladies.

Each morning Sachi put on a new pair of straw sandals, hitched up her kimono skirts, picked up her halberd and set off full of determination. She felt stronger with each day that passed, though her feet became more and more chafed and sore no matter how many times she changed her sandals.

Taki too was striding out like a country girl. She had colour in her pale cheeks and her big eyes were sparkling. She no longer complained about the cold and the hardship. Sachi could see that she was excited, knowing she was on her way to Edo – on her way home.

Sachi knew she should have been excited too. She was going back to the palace, to the princess – to the place where, she told herself again and again, she would find her mother. Yet with every day that passed she knew she was a day nearer to the moment when she would have to say goodbye to Shinzaemon.

In the evenings Shinzaemon and Sachi sat together. Sometimes they talked, sometimes they didn't. They spoke of the events of the day, of their childhoods, of books they had read and music and poetry they loved. Sometimes their hands brushed. They were both aware that what they were doing was wrong, but here on the road they were anonymous. Anyway, they were heading for war. Shinzaemon expected to die and Sachi had no idea what would happen to her.

Seven days after they had left the village they toiled up Usui Pass, the last of the four high passes along the Inner Mountain Road. It was a long hard climb. Standing at the top, breathing in the thin cool air, they gazed out across the Kanto plain. Somewhere way out there lay Edo. Shadowy peaks rose in the distance, fringing the plain like the battlements of a fortress. Shinzaemon pointed out the angular shapes of Mount Miyogi, Mount

344

Haruna and Mount Akagi. Far away to the south, shimmering on the horizon, was a ghostly shape – the perfect cone of Mount Fuji. They prayed at the Kumano Shrine at the top of the pass, then set off, slipping and sliding down treacherous shale, along the top of the ridge and down to the post town of Sakamoto. As they descended lower and lower the heat came up to meet them. They were moving from winter to spring.

The following evening they reached the castle town of Takasaki. They left before dawn. They could not help noticing bodies tied to crosses at the edge of the city as a warning to lawless characters who might think of taking advantage of the chaos to attack travellers. The mountains loomed behind them, monstrous shapes in the darkness, filling the sky. From now on they would be walking across the plains.

Around the hour of the horse, when the sun was high in the sky, they came to a river too wide and fast-flowing to ford.

'The River Toné,' said Shinzaemon. 'Once we've crossed it we're on the last stretch.'

The river was in flood, swollen with melting snow. The houses on the far side were like houses in a painted landscape. On the bank people peered anxiously out across the water. An ancient flat-bottomed ferry boat was zigzagging precariously towards them, propelled by a bald-headed ferryman heaving and shoving a long bamboo pole while another squatted in the stern, steering. The wind rustled the reeds at the water's edge.

A gnarled old man with a money belt around his waist growled something in a dialect so uncouth that Sachi couldn't make out a word.

'What? That's ten times the proper rate,' Shin-zaemon yelled. 'Greedy wretch! The country's up in flames and all you can think about is how much money you can make out of it?'

'Sorry, your lordship,' squawked the old man. Sachi was becoming attuned to the accent. 'That's the rate, your honour. Take it or leave it. Or find your own way across.'

The boat creaked and groaned towards them, so jam-packed it looked as if it would sink under the weight of people and goods. The boatman leaned hard on his pole, nearly toppling into the water with each stroke. There were porters crowded in the stern, standing miserably around a pile of strongboxes, shivering and pale, wearing nothing but loincloths. In the prow were some well-fed characters who looked like the owners of the porters. There was a furtive air about them. From time to time they glanced over their shoulders as if they were being followed. Keeping her scarf pulled well across her face, Sachi peeped at them curiously.

They looked like Edo merchants, like the merchants she used to see bringing rolls of silk to the palace to sell. They were wearing costly gowns in rich fabrics, drab on the outside but with lustrous linings visible at the cuffs and collar. But there was something strange about these supposed merchants. The men grouped around them had two swords poking out from beneath their towns-men's cloaks and seemed to be guarding the three in the middle, whose faces were shaded under travelling hats.

The prow of the ferry pushed up on to the riverbank with a great swell of water and the men stepped out, so close to Sachi that she could have reached out and touched them. As the first man brushed past her, the wind rippled his sleeves and for a moment a faint hint of perfume scented the air. Sachi closed her eyes and inhaled. It was a plum blossom blend, mild and sweet, a winter scent with a hint of camellias. This man was no merchant, she thought. No merchant would ever have access to a sophisticated fragrance like that or be allowed to wear it. There was something familiar about it. An obscure memory stirred in her mind.

For a moment she was back in the palace, gliding through the great chambers with their coffered ceilings and walls glimmering with gold, the quilted hem of her train swishing behind her. The women she passed were talking and laughing, each of them with her own distinctive perfume. She was hurrying, with Taki, following Lady Tsuguko who strode in front, her long hair streaked with grey sweeping the ground. But where to, and why? She groped in her mind, trying to remember. The fragrance gave her a terrible sense of foreboding.

She opened her eyes. Glancing down she saw the man's hand. It was soft and white, fleshy and manicured like a woman's. A shock tingled through her body. It had been pressed to the tatami in the princess's audience chamber. The scent was so overwhelming she felt herself growing dizzy. A man's silken tones echoed in her ears, whispering again and again in the convoluted

347

language of the court that His Majesty the shogun was gravely ill.

His Majesty the shogun. She saw his smooth pale chest, his boyish smile. She had thought with time the pain would become less intense but she felt hot tears spring to her eyes. Then she pictured the princess weeping behind her screens and heard her asking, 'Oguri. Oguri. His Majesty's illness – is it natural?' Oguri. That had been his name.

Recklessly she raised her head. There was no mistaking that bland, doughy face with the shifty-eyed look of the eternal courtier. For a moment their eyes met. His registered nothing. Of course, she had been hidden that day so he had not seen her.

A younger man followed him. He was still a boy, no older than Tatsuemon. Then came the third. She was so swept up in her memories, so shocked at seeing Lord Oguri again, that she let her scarf fall away from her face. She knew her white skin, delicately boned nose and dark green eyes stood out in the crowd and it was important not to draw attention to herself. But everyone was so concerned with their own business, no one would notice. Besides, these men had never seen her before. She meant nothing to them.

She recognized the craggy hawk-like face passing before her – a swarthy heavy-jowled face, scarred with the marks of smallpox, with a mouth that creased naturally into a scowl. The man's samurai topknot lay, hard and shiny, on top of his tanned, leathery head. It was Lord Mizuno, who had been Lord Oguri's companion on that

348

dreadful day.

His eyes met hers – and his face dissolved with shock. His thick-lipped mouth fell open and he started backwards as if he had seen a ghost.

'Go! Go! Let me alone! Leave me be!' he bellowed. His sword arm twitched – she remembered that odd twitch of his – and the guards reached for their sword hilts. His eyes were starting out of his head, his mouth wide open in a silent scream.

Oguri swung round, glaring.

'Silence,' he hissed in a strangled voice. 'You want to destroy us all with your madness?'

The men pushed through the crowds, the bodyguards thrusting people aside to make way for them, and scrambled into palanquins. Lord Mizuno was still looking back, staring at Sachi wild-eyed. She watched as they moved away from the river, towards the mountains, followed by a long train of porters staggering under the weight of strongboxes, four men to a box.

Taki was standing at Sachi's shoulder. 'Those men... Did you see them?' she murmured. 'Wasn't it...?'

But Sachi was still incredulous, aghast at Mizuno's behaviour. Had he somehow managed to see her that day? Surely not. It was impossible that he could know her. But there was no other time they might have met. That was the only time she had ever seen men of any sort in the women's palace. And to see these men out here on the road... She wondered what could have made him react like that.

'Things must be very bad in Edo if even they're

leaving,' whispered Taki. 'And the way he looked at you. What did it mean?'

Sachi shook her head. 'I suppose they're just not used to seeing women travelling freely,' she whispered. She flushed red, burning with shame that she had been so foolish as to draw these men's attention by letting her veil fall. She must never be so careless again.

The ferry going towards Edo was nearly empty. Besides Sachi, Taki and Shinzaemon and their porters there were only a couple of farmers on it. The water was in full flood and it was all the ferryman could do to hang on to his pole as the boat bobbed across the swell. Sachi, Taki and Shinzaemon were tossed from side to side while a cold wind whipped through their thin cotton clothes. Icy foam showered them with stinging spray. Gulls flapped overhead and wild geese shrieked.

The bank on the Edo side was crammed with frightened faces and heaps of baggage. People shoved and pushed, elbowing each other out of the way, yelling, 'My old mother's ill, she needs to go first,' and 'We're in a hurry, we were here first.' The boatmen shoved them off, bawling, 'Get back. Boat's full.' There were people clinging to the sides and crowded on to the bows. By the time the ferry left it was riding dangerously low in the water.

The three travellers tramped through woods and moorland and between brown paddy fields ploughed and ready for planting. Temples and villages jutted like islands in a sea of green and shops and stalls dotted the highway. Clouds scudded across the sky. It was only twenty *ri* to Edo – just a couple more days to go.

Shinzaemon slowed his pace and he and Sachi walked together. From time to time she glanced up at him – his broad nose, his wild hair, his big hands, his cheekbones – trying to fix the memory in her mind, knowing what a short time was left to them.

As they got closer to Edo they met more and more grim-faced refugees shuffling wearily along, hauling carts piled high with belongings. The road was overflowing with them. There were long processions of palanquins and litters jogging along at a trot, preceded by servants and followed by trains of packhorses and porters carrying baskets and trunks strung on poles. Poorer folk tramped along bent under bundles of bedding and clothes, overtaking oxcarts pulled by sleepy oxen. There were shaven-headed monks, nuns mumbling prayers and ragged beggars, all skin and bone, calling out for alms. Groups of pilgrims ambled along, gossiping, as if nothing in the world had changed.

Some were humming that maddening, defiant, hopeless chorus: *'Ee ja nai ka? Ee ja nai ka?* Who gives a damn? Who gives a damn?' Others took up the refrain and soon the whole road was full of people singing, some under their breath, others at the tops of their voices. The more they repeated the meaningless phrase, the more wild their eyes became. Some even began to hop and skip. With everything falling apart, the song seemed to say, what else was there to do except throw up your hands and dance?

Sachi and Taki scoured the blank, exhausted faces, wondering if there were any women from the palace among them. Every now and then there was a warning shout in the distance. As people scrambled to get out of the way an express palanquin would go flying by, the bearers kicking up the dust with their straw-sandalled feet.

Sachi and her companions were the only ones going towards Edo. Everyone else was fleeing the city.

They took the long bridge across the River Kanna at Honjo and rested in a teahouse on the other side. A group of men were sitting there, puffing small pipes. They were dressed as towns-men but talked like samurai. Everyone seemed to be in disguise.

'Which way are you headed?' asked one. He was a mousy little man – his false topknot had slipped a little – who looked as if he had spent his life bent over account books, lodged in one of the miserable apartment blocks where low-level samurai lived. Sachi suspected he would have no idea what to do if he ever found himself in a fight.

Shinzaemon took a puff of his pipe and jerked his head to the south, towards Edo.

The man drew his breath through his teeth with a sharp hiss.

'Wouldn't do that,' he muttered, blinking behind his glasses and glancing over his shoulder. 'Everyone's getting out. It's a dead city. The southerners are at the gates. They've got a check-point at Itabashi and they're interrogating every-one. Word is they're at Shinagawa too. They've got control of the Inner Mountain Road and the Eastern Sea Road. City's under siege. I should turn right round if I was you.'

'We're only women,' Sachi piped up. She spoke in Kiso dialect to conceal the fact she was a lady of the court. 'They won't bother us.'

'You can't go walking the streets,' said the man, nervously sipping his tea. 'Too dangerous by far. Most of the samurai have left and there's no one keeping order. Thugs and hoodlums all over the place. It's a free-for-all.'

'Most of those so-called hoodlums are south-erners,' said another man. He too looked like a samurai in disguise. 'Stirring up trouble.'

Sachi yearned to ask about the castle. But ordinary people like these knew nothing about the castle or its inhabitants. All she could do was listen hard and hope she might hear some news.

The road wound through marshland and paddy fields and great swathes of safflower just coming into bloom, stretching away to the distant hills. There were thatched teahouses and stalls at regular intervals for travellers to rest, and groves of cherry trees.

They were trudging on against the tide when they saw a group of southerners ahead of them. They were easy to spot – squat, brawny men with narrow eyes and leathery faces, dressed in those strange tight black uniforms. Some had conical helmets, others white headbands. They looked like a bunch of roughnecks who had broken away from the main army and were out for trouble, harassing the northerners fleeing Edo.

They were waiting belligerently, filling the

entire road. Sachi realized they had no choice but to try to weave their way through them. She walked quickly, head bowed, keeping her eyes on the ground, hoping that if she imagined herself invisible, she would be. She was right in the middle of the crowd of soldiers when she raised her eyes and peeked through the fabric hanging down like a veil from her hat. She started. It couldn't be... Desperately she prayed that it was not. She knew that swarthy pockmarked face.

At the same moment the man leaned forward, staring hard at her. A grimy hand shot out and snatched her hat off her head. She grabbed at it but it was gone.

'Well, if it isn't...' he shouted. 'That peasant. That pretty little pale-faced peasant!'

He gripped her clothes and dragged her up against him. She struggled frantically but he was very strong.

'Remember me?' he sneered, rubbing his greasy face against hers and squinting at her with his small close-set eyes. He reeked of dirt and stale sweat.

Sachi twisted her head away and recoiled in disgust. She knew that peasants were fair game and women even more so. Samurai could legally cut a peasant's head off with impunity – though she was not at all sure that this man was a samurai. In any case, it was wartime and soldiers did as they pleased. Passers-by were slowing their pace, turning to gawp. She knew very well that none of them would dream of getting hurt to defend her.

'No,' she muttered grimly, trying to push the

man away. Terrified not for herself but for Shinzaemon, she glanced around to see what was happening to him and to Taki. She knew these men had been looking for him the night they had burst into her parents' house.

Her heart pounding, she shoved the man in the chest with all her might. He let go his hold and stumbled back.

'Enough,' muttered one of the other soldiers. 'Let's go. Gonna be in trouble.'

But the pockmarked man's eyes were glittering. His hand was on his sword hilt.

'Excuse us,' Sachi said in Kiso dialect. 'Inexcusable to cause you trouble. Please allow us to pass.'

For a long moment the soldiers hesitated. Sachi took a few more paces through the crowd, followed by Taki and Shinzaemon. Passers-by were gathering to watch, keeping a safe distance. Smoke rose from the roofs of the little shops that lined the road. The cherry trees were covered in pink buds. Everything was very clear and sharp, as if she was seeing it for the last time. Her mind was clear too. She was ready for whatever might happen.

One of the soldiers stepped up to her, blocking her path.

'Hey. What you peasants doing with weapons like that?' he barked. 'It's against the law. Hand them over and you can be on your way.'

Then the pockmarked man barked, 'Wait.'

He was staring at Shinzaemon. 'This man 'ere. I've seen 'im before. Isn't he the one that killed our comrades back in Kiso? That ... that outlaw.

355

And on his own? Let's have a look at your shoulder, fellow!'

The soldiers turned to him, nodding. Shinzaemon had stopped in his tracks. He ran his eyes over them with a contemptuous curl of his lip. His eyebrows came together in a frown of concentration. Sachi could see he was working out the odds. Fifteen, maybe twenty, of them and one of him. But he had a couple of women to protect, so he couldn't take risks. He had to stay alive, no matter what.

He's lived all these years, she told herself. He's not going to die yet and neither are we.

She had her halberd in her hand. She had been using it as a staff. In a moment she had slipped off the cover and the scabbard. Dazzling shards of sunlight reflected off the blade. In her head she was back in the training hall at the palace. She could hear Lady Masa's deep voice urging them not to think, to empty their minds, to let their bodies move. The halberd was heavy, heavier than a practice stick. When she swung it, it had a momentum of its own. It made her feel tall and strong and confident to have it in her hand.

She glanced at Taki. She had never seen her look so alive. Her eyes were gleaming. She too had unsheathed her halberd. They had never yet had a chance to fight with them. Now was the moment to put all those years of training to the test.

If they died, Sachi thought, they would die all three together. She drew herself up. She was ready.

Without warning a couple of soldiers drew

356

their swords and lunged at Shinzaemon. But he was faster. With a yell he parried the blows. A hand flew into the air. The two men staggered back. One was still holding out his arm, blood spraying from the end.

Shinzaemon kept his eyes on the soldiers as he wiped the blood off his blade.

Several of the men drew their swords. Blades glinted in the sun, flashing like lightning. There was the scuffle of feet. Metal rang on metal with a deafening clang and clash. Then there were shrieks and groans. Men in black uniforms were staggering back, blood spurting. One had blood pouring from his arm; another's jaw was hanging loose. One was clutching at his stomach where his guts were spilling out.

Shinzaemon was still standing. Taki rushed to his side, swinging her halberd.

Sachi was behind her.

'These aren't peasants,' she heard one of the southerners say. She had known it would be obvious as soon as they took up their weapons. Only samurai women carried halberds or could fight with them. And they were not just samurai women but women of the shogun's court, trained to fight well enough to defend the shogun himself.

The pockmarked man had seen his chance. Sword drawn, he stepped in front of her. Sachi raised her halberd.

'Now don't do anything silly,' he jeered, his pitted face breaking into a grin. 'You'll only hurt yourself.'

He edged around, keeping a safe distance from

357

her blade. She stood, poised, halberd pointing towards him. As he moved round, she moved too. She knew the halberd could outreach his sword. She needed to keep him at a distance. If they got close enough to spar, he was stronger than her. Her heart was pounding but she kept her mind focused and her breathing very calm.

'Not gonna spoil your pretty face,' he yelled above the scrape and clang of blades. 'Just put down that silly weapon and you'll be fine.'

Sachi said nothing. She was holding the halberd in both hands, keeping her eyes fixed on his every move. If he came within reach she would have him.

They danced forward and back. Grinning, he took a step towards her. She saw the sun glint as he raised his sword. With a yell she lunged forward and swung the halberd, slicing through his trouser and nicking the front of his calf. She raised her weapon and spun round, ready for the next blow. He leaped back with a yowl, his face twisted in pain. There was a wet stain growing larger on the black of his trouser leg.

'Now I'm angry,' he roared. His face blackened and swelled like a bullfrog's as he bore down on her, swinging his sword with both hands. But the halberd was longer.

Sachi was poised, balanced, waiting. He raised his sword. She sprang forward and caught the blow on the blade of her halberd. There was an ear-splitting clang. The force of the blow sent her staggering back a few steps. She slipped and put her hand out to steady herself. As she looked up, she saw the sword flashing through the air towards her. Before she had time to breathe she had raised her halberd and parried the blow. She gave the blade a twist. She felt the rush of air, smelt the vile stale smell of the man as he stumbled clumsily forward, caught off balance by his own momentum.

She leaped to her feet and spun round on her toes, pointing the halberd at his chest. Her hair had come loose and fallen across her face. She felt no fear, only a sort of wild elation.

Out of the corner of her eye she could see Shinzaemon fighting like a madman, striking, stabbing, parrying blows, thrusting his sword into men's chests and slashing them about the face. Taki was at his side, lashing out with her halberd as the southerners' bodies piled up in a bloody heap in front of them. But they were being driven inexorably back by the onslaught. She needed to finish this quickly and help them.

The man scrambled to his feet, roaring like a wounded beast. He charged towards her. She saw the hatred in his little black eyes. The sounds and noise of battle – the metallic clangs and crashes, Shinzaemon's war cries, the yowls of pain – faded away. There was an eerie silence. In the whole world there were just the two of them. Her halberd had become a part of her, an extension of her body.

She focused on his eyes. He swung his sword. She leaped back as it crashed down on the blade of her halberd. Then she darted forward and dropped to one knee.

Very deliberately she swung the halberd, aiming for his throat. She could feel the heaviness of the blade, the momentum of it, and hear the hiss as it curved through the air.

Then suddenly the pockmarked head was spinning upwards. She looked at the halberd in amazement. The blade had passed through the man's muscular neck as smoothly as a knife through water.

The headless body staggered on, blood spouting in a fountain from the neck, then lurched to one side and crumpled. The head rolled across the road and flopped into the gutter. The water divided around it, running red where it had landed.

She awoke as if from a trance and darted into the fray. She could see that Shinzaemon had been hurt. He was fighting left-handed, with blood streaming from his right arm. And no matter how many southerners fell, more took up the attack.

Suddenly there was a bang, ear-shatteringly loud. Sachi started and looked around frantically. She knew the sound though she had never heard it so close to hand. Gunfire. Everyone froze. There was another shot.

Half the southerners were sprawled on the ground, groaning or screaming in pain. Some lay silent. Taki and Shinzaemon leaned on their weapons, wiping blood and sweat from their faces. Their clothes were in tatters, their hair sticking out wildly, but apart from the wound on Shinzaemon's arm they seemed to be all right.

Sachi ran up to him. 'I'm fine,' he said, grimacing as he tore off a piece of his kimono skirts to bind the wound. 'Just another scar.'

Passers-by were standing at a safe distance to watch, blank-faced. At the sound of the shots everyone had gone deadly quiet. Then they started shrieking and running in every direction.

In the turmoil, no one had noticed some palanquins appearing accompanied by an escort of samurai. Two creatures leaped out and stormed into the crowd, holding guns above their heads. Smoke coiled from the barrels.

But were they men or ogres? They had two eyes, two ears and two hands, but they were huge and brawny, like giants. Their heads and shoulders poked above the crowd. Their faces were craggy, not smooth and round, and their noses jutted out, monstrously big. Could they be *tengu*, the long-nosed goblins that lived in the mountains? But *tengu* had red faces. These creatures were deathly pale like ghosts. One had hair the colour of rice stalks in autumn, while the other's hair was the colour of earth. And they were wearing strange outlandish clothes like nothing Sachi had ever seen before.

The crowd surged back as the creatures burst through. Some fell to their knees and pressed their heads to the ground. Others stood transfixed, their mouths gaping in shock. Some of the women screamed and ran away.

The straw-headed one paid no attention. He marched straight into the middle of the battlefield, stepping across the groaning southern soldiers. A rank smell hung about him like fog. It was the smell of the outcastes, of those who dealt in butchery – the smell of meat, of dead flesh.

Of course. These were not *tengu* at all but

361

something far more frightening and weird. *Tojin* – foreigners. Sachi had heard talk of the 'stinking barbarians' but she had never met anyone who had actually seen one. As far as she knew, they were restricted to a tiny village outside Edo called Yokohama, a port near Osaka and a handful of other ports. She had certainly seen the Yokohama prints that depicted these exotic creatures with their fearsome noses, strange costumes and extraordinary dwellings. There had been plenty of these woodblock prints at the women's palace. She had also heard – indeed, everyone seemed to know – that the original cause of the southerners' uprising had been that none of the shoguns had been able to drive the barbarians out. That had been the pretext, at any rate, for their rebellion.

Now the foreigner opened his mouth and shouted. Sachi drew herself up and looked straight at him. She was not going to run away or shriek. She must never forget she was the Retired Lady Shoko-in, the concubine of His late Majesty. She gestured at his gun. What was he going to do? Did he mean to shoot them all?

He stared at her with his strange pale eyes. It made her feel uncomfortable. She wished she could conceal her face, but she had lost her hat and veil. He spoke again. His voice was so loud it made her start. To her amazement she realized she could understand him. He was speaking a stilted version of her language, though with an odd distorted accent.

'No worry, madam. I shoot in the air only. Can I help you? Are you all right?'

He barked at the southerners, 'What's this?

Attacking ladies? So many against one man? Shame on you.'

The few southerners still on their feet stared at the ground, scowling. They were panting, bruised, bloodied, their black uniforms ripped, their hair wild.

'This man is an outlaw,' snarled one, gesturing at Shinzaemon.

'That's not true,' Sachi protested fiercely. She was thinking fast. 'He's my ... bodyguard. He was protecting me and my maid – my friend.'

The southern soldiers were whispering to each other. Their swords were still unsheathed, their fingers twitching on the hilts.

'Interfering barbarians!' hissed one. 'We'll get you. Just you wait!'

'I think you have forgotten the emperor's proclamation,' said the foreigner smoothly. His gun was still in his hand. It looked new and shiny, quite unlike the ancient matchlocks that people had in Kiso. 'No more killing of foreigners. You southerners, you call yourselves the emperor's men. Do you have no respect for His Grace's decree?'

He turned back to Sachi.

'Madam,' he said. 'You go to Edo? We too. We escort you – you, your friend and your bodyguard. Travel with us. Our guards protect you. No need to worry.'

Sachi stared at him in shock. Travel with wild, unpredictable creatures like these? She knew nothing of them. With ordinary people – people of her country – she could read their faces, understand their feelings beneath the forms and

363

words that etiquette prescribed. But with barbarians like these, she had no idea what went on in their minds. It was the craziest notion she had ever heard.

Yet ... it was wartime. The road was undoubtedly dangerous and Edo even more so. The barbarians had guns and a samurai escort bristling with swords and staves – though who those samurai were was another question. Which side were they on? Who did they report to? They were undoubtedly spies, delegated to keep an eye on the barbarians. If she and her companions travelled with them, they would have to guard their speech.

But though Shinzaemon could fight like a demon, there was only one of him. The most important thing now was to finish their journey, to get to Edo – to the princess, perhaps to her mother – before the southerners sealed the city off completely.

She glanced at Taki. Taki was wiping her halberd blade on her skirts. Her hair had come loose and stuck out in a great tangled bush. Her thin face was sticky with southerners' blood but her big eyes shone with a mad triumphant gleam. She looked back at Sachi, raised her eyebrows and tilted her head to one side as if to say, 'Do whatever you like. Things can't get any worse.'

Shinzaemon had sheathed his sword and was tearing off a piece of cotton to make a sling for his injured arm. He looked at her, shrugged his broad shoulders and muttered, 'What choice do we have?'

She sighed and inclined her head. 'Thank you,' she said.

The barbarian took off his hat and bowed stiffly.

'My name is Edwards,' he said. 'Edowadzu.'

She tried out the syllables. 'Edo-wadzu.' Like Edo, the city of Edo. It was the strangest name she'd ever heard.

The man with the earth-coloured hair stepped forward.

'Satow. At your service. By all means, please join us.'

II

The two giants rode in ungainly palanquins built to accommodate their long legs, carried by six bearers each, followed by their servants in two normal palanquins and a train of porters with their belongings. Sachi, Taki and Shinzaemon walked behind with their packhorses. The samurai escort marched in front and behind. Mobs pushed in the other direction – samurai retainers from daimyo households trudging along with grim determination, merchants followed by endless trains of porters carrying baskets of belongings, beggars and threatening vaguely military-looking men hiding their faces under deep straw hats. But travelling with the foreigners and their guard they finally felt safe.

The next town was overflowing with people. Crowds filled the street, clamouring and pushing. *'Tojin! Tojin!* Foreigners! Foreigners!' they shouted. Sachi heard other cries: 'Stupid barbarians. Throw out the barbarians. Clear off!' She hoped the foreigners could not understand them. The mobs were all staring, elbowing each other out of the way, doing their best to get a glimpse inside the palanquins. The samurai shoved them aside with their staves, barking, 'On your knees. Get down!' No one paid the slightest attention to Sachi, Taki and Shinzaemon. Everyone was far too busy trying to see the *tojin*.

The highway wound on, along the side of a river, through rice fields bordered with cherry trees just coming into bloom, with misty hills rising in the distance. Once they were clear of the town, the bearers set down the palanquins and the foreigners clambered out, groaning and stretching their long legs. What strange creatures they were, thought Sachi. How could they be so uncomfortable when they were riding in such big luxurious palanquins? Instead of sandals, their sandal-bearers carried big, shiny boots for them which smelt of animal hide. They pulled them on with sighs of relief and set off again on foot.

Sachi, Taki and Shinzaemon kept their distance. Taki, usually so fearless, seemed terrified of these extraordinary beings. Shinzaemon had spent so much time on the road he had certainly come across such creatures before. No doubt he hated them as much as everyone else did, and would have loved to cut them down, but he was also aware that attacking foreigners was against not just the emperor's decree but the policy of the retired shogun, his liege lord. No matter what he felt, he had to behave civilly towards them. She could see from the scowl on his face and the way he held his shoulders, his fingers drumming

366

on the hilt of his sword, what a mighty effort he was making. Even worse, he had to bear the humiliation of being described as a bodyguard. No wonder he looked surly.

After a while the straw-headed man dropped back.

'May I walk with you?' he asked Sachi.

It was all Sachi could do not to laugh. He was hideous. He had hair sprouting from his face, like the fearsome moustaches that bristled on samurai's helmets. And the smell... Besides, the idea of a samurai woman walking alongside a man who was not even a family member (as Shinzaemon, in effect, had become) was totally improper. But then, she reflected, he was only a barbarian – and a barbarian was not a man at all. It would be like walking with a bear or a monkey.

She glanced behind her. Shinzaemon was loping along as if he was paying no attention to anything, but she knew he saw and heard everything.

'Where do you go in Edo?' the barbarian asked boldly, looking down at her.

She was shocked at the directness of the question and also afraid. Ordinary people didn't ask direct questions, especially at a time like this when nobody knew which side anyone else was on. 'Have you been to Edo before?' she asked, hoping that he might let slip some clue.

'We live there,' he said. 'We have a house. A small house beside a temple. On a hill.'

She had thought he must be old because of the hair on his face and his strange coarse-textured skin. But his voice was boyish. He couldn't be many years older than her. Where were his mother and father? What was he doing so far from home, travelling through this foreign country that was on the brink of war?

'Everyone else is leaving Edo and we're going there!' he said as if in answer to her unspoken question, showing his teeth in a grin. 'People say there's going to be a terrible battle but you don't seem worried, not at all. I've never before seen a woman who can fight like you!'

As he spoke he flapped his hands. They were large and powerful, bigger even than Shinzaemon's swordsman's hands. And the colour! As white as chalk. The pale hair on the fingers shone like gold threads in the sunlight. Perhaps he was not such a monster. Certainly he was not of the same race as her, but it seemed he was human after all.

Sachi had heard that barbarians were rough and uncivilized, that they had no manners, that they got violent when they were drunk, that they brawled and raped women. But close up they didn't seem so bad. It was hard to believe she was really walking and talking with creatures like these. If the country had not been at war, if she had not been full of apprehension about what would happen when they got to Edo, it might have been thrilling, an experience to savour, to tell her grandchildren about.

She could feel Shinzaemon's eyes on her. She was aware that while she might think the foreigner was only a barbarian, Shinzaemon knew perfectly well he was a man. She could sense Taki's disapproval too. But after all, she was the mistress and Taki the maid, and she had to be civil to their hosts. And actually she was rather enjoying herself talking to this great lumbering creature.

He worked for the British Legation, he told her, though he said little about where they had been and nothing about the purpose of their journey. No doubt they were on some secret mission.

'We've had great adventures,' he added. 'We've seen the most glorious things. Mount Fuji! Did you come that way? Did you cross Shiojiri Pass and see Mount Fuji on the horizon? I've never seen anything so beautiful. The weather was perfect!'

'Your country...' she murmured hesitantly, 'must be beautiful too.'

He came, he told her, from a small island a long way away. It had taken him two months to reach her country. His was ruled by an empress who lived in a palace nearly as splendid – though not as large – as Edo Castle. It was called England.

'Your country is ruled by a woman?' Sachi asked incredulously. Up to then she had believed everything he had said. But a country ruled by a woman – that couldn't be true. Maybe he couldn't speak her language as well as she had thought. Or perhaps everything he had told her was just stories.

England, he had said they were from. If they were English, these foreigners, they were on the side of the southerners. Did this Edwards really believe she was just a civilian who had been attacked by *ronin?* Surely not. After all, he had seen the dead and wounded southern soldiers littering the road. He had stepped right over

369

them. Perhaps he suspected that she was a lady of the shogun's court and a leading figure on the northern side whom the southerners would give anything to capture. She would have to be very cautious indeed.

That evening they saw lights twinkling far away in the distance, so many it looked as if the stars had fallen down to earth. There was a haze of smoke above the hills, half obscuring the sky.

'Watchfires,' said Shinzaemon. 'We're getting close. That monkey walking on his hind legs, talking like he thinks he's a human being,' he added in a growl. 'How can you speak to him? He's English. You know which side they're on. What's he doing travelling across our country? He must be a spy. They all are, these foreigners.'

'Don't be angry, not just as we're going to part,' pleaded Sachi. 'You know I have to be civil. We're their guests.'

'We would have been fine on our own,' grumbled Shinzaemon. 'Better off, in fact. I could have taken care of us.'

'We still have to get through the Itabashi checkpoint and Edo will be swarming with southerners. Dressed like this they'll think we're part of the foreigners' entourage. It's the perfect disguise. Don't you see? You'll be able to take a good look at the southern forces. There'll be a lot you can report to the militia – how many there are of them, what arms they have, that sort of thing.'

'I suppose you're right,' he grunted. 'Could be I'll see something useful.'

When they got to the post town of Urawa the following day there were red banners fluttering outside the gates, marked with a white cross in a circle. Sachi's heart sank as she saw it. The crest of the Shimazu, the most implacable of the southern warlords. So the enemy really was right at the gates of Edo. There were other banners too – scarlet, marked with the golden chrysanthemum of the emperor. She had heard rumours that the southerners were calling themselves the imperial army; here was the proof.

The highway was packed with enemy soldiers and they would have to walk straight through the middle of them. Sachi held her halberd low, hoping that in the crush the soldiers would think it was just a staff. With her head down she threaded her way through the throng, keeping close to the foreigners. Taki and Shinzaemon followed behind. She walked slowly and steadily, placing her feet carefully as if she was treading on egg shells, focusing her mind on walking, trying not to let the smallest twitch of her mouth or her hands betray her fear. Her heart was pounding. Thousands of soldiers, all converging, just waiting for the order to march on the city. And this was just the beginning. She prayed to the gods that there was an army just as formidable waiting to beat them back when they got there.

In the evening they came to Itabashi – 'Wooden Bridge' – the last post town on the Inner Mountain Road. They were almost in Edo. It was only two *ri* to the centre, where the castle was. Flaming torches were burning along the road and watchfires on the surrounding hills.

Long before they entered Itabashi they heard shouts and laughter and the twang of shamisens. The inns and hostelries were bursting at the seams. There were lanterns lit in front of every house. Enemy soldiers swarmed in the streets, swigging sake out of bamboo flasks, talking and guffawing in their boorish accents. Geishas and prostitutes were out in force, grabbing them as they swaggered by and trying to drag them into their establishments. Porters, bearers and stable boys were touting eagerly for work. Even the beggars were grinning, enjoying the merrymaking. So near to Edo, the shogun's city, and they partied so carelessly with his enemies! Didn't anyone care which side the soldiers were on, or were they only interested in their purses? She could guess what it was. Everyone knew the end was coming, so what did it matter any more? They might as well have fun.

They reached the checkpoint – the last they would have to pass before they got to Edo. Sachi and her companions kept their faces lowered, but when the guards saw the barbarians' palanquins they got down on their knees and waved the party on. As Sachi walked through the gates, she suddenly realized how exhausted she was. Her feet were chafed and swollen and her legs felt so heavy she thought she would never walk another step. The little toe of her right foot rubbed excruciatingly. It could only be another blister. She would have to bind it and put on new sandals.

Then she looked up. Through the houses that lined the road she caught a glimpse of paddy

fields dotted with farmhouses and beyond that...
Roofs, tiled roofs, a great ocean of roofs, sparkling in the evening light, stretching from horizon to horizon for as far as she could see. Edo.

For a moment it seemed as beautiful as the Western Paradise, as if Amida Buddha himself might be there to welcome them. On the darkening east side of the city, lights twinkled and threads of smoke coiled upwards like the smoke from a thousand incense burners. Between the roofs were splashes of pink – cherry trees, perhaps. And there were patches of darkness, groves of trees and broad sweeping roofs marking the estates of the daimyos. Was it just her imagination or could she make out, right in the middle, the battlements, landscaped pleasure gardens and wooded grounds of the castle?

Shinzaemon looked at the city. She could see on his face his eagerness to get there, to join his comrades, to prepare for war. Then he turned. Their eyes met in a long lingering gaze. Taki was staring at the city with a look of dazed relief.

But soon they realized something was terribly wrong. As they stumbled off again on their sore feet, they could see that shops and stalls had been wrecked and storehouses broken into. Doors were smashed and windows ripped out. Broken screens, shards of wood, abacuses and rolls of silk lay in the dust and barrels of rice spilt across the ground. The shops that had escaped damage were shuttered and bolted. They walked in silence. Sachi was afraid even to put words to the thought: if it was like this here, how would it be in Edo itself?

Shinzaemon had been walking behind. They were well inside the city when he caught up with her. He glanced at the samurai guards to check that they were out of earshot.

'That's where I'll be,' he said. A road led away to the left between dilapidated shops towards Kanei-ji Temple. 'The militia is barracked there, on Ueno Hill. I'll see you to the castle first.'

Sachi was speechless. Her eyes filled with tears. The idea of losing him was unbearable.

A while later they crossed the outer moat. To their right was the samurai section of town with its broad boulevards and high walls masking the daimyos' palaces, to their left the maze of narrow lanes where the townsmen lived. Sachi couldn't help noticing that the canals that had been full of people and boats when she last saw them were now empty. A terrible silence hung over the place, as if some deadly plague had fallen on the city. The smells of life had gone, and there was only a faint odour of dust. Some of the daimyos had even taken their palaces with them. The little convoy passed great gates standing open. Beyond the tiled walls Sachi could see nothing but an open expanse covered in sand, no buildings at all. How could everything have changed so quickly? When she had left in the imperial palanquin, the city had been a living, noisy place. Now it was a graveyard, populated by ghosts. She tried not to think of what might have happened at the castle and in the women's palace.

They crossed another moat, then another. Night was falling by the time they reached Hirakawa

374

Bridge. On the far side were a pair of massive wooden gates reinforced with bands of iron: the Tsubone Gate, the 'Gate of the Shoguns' Ladies'. They were at the entrance to the women's quarters of Edo Castle. The gates were set in a smooth granite wall that soared into the darkening sky. Sachi took Taki's hand and they stood side by side, looking across. A ray of sunlight sparkled on the still waters of the moat.

Sachi closed her eyes. For a moment that life came swirling back: the chambers glimmering with gold, painted with pine trees and cranes and birds; the fretted transepts, the exquisite coffered ceilings, the sumptuous kimonos. Even the maids had had magnificent kimonos, far finer than any she had seen since she left the palace. While she had lived there she had forgotten this other world where people were poor, where they sometimes did not have enough to eat. But now it was the palace that seemed like a dream, as unreal as the palace of the dragon king's daughter under the sea must have seemed to poor Urashima.

She had seen the palace in flames. But it had been only one section of one citadel in the great castle complex. Surely in the rest of the castle life must go on as it always had? The women must simply have moved to another part.

And what of her mother? She clutched the bundle containing the brocade and tried to picture the woman who had worn it. Was she too only a dream?

The moment had come, the moment she had been dreading. She had been trying not to think about it, hoping that it would never happen. But there was no avoiding it any longer.

Sachi and Shinzaemon stood together at the end of the bridge. The foreigners were standing nearby but they didn't matter. There were ducks swimming on the murky water of the moat. The moon already hung pale in the sky though the sun had not yet set.

Shinzaemon took her hand. His large swordsman's hand enfolded her small white one and held it tight. She felt the calluses on his palm where he wielded his sword. She could feel the dryness of his palm on hers, smell the faint whiff of salt on his skin, feel the warmth of his body. Tears sprang to her eyes but she choked them back. She wanted to beg him to stay but she knew she couldn't. She ran her eyes across the fine bones of his face, his full-lipped mouth.

'So you will be where you told me,' she breathed, 'on Ueno Hill?'

'With the *shogitai* militia. The southerners still have to conquer Edo. If we can hold it for the Tokugawas perhaps we can drive them back.'

They looked at each other. 'While I live I'll never forget you,' he said softly. 'I had never imagined the world contained someone like you – or that it could be so rich and colourful. You make it very hard for me to accept that I may die. No, not "may". I have to die.'

'I shall pray with all my might that you live,' she said. 'When the war is over, come and find me.'

She knew what she had to do. She reached into her sleeve for her comb, that precious comb that she had loved since she was a child, and held it out to him. The gold crest embossed on it gleamed in the rays of the setting sun and their two shadows stretched out long across the ground.

'This is the most precious thing I have,' she said. 'It's my good luck charm. I've had it all my life. It will protect you. When you look at it, think of me.'

'I can't take it,' he protested. 'I know what it means to you.'

'It will bring you back to me,' she said. 'It will protect you better than any amulet, better than a thousand-stitch belt. When you see me again you can give it back.'

She pressed it into his hands, letting her soft hands linger on his hard muscular ones. He lifted it gravely to his forehead in a formal gesture of thanks, then bowed and tucked it in his sleeve. They stood in silence for a while.

Suddenly Sachi had an idea. Impulsively she said, 'Meet me one last time, I beg you. Here, at the Tsubone Gate, tomorrow, at dusk.'

Even as she said it, she knew it was a crazy plan. In the past it would have been unthinkable to sneak out for a meeting with a man. She had no reason now to think things had changed that much. In a moment, when she passed through the gates, she would be the retired lady of the side chamber again. And him? A soldier didn't walk away from the barracks.

But no matter what, she would be there. 'I'll be waiting for you,' she said.

He looked away, then took a breath and said, 'I'll do my best.'

Sachi was expecting Taki to scold her. She

377

could almost hear her voice saying, 'Remember your place. Remember who you are.'

But Taki didn't. She was looking at Shinzaemon. There were tears in her eyes too. Suddenly Sachi realized that Taki was sad too, a deep hopeless despairing sadness. She was as far from Toranosuké as ever. Coming to Edo hadn't brought her any closer to him. She too had enjoyed the freedom of the road and seemed a little shocked to be heading back into the prison of the palace.

'I have a request too,' Taki said hesitantly in the tiniest of squeaky whispers. 'I know it's foolish but...' She took an amulet from her sleeve. Sachi recognized it. It was a long-life amulet Taki had brought with her from Kyoto. She pressed it into Shinzaemon's hand.

'Please give this to Master Toranosuké,' she said. 'Tell him I'll be praying for him. And for Tatsuemon too.'

Shinzaemon touched it to his forehead and said, 'I'll tell them. And I'll make sure he gets it.'

The sun had disappeared behind the great walls of the castle. Sachi and Shinzaemon still stood looking at each other.

'We have to go,' said Taki softly.

Sachi knew what had to be done – what a soldier's wife would do. She smiled and bowed as bravely as she could.

'Do your best!' she said in firm tones.

They turned towards the castle. Sachi hesitated. Once she crossed that bridge, she knew, she would be back in that other world again, a world that didn't contain Shinzaemon. She felt dead in her heart. She recognized the feeling. It

378

was the same as she had felt just before she heard that the young shogun was dead.

A breeze stirred the waters of the moat and the pond weed rippled. On the other side the ramparts swept upwards, seemingly impregnable.

'It's nearly nightfall,' whispered Taki. 'Suppose we can't get in? How are we going to persuade the guards that we are who we say we are?'

She was quite right. With her shabby clothes and travel-stained face Taki looked like a peasant or a beggar, not remotely like a court lady. Sachi realized that she looked exactly the same. They'd been on the road for so long and had so many adventures, they'd become completely different people.

The castle walls loomed in the dusk. But something was missing.

'Look,' Sachi whispered. 'There's no smoke. It's dinner time but there's no smoke.'

The wooden gates with their iron bars and huge bolts were tightly locked. Sachi had thought there would at least be a battalion of guards on duty outside. But there was no one. Cut into one of the side walls next to the gates was a small door. She knocked then gave it a shove. It creaked open.

The foreigners and Shinzaemon were waiting in the darkness on the other side of the moat.

Swallowing hard, Sachi turned and gave a brave smile and a wave. She could hardly see for tears. Then she and Taki stepped through the door. It clanged shut behind them.

Part IV

City of Ruins

9

The Secret of the Brocade

I

The blackness was as dense as if they had fallen into a well. Only the sky was visible, a small square of dark blue above them. Stars were coming out one by one. An owl hooted in the silence. The sound was still echoing around the battlements when there was a hoarse caw close to Sachi's face and a raven flapped off with a rattle of its great wings. She stumbled backwards, shuddering. Birds of ill fortune, birds of death.

As her eyes grew used to the gloom she saw where they were in the enclosure between the outer and the inner gates of the Tsubone guardhouse. She had been there before, when she had walked in with the princess's train and when she left, racing through in the imperial palanquin.

She was back in the palace, where she had decided she belonged, where perhaps her mother was: but all she could think was that Shinzaemon was gone. It was as if half of her had been wrenched away and all that was left was an empty shell, drifting like a ghost.

Then she heard the scrape of gates creaking open and lights appeared, darting here and there like fireflies. Straw-sandalled feet came running, crunching across the paving stones. Men swarmed around them, swinging lanterns. There were rough shouts.

'Hey! What's this? What we got over 'ere?'

'Halt! Where do you think you're going?'

'Intruders. Spies, trying to sneak in!'

A forest of pikes and spears appeared, thrusting towards their throats.

Sachi stood still. Although she and Taki were dressed like a couple of peasant women, somehow they had to persuade the soldiers that they were court ladies with every right to be there. The best thing was to behave in a manner appropriate to their rank, with icy disdain. Soldiers were like dogs, she told herself, and could sense fear.

'Taki,' she hissed. 'Say something.' As the Retired Lady Shoko-in, it was not for her to address these inferior creatures.

Taki drew herself up. 'I am Lady Takiko, lady-in-waiting to the Retired Lady Shoko-in,' she squeaked in her haughtiest tones, using the language in which court ladies addressed servants. 'We have returned to the palace. We require to be escorted to the presence of Her Highness.'

There was a long silence, then a chorus of hisses as the soldiers stumbled back, sucking their breath through their teeth and muttering to each other. An old man hobbled out of the darkness.

'Forgive me,' he croaked. He raised his lantern, casting a beam across Sachi's face. Dazzled by the brightness she looked away, keeping her expression coldly impassive. The man squinted up at her, then bent his bandy legs and pressed

384

his ancient leathery face to the soil.

'Your ladyship.' It seemed an eternity since anyone had called her that. 'Take our heads for our impertinence, ma'am.' Sachi guessed he must have seen her from a distance when she was getting into the imperial palanquin and about to flee the palace. How else was it possible that a member of the outer guard would know her?

Tumbling over each other, the soldiers fell to their knees and rubbed their heads in the dirt. Sachi stared in relief at the hunched backs and topknots quivering on top of shiny shaven heads.

The old man was snivelling and wiping his eyes. 'Your ladyship,' he babbled, 'is it really you? We missed you.'

Sachi knew she ought to be outraged by the fellow's presumption but she was still the village headman's daughter. She had yet to put on her concubine's robes again. She had spoken to so many people of so many different classes – she had *been* so many people. Now she was back at last. She should have been pleased, but all she felt was dazed.

'But ... ladyship, forgive me,' the old man whimpered. 'Forgive me for speaking. But ... since your ladyship left ... since the fire... There is nothing here now, your ladyship.'

'Nothing? The ladies? Her Highness?'

Another soldier butted in. 'Your ladyship, we will escort you to Her Highness's apartments.'

'What are you doing polluting her ladyship's ears with your voices?' snapped Taki. 'Take us there immediately.'

Holding their lanterns high, the soldiers led

them into the palace grounds. Every corner of the gardens had always been perfectly trimmed, but now there was grass between the paving stones and ivy climbing the walls. The trees stretched out long branches, threatening to engulf them all.

They climbed a winding path lined with rhododendron bushes and stepped out into an open space.

In front of them were the outer walls of a huge tumbledown ruin, stretching as far as they could see. The great slabs of stone were blackened and cracked. Beyond, charred timbers stabbed the sky like the spears of a ghostly army. Huge beams had fallen to the ground. Roof tiles lay in heaps, grotesquely fused together. The pale light of the moon sparkled on chunks of coffered ceiling and fragments of gold screens that had somehow escaped the conflagration. A dank acrid smell hung over the place. The smell of burned wood. The smell of death.

'Don't look, ma'am. Don't look,' said the old man, hurrying them on.

But how could Sachi not look? They passed the remains of the great hall where she had sheltered with Lady Tsuguko and Taki that terrible night before rushing out into the snow. The roof had collapsed and fallen beams lay across the entrance. She could still see the pall of smoke and the flames leaping from roof to roof and hear the horrific whoosh as they sucked up everything in their path.

'We searched and searched,' faltered the old man. 'We buried the dead. But by then ... By then...'

The dead... Sachi pressed her sleeves to her eyes as memories came flooding back.

Faces floated before her. Her Highness – at least she was still alive, or so the men had told her. Formidable Lady Tsuguko. Haru, dear Haru, her teacher. Sachi's ladies-in-waiting and her maids and attendants. The fearsome Retired One and her retinue of grand ladies. Old Lady Honju-in and hers. The princess's withered mother, the Old Crow. Lady Nakaoka and the other elders. The shaven-headed lady priests. What had become of all those women?

And what of all the others, all those three thousand who had filled the palace, from the highest-ranking ladies-in-waiting, entitled to look upon His Majesty, to the lowest? The administrators, negotiators, office workers, time keepers, seam-stresses, fire wardens, errand women, cooks, singers, dancers, musicians, altar-room attend-ants, kitchen staff, ladies of the bath, scribes, maids in charge of tobacco and hand water, cleaners, guards, maids, maids of maids, maids of maids of maids – what had become of them all?

An icy breeze stirred the ashes and rippled her miserable cotton garments. Sachi shivered. The ruins seemed to be full of the wails of all the women who had died. They had given their lives to serve a man whom most of them would never even see. And then to suffer such terrible deaths – to burn to death in a fire!

She and Taki stumbled on through the never-ending grounds, across streams and bridges, around the boating lakes with lacquered pleasure barges pulled up forlornly on the banks, past gardens overgrown with weeds and pavilions with moss creeping across the roofs and holes in their walls. Much later, across another moat, they saw sweeping roofs and wooden shutters.

'The Second Citadel,' whispered Taki. Ninomaru, the Second Citadel, where the widows of past shoguns lived. Was Sachi's mother still there? Sachi had come all this way in search of her, but now the thought of meeting her filled her with dread.

They skirted building after building until they came to the women's palace of the Ninomaru. Women guards escorted them inside and led them through a warren of chambers and corridors. In some, tapers and candles cast a wavering light, in others they fumbled their way through shadows with only the faint glow of the guards' lanterns bobbing ahead of them to light their way.

Sachi kept expecting to open a door and find a room full of women with their skirts spread like water lilies, sewing or combing each other's hair. But it was utterly silent. No chatter and laughter, no rustle of silk, no clatter of dishes, no singing and strumming of kotos. The only sound was the whisper of their own footsteps sliding across wooden floors and tatami mats.

There was a musty smell about the place. She noticed cobwebs glittering on the transepts and the corners of the ceilings and draped across the ornamental shelves. So even the honourable whelps – the children who took care of menial tasks, shadowy young girls who didn't exist as far as noblewomen like her were concerned – had gone.

In the dim light she caught a glimpse of something humped and bristly, like a monstrous hedgehog, in the shadows in a far corner of one of the chambers. The guards hurried her past. Then she saw another behind a door. It was a great mound of brushwood. In chamber after chamber there were heaps of brushwood and bundles of dry grass hidden in dark corners. Instinctively she knew what it was for, and the thought made her cold with dread. So this was the destiny that the gods had brought her here to share.

Finally they came to a set of closed doors hung with giant red tassels. The guards knelt and intoned, 'Her ladyship, the Retired Lady Shoko-in.'

A door slid open. A woman was on her knees with her head pressed to the tatami mats. Sachi gasped. She knew that plump back and thick hair tied into a simple knot. Every morning, throughout her life at the palace, that same head had been there, bowing at the door to her chamber. Seeing her, the palace no longer felt so strange. She was home after all.

The woman raised her head. She put her hand over her mouth and smiled until her eyes disappeared in the folds of her round pink cheeks. Tears ran down her plump face.

'Well, I never!' she said. 'Well, I never! Your ladyship! I never thought I'd see you again.'

'Haru! Big Sister!'

'Welcome home. Welcome home!'

Haru – who had taken Sachi under her wing when she had just arrived, new and frightened, from the village and had made her into a lady;

who had taught her how to talk like a lady of the shogun's court, how to glide with slow, dignified steps instead of bounding like a peasant, how to write beautifully, to eat politely, to sing, to dance, gently explaining everything, correcting her kindly. The day Sachi had been ordered to go to His Majesty's chamber, it was Haru who had told her what to do and not to be afraid. Haru with her stories and jokes – the tale of the body in the palanquin, the talk of roasted lizard powder and mushroom stems...

Sachi tried to speak but tears spilled down her cheeks. Taki was weeping too.

Brushing her sleeve across her eyes, Sachi knelt. She took Haru's soft hands in hers and held them tight. She needed to be sure this was a real woman, not a ghost. She gazed at her face. There were lines on her forehead, streaks of grey in her hair. Her eyes still crinkled when she laughed, but there was a new sadness in them.

'Big Sister. Thank the gods, thank the gods. You survived the fire.'

'Yes, the gods were on my side,' smiled Haru. 'And yours too.'

'Big Sister, where is everyone? Her Highness, how is she? Where are the ladies?'

But Haru didn't answer. She was staring at her strangely, as if she in turn had seen a ghost.

'Well, I never!' she said again. 'You look just like...'

Sachi could imagine what she must look like – like a savage or a madwoman, with her wild hair and gleaming white teeth and shapeless peasant's clothes.

Haru shook her head. 'I must be getting old,' she said. 'Come, both of you, you must bathe and change. I will notify Her Highness. But ... how did you get here? How did you manage to cross the city unharmed? I heard it was swarming with southern hoodlums and the entire populace had fled. You should have stayed away. There's nothing here except death, for all of us.'

Not everyone had left. There were enough serving women still to make sure the great baths were overflowing with steaming water. It really would have been the end if that had not been the case, thought Sachi. Sitting side by side on small wooden stools beside the baths, she and Taki took turns to scrub each other's back; there were no bath maids any more, and anyway she was used to having Taki around.

'Come and soak with me, Taki,' she said.

Having washed off the dirt of the road as thoroughly as possible, they stepped into the scalding water, sank up to their necks and sat together for a while, feeling the tiredness of the journey ebb away. Sachi was grateful for the steam that swirled around, hiding her tears. This was not the home she remembered, this grim echoing palace. She had convinced herself that even though the rest of the world had changed, inside the castle walls she would still find a haven. How wrong she had been.

Shinzaemon... Shinzaemon... If only he were with her! It was as if a part of her was missing. Without him the world was a desolate place. She felt more forlorn than she could ever have imagined possible.

She tried to picture his face – his slanting eyes, his thick brows, his fine nose, his full mouth. In her mind she ran over every day, every moment of their time together, all the things he'd done and said – the time he had given her the wild orchid, the moment he had said he would go to the village with her. She tried to remember the touch of his palm and his salty smell. She had been foolish to let herself get so caught up but she didn't regret it at all. It made her happy just to remember being with him.

Taki's thin hollow-cheeked face had turned peony red from the heat. Sachi could see that she was weeping too.

'I thought once we got back to the palace I'd be myself again,' sniffed Taki. She shifted a little and Sachi felt the heat on her skin as the scalding water rippled. 'I never imagined it was possible to have such feelings for someone. I didn't know such feelings existed. If we'd stayed here, none of this would have happened. All that freedom went to our heads. That's what I keep telling myself. We just got carried away, you and I.'

But she and Taki were not the same, thought Sachi. Taki had never been further than her family home or the women's palace before. She had never known any other life. It was perfectly possible that being out on the road, mixing with men, really had gone to her head. It had all been so new for her, it must have been utterly intoxicating, so it was hardly surprising that she had fallen for the handsome Toranosuké. But Sachi had grown up far away from the palace and had always known it was not the only world there was.

'When we got back here I thought it would be like waking up from a dream,' sighed Taki. 'But I don't seem to be able to wake up. I feel as if this is the dream.'

'It's like Urashima and the dragon king's daughter,' Sachi said softly. 'Which was real and which was the dream – his village after he had been away for three hundred years or the palace under the sea?'

Taki murmured the first lines of a poem:

'*Kakikurasu*   Through the blackest shadow
Kokoro no yami ni Of the darkness of the heart
Madoiniki   I wander, lost...'

Sachi knew it well – a wonderful poem, written hundreds of years earlier by the great poet and lover Ariwara no Narihira. It seemed to chime perfectly with her feelings. Forgetting their gloom for a moment, Sachi and Taki recited the coda together, their voices ringing around the great bath chamber:

'*Yume utsutsu to wa* Whether dream or reality
Koyoi sadame yo   Tonight let us decide.'

Taki sighed. 'We'll wake up soon enough,' she said. 'We're not living in a fairy tale. We're not peasants or children, to follow our emotions blindly. That's only ever led to disaster. The quicker we disentangle ourselves, the better.'

She was right, Sachi thought. Yet she had not forgotten that the following night Shinzaemon might be waiting on the bridge. After tomorrow night, she told herself sternly. That would be the time to rein in these childish feelings.

After the bath she sat in silence while Taki fussed around her, blackening her teeth and shaving her eyebrows. Before, when she had looked at herself in the mirror, she had seen the glowing face that Shinzaemon saw. Now her reflection was pale and wan.

Carefully Taki painted her face porcelain white, rouged her cheeks and made her mouth small and red like a rosebud, then brushed in two moths' wings on her forehead. Then she combed and oiled her hair until it swung at her shoulders, gleaming and black. She lifted it strand by strand and held an incense censer under it to perfume it and laid out layer upon layer of kimonos suitable for a widow who had taken holy orders.

Little by little Sachi the village headman's daughter, the anonymous traveller on the Inner Mountain Road, disappeared. There in the mirror before her was the Retired Lady Shoko-in, the widowed concubine of His late Majesty, Lord Iemochi. Taki made the final adjustments to her robes, tweaking and smoothing the collars until they were perfectly parallel. As Taki helped her into her overkimono, Sachi grew grave and serious, feeling the cares and responsibilities pressing on her shoulders again along with the layers and layers of clothing.

But inside herself she knew she was not that person any more. Beneath the white powder there was colour in her cheeks and a new light in her eyes. She had seen too much, been to too many places. She knew what was expected of her and she would do her duty. Nevertheless she had tasted freedom and she could never be the same again.

Sachi hurried to the princess's rooms and knelt outside the door, terrified of what she might find and of how she might be received. She took a breath, then softly slid it open.

Despite the heavy silence, she had been half expecting to find an antechamber lined with gold screens, full of gold-encrusted boxes set on lacquered shelves, with crowds of ladies-in-waiting chattering and laughing together, running in and out with lengths of kimono fabric, their magnificent silk robes rustling as they moved. But the room was nearly empty. There were just a few kimono stands with kimonos airing on them, a single kimono chest and a cosmetics box.

The princess was almost entirely alone. She was not even hidden behind screens. She was kneeling at a small table in the middle of the room, holding a brush upright in her thin fingers, writing. She finished the stroke and laid the brush down. Then she glanced around, inclined her head and touched her fingertips to the tatami.

'I have put thee to much trouble,' she murmured. She spoke the formal words of greeting in the archaic language of the imperial court. Her voice had not changed. It was that same piping birdlike whisper that Sachi knew so well. 'Thou must be tired. Thou hast come a long way. What a journey thou hast had.'

She smiled her gentle sad smile and slipped into the language of the Edo aristocrats.

'Welcome, child,' she said. 'Haru told me you were back. Come and sit by me.'

Tears pricked Sachi's eyes. To see this woman who had always been surrounded by crowds of ladies-in-waiting, who throughout her whole life had never had to do anything for herself – to see her sitting alone like this was too poignant for words.

Silently Sachi knelt before the princess and peeped up at her face. It was a deplorable breach of protocol, but she needed to see this face she loved so well.

Beneath the white make-up the princess's skin was still transparently pale. The delicately arched nose, the large sad eyes, the tiny pursed mouth – nothing had changed. She was so thin she looked as if she might vanish at any moment into the world of ghosts. A few strands of her hair were out of place as if she might even – impossible to imagine – have had to comb it herself. Between her shaved eyebrows Sachi made out a faint line, a mark of her suffering.

Yet something was different. She held herself more upright. There was a spark in her eye as if she had found something to fight for after so many years listlessly watching her life go by. She looked bolder, more commanding.

'Come,' the princess said softly and led Sachi to the side of the room. On the altar was a funerary tablet and a small daguerreotype. That picture! Sachi remembered it so well. She took it in both hands and raised it reverently to her forehead. She could hardly see through the tears that sprang to her eyes and coursed down her cheeks,

396

streaking her make-up. It was His late Majesty. In her memory he had always been so knowledgeable, so grownup. But she had been only a child at that time. Looking at the picture now she saw he was just a vulnerable boy. The two women knelt together, mumbling prayers, running their beads through their fingers.

'I'm happy Your Highness saved these,' whispered Sachi.

'Seeing you reminds me of happier times,' said the princess. 'And yet... Were they so happy? If only I had been a better wife to him.'

'I'm sure he...' said Sachi. She stopped. It was not her place to speak of such things.

Princess Kazu dabbed her eyes with her sleeve. 'It's good that you've come back,' she said. 'There is a lot to tell you. Much has happened since you've been away.'

Silence filled the room. Sachi waited respectfully for her to continue.

'You completed your mission well.'

Mission? Sachi had forgotten that she had had a mission.

'We heard the imperial palanquin had been attacked by rebels. People were saying I had been abducted – I or the Retired One or both of us – and taken off to Satsuma, the southerners' stronghold. Yes, people were filled with anger. No one doubted it was southerners who had set fire to the castle. Our men burned the residences of the Satsuma clan and drove them out of the city. Later they found the imperial palanquin, somewhere ... somewhere far from the city.'

She glanced down at her thin hands folded on

her lap, then glanced up again.

'We thought we had lost you,' she said softly. 'We mourned for you. We thought you had gone for ever...' Her voice trailed away. She looked around at the empty room and opened her hands in a gesture of helplessness. 'Our life is changed. Our world is at an end. I would never have imagined it could come to this. Never. Never!'

Startled at the intensity of the words, Sachi looked up.

'I have missed you, child,' the princess murmured. 'I was sad I had sent you on such a terrible mission, with no retinue, not even a single servant. How did you survive? It must have been terrible ... out there, away from all our comforts. I am glad to know you did your duty. But it was cruel of me – unforgivable – to cast you out like that. I am reassured to see you back and in good health.'

Sachi looked at her in amazement. There were tears in the princess's eyes. That she had even thought of Sachi – that she could even try to imagine what had become of her – showed how much she had suffered, how much she had changed.

'Your Highness. It's very rude of me but...What of the ladies? Lady Tsuguko...?' The princess's chief lady-in-waiting had always been at her side. Sachi dared not think what had happened to her.

'Lady Tsuguko...' repeated the princess. A shadow crossed her face.

Footsteps whispered across the tatami outside the princess's chamber. The door slid open. A tall figure was on her knees outside.

'Your Imperial Highness. Excuse my rudeness. I heard she had returned. My Lady Shoko-in! Daughter-in-law!'

Sachi knew that commanding presence and deep resonant voice. Hastily she bowed to the ground and pressed her face to her hands.

The Retired One was wearing an elegant kimono in a modest shade of grey. Her hair, which hung to her shoulders, was glossy and black. Her eyes were jewel-bright, her beauty undimmed. Sachi remembered the ice queen in the folk tale who lured men into the snowy wastes with her beauty and then left them to freeze to death. She was just as perfect and as blood-chilling. She was looking at Sachi with a honeyed smile. Sachi's heart sank. Had she come all this way only to be the butt of her sarcasm again? She braced herself.

'Welcome,' the Retired One said smoothly. 'You've come a long way. How very brave to return. You show great loyalty to the Tokugawa clan. We gather you back into our embrace.'

The princess returned her bow, taking care not to incline her head even a fraction lower than the Retired One's. So they were still battling over who took precedence, even now when there were only the two of them left.

'Of course I am very happy to see you,' said the Retired One, addressing Sachi. Sachi bowed. It was far more disconcerting when the Retired One was polite than when she showed open hostility.

'We thought you'd gone back to your own kind,' the Retired One continued, enunciating each

399

syllable with icy clarity. 'We didn't expect to see you again. Why did you return?'

Sachi shivered. The words were like a shower of sleet, chilling her to the bone. But the Retired One's harshness no longer hurt her as it had.

'You must realize it's all over,' hissed the Retired One. 'There is nothing here now. No more luxury. Nothing left except death. There's no need for you to stay. Everyone has gone. Everyone but us.'

Everyone gone... So if her mother had been here then she too... Sachi tried to swallow but couldn't.

'You don't belong here,' said the Retired One in tones of sneering condescension. 'We release you. I suggest you leave while you have the chance.'

'It's very good that you returned, dear child,' said the princess hastily. 'We are happy to see you. Happy that you feel such loyalty to us and to the Tokugawa clan. Happy to have the chance to say goodbye. But you must leave, and quickly. We belong to the Tokugawa clan, the Retired One and I. We are wives, we married into the family. But you are young. Life is before you. It was me who brought you here – you did not choose to come. Now it is my responsibility to release you. You must go.'

But the princess had not chosen either. Sachi knew that very well. This was not a world in which anyone could choose any part of their life, the princess least of all.

'And ... and what will you do?' she whispered.

'We are expecting an attack at any moment,' said the princess. She spoke lightly, almost carelessly, and Sachi could see that her face was serene, her eyes bright. It was as if she were discussing her wedding, not a terrible battle. 'The city is under siege. We hear there are fifty thousand southern troops at Shinagawa and Itabashi, waiting for the order to attack. When the time comes our men will fight to the death. The city will go up in flames. We will stay here, her ladyship and I. It is our place. If they take the castle, it will be with us in it. We will burn it and kill ourselves. Leave, child. Leave now.'

So that was why the princess looked so different, so alive. Here was the destiny she yearned for. To be present at the end, to go up in flames along with the greatest castle in the land – it was a fate to be grasped with joy.

For a moment Sachi too felt intoxicated, swept up in the princess's excitement. But then she thought of Shinzaemon. She no longer wanted to embrace death like a lover, as a samurai would. The princess and the Retired One had no reason to live, to grow old. She did. In her imagination she was stealing out of the doomed castle. Taki would come too. They would wait at the Tsubone Gate for Shinzaemon to appear. She would beg him to flee with her. Of course he would refuse, he would speak of honour and duty, but she would think up argument after argument: he had to protect her, that was his duty too. Finally she would succeed. She pictured the three of them on their way out of the city, somehow evading the troops, setting off along the Inner Mountain Road again, disappearing into the hills.

But then Sachi remembered her quest for her

mother. She needed to find out what had happened to her. How could she leave now if there was even the slightest possibility that her mother was still alive, waiting for her? In any case, she had no choice. She knew what her duty was and what she had to say. She was a warrior woman, a samurai, and she must be ready to die as a samurai would, proudly and bravely. No matter what she might feel in her heart, no matter what she herself might want to do, it was her duty as the late shogun's concubine to join the princess and the Retired One in death. She could not do less.

'Never!' She spoke quietly and firmly. 'I too am a Tokugawa, unworthy though I am. His Majesty graciously deigned to take me as his concubine – his only concubine. I will share the Tokugawas' destiny, no matter what it is.'

The Retired One fixed her fierce black eyes on Sachi. 'Call yourself a Tokugawa?' she snapped, her lip curling into a sneer. 'You forget! You are not even a samurai. You're a peasant. Don't presume to think you can follow our code. Leave now while you can.'

But Sachi was no longer afraid of the Retired One.

'Madam,' she said calmly, 'I am as much a Tokugawa as you are. I did not choose my birthplace but I can choose my place of death. No matter what I am, I know my duty.'

'Child, I order you to leave,' said the princess. 'Time is running out. You are under no obligation to stay. You must obey.'

'Never. If you die here then I will too.'

402

The Retired One sighed. Her face softened. Was it Sachi's imagination or was there even a tear in those fierce black eyes?

'You have great strength of spirit,' she said finally.

'Her ladyship ordered our ladies-in-waiting to leave,' said the princess. 'She shouted at them, told them that it was an order. But she didn't think they would.'

'They call themselves samurai,' said the Retired One, 'and they're afraid to die! I thought they would be proud to stay and die here together. But they've all fled.' Her lip curled again. 'Crawled back to their families. In the old days everyone would have stayed.'

The princess and the Retired One glanced at each other and smiled – triumphant smiles. Sachi had never seen them look so happy and proud, as if their moment had come, as if they were about to fulfil the destiny they had been awaiting for so long. They were no longer victims who had been married against their will. Their eyes were shining like young girls tremblingly awaiting their first lover, as if all of life was before them. But it was not life but death that they yearned for with such impatience.

'Times have changed,' said the princess. 'We are no longer in the Warring Period, when people would elect to die together.'

'It saddens me that standards have fallen so far,' said the Retired One. She looked straight at Sachi, smiling. 'You began life as a peasant, but truly you have the heart of a samurai.'

II

'After the fire the princess told everyone to leave,' said Haru. 'It was too dangerous to stay. The Retired One said it was an order. We are in great peril here in the castle. The southerners have the city in a stranglehold. If they can take the castle, they'll have the country.'

Haru had cleared away the dinner trays and now knelt, turning her fan over and over in her plump hands. Candles in tall golden candlesticks stood around the chamber, crackling and sputtering. The flames threw a yellow glow across her face, flickering across her round cheeks, the fine wrinkles of her forehead, her small nose, the gleaming coils of her coiffure. The kimono stands cast long shadows. Sachi imagined being outside in the castle grounds, seeing the huge silhouette of the castle looming above her with only a few needle-thin slivers of light to break the darkness.

'But you didn't go, Big Sister,' said Sachi. 'The princess said you could leave but you refused.'

'Why would I go?' said Haru abruptly. 'Go where? To what?' Sachi glanced at her, surprised. Her plump face had changed. Her small eyes had widened and her eyebrows were pressed together, as if some painful memory had leaped unbidden to her mind. She was staring into the distance as if gazing into some long-forgotten past. 'To a family and country I don't know at all?' she demanded. 'That remote place I came from – it's nothing to me. I've been here my whole life. This

404

is my family and my home.'

'But...' Sachi was remembering the stories Haru had told her about the body in the palanquin and the many other strange and terrible things that had happened in the castle. Haru had always complained about what an unhappy place it was, how she missed the company of men. Yet when she had had the chance to leave, she had chosen to stay.

Haru was looking at Sachi intensely. Sachi shifted and looked away, suddenly uncomfortable.

'And Lady Tsuguko?' she asked hastily.

Haru shook herself back into the present.

'No one knows. You were the last to see her. Did she not take you to the imperial palanquin?'

Of course. That tall figure striding through the smoke-filled rooms while the flames crackled louder and louder. She couldn't possibly have survived the journey back through that inferno. She must have perished there. It was a good death, an admirable death: she had died while carrying out her duty. Still, Sachi's eyes filled with tears. Lady Tsuguko had taught her so much and always taken her side. Why did life have to be so full of sadness?

Haru was usually so sunny and cheerful, but tonight she seemed restless. She was looking at Sachi as if she couldn't take her eyes off her. She opened her mouth as if to say something, then closed it again, then took up some sewing and put it down again. With a start Sachi realized Haru's eyes too were brimming with tears.

In the corner was the bulky, shapeless bundle

Sachi had brought all the way back to the palace. The brocade inside seemed to glow, to draw her eyes towards it. Sachi remembered that Haru had seemed to recognize the crest on the comb. The same crest was embroidered on the brocade. She put the bundle on the floor in front of her and started fiddling with the knot. Haru reached out and took it.

Sachi watched curiously.

As Haru finished unpicking the knot, the thin silk wrapper fell open. There was the folded brocade, brilliant as the sky. It lit up the dark corners of the room.

Haru gasped and turned as white as if she had seen a ghost. She stared at the fabric, stretched out a trembling finger and touched it as if she could hardly believe it was real, as if she was afraid it would crumble away into dust. Then she picked it up and shook it out. A faint musty fragrance, as ancient as time – of musk and aloe, wormwood and frankincense – swirled into the air. She held it to her face, took a deep, convulsive breath and started to cry. She cried until Sachi thought she would never stop.

Sachi stared at her, aghast. Haru hadn't even looked at the crest; it was the brocade itself that had had such a dramatic effect. Fear clutched at Sachi's stomach, held it in an iron fist. Finally she forced herself to speak.

'You ... you know it, Big Sister.'

'It's been so long. So many years.' Haru mopped her face with her sleeves and laid the brocade carefully on her lap. 'You look just like her, Little Sister,' she breathed. Her voice was a hoarse whisper. 'I thought as much but I couldn't let myself believe it. I told myself it was a coincidence, that my memory was failing me. How could such a thing be possible?'

Sachi put her hands on the tatami to steady herself. The truth about her mother – about who she was – was so close, yet suddenly she wasn't sure she could bear to hear it. She was afraid.

'Who do I look like?' she whispered. 'Big Sister, who do I look like?'

'It's so long since I saw her. And then you came. At first you were just a little thing. And then as you got older you looked more and more... And now, now you've been away and I see you afresh... It's as if she's come back. As if she's here again.'

'My mother...' Sachi had to say it.

Haru was weeping. For a while she couldn't speak. The scent of the brocade filled the room. A candle guttered and went out. Moonlight poured in through the fine white paper of the windows. Where once the castle would have been full of voices, footsteps and laughter there was utter silence, broken only by the sighing of the wind in the trees outside, the shriek of a night owl and the sound of Haru's sobs.

'She was so beautiful. So beautiful,' said Haru brokenly. 'No one could lay eyes on her and not love her. And you... You are the same.'

'Is she here, Big Sister?' Sachi's voice was shrill in the silence. 'If I could only see her, just once.'

Haru turned her face towards her. She was no longer the plump cheerful Haru that Sachi knew. In the sickly light of the flames she had shrivelled into an old woman. She shook her head.

407

'I ... don't know where she is,' she whispered. 'I haven't seen her since ... that day. Since the day you were born.'

III

Sachi woke well before dawn and lay waiting impatiently for the first threads of light to come slanting between the wooden shutters. Taki had spent the night there in attendance. Sachi called to her to slide them back.

In the distance cocks were crowing. Another answered from the palace grounds. Birds sang, insects twittered, the sweet smells of spring came pouring in. Dogs barked madly as the city came to life. Temple bells tolled and drums sounded the hour but the sounds were thin and sparse, as if half the populace had disappeared.

As the late shogun's concubine, Sachi had been given one of the finest rooms in the palace. She set a mirror on a mirror stand and, as pale light filtered into the room, gazed at the face that glimmered back from the polished metal surface. She studied the smooth pale oval, the straight, almost aquiline nose, the narrow slanted eyes, the small pursed mouth. There was something she was missing, something else there to be seen if only she could see it. For it was not only herself she saw there but a stranger: her mother, gazing back at her from some deep distant place.

Taki knelt behind her and started combing her hair.

'Haru seems to know your mother,' she said,

408

'yet she never said anything all these years. Something must have happened, something terrible, to make her cry like that. It's not like her at all.'

There was so little time, so little time, and so much Sachi needed to know.

Haru was waiting in the outer chamber. In the daylight the brocade had lost its glow. Sachi ran her fingers across it, as if afraid that if she put it away she would never see it again – that the spell it cast would be broken, that the woman who had come back would disappear. She looked up at Haru.

'Tell me her name, Big Sister,' she said. 'What is her name?'

'I shall, my lady.' Sachi frowned. Haru had never called her 'my lady' before; she always called her 'Little Sister'. 'But first, I beg you, please tell me about this brocade. Where did you get it?'

Sachi smiled. 'I had it all along but I didn't know it,' she said. 'We went back to the village where I used to live. They told me there – my ... parents. They told me my father brought me to them, wrapped in the brocade.'

'Your father...!' Haru went pale. Her eyes opened wide and her plump hands fluttered up to cover her mouth. 'He went all that way ... to the village?'

'He's a distant cousin of my parents. He visited again recently,' said Sachi, trying to hide her amazement. Could it be possible that Haru knew her father too?

Haru gasped. 'You mean ... he's alive?' she asked eagerly. 'Did you see him?' She was staring at

409

Sachi, half smiling, as if memories were reawakening.

'No,' said Sachi. 'But my parents did.'

Haru drew back as if she had suddenly remembered who and where she was. 'And he was ... well?' she asked rather formally.

'He's well. He was...' How could she tell her that he was with the enemy?

But Haru had clasped her arms across her obi and was rocking backwards and forwards. 'Daisuké-*sama*, Daisuké-*sama*,' she murmured, her eyes filling with tears. 'It would have been better if we'd never seen him, your mother and I. But then ... you wouldn't be here either.'

A maid was bringing in tray after tray of dishes the likes of which Sachi hadn't seen since she left the palace.

'Tell me ... tell me about my mother, Big Sister. How did you know her?'

'We grew up together, my lady,' she said. 'My father was a retainer of her father's. I came with her to the palace. I was her maid. We were always together – like you two. I miss her still, I can't tell you how much.'

Her maid...! Taki gave a slow rumble of amazement, rising from somewhere deep in her throat. There was a long silence.

'What was her name?' whispered Sachi.

'Okoto,' Haru whispered, savouring each syllable. '*Okoto-no-kata*. Lady Okoto.'

Lady Okoto. In the shadows a kimono hanging over a stand stirred as a draught eddied through the room.

'She was of the House of Mizuno. Her father

410

was Lord Tadahira, chamberlain to the lords of Kisshu.'

Lord Mizuno... Was that not the man who had come to the palace to announce that His Majesty was ill, that dreadful man she and Taki had seen getting off the ferry only a few days earlier? Sachi could see his swarthy hawk-like features as he shuffled past her behind Lord Oguri, disguised as a merchant with a travelling hat pulled well down over his face. The way he had stared at her and cried out, as if she was a ghost... It must have been because she looked like her mother!

Haru picked up the brocade, shook it out and ran it through her fingers till she found the crest embroidered on the shoulder. Sachi looked at it, mesmerized. It was the Mizuno crest: she should have recognized it.

She was opening her mouth to speak when she felt a thin hand grasp her arm. She had forgotten that she and Taki were sworn to secrecy. Besides the princess and Lady Tsuguko, only the two of them even knew he had been in the palace.

Sachi could still hear him shouting, 'Go! Go! Leave me alone!' If her mother was of the same family as that dreadful man then so was she. They shared the same blood. The thought made her go quite cold.

'My mother was ... your mother's wet nurse,' said Haru. She was so caught up in her story she seemed not to have noticed Sachi's reaction. Her face was alight. She was in another time, another place. She sat back on her heels as the words came tumbling out. 'She was Lady Ohiro then, the little Lady Ohiro. She was lovely even then,

411

when she was tiny. She had the sweetest face. She was not shy at all, as if she knew from early on what a great future she would have. We always played together. Tankaku Castle in Shingu, in the country of Kii – that was where we lived. When it was stormy you could hear the ocean outside. I used to lie in my futons and listen to the waves crashing up against the rocks below the castle walls. Sometimes I hear it still.

'We studied together. Whatever she turned her hand to she did brilliantly – reading, calligraphy, poetry-writing, tea ceremony, incense-guessing, the koto, the halberd, all that. She was very clever, much cleverer than me. But wild, so wild. She went walking, climbed trees, climbed the cliffs. Imagine that! My father used to say she should have been a boy, that she had too many ideas of her own for a girl. She always got what she wanted. She could charm anyone.

'But she was good to me. She treated me like a sister. We were still children when the Mizuno family were ordered to move to their Edo mansion. She said she would only go if I went too. But we didn't stay there long, she and I. A couple of years later she went into service at the palace and she took me with her as her personal maid.

'I was not much older than you were when you arrived, my lady. The palace was so huge! It was like a labyrinth, it went on and on. And the ladies with their gorgeous kimonos, and painted faces. So grand, so haughty. I was terrified of them.'

Haru sighed and wiped a tear from her cheek.

Sachi was half kneeling, half lying on the tatami, her chin cupped in her hand, gazing up at

412

Haru, gripped by her story, drinking in her words. Taki knelt beside her, listening too.

At least now she knew that noble blood flowed in her veins, Sachi thought. That was why she was so pale, like a ghost or an aristocrat, not nut-brown like the peasants of the Kiso valley. And perhaps it was why fate had brought her to the women's palace, just as it had her mother. But more than that: she too was wilful. She shared the same blood as crazy Lord Mizuno.

'Old Lady Honju-in was the number-one concubine back then,' said Haru. 'Her Majesty the *midaidokoro*, His Majesty's wife, had long since passed away so Lady Honju-in was in charge. She ran this place with a rod of iron. You think the Retired One is tough. Lady Honju-in was worse, far worse. The beatings I got! I was black and blue. She was chief concubine because she was the mother of the heir. A hopeless, lolloping boy. He must have been twenty-one by then. I told you about him. Weak in the body and weak in the head. Everyone hoped and prayed for another son to be heir instead.

'The moment His Majesty Lord Ieyoshi saw my lady he fell for her. I wasn't surprised at all, not one bit. Who could resist her? She was so lovely and bright and full of sunshine – like you, Little Sister. Just like you. He was old and bald but a dear man, very kind. Of course he had plenty of concubines. But he was not like his father, he didn't collect women like so many ceramics. He had a tender heart. He always had a favourite. His last had died in childbirth. He was so sad, we heard, he couldn't sleep, he wept all the time.

413

Then we arrived.'

'What happened then?'

'He took one look and asked, "What is her name?" I didn't even know what the question meant. I didn't realize he wanted my lady to be his concubine. She was scared too, like you were when His young Majesty asked for you. But she had to do it, she knew that. So she became Lady Okoto, the lady of the side chamber.

'What a life we led! We lived in a magnificent suite of apartments. I was the head lady-in-waiting. Merchants would be lining up at the palace gates with trunks and boxes full of kimonos, obis, hair ornaments, cosmetics sets, all for her. The lords and officials and courtiers and merchants all wanted to be sure she was on their side when they petitioned His Majesty. They knew the only sure way to His Majesty's ear was through her. It was my job to sort out all the presents they gave her.

'There were many concubines, but His Majesty cared only for her. Night after night he summoned her. The year after we came she had a son, Prince Tadzuruwaka. There were huge celebrations and a ceremony to make him His Majesty's heir. But His Highness didn't live long. He passed away when he was still a baby. Then my lady had a daughter, Princess Shigé. She passed away too...'

Haru's voice trailed away. Sachi glanced over her shoulder. She could almost feel the presence of her mother, the beautiful Lady Okoto, there in the room with them, kneeling by the window, her hair in gleaming oiled loops, wearing the glorious

414

brocade over-kimono, the colour of the sky. Maybe she had felt trapped in the palace, this vibrant, lovely woman. Maybe she had looked out at the gardens and wished she could escape, remembered Tankaku Castle and the waves breaking on the shore. Maybe she was lonely in the middle of all the gifts.

'No one would have imagined it would come to this,' Haru murmured. 'I can't say if we were happy or sad. We lived out our lives, here in the palace. And she was young still, your mother, she hadn't even reached her twentieth year.' She buried her face in her hands. 'I tried so hard to forget!' she wailed suddenly. 'I thought I had succeeded. But then you appeared.' She gazed at Sachi, tears running down her cheeks.

Sachi leaned forward, acutely aware of how little time they had, of the danger they were all in.

'Big Sister,' she began urgently. 'I beg you to tell me: who is my father? How did he ... meet my mother?'

The light was beginning to fade. Flies buzzed. A shiny black cockroach skittered across a wall. Taki too was staring into space. Sachi could see she was thinking hard, trying to fit together the pieces of the puzzle.

Haru was gazing at the brocade. She picked it up reverently and held it to her cheek. As she touched it the rich dark scent swirled about the room, ebbing and flowing like a tide.

'Your father,' she said softly. 'If only you could have seen him, perhaps then you would have understood. I can see him too in your face.'

Sachi's father... The man who had carried her

415

to the village when she was a baby; the man who was now the enemy.

'But Haru, how could you possibly have known my lady's father?' demanded Taki, voicing Sachi's thought. 'You've never once left the palace!'

'I will tell you,' Haru said slowly. 'I have kept my secret for so long. But now everything is coming to an end. Nothing makes any difference any more.

'It was ... the year of the rooster, the second year of Kaei. The year before you were born. Some master builders had come to draw up an estimate for the annual repairs.'

Her eyes disappeared in the folds of her pink cheeks as a wicked smile crinkled her face. For a moment she was the old Haru again.

'There was always such a fuss whenever men turned up. We women would all be peeking through the lattices at them. Of course my lady, your mother, never took part in such nonsense. After all, she was His Majesty's concubine, she had her dignity to maintain. By then His Majesty... What can I say? He needed an heir. He was the shogun, after all. In short, he never summoned her any more. My lady tried hard to endure. She had always been so full of life but now she grew pale and sad.

'That summer the ladies were all a-twitter, like a forest full of birds, spying on these men with their belts laden with tools. They were ugly fellows, most of them, not like samurai at all. They crept around looking scared half out of their wits. After all, they only had to offend someone and they'd get their heads lopped off. Normally we

416

wouldn't have paid the remotest attention to such creatures. But what other chance did we get to see men?

'My lady was in her room, along with her ladies-in-waiting, when the door slid open and some builders came in to examine the ceiling. Some of the bamboo slats were fraying and falling apart. We shouldn't have been there at all, but no one had told us they were coming. My lady stood up immediately and out we all swept. But I couldn't help noticing that she glanced at one of the carpenters and he glanced at her. Just for a moment, nothing inappropriate.'

Haru closed her eyes. She was far away, back in that distant time. The room was utterly silent. Sachi sat mesmerized, trying to catch every word. Taki was holding her hand tightly.

'My, was he handsome!' Haru said softly. 'He wasn't anything like the other carpenters, not one bit. He looked like one of those kabuki actors we all admired so much. We weren't allowed to go to the theatre but some of the ladies had managed to sneak out. There was a really famous actor we all adored – Sojiro Sawamura. He looked just like him. That was Daisuké-*sama*. Your father.

'Afterwards we were chattering away about him. But not my lady. She didn't say a word. She was far too grand. But as the days passed she started to get paler and paler. She couldn't eat. She grew gaunt and black around the eyes, as if she'd taken opium or absinthe. I was afraid she was coming down with consumption. People always said it was a disease of the rich. But then I began to wonder if someone had sneaked powder of

417

roasted lizard into her food. That was what it looked like, that faraway look in her eyes, as if she wasn't really there in her body at all any more.

'Then one day she said, "Haru. Haru, I think I've fallen under a spell. It's like a spiritual starvation." Spiritual starvation, that's what she said. "Day and night I can't think of anything else. I've never felt like this before. I've become a hungry ghost. I shall die unless... Somehow I have to see this man again."

'We all yearn for the company of men, but what can you do except endure it? Endure the loneliness, endure the solitude, live without our bodies ever being set alight. But she never cared what anyone thought. She always had to have what she wanted. I asked a priest I knew to help us. We found out the name of the man and the priest sent a message. I knew Daisuké-*sama* would come. I could tell from that single look I had seen pass between them.

'We made up a story. My lady said she was going to Zojoji Temple to pray at the tombs of His Majesty's ancestors. What other reason could there be to leave the palace? We boarded palanquins and set off with a party of ladies-in-waiting and foot attendants. We'd taken a couple of ladies into our confidence. They stayed with the palanquins at Zojoji while we crept away. The priest I knew had had affairs with palace ladies himself. He had a secret room in his temple for that very purpose. Your father was waiting for us.'

Sachi put her hands over her mouth. So that was what she was, that was where she came from. A spiritual starvation... She knew that feeling.

That same madness surged in her veins. But at least... At least she had not gone as far as her mother. She had not thrown duty and honour away.

'Afterwards she didn't say a word. But it didn't quench the hunger. In fact her hunger grew fiercer and fiercer until I thought it would eat her up. Again and again we visited the tombs of the shoguns' ancestors. His Majesty must have thought she'd become very pious all of a sudden – except that he never thought of her at all any more. That was the pity of it. I kept telling her she must stop. But she couldn't. She just couldn't stop seeing Daisuké.

'I used to sit in attendance serving sake while they talked. After a while it didn't seem to matter any more that he was handsome or she was beautiful. They just had to be together.

'My lady grew plump again. She bloomed like a flower. Her eyes shone, she had colour in her cheeks, she laughed and chattered. When we were alone, she talked and talked about him. I was afraid the palace women would notice how different she was. Soon I started to hear murmurs and gossip. The other concubines were jealous of her because she had been the shogun's favourite. She had plenty of enemies.

'The next thing we knew she was with child. But His Majesty hadn't summoned her for months. It was obvious she'd have to get rid of it – but she couldn't bear to. It was wintertime. My lady put on layers and layers of kimonos to hide her belly. She took to staying in her room all the time except when she went to the temple to meet your father.

'She had the baby in the temple. I helped her. I brought you out into the daylight. I remember you still – such a tiny little wizened thing.'

Haru looked at Sachi and smiled a motherly smile. Reaching out, she laid her plump hand softly on Sachi's cheek, as if to reassure herself that she hadn't disappeared.

'At first they were so happy, your mother and father. They held you, they looked at you, they couldn't stop looking at you and at each other. But then my lady began to panic. "We must get back to the castle," she said. "They're going to come after us and kill my baby." "You must rest," I told her, but she was too afraid.

'My lady began to weep. She couldn't bear to leave you, even for a short time. She knew she'd gone too far, that she'd committed an unpardonable crime. She was wearing that brocade you have. She wrapped you up in it and tucked her comb into the folds. "There, little one," she said. "With this you'll be able to find me some day." And it worked, you see? In a strange way it worked.'

Haru pressed her sleeves to her face. She clasped her arms to her bosom, rocked back and forth, then took a deep breath.

'Then ... she put you into your father's arms. We carried her to the palanquin, she couldn't walk. So... So that was how we got back to the castle.'

A large grey rat scuttled into a corner. The shadows in the room were growing longer and the candles glimmered with a bright yellow light. It was nearly nightfall.

'When we got back there was news. My lady's brother was ill. Desperately ill.'

Sachi started. Her mother's brother – Lord Mizuno; perhaps the very Lord Mizuno she had seen crossing the river. Taki frowned at her, warning her to say nothing.

'She was to go to the family's Edo residence right away,' Haru continued. 'I thought I'd go with her, but she told me to stay. "If I'm not back tomorrow," she said, "tell Daisuké not to wait. Nothing matters, only my baby. She must be kept safe." She swore me to secrecy. "Never tell this tale to anyone except my child," she said. She didn't come back the next day or the next day either. I sneaked out and went to the temple. Daisuké had already left and had taken you with him. The priest didn't know where he'd gone.

'That was the last time I ever left the palace. I couldn't even weep, nor could I tell anyone what had happened. My life was over. I just stayed here, doing my work. I concentrated on teaching the new girls.

'And then ... you came. You were just a child but there was something about you that made me think of that baby. If she had lived, I thought, she would have been exactly your age. And then I saw that comb of yours. Such a fine comb for a little country girl. It was exactly like the one I used to comb my lady's hair with, hour after hour. I told myself some merchant must have left it in your village – but all the same I couldn't help wondering. And now – now it's as if she's come back. She's here again, my dear mistress, in you.'

Sachi was caught up in Haru's story – in her

own story. But the comb, the comb... She had given it to Shinzaemon, with whom she was entwined in a passion nearly as obsessive, as mad – as dangerous – as the one that had bound her mother to her father.

Suddenly she was aware of the guttering candles and the fading light. She shook herself and scrambled to her feet. She felt strangely disembodied, as if she had no control over her limbs.

'You have your mother in you,' said Haru. A smile flickered across her face.

For a moment Sachi wondered what she meant, but she had more pressing matters to think of.

'Go,' said Haru. 'Go now, my lady. Go to him.'

IV

Sachi hurried across the palace grounds with as much speed as she could muster. She had flung a townswoman's cloak over her court robes and wrapped a scarf around her head. Her skirts clung to her legs, making her mince with tiny steps. She was flushed and panting, damp with sweat. She could hear her breath, loud in the silence. Court ladies were supposed to glide at a glacial pace, she told herself, not charge about like peasants. She hardly noticed the mud clinging to her shoes and spattering the bottom of her skirts. All she knew was that she had to get to the Tsubone Gate by dusk.

The gardens were overgrown and cherry

blossom floated down like snow. It clung to her clothes and lay in damp mounds, clogging the path around her feet. It made her think of all those young warriors, doomed to die in their prime. Blindly she hurried by the sprawling palace buildings, the streams and bridges and pavilions and the burned-out ruin of the women's palace. She could hear Taki's footsteps, scampering along behind her. The old man too whom they had met when they arrived had appeared from nowhere. When patrols crossed their path he warned them off and sent them on their way.

The grounds were swarming with soldiers. The women might have left but the men were there in force, regiments of them bristling with rifles, marching about, doing all they could to protect the castle.

The Tsubone Gate – the Gate of the Shoguns' Ladies, the entrance to the women's palace – was tightly barred and bolted. Escorted by the old man, the two women slipped between the patrols and hurried through the small door beside the outer gates. Taki stayed in the shadows while Sachi went out on to the bridge. She knew there was very little time, that the door would be locked at nightfall. To be trapped outside the castle after dark, at the mercy of southern soldiers, would be too dreadful to imagine.

Standing alone on the bridge, outside the soaring ramparts of the castle, she suddenly felt very small. On the other side was a huge plaza and beyond it, small in the distance, a great wall bordering one of the daimyos' palaces. Broad boulevards led away in each direction. The waters

423

of the moat sparkled in the last rays of the dying sun. Bats flittered and wheeled against the vast arc of the darkening sky.

She began to realize how reckless she was being. The streets were entirely empty, and if robbers or gangsters or southerners appeared she would have to race back to the gate. From somewhere not far away came rough shouts and running feet and the sound of gunfire. A spasm of fear ran down her spine. She clutched her dagger, hardly daring to breathe.

The moon was rising behind the trees like a huge round lantern, the image of the rabbit pounding rice cakes marked clearly on its surface.

Of course Shinzaemon would not be here. He was a man, a soldier, and would not be driven by foolish feelings, particularly not something so absurd as weakness for a woman. In any case, to get here he would have to pass through these streets crawling with enemy soldiers. She should leave now, she told herself sternly, not linger like some low-class courtesan.

But no matter how much she upbraided herself she couldn't help feeling a gaping well of emptiness inside her. She knew now what it was – that spiritual starvation that had been the ruin of her mother. But she didn't care how mad and reckless and wrong it was – she would wait just a little longer. It was not quite dark yet.

There was a movement in the trees on the other side of the road. A man. In the moonlight she could see the face she had pictured so many times since they had parted – the broad nose, the

424

full-lipped mouth, the glossy hair tugged back. He walked with that lazy cat-like grace she knew so well, his two swords tucked firmly in his belt. She stood like a statue, her heart pounding, gripping the smooth wooden railing of the bridge, as his eyes met hers. She tried to look away, to break the spell. But she couldn't.

His eyes were shining with a fiery, devil-may-care madness – as if nothing mattered any more, as if he could see death holding out its arms, waiting to take him in its icy embrace. She had thought he would stop, speak, say something, but he walked straight up to her.

'You,' he said softly. The sound of his voice, gruff and tender, sent a shiver through her.

He pulled her towards him. She could feel the firmness of his body pressing against hers, crushing her. She felt his heat, smelt the salt of his sweat.

He pressed his face to her hair. Then he ran his lips greedily across her ear and the back of her neck as if he was going to eat her. The sensation of his mouth on her skin made her shudder. Almost fainting, she let her body fall against his. She was aware of nothing but a burning desire to be one with him.

Somewhere in the depths of her mind she was aware that decent women didn't behave this way. Maybe in the pleasure quarters, but not samurai and certainly not court ladies. But her mother... She had to save herself. She would not repeat the pattern, she would not.

'Stop, stop,' she gasped. 'I'll be … ruined.'

He took a deep breath and stepped back,

gazing at her.

'We don't have much time. I had to dodge a gang of southern soldiers heading for the castle. You need to get back inside. It's too dangerous out here.'

He grinned at her, that conspiratorial grin of his. She was aware of how different she must look in her nun's robes, even though it was nearly dark and she had thrown a cloak over them. She was dressed as she had been when he first saw her.

'I didn't think you'd come,' she whispered.

'I couldn't stop myself. I've thought of nothing but you. How can I be a soldier when you turn me into a woman?'

'I missed you.'

They stood in silence, held in each other's gaze.

'We're alike,' he said, 'you and I. All ... this.' He gestured at the castle ramparts and the great white-walled fortifications looming on the other side of the moat. 'We're outside it. I ride alone. You do too. I still don't know who or what you are, but I know that.'

For a moment she wanted to tell him everything – that she was the Retired Lady Shoko-in, the concubine of the late shogun, that she had taken holy orders. That she was the daughter of another concubine, of the Lady Okoto. But he was soon to die and they would never meet again.

'Everyone is mad for bloodshed, mad for war,' he said. 'Only I have anything else on my mind. But...' In the dying light she could see his eyes flash. 'I shall fight all the better. I shall fight for you.'

He took her in his arms again and everything

faded away. There were just the two of them, standing on the bridge while above them the moon shone, reflected in the water rippling below. In the whole universe there was only her and Shinzaemon.

Footsteps were approaching. There were shadowy figures at the top of the rise, approaching along the road. She realized the door in the gate would shut at any moment.

He took something from his belt.

'Take this,' he said, reluctantly drawing apart. 'For you. A keepsake. The clasp of my tobacco pouch.'

She felt the rough skin of his hands on hers as he closed her fingers around it. It was small and heavy, like a pebble, and warm with the warmth of his body. Tears welled in her eyes.

'I have to get back,' he said.

'To Kanei-ji Temple?'

He nodded. 'On Ueno Hill. The retired shogun, Lord Yoshinobu, is there. There are thousands of us. We have men up in the hills, picking off the southerners, holding them off for as long as we can. I can't wait to feel my sword cutting southern flesh again. We'll put His Majesty back where he belongs, up there in the castle. It'll be glorious!'

He held her with his eyes.

'I look forward to the honour of dying in battle for my lord. But if I survive I shall come and find you.'

She nodded, her lips trembling.

'I'll wait for you – in this world or the next,' she said.

Reluctantly she turned and ran back up the

bridge to the great gate of the castle. As she pushed the door, it creaked open. She looked back and saw him standing on the bridge still, a dark shape, keeping watch. She bowed. He raised his hand and strode away.

Safely inside the gate she opened her hand. Taki held up a lantern. He had given her a *netsuke*, a wooden toggle, carved in the shape of a monkey. His birth year. She held it to her nose. It smelt of him, his body.

Tears filled her eyes and poured in a hot stream down her cheeks. If he had asked her to run away with him... What might she have done? She told herself sternly not to be so foolish. They had made their farewells. They had had their last moment together. There was nothing left now to look forward to but death – his ... and hers.

V

Sachi ground a little more ink then dipped her brush and wrote some characters in a few elegant strokes, letting the brush rise and fall like a plover in flight. She should have been composing her death poem, but instead the passionate lines of the Heian-period poetess Ono no Komachi thrummed insistently in her mind:

Yumeji ni wa	On the path of dreams
Ashi mo yasumezu	My feet never rest
Kayoedo mo	As they run to you:
Utsutsu ni hitome	But such visions cannot match

Mishi goto wa arazu. One waking glimpse of you yourself.

'One waking glimpse of you yourself...' One moment of closeness. As she wrote, she was back on the bridge. She could feel Shinzaemon's arms around her, the muscles of his body pressed against hers, his lips rough on her neck. The fact they might never meet again made it all the more poignant.

She looked at Taki. They had been through so much together. She was such a tiny, thin little creature, like a bundle of sticks inside her clothes. Yet she was so strong, so indomitable, so dependable. She was like a sister – as Haru had been for her mother.

Taki was frowning at her. 'She's not you,' she said severely. 'Your mother. That was a long time ago. She was a samurai's spoilt daughter. You're different. You grew up in the countryside, your parents were down-to-earth people. Don't let Haru's story confuse you.'

Then she smiled and looked down. 'But who am I to talk?' she said, blushing. 'Look at me, I'm just as foolish.' She whispered hesitantly as if she almost dared not ask, 'Did Shin ... have any message for me?'

Sachi took a breath. 'Toranosuké sends greetings and says he's thinking of you,' she said. It was a lie, but she needed to tell it. It was what Taki needed to hear.

Taki nodded, satisfied. Then her eyes opened wide. She tipped her head to one side like a bird and took a breath.

'Listen,' she said.

Somewhere in the distance they could hear footsteps. People were walking through the empty rooms, not scurrying like women or sliding their feet deferentially like courtiers but moving, many of them, with an urgent heavy tread. There were voices too, loud, deep voices. Men's voices. And laughter, men's laughter.

Men? In the women's palace? But that was ... impossible.

The door slid open. Haru was outside. Her plump face was drawn, her lips trembling.

'Her Highness requires your presence immediately.'

Women were emerging from the depths of the palace, the younger ones like great flowers in their full-skirted, brilliantly coloured kimonos, the older ones autumn leaves in sere drab colours. Lady Honju-in appeared, hobbling along, more tiny and withered than ever. Of her three hundred aged ladies-in-waiting, there were only two left. The Old Crow, the princess's mother, shuffled in too, accompanied by a single attendant. Without their pomp and finery they were just tired old ladies, sallow-skinned and wrinkled. But their faces were alight with a fierce joy, as if they could already see their heroic deaths. Sachi hadn't realized there were so many women left in the palace.

They flocked towards the great hall, the heavy trains of their robes swishing along the tatami mats with a sound like waves breaking on a distant shore, and took their places inside on their knees.

The princess and the Retired One knelt on a

430

dais at the far end of the room. On the wall behind them a gnarled cherry tree spread its branches, covered in clouds of pink blossom. It was so perfectly painted that if it hadn't been for the background of glimmering gold leaf you might have thought it was a real tree. It spoke of life but on their faces there was nothing but death. They knelt like statues, ominously calm.

A hush fell over the room. The Retired One drew herself up. Her face seemed to have sunk until it was nothing but bone, yet her eyes gleamed feverishly like coals. A vein throbbed in her neck.

'My ladies. It's over for the women's palace – for us, for our world, for our way of life. This great castle, this life of beauty we have led, these traditions we have preserved for hundreds of years, ever since the days of the first shogun, Lord Ieyasu, are at an end.

'Edo Castle ... is to be surrendered. It is to be evacuated within seven days. The imperial envoys have arrived. They have read out the terms of surrender in the Great Audience Hall of the Main Citadel. They will be here at any moment to demand our compliance.'

Stifled gasps and sobs filled the hall.

'Surrender?' It was Lady Honju-in's croaky old voice. 'Whoever heard of such a thing? You, daughter-in-law,' she shrilled, shaking a gnarled finger at the Retired One. 'You should be the last to accept such ignominy. Give ourselves up to the enemy? Never! We've been betrayed. But there is still time. Ladies, we must kill ourselves now!'

The Retired One grew paler still. 'On the

orders of His Majesty the retired shogun, Lord Yoshinobu,' she said, her voice shaking, 'we are denied the privilege of suicide. We have no choice but to obey. We are to leave without a fight.'

'Like dogs, with our tails between our legs!' snarled Lady Honju-in. At her age she could say what she liked. 'The Two-Faced One, up to his tricks again. Hardly a surprise.'

Sachi could hardly breathe. Her heart was pounding, her throat constricted, her breath coming in short gasps.

To Lady Honju-in, to surrender was the ultimate disgrace, to die with honour what every samurai yearned for. But Lady Honju-in was old. Things were different now, Sachi could see that. The shogun was no longer at the head of his troops. He was in hiding and had already surrendered. So why should the castle hold out? Why should they fight and die for a shogun who was not prepared to die himself?

She looked around at the princess and the Retired One and the women. The princess was deathly white, so pale Sachi was afraid she would faint. The glorious destiny they had foreseen for themselves had been ripped from their grasp. There was defiance on every face, yet they were the shogun's household, bound to him for ever and they would do whatever he ordered them to do. In the past they had shared in his wealth and power and glory. Now they would share in his disgrace. It would have been better by far if they had died.

Sachi understood all this. But deep inside she felt something else so shameful she hardly dared acknowledge it, even to herself. It was a kind of relief. She was going to live.

The shuffle of footsteps grew louder and stopped right outside. The doors slid open.

As one the women dropped their heads, as if afraid that if they glimpsed the enemy even for a moment they would be turned to stone. No man but the shogun had ever seen their faces. It was unthinkable to let these hateful intruders violate them with their eyes. There was to be not a sound – not a sob, not a sniffle. They still had their pride, at least. But though their eyes were cast down, every hair on the back of every neck was prickling. Everyone was determined that the arch of their backs should communicate not deference but defiance.

Sachi stared hard at the tatami as men swaggered in, their voices incongruously loud in the hush. A complicated mix of odours swirled in with them. She made out a delicate perfume redolent of the imperial court, so there were imperial envoys present. But it was overwhelmed by earthier smells – the stench of sweat mixed with tobacco smoke, of leather, horses, dirty clothes. It was the reek of samurai of the lower ranks. She wrinkled her nose as the sharp tang of clove oil assailed her nostrils. The oil that was used for polishing swords. How could that be? It must mean... Surely even ruffians like these could not be so ignorant as to wear their swords in the women's palace!

At least she had mixed with men on her travels, she thought; it was not such a shock for her. But these women had not been near a man for twenty

433

or thirty years or even more, and in all those years the only man they had ever glimpsed had been the exquisitely perfumed shogun. For them the contrast between those days of culture and beauty and the grim reality of the present must be almost too much to bear.

A voice grunted in a gruff southern burr so outlandish it was almost impossible to understand him.

'Well, 'ere we are ... er ... ladies.'

The women froze. There were stifled gasps, a few horrified titters. He didn't even know the proper language to use to address ladies of rank. And these were to be their new masters. Victors or not, for such lowly men to set foot inside the palace and look upon the most powerful women in the land, beautiful enough to have been chosen for the shogun's household... If Sachi had not been present she would never have believed it. Before this war, men such as these could never have dreamed of finding themselves in such a place. The man even sounded a little awestruck, as indeed he should.

'As from now, Edo Castle belongs to the emperor...' It was one of the envoys, speaking in the formal language of the court. 'The castle is to be handed over to the imperial troops. We are taking possession of it in seven days. The ladies are required to leave.'

'When we arrive we expect the castle to be empty,' said another. 'The ladies will be suitably accommodated outside the castle. They will remain in seclusion, under our orders.'

'You'll have to kill us first.' The Retired One's

voice was as sharp and clear as a sliver of ice. 'This is where we belong. This is our home. If you want us to leave you'll have to remove us by force. We'll die by our own hands.'

'Excuse me, my lady.' It was the princess's voice. She chose her words with care, speaking calmly and with dignity. 'I bow to the command of His Grace my nephew, the Son of Heaven. I will take it upon myself to ensure that your orders are carried out.'

In the gardens a heron shrieked. The scent of spring wafted through the thick gold leaf of the walls, drenching the darkest corners of the great hall with the odour of earth and wet leaves and trees and plants bursting into bud. It had been on a fragrant spring day just like this that Sachi had first seen His Majesty, the late shogun, in the gardens, so many years ago. She felt a spasm in her throat as she remembered and swallowed hard.

Harsh male voices crackled from the other side of the room.

'Just in time to see the cherry blossom.'

'Lucky, unh?'

The women knelt, staring defiantly at the tatami. It was a cruel reminder that everything was about to change. They would all be gone before the cherry blossom had reached full bloom.

Among the murmur of voices Sachi heard a stifled sob. Startled, she looked around. Haru, of all people. And she a samurai!

The room was packed with men, pressed around the edges of the great hall and crammed beyond the open doors. Two envoys in full court regalia faced the princess and the Retired One.

435

Four or five other men stood there too. They looked like officers, perhaps generals. They were wearing splendid red and gold *haori* surcoats with starched wing-like shoulders, but instead of the usual formal dress they had black southern uniforms underneath. A wild-looking bunch with swarthy faces and fierce black eyes, some had moustaches and beards and hair as long and bushy as a bear's mane. Others wore their hair oiled and tugged back into a horse's tail, held in place with a red and gold headband.

The rest were ordinary soldiers – burly leather-skinned veterans of battle, hard-eyed profes-sionals. Some held red banners marked with a white cross in a circle – the crest of the Satsuma, the most intractable of the southern clans. Just as she had thought, they were all wearing their swords.

Some were yawning, looking bored. Some were gloating, stifling grins as if they couldn't believe their luck. They seemed a little shamefaced too, like children who had been caught fighting or stealing or running away. Here they were right inside the forbidden palace, in the innermost sanctum, the most secret part, walking where no man had ever walked before, seeing women no man had ever been allowed to cast eyes on. And without even removing their swords! It was unbearable.

Haru was kneeling bolt upright, her fists clenched. Her eyes were wide and her plump cheeks were as pale as the straw of the tatami mats. Tears ran unheeded down her cheeks. She was staring transfixed at someone in the crowd.

At the far end of the hall was a middle-aged man, standing a little apart from the rest. He looked like an official of some sort. He was dressed formally in stiff black *hakama* trousers and a *haori* jacket. He had two swords but he didn't seem to be a samurai. His head was not shaved and he didn't have a topknot. His thick hair, greying at the temples, was cut short like a foreigner's. He was peering around with unabashed curiosity, studying the ranks of bowed heads as if he was trying to make out the faces beneath the gleaming coiffures sparkling with hairpins and combs.

Sachi couldn't help noticing what a fine-looking man he was, despite his age. Maybe it was the way he held himself, with a kind of quiet confidence. Maybe it was his broad high-cheekboned face, or the way he gazed so steadily from under his thick brows, or the laughter lines around his eyes, or the half-smile lurking on his full, rather sensual lips. For a southerner he looked almost human.

For a moment their eyes met, and he started. She could see his throat move as he swallowed. He clenched his fists so tightly his knuckles went white and he clutched at his sword for support.

Sachi looked away quickly. In her mind something was falling into place. It was as if she had been trying to open one of the puzzle boxes some of the women in the palace had. Only the owner of the box knew the secret sequence of moves, which small slat of wood to slide first and which after. Some of those beautiful boxes took a hundred different moves to open. Sachi felt as if

437

she had worked out which piece to move but she didn't know yet which way it went.

As soon as the formalities had finished, the man strode across to her. He knelt, slid his fan from his obi, laid it on the tatami in front of him, and made a formal bow.

There was a sickening feeling in the pit of her stomach. Suddenly Sachi knew exactly what he was going to say.

He spoke the words softly but clearly: 'I am your father.'

10

Falling Blossoms

I

The great hall seemed to have grown quiet. Somewhere in the distance men's voices and laughter echoed dully. Not a sound came from the ranks of women, only a soft rustling from the movements of their voluminous skirts.

Sachi looked at the hands resting politely on the tatami in front of her. They were big and muscular with broad nails and black hairs sprouting between the knuckles. Carpenters' hands, she thought with a sort of dazed wonderment. But surely a carpenter's would be ingrained with dirt and have chipped, broken nails? These were scrubbed, trimmed and faintly perfumed. They had not seen manual labour for years.

So this was her father. She knew he had asked for her at the village when he had been on his way to Edo with the southern forces. But a father! He was an outsider, a townsman, a southerner with an outlandish haircut, utterly wrong and foreign.

She stared down at her own hands, so small and thin and pale. She was not going to look at him. But she could feel his eyes probing her downturned face, hear the rasp of his breath, smell the pungent scents of sweat and tobacco and southern spices.

Then Taki spoke up. She seemed to sense what Sachi was feeling.

'You are mistaken, sir,' she said in her most fiercely protective tones.

'There's no mistaking,' he said. His voice was a low rumble. 'My daughter. My child. I knew straight away. You are exactly...'

He spoke in rough townsman's Edo overlaid with what sounded like broad Osaka. Sachi knew what he wanted to say: exactly like her mother.

'I waited so long,' he said, softly but clearly. 'So many years. I thought I would never set eyes on you again. And now... To find you in this place of all places, at this time of all times ...'

Sachi was staring at his hands. She looked back at her own. There was something about the way the fingers lay. The tip of his middle finger inclined ever so slightly towards the finger next to it. The same as hers. She looked away, focused her mind, took a deep breath. She had to remember she was a samurai.

'Who is addressing me?' she asked. For all her efforts her voice was shaking and her breath came in short gasps.

'So rude of me,' he grunted. She glimpsed the stubbly grey hair on the top of his head as he bowed. 'Allow me to introduce myself. My name is Daisuké, humble servant to His Grace the emperor, the Son of Heaven. I am charged with ensuring the smooth transfer of Edo Castle to the imperial command. At your service, madam. I will do all I can to help you and all the ladies.'

Sachi couldn't resist any longer. She was too curious. She raised her head a fraction and peeked at him through her lashes.

Close up his face was lined and weathered, a little jowly around the cheeks and baggy around the eyes. She could see the pores on his nose, the thick black hairs of his eyebrows. Hairs prickled above his upper lip. His eyes roamed across her nun's garments, her cowl. He was looking at her as if nothing else existed in the world, studying her face as if he wanted to fix her image in his mind for ever. It was a rather kind face, she thought, not villainous at all. He was not scowling like an enemy or gloating with triumph but gazing at her with a look that was excited and hopeful, sad and despairing all at the same time.

For a moment their eyes met. His were narrow, slightly puffy, a little bloodshot. She started as she realized they were glittering with tears.

Behind him the pompous court envoys and generals in their gleaming red and gold surcoats had disappeared. The lower ranks were milling around in a clot of sweaty black uniforms, pomaded ponytails and oiled rifle butts. They were trying to keep their expressions cool and indifferent, like professional soldiers who strutted through conquered castles every day; but she could see the corners of their mouths twitching and the gleam of triumph in their eyes.

The women pressed their faces to the floor, refusing to let the men see them, but Sachi knew exactly what they were thinking. For ladies such as they, the greatest ladies in the land, to be evicted by this mob of ignorant bumpkins – the ignominy was more than they could endure. Some would go back to their families but many more were vowing to be dead by their own hands long before the seven days had passed.

There was a rustle. Haru slipped forward on her knees. Her plump cheeks were redder than ever and her lips were trembling.

'My lady,' she said. 'I know this man. I can vouch for him.'

The man spun round. 'Haru,' he said. 'Is it really you?'

She nodded.

He turned back to Sachi.

'My child,' he said. His voice was a groan. 'My Sachi.'

She stared at him wildly. He knew her name, her childhood name! She had always thought it was her parents in the village who had given her that name. He could only know it if... She looked at his face again, at his eyes, like bitter almonds, barely slanting at all... It couldn't be denied. There was a connection between them stronger even than the bond that united the northerners

441

against the southerners. A bond of blood.

The last soldiers were straggling out of the great hall, scuffing their feet across the exquisite tatami with its woven gold edging. Their voices and raucous laughter, the noxious odours of sweat and clove oil disappeared into the distance.

'I have to go,' the man said, still gazing at Sachi. 'But I beg you, let me return. I know you see me as your enemy. Give me a chance, a chance to get to know you.'

Sachi tried to speak but couldn't. She was trembling too much.

'Daisuké-*sama*.' It was Haru. 'Please visit us. Her ladyship would like it too, I promise.'

Sachi bowed stiffly. Haru understood everything, yet it was still a struggle to force out the words.

'You are welcome ... to come.'

His eyes lit up.

'Nothing will stop me,' he said. He bowed and hurried out.

The women made their way slowly through the labyrinth of rooms. For a while there was no sound except the swish of their quilted kimono hems trailing across the tatami and the trilling of birds in the gardens. Then Haru turned to Sachi. She was dabbing her eyes with her sleeve.

'What did I tell you?' she said, smiling ruefully through her tears. 'Is he not the handsomest man you ever saw?'

'Be careful, my lady,' said Taki in thin clipped tones. 'He's not a good person for people like you to consort with. He's a townsman. He has no

442

idea of proper behaviour among our class of people. He persuaded your mother – a concubine of the shogun – to neglect her duty. Don't forget that. Don't be taken in by him.'

Sachi had never heard Taki speak so disapprovingly before. She was not sure about this man either but Taki's attitude made her leap to his defence.

'Taki!' she said fiercely. 'You forget. He's my father.'

Taki bit her lip. With a jolt Sachi realized what she had said – that she had acknowledged their blood relationship, voiced her acceptance of it.

'He isn't a good man,' said Taki, setting her jaw stubbornly. 'He's a traitor. He's an Edo man who's with the southerners. I don't know what you can be thinking, Haru-*sama*. If he comes, you can see him, but *my* lady needn't ever see him again.'

'My lady's destiny is intertwined with his,' said Haru. 'Now they've found each other it's only the beginning.'

II

Seven days to pack up and leave. In seven days it would all be over.

Sachi was kneeling on a dais, plucking out a melody on a koto. The notes echoed hollowly in the empty room. She was hardly aware of the tune she was playing. Her fingers moved by themselves across the strings. In her thoughts she was far away, outside the castle, up on the hill where the militia was billeted.

443

Shinzaemon... They were nothing but autumn leaves whirling in a typhoon, the two of them, tossed by events far bigger than themselves. Without him the world was an empty place, a howling wilderness. In front of the others she hid her pain, but she had to force herself to smile and laugh.

She carried his toggle tucked into her obi. When she was alone she brought it out, raised it to her nose, inhaled his smell. Now she felt it there, pressing against her stomach.

If only there was some way to get a message to him, to tell him that the castle had been occupied, that she was not going to die. But she couldn't even tell him where she was going because she didn't know herself.

Taki's voice broke into her thoughts.

'Please, my lady,' she squeaked. 'Something different, I beg you. Play something different.'

Sachi was playing one of the songs they used to sing when they went to view the cherry blossom. She came back to the present with a start and pushed the koto away. The memory of those happy times was too much to bear.

Already the palace was starting to feel deserted. Haru and Taki were rushing around in a panic, packing as quickly as they could. Carefully they lifted a last kimono off its rack. It was white with a pattern of phoenixes woven into the cloth. With every movement of the fabric fragrance wafted through the room, a complex scent of eight or nine different ingredients – sandalwood, myrrh, a heady hint of fragrant spikenard oil on a base of aloe, with a grace note of some secret ingredient that only the princess knew. The scent took Sachi

444

back to the day when His Majesty had made his last visit to the women's palace. It was the gown the princess had worn that day. Sighing and brushing away tears from their cheeks, the women smoothed the beautiful robe, then folded it, wrapped it in paper, put it in a drawer and laid it gently in a trunk.

Footsteps sounded in the distance. Men, stomping unceremoniously through the palace. The women bowed their heads in resignation. They must show a strong face to these intruders.

The doors slid open. Daisuké. This man who claimed to be ... who was ... Sachi's father. He strode in, tall and burly and commanding, followed by a party of uniformed soldiers.

Sachi stared at the floor as a terrible idea occurred to her. Maybe everything that had happened was her fault? Maybe it was she, the offspring of an unnatural union of high and low, the shogun's concubine and a low-class townsman, who had brought this ill fortune on the palace. Maybe it was because of her that these southern barbarians – low-class samurai and townsfolk so base they barely counted as humans – swarmed like a plague of rats into every corner of the magnificent halls.

'We are under orders to inspect the chambers,' said Daisuké. Sachi detected a note of apology in his voice. Even the princess's chambers? Surely not. Even these loutish southerners could not be so ignorant of the proper order of things.

Daisuké clapped his hands and men of the merchant class appeared, bobbing and bowing timidly outside the door. In the old days under-

445

maids of undermaids would have gone to the gates to deal with such creatures. Never in a million years would these men have dreamed of setting foot within the sacrosanct precincts of the palace. They would have been dead, their heads severed from their shoulders, if they had even thought of it.

Now here they were in their merchants' garb, dull and drab as the rules required but with a flash of gold at the cuffs, a reminder that for all their grovelling humility they were hugely rich. They crept in, trembling, on their hands and knees, rubbing their noses along the matting, bowing again and again. Every now and then they twisted their heads to steal a glance at the forbidden interior and even more forbidden women. The women shrank back and turned their heads away, trying to conceal their faces from these vulgar eyes.

Servants scurried behind the merchants carrying lengths of silk. 'To make your days of seclusion more endurable,' said Daisuké as he presented the gifts to Haru and Taki.

One servant held a cage of finest paulownia wood, exquisitely carved and embossed, fitted with opaque paper screens in rose-wood frames. A tiny brown bird crouched in the shadows. It cocked its head, blinked a black eye and trilled out a plangent melody, slow and sweet, rising to a passionate warble. In the gardens a wild nightingale took up the song.

'A good omen,' said Daisuké, smiling. 'Nightingales never sing when people are watching. But he sings for you.'

446

Sachi bowed. The little bird's plight reminded her all too fiercely that she too was about to lose her freedom. She murmured a poem:

'Taguinaki	Were it not for
Ne nite nakazuba	The peerless sweetness of its song
Uguisu no	The nightingale in its cage
Ko ni sumu ukime	Would never suffer
Mizu ya aramashi	So harsh a fate.'

For a moment she looked up at this face – her father's. The sags and bags were kindly but there was something disturbing about him too. It was the way he looked at her, she thought, the fiery intensity of his eyes.

There were other gifts – an urn of the finest Uji tea, boxes of rice cakes stuffed with bean jam, last season's Edo oranges. Sachi had been dreading this visit, fearful he was going to make demands, try to persuade her to do this or do that. But he didn't. They sat in silence, puffing on long-stemmed pipes, listening to the nightingale's song. Little by little she was getting used to his presence.

Haru was leaning forward, gazing at Daisuké bright-eyed as if she was afraid that if she once took her eyes off him he would disappear back into the shadows from which he had so unexpectedly emerged. Every now and then Taki glanced at her with a frown of irritation on her thin face but Haru seemed not to care.

'It must be ... eighteen years!' she said suddenly, then clapped her hands over her mouth and turned a deep shade of red, glancing around as if the words had burst out of their own accord.

'You weren't much more than a child when I saw you last,' said Daisuké, smiling. 'You haven't changed, not one bit.'

Haru flushed even redder. Sachi smiled to herself at the thought of plump-cheeked Haru, with her heavy face and forehead covered in fine lines, being like a child.

Daisuké was staring into the distance.

'This palace,' he said with a wry smile. 'I used to come here even when I was just a boy. Climbing around the roofs – roof after roof after roof. Checking the lead tiles – hundreds of thousands of them. Then there were the beams, the support pillars, the joists, the floors, the transepts... There was so much that needed seeing to. My father was so proud we had the contract. We had the sign outside our shop: "By appointment to the shogun".'

'We weren't supposed to see you,' said Haru. Her round face was wreathed in smiles. 'As far as we were concerned you didn't exist. That was the theory, anyway.'

The faintest of scents spiked the air, a mysterious silky odour like the perfume of some great lady. Musk, aloe, wormwood, frankincense... The candle flames flickered and a whorl of dust spiralled in a corner. Was someone else there with them? A beautiful woman dressed in the gorgeous overkimono of a concubine?

Sachi sat still, her hands folded in her lap. She had been expecting Daisuké to bombard her with questions and arguments, to try to get to know her, justify why he had taken the path he had. She had sworn to herself she wouldn't speak to him, but now, when he sat so quietly, she found questions bubbling up inside her.

'Did you really carry me through the mountains?' she whispered shyly. His face lit up as if he was amazed and delighted she had spoken to him at last. She looked down quickly and stared at the floor.

'You were such a little thing, so tiny and so light,' he said in his gruff tones. 'Your mother had wrapped you in her overkimono. I bundled you up, brocade and all, in a scarf and tied you to my back. I was afraid someone might question me at a checkpoint. They would have if they'd seen the brocade. They'd have thought I was stealing a daimyo's child – a beautiful baby like you, with your face like a pearl. They'd have thrown me in prison and taken you away. They'd have tried, anyway.'

He bunched his big fists for a moment. A shadow of a grin lit the corners of his mouth and gleamed in his eyes.

'And so you got to my village...' Sachi said in a tiny voice.

His face softened.

'I'd never met those good folk, I only knew they were my relatives. But it felt like home. I was afraid you might die, a newborn child like you, but you were well wrapped up.'

'It's here,' breathed Haru. 'My lady has it still. The brocade. My lady her mother's...'

She had brought it out from its drawer and it lay folded beside her like a little piece of the sky,

449

blue and shimmering, exuding its delicate perfume. There was no ghost there, only the brocade.

Daisuké's brow furrowed as he reached out and laid his big carpenter's hand on the delicate fabric. He picked it up, held it to his cheek, inhaled the scent.

'You. Your perfume,' he murmured. 'You are here with us. Not a day has passed, not a moment, when I haven't thought of you, when I haven't prayed for you.'

He looked at Sachi as if suddenly remembering she was there and smiled. She hadn't noticed before what a reassuring smile he had – a fatherly smile, she thought to herself uneasily.

'She was a fine woman, your mother,' he said softly.

'Was she like me?' whispered Sachi.

'Just like you,' he said. 'Full of life. And very brave. She didn't care about anything. This world she lived in, this palace full of hatred and snobbery and in-fighting – it was like a prison for her. She hated it. I wanted to take her away from it. If I could, I'd take you too. But it's all over now.'

'All over for who?' Sachi glared at him. 'For the shoguns? For the Tokugawas? You're wrong. The war isn't over yet.'

'Maybe. But we can never go back to the old ways where men die at a word from their lord or kill others without a thought because it's what the clan orders. It was that rigid system that forced us apart, your mother and me. Before we met I never thought about anything except getting up in the morning, doing my job, keeping on the right side of the shogun's police.

'We were from different castes, you know that. What we did was a crime. The only choice we had was to kill ourselves together like people do in the old plays. But I'm not a samurai. I'm not so eager to die.'

Silence fell across the gathering like a pall. Even the little bird had stopped its singing. Sachi thought of her mother. Her presence was almost palpable – her brightness, her laughter, her mysterious smile.

'You talk about her as if she's dead,' she faltered.

Daisuké looked at Haru. In the candlelight his face was haggard. Haru was staring at the tatami.

'So what did you do after you left my lady at the village?'

Everyone whirled round. It was Taki. It was the first time she had ever addressed Daisuké.

'I've been to the village too, you know. With my lady. We heard about you, there. We heard you had passed through.'

'Well...' said Daisuké slowly, returning to the present. His face relaxed. 'I ended up in Osaka. I settled down. I found work. It wasn't so hard, I had a trade.' He looked at Sachi, held her in his gaze as if she was a precious treasure. 'I wanted to get you back but I had to be able to support you first. Whenever I had spare money I sent it to your parents. I wanted to become a father you could be proud of, then I'd come and claim you.'

She looked at him. He had tears in his eyes.

'The years went by. I struggled. Then the Black

451

Ships came.'

'Bringing the foreigners.'

He nodded. 'Bringing the foreigners.'

Sachi remembered when she was a child, growing up in the village, hearing of the Black Ships that had anchored, belching smoke, off the coast at Shimoda and disgorged a delegation of red-haired barbarians. It was the first time barbarians had ever stepped on to Japanese soil, apart from a small group of Dutch merchants who lived on an island off Nagasaki, a good way from Edo. After that no one had been able to stem the tide. Many samurai had made it their business to cut down foreigners whenever they could, though they had often had to pay with their heads for it. Now, of course, Sachi had met foreigners herself and discovered they were not so fearsome after all.

'I had made new friends by then,' said Daisuké. 'Good men, brave men. They didn't care what caste I was. High-level samurai, low-level samurai, peasant, townsman – there was room for all of us. We spent night after night talking politics. Most were from down south – a long way from Edo. It's a lot freer down there, where the shogun's grip is not so tight.'

'We know about those southern lords,' said Sachi softly. 'They're the ones who started all the trouble.'

'They could see that the country had to change, that there were foreigners right here, on our sacred soil. We all felt the same about that. We read books, we read news sheets. We knew they'd carved up China and India and other countries

452

beyond the seas. If they had half a chance they'd grab our country too, that was for sure. But the government – this government...' Daisuké gestured around at the empty room, the cobwebs glistening faintly in the corners.

Sachi frowned. For a moment she could see it through his eyes – this world of women with their lives of luxury and privilege; the innocent young shogun, so weak, so ignorant of everything, dependent on his advisers... Angrily she pushed away the thought.

'The government didn't seem to understand the peril,' said Daisuké. 'Or maybe it was too weak to drive them out. We realized it was time for change, time to give power back to the emperor. "Restore the emperor and expel the barbarians." That was our slogan. Those were our aims.

'Suddenly it seemed that we – carpenters like me, ordinary people – could make a difference. Instead of just earning money, spending money, worrying about money, we could change the world, make it a better place. It actually seemed possible.'

Sachi shook her head. When she was growing up she hadn't even known there was an emperor. Each daimyo – all two hundred and sixty of them – ruled his own domain and over them all, keeping peace in the whole great land of the Rising Sun, was the shogun. That was how it had always been.

Now she knew very well that the emperor was a holy being who lived in seclusion in Kyoto and communed with the gods to ensure that the country was prosperous and crops were good.

With a pang of sadness she remembered Lady Tsuguko. It was she who had explained to Sachi and Taki how the southern lords – those who were furthest from Edo and from the control of the shogun – had put about the theory that the emperor, aeons earlier, had given the shogun authority to rule, and that that authority should now be returned to the emperor. Not that they intended the emperor truly to rule: far from it, they were determined to use the emperor's name to take power themselves.

Daisuké must think they were foolish gullible women to tell them such stories, Sachi thought. Didn't he realize that the women of the shogun's household knew as much about affairs of state as any man? And surely it must be obvious where their loyalties lay.

'Give power back to the emperor?' demanded Taki, bristling. 'You mean take power into your own hands. Those friends of yours, those southerners – they killed His Grace the old emperor. They murdered him. His present Grace is a child. You'd kill him too if he didn't do what you wanted. *You* brought war on this country.'

She glared at him accusingly. 'You were in Kyoto,' she snapped. 'You! You were fighting there.'

Daisuké looked away. 'There was fighting there,' he muttered. 'And I was involved in it. We're making a new world.'

In the distance there were footsteps – the soldiers returning. Daisuké looked relieved. He shifted back a little, adjusted his posture, put on an official face.

'What will become of us?' Sachi asked urgently. 'Can't you help us?'

'I don't have that power,' he said. 'But I'll seek you out, wherever you are, and do my best for you. I'll watch over you, no matter what. I haven't found you just to lose you again.'

III

The door of Sachi's palanquin was open but she didn't get in. She was trying to imprint the image of the palace and the gardens on her mind. She knew with terrible certainty that once the door closed she would never see any of it again.

In the spring sunshine the palace looked lonelier than ever. Moss sprouted between the roof tiles. The buildings were beginning to crumble. Ferns and horsetail shoots burst out between the moss-covered boulders of the ramparts. The gardeners had long since fled. Wild grasses, tall and pale, swayed in the wind. Reeds darkened the grey and silver waters of the lake and ivy clung to the tree trunks and hung in festoons from the branches. The air was full of the warm scent of moist earth, leaves and grass.

For a moment Sachi thought she glimpsed a fox, poking its head out of the bushes and peeking around. Then it disappeared. Perhaps it was a fox spirit, the ghost of one of the myriad women who had died there.

She took a last look then stepped into the palanquin. As the little box rose gently into the air, she could hear the shouts of the bearers and the crunch of their straw sandals.

Five days had passed since the arrival of the envoys. Sachi's fate had been decreed. Together with the princess, the Old Crow and their entourages, she was to move to the mansion of the Shimizu family and stay there in seclusion. None of them had the slightest idea what would become of them.

She had not managed to get a message to Shinzaemon. It would have been better to have died, Sachi told herself. That way she could at least have met him in the next world, as she had promised.

It grew dark inside the palanquin. They were passing into the shadows of a gate, on their way out of the castle. The bearers' footsteps echoed with a hollow sound. She heard guards shouting. The footsteps rang out with a different tone as they ran across the moat. Again they passed into shadow.

Then doors clanged shut. She heard grinding and crashing followed by a thud as a mighty wooden bolt slammed into place. She had left the women's palace for the last time.

IV

Spring ended and with it the nightingale's song. The little bird huddled in its cage, a forlorn ball of brown feathers. Every day Sachi sat by it as the servants gave it its food. She was sure its eyes were growing dimmer and its plumage dull. Sometimes she hoped she might share its fate.

She hadn't even bothered to order the attendants to unpack. She told herself she wanted to be ready to leave at any moment, but in truth she felt so sad and lethargic she couldn't summon up the energy.

She thought about the village, about Otama and Jiroemon, the kind and loving parents who had brought her up, and about these other 'real' parents who had suddenly appeared: the mother who was perhaps no more than a ghost and the all-too-real father. If anyone could save them, her father could.

And silently, secretly, she yearned for Shinzaemon. At first she was ashamed that such unruly feelings burned inside her. She knew that a woman was a creature of no account who was duty bound to obey her father until she was given away in marriage, then her husband until he died, and after that her son. That was the natural order of things. But her husband and liege lord – His Majesty the shogun – was dead and she had no son. In such a case in normal times a woman would return to her family, to her parents. But these were not normal times. There was nothing for it but to take her life in her own hands and follow her feelings, wherever they led. That was what her mother had done. But for the time being it made no difference what she felt or what she thought. It was all no more than idle daydreams as long as she remained immured in the Shimizu mansion.

So the days passed, merging seamlessly one into the next. The princess had shut herself in her room. She had set His Majesty's funerary tablet and the daguerreotype image of him, looking so boyish and vulnerable, on the altar. Hour after hour she knelt, telling her beads, murmuring prayers and sitting silently in meditation. When he had died she had taken holy vows; now it seemed she had decided to lead the life of a nun in earnest.

The rains came, thundering on the roof tiles like an army of horses. Water cascaded in sheets from the eaves and the gardens turned into a lake. The heat was unbearable. Sachi's thin summer robes stuck to her like the bandages of a corpse. Mould glistened in every corner, encrusting the wooden drawers, the chests and the wooden sandals on the step outside the veranda. In the evenings bullfrogs brayed raucously in the ponds and owls hooted in the trees. Insects dashed against the paper screens. Taki's fan was perpetually flapping, beating off the flies that settled on everything and everyone. Mosquitoes filled the airless nights with incessant buzzing.

Taki had grown even thinner and paler. She too seemed sad and listless. She never spoke of Toranosuké but Sachi could see that her journey into the world outside the palace had changed her. Like Sachi, she could no longer be contented with a life of seclusion, no matter how pampered.

Eventually Sachi couldn't bear it any more. She shoved back the heavy wooden shutters and stepped outside. Splashing through the puddles, she was oblivious to the water soaking her legs and the mud clinging to her sandals and squelching between her toes. As the hot dank air filled her lungs she felt herself coming back to life. Taki scurried beside her, holding an umbrella over her head.

At the edge of the grounds they found a wall with steps leading up it. Sachi scrambled to the top with Taki on her heels and emerged, laughing and panting, soaked with sweat and rain, on to a parapet.

The city spread before them, a sea of glistening roofs stretching as far as they could see, dotted with trees and splashes of green. A haze of steam shimmered above the hot wet tiles. Below them the wall plummeted towards the dark waters of the moat. A little way away was a gate, leading to a bridge. From their perch on the parapet they could see the sweeping roofs and tiled walls of daimyos' estates and an expanse of grassland dotted with pines and cedars. A teahouse peeked from the trees.

'Goji-in Field,' said Taki, raising her voice above the clatter of rain on the umbrella. 'His Majesty's hunting ground where he used to exercise his falcons.'

Nearby were rows of barracks shaded by cypresses and cedars. But the place looked empty. The buildings were beginning to fall down and packs of dogs slunk about the grounds.

A river glinted in the distance. Beyond it the roofs became a jumble, small as the squares on a go board and tightly packed, squashed together higgledy-piggledy until they faded across the horizon. Threads of smoke wavered skywards, merging into the clouds. There were glimpses of movement, the hum and thrum of life.

'The townsfolk's section of the city,' said Sachi.

459

'At least it's alive over there.'

'I suppose they have nowhere else to go,' said Taki. 'Everyone who can has already left Edo.'

They stood and watched while the watery sun climbed in the sky. They were looking towards the north-east section of the city – in the unlucky direction of the 'demon gate' where evil spirits came from and where the execution grounds were. A couple of hills rose from the muddle of roofs. On one they could clearly see red buildings with gleaming black roofs dotted across the hillside.

'Isn't that ... Kanei-ji?' whispered Sachi. Kanei-ji Temple, the chief temple of the city, one of the greatest in all the land, built to protect the populace from the evil spirits of the north-east. It was the temple of the Tokugawa clan. In quieter times she had gone there to pray at the tombs of His Majesty's ancestors. She remembered it still – the great red-painted halls, covering the entire hilltop, breathtakingly magnificent. Kanei-ji, on Ueno Hill, where the retired shogun, Lord Yoshinobu, had taken sanctuary: where the militia was billeted, where the resistance had their headquarters. Shinzaemon was there, somewhere on that hill. She put her hand on her obi. She could feel the small round toggle in the shape of a monkey tucked firmly inside.

Every day after that Sachi went out and stood gazing at the city. In her imagination she crossed the bridge, skirted Goji-in Field, hurried along the broad empty boulevards that cut through the daimyos' section of town, crossed the river and entered the cramped maze of streets where the townsfolk lived until finally she came to Ueno Hill. She could see the great roofs and red walls of buildings covering the entire hill, surrounding courtyards crowded with people and edged with groves of trees. If she looked hard she could make out individual figures milling around the grounds. Sometimes she heard the crack of rifles and distant shouts and yells.

She yearned to be there with them. The princess's few remaining attendants and ladies-in-waiting, the Old Crow's much-depleted retinue and the ladies and maids of the Shimizu family were all used to living their lives indoors; inside the women's palace or inside the Shimizu mansion, it didn't make much difference. That was what they expected of life. Sachi and Taki seemed the only ones who were not prepared to endure whatever fate thrust in their way.

V

Early one morning Sachi was sitting with the women who had moved with her to the Shimizu mansion. Some of them were sewing, some completing their toilette. Sachi was trying to read, waiting for the moment when everyone would be absorbed in their tasks and she could slip away to her favourite place on the parapet.

Suddenly there was a boom like thunder breaking right overhead. Everyone flinched.

Then came another, then another – massive explosions that shook the walls and rattled the paper screens in their frames. The air quivered with the noise. The women looked at each other, all with the same expression of calm, luminous exhilaration, almost relief. They were warrior women, all of them; they knew what the booms were and what they meant. Cannon fire. The city was at war. The tedious waiting was over.

It was the fifteenth day of the fifth month. They had been in seclusion for more than two months.

Sachi leaped to her feet and darted outside. Rain was coming down in sheets. Taki raced after her, struggling to keep the umbrella over her head. They splashed across the grounds to the wall and scrambled up blindly, feeling their way in the murky light. Sachi's small hands were covered in mud and her sodden kimono skirts clung to her ankles.

Low cloud hung over the city. Through the mist and driving rain Sachi could see flashes lighting up the hills. Plumes of smoke, whiter than the clouds, rolled above the trees. The booms and bangs and thuds were deafening.

'What's going on, Taki?' she demanded.

There were other people on the parapet peering anxiously into the rain, their faces ghastly. Some were women she recognized, others men. They looked like servants and retainers who had moved there from the palace or worked for the Shimizu family. They bowed when they saw Sachi. Among them was the wizened old man who had let them into the palace grounds, a lifetime ago. He started to get down on his hands and knees in the mud. Sachi gestured impatiently.

'Old man, what's happening?'

'There's a lot of our fellows over there, my

lady,' he said. 'Wish I was too. But I'm too old. I'd be no use to them.'

'Our men?'

'Palace guards. They made off before the castle was taken over. A lot went to bolster the militia. The rest went north to join the army up there.'

'So it's the militia over there on the hill,' Sachi said, trying to stop the quiver of excitement and fear in her voice.

'We're doing well,' said the old man. 'Them southerners talk big but they got their backs against the wall. Our men have had command of the city. Helps that the townsfolk are on our side. We been out there skirmishing, ambushing their patrols, cutting down southerners every day. We even launched a full-out assault on their barracks. It's a regular uprising. Anyway, seems the southerners've had enough. There's been a lot of talk these last few days that they are going to send in an army, wipe out the militia once and for all. There's been leaflets all over the city telling us townsfolk to keep away.'

He took a tattered piece of paper out of his sleeve. Raindrops pounded it, blurring the ink. Sachi stared at it, trying to concentrate, but her heart was beating so hard she could barely make sense of the words: '... assassinating the soldiers of the government ... rebels against the state... It has been found unavoidable to use force against them.'

So that was it, an offensive against the militia. Well, they would fight back. Those southern cowards would find out what the northerners were made of. The northern forces would send them fleeing from Edo back to their miserable southern holdouts.

'Our men will stand firm, of course,' she said.

The old man sucked his breath through his teeth with a long hiss.

'Well,' he grunted, shaking his head. 'I'll be honest, my lady. It doesn't look good. The southerners have a huge army, maybe ten for every one of our men. I heard they got arms from the English, too – big cannons, modern ones, and fancy rifles. We got guns but not as good and not as many. But our men have spirit. They'll fight to the death, that's for sure. For the honour of His Majesty the shogun. You can depend on that, my lady. They'll die good deaths.'

Cannons, rifles. Of course. The southerners had to hide behind fancy foreign armaments. They would have no chance in honourable man-to-man combat. They were out to destroy the militia, to kill every one of them.

Fine swordsman though Shinzaemon was, his swords would be no use against weapons like that. Sachi could hear his voice: 'I look forward to the honour of dying in battle for my lord.' Every day she had wondered whether he was alive or dead. She bowed her head, praying to the gods. Like a proud samurai woman she prayed for victory, but she added a secret prayer of her own. Gods of the Tokugawa clan, please protect him. Protect Shinzaemon. Please keep him safe.

The booms seemed to be coming from the smaller of the two hills. Through the mist and scudding cloud Sachi could see white flashes, blindingly bright, and hear the whoosh of shells.

464

Explosions splintered the sky. She watched as the shells plummeted to earth, sending timber and tiles and bodies spinning into the air. Fires were breaking out among the densely packed roofs in the valley between the two hills. Here and there tongues of flame licked the red temple buildings on Ueno Hill.

Then came a barrage of flashes at the base of Ueno Hill itself and crackling filled the air. The flashes and cracks were like a gigantic never-ending fireworks display. Mesmerized, Sachi stood listening and watching, staring as hard as she could. Despite Taki's umbrella she was soaked from head to toe. Through the roar of the rain she could hear the boom of war drums, the wail of conch-shell trumpets, the distant clang of steel striking steel. The southerners were trying to take the hill. In the distance she could make out figures, men fighting, tiny and far away but clear as day. Sachi ached to have her halberd in her hands, to be fighting alongside them. Instead here she was, trapped, with nothing to do but stand and watch helplessly. She looked down towards the gate and the bridge, thinking hard. There had to be some way she could help them.

On the other side of the moat mobs of people had appeared from nowhere. They filled the streets, motionless and silent, staring towards the noise and smoke.

All day long the battle went on. The plumes of smoke grew until the hillside was enveloped in a thick white pall, though Sachi could still see flashes like lightning bursting through the clouds. Then late in the afternoon the guns fell silent.

There was a terrible hush. Even the cicadas had stopped their ear-piercing noise.

Then flames shot up. The wind fanned the blaze, sending sparks leaping like will-o'-the-wisps, setting roofs afire. The temples on the hillside and the flimsy wooden houses in the valley below were ablaze.

There was a roar as if a dragon had opened his mouth and sent a fiery blast to consume them. From the parapet Sachi could see flames racing towards them as heat seared her face and smoke tickled her nostrils and filled her lungs. The people crowded up there were tumbling down the steps, coughing and choking, tears pouring from their eyes, handkerchiefs clamped to their mouths and noses. The whole city seemed to be on fire.

Taki grabbed at her, trying to drag her away, but Sachi shook her off. The wall of flame swept as far as the river then leaped across to the Goji-in Field. But the broad empty spaces of the field acted as a firebreak and the flames dwindled, leaving sparks dancing like fireflies on a smouldering sea of ash and rubble.

Sachi knew she had to get to the battlefield, had to find out what had happened, which way the battle had gone. There must be wounded there who needed help. And dead there, many dead. Above all she needed to look for Shinzaemon.

She stared down at the smouldering city. She would put on plain clothes, like a townswoman or an ordinary samurai. She wouldn't take anything with her, not even the brocade. Just some money, something to sell.

The old man was standing next to her. Everyone else had gone. Only Taki was there, her thin face haggard and pale, her eyes wide.

'My lady,' the old man said. His face was expressionless, but there was a hint of something – sympathy, perhaps understanding – in his eyes. 'I'm on guard duty tomorrow.'

Sachi glanced at him, startled. She couldn't believe she had heard him correctly.

'Tomorrow? You?'

'Every southerner in the city is out there, fighting,' he said. 'They left us in charge.'

'You mean ... there are no southern guards?'

'No. Of course a fine lady like you wouldn't be interested in such matters. You wouldn't even be outside the women's quarters, I shouldn't think. But if some unknown lady or two happened to slip by, well, I probably wouldn't even notice. My eyesight's no good these days. My ears aren't too good either.'

VI

Sachi waited for the first glimmer of light to pierce the shutters then slipped quietly from beneath her bedclothes. She coiled her hair into a clumsy knot and put on a plain indigo-blue summer kimono. It was the first time in years she had had to do her own hair and dress herself. She had almost forgotten how. She took out Shinzaemon's toggle, which she had hidden under a corner of her bedding. The monkey's carved wooden face looked up at her knowingly as if it agreed that it was time to go. She tucked it into her obi then gathered up a few belongings and wrapped them in a bundle.

She looked sadly at her halberd. It was too long and awkward. She would have to leave it behind. But she made sure she had hairpins in her hair and her dagger in her obi.

She had meant to sneak out alone, but she should have guessed that no matter how early she got up Taki would wake up too (though she was vexed that she was not early enough to help Sachi dress). Not just that, but Haru also seemed to sense something was afoot. In no time the three of them were outside the gates, hurrying across the bridge, looking for all the world like nondescript townswomen.

At the end of the bridge they paused. A broad road led along the edge of the moat. Another disappeared down the hill in front of them. The walls that edged them were grimy with soot, the tiles scorched and broken. Huge charred trees filled the sky. Here and there were blackened ruins, unrecognizable as places where human beings could ever have lived.

Sachi turned to her companions. She hadn't dared speak while they were in the grounds of the mansion for fear of drawing attention.

'Go back,' she said quietly to Taki and Haru. 'I release you from my service. I don't need you. I can't be responsible for you. You're better off staying behind. This...'

She gestured towards the desolate scene before them, as the sour smell of wet ashes pricked her nostrils. The rain had stopped, for the time being at least. The sun had barely risen but already it was so hot that she was sticky with sweat. The water that puddled the road was quickly evaporating, steaming in the heat. The incessant shrilling of the cicadas split the air.

'It's my choice, my lady,' said Taki, meeting her eye. 'I'm coming with you. You must have known I would.' Her small mouth was set in a stubborn frown. She had scrambled into her clothes so quickly that the knot of her obi was askew.

Sachi shook her head and stared at the ground.

'I'm not "my lady" any longer,' she said. 'Can't you understand that? I'm not the Retired Lady Shoko-in. I'm Sachi, just plain Sachi.'

Haru was staring around wide-eyed, biting her lips. Bundled in a simple summer kimono, she looked afraid, excited and apprehensive all at the same time, like a little girl who has run away from home or a prisoner who has escaped a death sentence. It was the first time she had left the castle in eighteen years.

'I'm bound to you for ever, my lady,' she said quietly. 'You're the closest to family I've ever had. If you're going to Ueno Hill, I'm going too. I'm not losing you now. Anyway, there might be men there that need help. I brought some fabric to wrap up wounds.'

Sachi sighed and shook her head. Nothing made any difference any more. She knew what she had to do and she would do it. If they wanted to come along, they could. She had a feeling there would be a lot of work to be done. If they were with her ... she had to admit, it would be a comfort.

469

'Hurry,' she said. It wouldn't be long before someone noticed her absence. She would not be safe until she had disappeared into the bowels of the city.

Outside the high walls of the mansion she felt small and vulnerable, and at first she was careful to keep her face hidden. But soon the horror of the scene overwhelmed her and all she could think of was getting to the hill.

So many times, standing on the parapet, Sachi had imagined herself crossing the moat and setting off along the road. She had worked out that if she kept the moat behind her and the sun on her right she would be heading in the right direction. But now she was outside, with the fire-scarred walls of daimyos' estates all around her, blocking her view, it was hard to keep her bearings. The road led down one hill and up another, running beside great silent estates until it emerged on the bank of a river. On the other side was a wasteland of blackened rubble, the aftermath of the fire, and behind that the hill Sachi had gazed at so longingly.

The rain had stopped the fire from spreading too far. Nevertheless whole sections of the town had vanished, swept up by flames or dismantled by firemen. A few stout clay-walled storehouses still stood, like healthy teeth in a gaping mouth. People were out sweeping away the ash and clearing the rubble. Here and there corpses had been laid in pitiful rows, so badly charred they had shrunk to the size of dolls. They were more like burned logs of wood than human beings.

Tucking the hems of their kimono skirts into

their obis, the women picked their way through piles of ash and fallen timbers. In no time their legs were black and their robes spattered. Every now and then Sachi caught a glimpse of the hill across a pile of rubble or through a gap where a row of houses had disappeared. But they were soon shuffling along in a crowd so dense that even if they had wanted to go somewhere else, they couldn't.

Young women and old people with babies tied to their backs wandered like sleepwalkers, blank-eyed. Sometimes a baby yowled. Street hawkers yelled out their wares, selling food to the crowds, taking advantage of the catastrophe to turn a profit. But for the most part the crowd moved in eerie silence.

As Sachi, Taki and Haru got nearer the hill they heard the rhythmic toll of handbells being struck again and again – the sound of prayers spiralling to heaven. A nauseous stench began to fill the air, faint at first but growing stronger. People raised their sleeves to their mouths while others took out handkerchiefs and pressed them to their noses or tied them round their faces. Some stopped in their tracks or turned, pale and ghastly, and fled. It was the smell of the slaughterhouse – sweat, blood, excrement, decomposing flesh; the all-pervading smell of death.

Gagging, Sachi grabbed her handkerchief and clamped it across her nose and mouth. For a moment she wanted only to flee. She had never imagined it would be like this.

Swarthy-faced soldiers stood guard, toting rifles. They were wearing the black uniforms and tall conical helmets of southerners. They were holding the crowds back, turning them away.

'Stop!' they barked. 'No entry. Out of bounds.'

People surged against the cordon, trying to break through. In the shadow of the hill Sachi could see that the ground was heaped with slumped shapes. Even from a distance she could make out the black of their hair, the white of their faces and the glint of their pale blue *haori* jackets.

A stream trickled across the foot of the hill. Bodies filled the water and dangled from the three small footbridges. Beyond that, a cleft lined with steep rocky walls cut into the hillside and disappeared around a corner towards the temple compound. A palisade stood across it, barring the way. The famous Black Gate. The great double gates hung crazily on their hinges, the posts and crossbeams smashed and pocked with bullet holes. Soldiers in black uniforms strode about, shovelling bodies out of the way as if they were bundles of wood. A couple emerged with a comrade slung over their shoulders. Here and there were women, moving about silently.

The crowd began to grumble. 'Hey! There are women over there. Let us in too.'

An old man, thin and bent with white hairs straggling from his chin, was pleading with the soldiers.

'You've won. We can see that. At least let us take away our dead.'

'Those traitors stay right there,' barked one of the guards. 'Think you can rebel against the government, huh? They're traitors to the emperor.'

'Government!' sneered someone in the crowd.

472

'Ragtag impostors more like.'

But the old man was trying to mollify the soldiers. 'You have a father, young man,' he croaked. 'How would he feel if it was you there? At least let me see if my son is here.'

The soldiers were discussing the matter. One relented.

'All right. You and you and you. Helping those criminals is punishable by death, mind. Don't forget that.'

Sachi, Taki and Haru slipped through along with the old man and a few others before the soldiers closed ranks again.

Beyond the cordon the ground was littered with corpses and the smell was overwhelming. At first Sachi couldn't bear to look. When she forced herself, she saw that some of the bodies were blasted apart, not even visibly human any more but reduced to chunks of meat. Others had committed suicide and lay with their bellies ripped open. Intestines coiled out of gaping wounds. Some of the dead men looked no more than fifteen or sixteen. Gangly legs were bent at impossible angles, skinny arms twisted or broken. Some were no more than bloody stumps. Scrawny youths who hadn't even finished growing lay frozen in death.

Horrified and sickened, Sachi stepped over men lying where they'd fallen, with their heads or bellies ripped apart. Some clasped their hands pathetically over gaping wounds where great chunks of flesh were hanging out, as if they had been trying to hold themselves together, to staunch the bleeding, when death struck. Others

473

looked as if they had turned to flee and had been struck down from behind. But most lay on their backs. They had been facing the enemy till the last.

The women stood for a moment catching their breath, overwhelmed with the horror of it all, wondering what to do, where to start. Mosquitoes besieged them, nipping their arms and legs, but they were too numb even to notice.

Ravens with big black beaks and yellow beady eyes cawed incessantly in the pine and cherry trees. It was a dreadful, ominous sound. Some birds had settled on the corpses and were pecking at the eyes. Dogs prowled, ripping at bodies and gnawing at the faces. Sachi grabbed a stone and threw it at one and the dogs backed off, snarling, and hung skulking in the trees at the edge of the hillside. A skeletal dog scurried by, belly low to the ground, a glint in its eye. In its mouth was something white. Sachi realized with a shock of horror that it was a human hand.

A broad-shouldered man lay across their path, face down in a pool of bloody water. One arm was bent back, the other flung above his head. There was a jagged tear in his *haori* jacket. A stain spread across his back. It had seeped into the pale blue fabric, turning it puce.

Sachi shuddered, her hand at her throat. Her gorge rising, she reminded herself why she was there. The man was big-built, like Shinzaemon. It would be typical of him to be right in the front line when the southerners attacked. She wrapped her handkerchief around her face, tucked up her kimono skirts and tied back her sleeves.

The hands were not Shinzaemon's, but she needed to be sure. Clamping her lips together she reached down and touched a shoulder with her fingers. It was rubbery and cold, not like human flesh at all. She cupped her hand firmly under it and heaved. She had never thought a human being could be so heavy. She managed to pull the body round just enough to see the blackened, swollen face. It was not him; she could see that straight away. She felt a frisson of relief so powerful it made her head spin, as very gently she laid the body down again.

She stumbled on. She was picking her way between the bodies when something like a raw oyster squashed under her foot. It was a human eye. She couldn't even feel horror any more. She felt as if she had become a corpse herself.

Around her, the southern soldiers were tugging out their dead and wounded and carrying them away. One of the pale blue jackets, half hidden beneath a pile of bodies, gave a sudden spasm. There was a flash of steel as a southerner raised his sword and then the movement stopped.

Sachi became aware of eyes turned on her. In a daze she pulled her scarf round her face. A pair of filthy boots in some foreign style, coated with mud and blood, planted themselves in front of her. The foreign leggings above them steamed in the heat, giving off a rancid smell of dirty damp fabric.

'You're wasting your time, lady,' growled a voice in a sneering southern accent. It was the final insult – these savages gloating at the carnage they had caused. 'Nothing alive here. Not a cockroach. Nothing.'

A hand grabbed her sleeve and she shrank back. It was more than she could bear. In this holy place, surrounded by bloated corpses, the bodies of the dead. Surely even the most brutal southerner would not defile such a place?

'Hey, here's a pretty face. What do you say, Wakamoto? Fair prey, isn't it? Spoils of war?'

Sachi tugged her arm away. She knew it was madness to fight back. The best she could manage would be to strike down one soldier before she was felled herself – or, worse still, dragged off as a hostage. But she couldn't think clearly any more. She reached for her dagger.

Then footsteps came squelching through the mud.

'Leave them be,' barked another voice. 'We've done our work. Let them look for their menfolk. But keep an eye out. No removing of bodies.'

Sachi glanced at Taki and Haru and their eyes met. Their hands too were on their daggers. She was so numbed with horror, she'd forgotten what danger they were in. If these southerners arrested them, they would discover they were fugitives, high-ranking ladies on the northern side who had escaped their sentence of seclusion. They risked being not just returned to the mansion but imprisoned or even executed.

Keeping their heads bent and watching out for southern soldiers, they turned back to their task. Silently they picked their way across the battlefield, bending over any corpse that looked remotely familiar, checking the head and hands, examining clogs and sandals, searching for any clue. Some of the bodies were already beginning to swell and their faces were puffy and unrecognizable. Others were faceless or horribly disfigured. When they lifted one, the guts came spilling out.

The narrow pass around the Black Gate was piled high with bodies. Slowly, painfully, the women worked their way up the incline towards the temple on the top of the hill. There were bodies every step of the way, lying slumped on the steep slopes that lined the path and sprawled across the ground.

Dazed by the heat, numbed by the horror, Sachi was staring at a pile of bodies when she caught a glimpse of a face she thought she recognized. A shock of dismay jolted through her. She jerked her head away and staggered back, her hand to her throat. She stood, panting, her fists clenched so hard she could feel her nails cutting into her palms. Gasping for breath she forced herself to take another look. The hollow-cheeked face, the bristly hair sticking out in unruly tufts around the white headband, the gangly limbs... There was no mistaking him.

Sachi fell to her knees, retching. Great sobs convulsed her. There was a skinny arm around her shoulders, holding her tight.

'Gen,' whispered Taki. Sachi nodded, speechless. Genzaburo, her childhood friend, who had survived so many scrapes and embarked on so many crazy adventures. She had never before seen that face without a mischievous smile playing across it. Now it was blank and waxen, the eyes opaque, the lips drained of colour. He

477

looked terribly young. He was sprawled on his back, his chest soaked in blood. Flies buzzed around the black stains and swarmed across his eyes and mouth.

'There are southern soldiers coming,' whispered Taki, tugging at her arm, trying to pull her up.

'We can't just leave him here,' groaned Sachi.

'Pray if you like but no moving the bodies,' barked a rough southern voice.

Sachi took a deep breath. She reached out a hand to brush Genzaburo's cheek. It was cold and rubbery. Quivering with horror, she waved away the flies and closed his eyes. Weeping, she knelt and said a prayer.

Taki took her arm and squeezed it.

'He was a peasant but he died a samurai's death,' she said, leading her away. 'A good death.'

When they emerged at the top of the slope there was nothing but a sea of mud, pitted with craters where shells had fallen, overflowing with water and blood. The magnificent red halls with their gleaming tiled roofs had entirely disappeared. There was no sign there had ever been a temple there. A single building stood forlornly in the middle. The great copper bell with its stone base, its housing of wooden scaffolding and tiled roof had somehow survived. Priests walked around striking bells, sending prayers circling towards heaven – prayers for the souls of the dead.

As the midday sun beat down Sachi and Taki stumbled about, sweat pouring from their bodies, trying to examine every corpse. All around were women engaged in the same grim work. No one spoke. Every now and then one stopped in her tracks, bent down to peer at a face, then bowed her head. Here and there were women kneeling in silence, keeping watch beside a body. Soldiers strode around, making sure no one tried to take one away.

Sachi stood up painfully. Taki looked like a ghost, exhausted and filthy. There was a blankness in her eyes as if she had seen so much she couldn't feel anything any more, as if she had died inside. Wearily Sachi guessed that she must look the same. She suddenly became aware of how her back ached, of the mosquito bites on her arms. Her hands were raw, her feet bleeding from the grit and stones and broken metal that littered the ground.

'I can't search any more,' she muttered. 'Thank you for helping me.'

'I wasn't helping you,' said Taki. 'I wanted to look too. I care, too, about those men. You know that. Shinzaemon, Tatsuemon and ... and...'

Her voice was dull, her eyes bright with tears. Sachi knew what it was she couldn't bear to say: '...and Toranosuké.' She put her arm round her thin shoulders and held her tight.

The sound of a bell echoed across the hilltop, ringing monotonously. A priest was stumbling towards them, his black robes smeared with ashes and mud. His face was grey, his chin covered in stubble. One arm was in a sling. In the other he held a handbell. As he reached them he rang the bell once more, then stopped.

'Looking for your dead?'

Sachi and Taki nodded. It was good to see a

living human being who was not an enemy, who looked as if he had seen the fight and lived through it.

'A lot went north. The southerners think they beat us here but we'll get our own back. His Reverence the abbot escaped too.'

The priest gestured around at the sea of mud. 'Look at this,' he said. 'Savages.' He spat on the ground. 'Until yesterday this was Kanei-ji Temple. Now the treasures have gone – the halls, the books, the libraries, the statues, all gone. At least His Reverence escaped, the gods and the Buddhas protect him.'

'You were here?'

'I was,' the priest told them. 'We put up a fight but they trapped us, killed half our men with their shelling. Call themselves samurai! They hide behind foreign weapons. Can't even see them, let alone get close enough to put a sword into them. Then they send a rain of bullets down on us. We held them back at the Black Gate till mid-afternoon. A lot of men died. If your men were here, I tell you, they fought like heroes. You can be proud of them.'

He wandered off, moving from corpse to corpse. They could hear the lonely sound of the bell across the hilltop.

Haru was kneeling some distance away at the edge of the plateau, where the woods began. She had found an injured man. He was small and slight and looked no more than fifteen. His pleated trousers and *haori* jacket were covered in mud and one arm was twisted at a strange angle. Blood seeped from a wound on his head.

But he was moving and moaning faintly. His lips were cracked, his face burned and blackened and covered in dust. Haru had torn off some of the fabric she had brought and wrapped it round his head. She was cradling him in her arms, flapping her hand, trying to drive away the flies that swarmed around his bloody wounds.

'You'll be fine,' she whispered again and again.

She turned to Sachi and Taki. 'He needs water and help, quickly. Those southerners are butchers. They're beheading the wounded men.' Her tears dropped on the soldier's bloody face. 'Lying here alone among all these corpses, waiting to die. Look at him. He's only a boy.'

'If we're caught we'll be in trouble,' said Taki. 'Crying over them is one thing, helping them's another. We're fugitives, don't forget. They'll be out looking for us.'

'But if we leave him here he'll die,' said Sachi. This boy-man seemed to represent the whole of the militia. If they could only save him it would be worth dying for.

'If only your father was here,' said Haru, glancing up at Sachi. 'Now's the time we need him.'

Sachi was staring at the youth. His hands were thin and boyish – a lot like the hands that had held out her halberd to her, it seemed a lifetime ago. His face was grey, caked in blood and dirt – that round face with the forelock still untrimmed... Her heart stopped. She was back on the road walking towards Kano, saying farewell at the village when he had ridden off so bravely with Toranosuké. And now here he was, dying

481

before her eyes.

'Tatsu!' she gasped. 'Tatsuemon, it's us! Sachi and Taki!'

She took his hand and squeezed it, rubbing his palm, trying to rub a little life into it, and the boy groaned faintly. The women stared wildly at each other. If Tatsuemon was here, Shinzaemon and Toranosuké couldn't be far away. They would surely have fought shoulder to shoulder. Frantically they began heaving at nearby bodies, trying to turn them over, to glimpse the faces. But there was nobody that looked like either of them.

From across the plateau came the sound of southern accents. They could hear men talking and laughing, the tramp of feet squelching across the muddy ground. Then another voice floated across. The speaker barked angrily, in a strange accent.

A foreigner.

Sachi looked up. Southern soldiers were approaching with a group of foreigners. One was a fearsome-looking creature, a giant of a man. He towered above the southerners and even dwarfed the other foreigner. Thick black hair curled on his cheeks.

Then she noticed the second man. Could it be...? Surely this was the foreigner who had rescued them when they had been attacked by marauding southern soldiers. She remembered his golden face and shining hair and how he'd suddenly appeared, firing his gun, scattering the soldiers. She recalled how she and Taki and Shinzaemon had travelled with him and his friend in their ungainly palanquins, specially shaped to hold their long legs, and how they had escorted her and Taki right to the gates of the palace.

Sachi felt a surge of joy and relief. He would help them. He would rescue them again.

But she was covered in mud and blood. How would he even recognize her?

Desperately she tried to remember his strange barbarian name as the group bore down on them. Her mouth was parched, her mind a blank. She had to think, to concentrate. She made a supreme effort. His name – it was like the city of Edo, wasn't it?

Then it came to her. She croaked out four syllables: 'Edo ... Edowadzu.'

Edwards.

What would he do? He knew she belonged to the palace. He had only to say the word and she would be handed over to the southerners, held as a hostage, maybe executed. Foreigners were so guileless, they could never dissemble.

For a long moment there was silence. Sachi could hear her heart beating, feel the rivulets of sweat running into her eyes. The southern soldiers were staring suspiciously at the little group of women, fingering their guns. Then Edwards looked at her and Taki, his round eyes widening in surprise. Sachi saw a gleam of recognition, then his brows came together in a furious scowl.

'So that's where you got to,' he exploded. 'What do you think you're doing here?'

His bark was so fearsome the birds settled on the corpses flew off with a great rustling of their big black wings. He said a few words in an angry tone to the other foreigner, then he turned back

483

to the women.

'I can't believe it,' he shouted. 'I pay you people, you live in my house, and look how you repay me. This Jiro, this half-wit boy. Getting himself into trouble like this. And you women – you're supposed to be cleaning my house, cooking my food.'

Sachi was gawping at him in such amazement that she really did look like a servant, she thought to herself.

'Didn't expect to see me here, did you?' he barked. 'You're coming straight back with me, all of you.'

Coming to her senses, Sachi fell on her knees and pressed her forehead in the mud.

'Sorry, master,' she bleated. 'Straight away, master. Our boy, our Jiro...'

Taki knelt too, her thin shoulders hunched. She didn't need to play-act exhaustion and fear.

The southerners were gaping, uttering throaty inarticulate grunts of amazement. Sachi could hear them muttering to each other. 'His household? Likely story. Then again, he seems to know them. They knew his name...'

'So-called housekeeper,' snorted Edwards.

'His housekeeper?' mumbled one.

'Hold on,' muttered another. 'So how'd he get that uniform, that boy?'

'Well, if the foreigner-*sama* says so...' grunted another. They all turned towards Edwards and bowed, twisting their mouths into ingratiating smiles.

Sachi was overcome by a weariness so deathly she wondered if she would ever be able to stand up again. She wanted to weep for sheer relief, but she knew it would never do to show weakness in front of the hateful southerners.

The huge black-haired foreigner had stooped down and put a flask to Tatsuemon's lips. Gently he lifted his damaged arm and tied a cloth around it to make a sling. Then he scooped him up as easily as if he was a child. The injured boy's limbs dangled like a doll's.

The women followed the foreigners back down the hill, picking their way carefully between the corpses. They stumbled past wives – widows – keeping watch, kneeling on the muddy ground beside one fallen man or another. Some knelt in silence, heads bowed. Every now and then a sound mingled with the cawing of the crows, the buzzing of flies and mosquitoes and the monotonous shrilling of the cicadas: a thin keening like an animal trapped in the woods, a hopeless, anguished wailing.

Once they had passed through the Black Gate and across the bridge the southern soldiers disappeared. Dazed and filthy, the women looked up at Edwards.

'Thank you,' whispered Sachi.

'This is Dr Willis,' said Edwards. 'He will take care of your friend. He's lucky. If he'd shown the slightest sign of life the southerners would have had his head off long ago.'

'My hospital is full of southerners,' said Willis. 'I can't take him there. They're beheading all the prisoners. What about–'

'My house?' said Edwards. 'I have room. After all, he's one of my staff.'

'Will he be all right?' asked Sachi.

'I don't know,' said the doctor. 'You will have to pray to your gods.'

11

Before the Dawn

I

Sachi was back in the Shimizu mansion. She had been so determined to leave for ever but in the end there had been nowhere else to go. Now she lay tossing on her futon. The heat was unbearable. Again and again her head slipped from the wooden pillow. She pushed it away and lay flat on her bedding.

In her mind she was stumbling through the Black Gate. Her feet brushed against the rubbery flesh of corpses and the foul taste of death was on her lips. Images of broken bodies and the dog with a human hand hanging from its mouth swam before her eyes.

So many men, hundreds upon hundreds, left to rot. She had been so busy searching for Shinzaemon she had hardly thought about all those others – all those shattered bodies and faces she had looked at that had not been his. They must all have had wives, lovers, children, parents. They must all have said goodbye with bravado as they went riding off with their comrades, eager for glory.

Those wives and lovers must have hoped and prayed that they would see their men again, despite the odds. Many were hoping and praying still. She had seen a few out on the hill, searching. But most would never know what had happened and their men would lie rotting until they were ripped apart by crows or wild dogs.

And for what? To fulfil their duty to their lord the shogun, to hold back the barbarous southern clans who were overrunning the country. The war was not finished yet. There would be other battles, Sachi told herself, other battlefields just as grim or worse. And yet... To have fought so bravely and now to lie unburied. Having seen such a sight it was hard to think any longer of death in battle as honourable and glorious. It was nothing more than carnage and butchery and terrible waste.

And Genzaburo... He had been so young and, for all his love of mischief, so innocent. He hadn't been fiercely committed to the shogun, yet he had been on the hill all the same. Wherever danger or adventure was to be found, he had always been there. Sachi remembered their childhood together: the time he had wrestled a wild boar and how proud he had been of the scar where it had gored him; the way he used to dart about in the river like a fish and pluck hairs from horses' tails to make fishing lines; the time they had gone off together to watch for the princess's procession. He had whispered to her that they should hide in the eaves; but instead she had been snatched up, taken to Edo, and by the time she saw him again she had become a different person.

She remembered the wistful way he had looked at her when they met in the village a few months earlier. He had been so alive; now it felt as if her childhood had died with him. After all their years together she had not been able to do anything for him, had not been able even to bury him. In her mind she said goodbye to him. It was like the end of a chapter in her life.

When she finally drifted off to sleep, she saw not Genzaburo but Shinzaemon sprawled among the dead. His eyes were wide open, staring at her. He stretched out his hand but she drifted past like a ghost. She heard the roar of a great wind, saw the spirits of the dead warriors rising like columns of smoke, hovering whitely over the hill. She heard their wails, felt their chill breath. She jerked awake with a start, shuddering with horror, drenched in sweat.

From the next room came the sound of a bell. Light glimmered through the gap between the doors. Haru had been up all night. She was chanting sutras, praying to the Buddhas for the souls of the dead. Then she called on Lord Amida to save Tatsuemon.

Sachi scrambled to her knees, lit a candle and prayed too. She prayed first for Genzaburo, for his spirit to find peace, then for Shinzaemon and Toranosuké too, to keep them safe, wherever they might be. Then she rubbed her beads hard and whispered, 'Dear gods, dear ancestors, Lord Amida Buddha: keep Tatsuemon here, don't send him to join those dead warriors. He is so young. His life is just beginning.' She was ashamed for thinking it but she couldn't help herself: if he

488

lived, he might be able to tell her where Shin-zaemon was, whether he was alive or dead.

'They've gone north,' the priest had said. 'A lot have gone north.' Shinzaemon had surely been among them. He'd be back one day, standing in the great entrance hall of the mansion, looking at her with his slanted eyes, his hair bushing out around his head. If only she could hold on to that belief, it might happen. She prayed to Amida Buddha to keep him safe.

Morning came at last, even hotter and closer than the previous day. Sachi's clothes clung to her. Her face was sticky with sweat, she couldn't eat, she hardly dared breathe. She could think of nothing but the men dead on the hill and those who perhaps were not dead: Shinzaemon, Tora-nosuké – and Tatsuemon. Young Tatsu.

Taki and Haru had pulled back the paper doors that divided the silent rooms. They were lifting them out of their frames, turning the rooms into a big open pavilion so that any passing breeze would waft in. The shrill of cicadas shattered the still air.

Far in the distance there was a faint noise: the clatter of hooves pounding up the hill.

Supposing the news was bad? Supposing Tatsu had died in the night? For a moment Sachi was frozen with fear. Then she leaped to her feet, hitched up her kimono skirts and darted through the sombre rooms. Taki and Haru pattered across the tatami behind her.

Barely stopping to slip on sandals, she stumbled out of the shade of the entrance hall and into a wall of heat. In the courtyard the light was so intense that for a moment she was blinded. Each stone in the gravel, each leaf, each tiny piece of moss stood out in dazzling relief. Then she was in shadow again. Taki had rushed out and was holding a parasol over her head.

Sachi stopped short, staring into the brightness. A man was striding through the dark shadows under the heavy overhanging eaves of the gate. The previous day she had seen only that he was familiar, that she knew him. But now she couldn't help being struck by what an extraordinary creature he was. He was a giant! As he stepped into the sunlight his feet and legs and arms were huge. Even his nose, jutting out like a *tengu*'s, cast a long shadow. Hair, yellow like sunshine, sprouted from his cheeks and chin. He was wearing a hat, the strangest hat she had ever seen, black and cylindrical like a hand drum.

Yet for all his foreignness, there was nothing frightening about him. He had saved her life not once but twice. He was like a bodhisattva, a guardian being from another realm.

She fixed her eyes on his face, trying to read it, and walked slowly towards him. The shadow over her head quivered. Taki's hand holding the parasol was shaking.

'How is he?' she asked breathlessly.

Edwards shook his head. He bunched his forehead so that his eyebrows came together. His skin was ruddy, darkened by the sun. She could see the pores in it and the glow of his pale eyes.

'We can't tell yet,' he said. 'He's sleeping. He has fever.'

At least he was alive. Sachi felt weak with relief. The women clamoured around Edwards, bombarding him with questions. 'When did he wake up? Did he say anything? What did Dr Willis say?'

'Dr Willis took out a bullet from his arm but the bone is badly broken,' said Edwards. 'The wound may be infected. He's not sure if he can save the arm. He may have to amputate.'

Sachi gasped and put her hands to her mouth.

'It is wartime,' said Edwards gently. 'Many men lose arms and legs. Perhaps your doctors do not do such things but ours do. Often it's the only way to save the patient.'

Sachi knew this perfectly well. But she also knew that people sometimes died after having a limb cut off.

'Our medicine works as well as yours – in some cases better,' said Edwards. 'Your friend is very ill and is burning with fever. Dr Willis is a famous surgeon. He's saved many men.'

'We must go to Tatsu now,' said Sachi. 'Please take us.'

'Out of the question,' said Edwards. 'Dr Willis said he must rest.'

'But supposing he ... gets worse? He knows us. It will be a comfort to him if we're there.'

'There are women there. I'll come with a wheeled carriage for you when Dr Willis says he can have visitors.'

'A wheeled carriage?' gasped Taki. 'Like in the woodblock prints?'

'Don't be silly,' said Sachi, smiling despite herself. 'We'll walk. Nowhere in Edo is that far.'

Under the brim of his hat Edwards's forehead

bunched again.

'I live out near Shinagawa, near one of the execution grounds. I shouldn't think you've ever been there. It's very dangerous round there. Your militia were the only police in Edo. Now there is no one; the southern army cannot keep order. There are looters wrecking storehouses and stealing rice and thieves and robbers and murderers roaming about everywhere. The city is in chaos.'

'We're samurai,' said Sachi quietly. 'We are trained to fight. We walked to Ueno yesterday. We can walk anywhere.'

Edwards glanced at her. His eye seemed to linger a fraction longer than was necessary.

'And how are things ... otherwise?' Her words hung in the silence.

'Everyone is waiting to see what happens next.'

It was all too clear that the city belonged to the southerners. But the citizens of Edo were with the north. They belonged to the shogun, every last one of them. The southerners would have to fight long and hard to win them over.

II

A few days after they returned from the hill there was a rumbling and clattering in the distance, the clopping of hooves and yells of male voices. It was as noisy as if a battalion of soldiers was marching up to the gates.

Edwards was waiting in the courtyard. He took off his hat and bowed.

'Time to go,' he said, grinning. 'Bring your

492

travelling hats and tie them on tight.'

They had to push their way through tangles of long grass and weeds and knots of morning glory to get to the gatehouse at the edge of the estate. Cuckoos piped above the incessant shrilling of cicadas. The kind old man who had let the women through when they had gone to the hill was on guard, holding a hefty stave. His face crinkled into a smile as he bowed.

Standing at the gates was the most extraordinary contraption. Sachi stopped, gaping in amazement. She had seen such things in woodblock prints of foreigners in Yokohama, but she had never expected to see one in real life.

She felt a pang of superstitious dread. Nothing but palanquins and horses had ever passed through these ancient gates before, and now here was this foreign contraption. It marked the end of something, something that was important to her.

It was a bit like a giant palanquin on wheels or an oxcart such as farmers used. There was a trunk inside, with some coarse foreign fabric thrown over. It was huge. Even the horses that stood pawing the ground and snorting, beautiful beasts with long manes and glossy coats, were larger than life. Sitting up in front, holding the reins, was another hairy-faced foreigner. He too took off his hat and bowed.

There was also a troop of guards armed with swords and staves, the same men who had accompanied them when they had travelled with Edwards along the Inner Mountain Road. They shuffled their straw-sandalled feet and glanced at her then at each other, exchanging knowing looks. She looked back at them, wishing she could work out who they belonged to, who they reported to. But they turned their eyes away immediately and their crests revealed nothing. She would have to be very careful about what she said in their hearing.

Taki and Haru were standing a safe distance away, squeaking excitedly.

'*Dozo*,' said Edwards. 'Ladies, please, take a seat.'

'Isn't it dangerous?' said Taki, shrinking back – Taki, who was always so brave.

Sachi put her foot on the step. She was about to climb in when Edwards took her hand. She started, feeling the touch of his rough skin on hers. Before she had a chance to pull her hand away he had lifted her up into the carriage. She stared at him in bemusement. Fancy a man behaving like a servant!

It felt very odd indeed to sit with her legs dangling instead of tucked up beneath her. Edwards helped Taki and Haru too into the carriage and they squeezed in beside her. The carriage rocked a bit. It was not as stable as a palanquin.

The other foreigner – whom Sachi took to be a kind of groom – gave a yell and shook the reins. They lurched into motion, Edwards cantering alongside and the guards running a little way behind. With a great shaking and rattling they rumbled off across the bridge and careered around the corner on to the roadway beside the moat, clattering and bumping along. The earthen road was meant for feet, not wheels.

The city flew by dizzyingly fast. Taki and Haru clung to each other, squealing. Sachi did her best to remain calm and dignified as befitted a lady of the shogun's court, though she had never in her life travelled faster than walking pace before. Messengers, that sort of person, might go fast, soldiers maybe, but not ladies, especially not the shogun's ladies and least of all the shogun's concubine.

But as they bounced along she couldn't help laughing with excitement. Every time they rounded the smallest curve she was thrown to one side or the other. In the end she grabbed on to Taki and Haru and held on for dear life. She looked out at the world from her high perch, the wind rippling through her hair. Birds must feel like this, she thought, when they fly. Beyond the broad back of the foreigner sitting at the front she caught glimpses of the horses' heads and flying manes and heard the pounding of their hooves. She had put on a large flat straw hat to protect her face from the sun, wrapping the strings round and round her coiled hair. It flapped alarmingly, threatening to fly off. She clutched at it with one hand to make sure it stayed securely in place.

Then she became aware of what she was seeing and gasped in horror. Across the water the great wall of the moat spun by. Parts had collapsed completely, chunks of granite poked from the water and ragged figures who looked like nothing so much as outcastes lurked in the shadows. There was even a tumbledown shack in one of the gates. The roadway that had always been perfectly raked and swept was rutted and overgrown

495

with grass and weeds.

They whirled past a bridge. 'Taki,' she shouted over the clattering and rumbling, as the wind soughed past their ears. 'Look. Look – back there.'

They had just passed the Bridge of the Shoguns' Ladies, where she had stood with Shinzaemon as darkness fell and the moon rose and they had said their farewells.

It had been sixty-six days since then, sixty-six long dreary days. It was so hard waiting without any message, any sign that he was thinking of her or even that he was alive. She tried to picture his face as it had been that night but she couldn't see it any more. There was nothing but a shadow.

She thought back to the moments of closeness – when they were together on the mountain, when they had said goodbye on the bridge. Even if he returned, the best they could hope for would be to continue meeting in secret, pursuing a forbidden passion. She knew very well that a future together was out of the question. They couldn't marry. People didn't choose their own marriage partners – it wasn't the way the world worked.

Day after day she clung to Shinzaemon's memory. Now she wondered whether he felt the same way about her. If she was honest with herself, what had really gone on between them? Nothing but a few glances, a moment when they had been carried away by foolish passion. The more she thought about it, the more hopeless her feelings seemed. But still she couldn't help yearning for him.

With an effort she brought herself back to the present.

They were whirling along the very road she used to take when she went to pray at His Majesty's tomb. In those days she had travelled in a long procession of palanquins of which hers was the most magnificent, accompanied by guards, attendants, porters and ladies-in-waiting. She remembered pushing up the bamboo blinds every now and then to peek at the castle walls across the moat. After they left the castle area they had turned away from the moat into one of the daimyo districts, lined with vast walled estates.

Now they rattled past broken walls and gates. Every flake of gold leaf, every copper crest, every bronze ornament that had marked the greatness and wealth of the lords had been stripped away. Nothing but the skeletons of palaces were left. Through the gaping holes in the walls she glimpsed tumbledown buildings blanketed in weeds with charred timbers poking through, more like the haunts of foxes and badgers than places where human beings lived.

From time to time they passed groups of villainous-looking men loitering by the road or squatting in the shadow of a tree. Once Edwards brandished his pistol. But they trotted on without incident.

Finally they saw a bustling highway ahead of them. It was a relief to be surrounded by people after the ominously empty streets of the daimyo districts.

'The Eastern Sea Road,' Edwards shouted above the clattering of hooves and the noise of people. It was the highway that led to Kano and Kyoto, many days' journey away. The road was crammed with people struggling along, pushing carts piled high with bedding, food, kimono chests, trunks, dishes, pots and pans.

They slowed to a walk, skirting a cart that had toppled over sending luggage rolling across the street and tumbling into the drainage channel. A woman, pitifully young, stared up at Sachi with a dazed blank look. She had a child tied to her back and another clinging to her sleeve and was scrabbling about, grabbing at kimonos which had fallen out of their wrappings and lay crumpled in the dust. Her clothes were stained and ragged and her mouth twisted into an expression of fear and horror. But beneath it all her face was pale and aristocratic. She might have been a maid in a daimyo mansion or even somewhere in the women's palace. Perhaps she was a samurai woman whose husband had been there on the hill – and who had never come home.

Sachi noticed that there were hardly any young men among the crowds. Families of women, children and old people drifted along, their faces pale and empty. The whole population seemed to be fleeing the blighted city.

The road was tightly packed with inns and shops, some boarded up, some open, offering tea or lodging or supplies. Then they passed an open space between the shops. Behind the buildings water sparkled, dazzlingly blue, as far as Sachi could see. She had never seen anything wider than the River Kiso before. She peered into the distance, trying to see the far bank, but there were no hazy mountains covered in pine trees. There was no other side at all. The water shimmered on for ever until it disappeared into the sky.

It was crammed with craft of all sizes and shapes – big boats, small boats, ferry boats and boats with masts and tall sails hanging limply in the heat. Overshadowing them all was a huge black craft that loomed like a mountain. It puffed smoke from tall chimneys and had masts that poked the sky like burned and blackened tree trunks after a forest fire. There were people running around on it and guns bristling from the sides. There was a second riding a little way from shore.

Sachi knew what they were. Ships, like the Black Ships that had brought the foreigners. She had seen pictures of them in wood-block prints, but she had never guessed they could be so huge. They were like cities floating on the water.

Taki and Haru's eyes and mouths were as round as hers. They smiled at each other uneasily. It was a most thrilling sight. Yet it was disturbing too, in the same way that the carriage was disturbing. Sachi had never imagined that the world could contain such things.

'Don't you know what that is? It's Edo Bay,' said Edwards, grinning, seeing their faces all turned towards it. 'That's the *Fujiyama* – one of your country's warships. The ship behind is one of ours.'

Edwards's house was at the top of a hill over-looking the bay, surrounded by pine trees. Sachi had expected that he would live somewhere extraordinary but it was just a normal house, part of a temple complex. The carriage rumbled into the grounds and jolted to a halt, sending gravel spraying from the wheels. Grateful for Edwards's hand, Sachi stepped down, her legs shaking. She was dazed from the bumpy ride and covered in dust. For a moment she stood collecting herself, feeling her feet connect with the ground again.

Impatient to see Tatsuemon, she raced to the door, then stopped, suddenly afraid of what she might find.

There was a strange smell about the place – the smell of the sick room, of camphor. Tatsuemon was lying on a futon, propped on cushions, looking terribly young and thin and vulnerable. There was a big white bandage wrapped around his head and bandages on his arms and legs. One arm was in a sling – but at least it was still there, Sachi thought. His small round face was waxen and his forehead beaded with sweat. His eyes looked huge above his pale cheeks.

A maid was sitting with him. She bowed and scurried away.

Tatsuemon looked at Sachi blankly for a moment, then his eyes widened in recognition. He struggled to pull himself into an upright position and managed a bow.

'Tatsu, I'm so glad to see you,' said Sachi softly.

'I'm sorry, my lady,' he croaked. 'Was it... Was it you? Edwards-*dono* said it was some ladies. But I didn't realize...'

'It was Big Sister who found you,' said Sachi.

Haru had taken the maid's place and was dabbing Tatsuemon's forehead with a damp towel. She beamed at him.

'How are you?' asked Sachi.

She was about to take his hand, then stopped. He was no longer the shy pretty boy she had known a few months before. He had grown up. His forehead and cheeks were cracked and blackened still from the sun and when he looked at her there was an emptiness in his eyes. He seemed to drift away, as if he couldn't stop himself seeing sights he would rather forget.

'Fine,' he said in the clipped tones of a soldier. For a moment he was not in that cool room but on a steaming rain-sodden battlefield, reporting to his commanding officer. 'Back on my feet in no time. Got to ... get back to the front.'

She wondered where he had been, what he had done, what he had seen. When she had last seen him he had been such a boy, obediently following wherever Toranosuké, his handsome idealistic master, led. Ever since she had known Shinzaemon all he had talked of had been war, the glory of war, the glory of death. She too had been seduced by it, swept up in his fervour. But now she had seen those dead bodies. War was not glorious at all, whatever men might say. It was a slaughterhouse.

'But why were you there?' Tatsuemon asked, as if it had only just struck him how odd it was that these ladies he had last seen in faraway Kiso should have been wandering around on a battlefield in Edo.

'It was the cannons,' said Sachi. 'You could hear them all over the city. Like thunder. I couldn't just do nothing. There were many people – many women – up there, looking to see if there was

501

anyone alive and needing help.'

It was all she could do to stop herself demanding, 'What of Shinzaemon? Where is he? What became of him?' She had to squeeze her lips together to stop the words coming out.

He fell silent again.

'Edwards-*dono* told me,' he muttered after a while, 'the southerners took the hill and destroyed the temples.' He stared painfully into some unknown void.

'They're cowards, those southerners,' he said suddenly. 'They don't fight face to face like men. They hide behind guns. For half the day they were shelling us from across the valley. We couldn't even see them. The noise was terrible. And the sound of the shells flying through the air, like ... a wailing whooshing scream, like ghosts. You didn't know where they were going to land. There were shells crashing into the ground and exploding, making huge craters, sending mud and earth spewing into the air and bits of men – whatever men were unlucky enough to be there. Arms, hands, feet, legs, guts, chunks of bone flying through the air. Men blown to pieces. That's not a way for a man to die. How can you fight an enemy who fights like that?

'The smoke – I was choking from it; and the stench, the foul stench of blood and brains and men's innards. When I killed men in Kyoto it didn't bother me. It was just the enemy. I was proud. But this was our own men dying.

'We were sheltering in the trees, trying to keep out of the way, trying not to tread on dead or dying men, feeling their bodies squelching under

502

our feet. And the sound of men screaming. You always hope that when it's your turn you'll die like a samurai, in silence. But not all of them did.

'It was raining,' he continued. 'We were soaked to the skin. We kept slipping. We were running here, running there, trying to dodge the shells.'

His voice trailed away. Sachi saw that his forehead was sticky with sweat.

'By afternoon the shelling had died down. We went down to the Black Gate.'

'You...?' breathed Taki. They were all hanging on his words.

'Me, Tora and Shin. We all made it through. And Gen – Genzaburo – a friend of ours we'd known in Kyoto. Shin had met up with him again in Kiso.'

'I know,' Sachi whispered.

'The men at the Black Gate needed reinforcements. The southerners had cannons there too. They were out to kill us all. We just kept firing and firing, squatting down to load our guns and standing up and firing, like we'd been trained to do. At least we could see them, in their black uniforms, and the Tosa guys in their red wigs. At least we didn't have to fight an invisible enemy. I was deaf from the noise of my rifle, all I could taste was gunpowder in my mouth.'

He squeezed his eyes tight shut, frowning. 'Hold the Black Gate: that was the order. We stuck together, we four. Once they broke through our ranks we crouched behind rocks and picked them off.'

'With swords?' asked Taki. She was looking at him, her eyes blazing, as if wishing that she too could have been there, fighting alongside them; as if seeing him there reminded her of being back on the road, like a breath of fresh air after being imprisoned in the mansion for so long.

'We had rifles, French rifles. We'd done a lot of training – target practice, learning how to load and shoot fast. Tora was brilliant. He could hit anything. There'd be a man charging towards him and he'd get him right in the face. Shin was yelling like he was crazy, shooting and stabbing with his bayonet. Half the southerners ran away when they saw him. I saw him do in ten men. No, more like twenty men. You would have been proud.'

He was gazing into the distance. Sachi smiled. For a moment she was picturing Shinzaemon, fighting in that reckless way of his, utterly fearless.

'Gen was a terror too. Took down a lot of the enemy. Yeah, we could use our guns. But we had to keep stopping to put in more bullets. The enemy had rifles that never stopped firing. It was like it was raining bullets. Then they charged, hordes of them. Every time we killed one, another one came. They just kept coming. They forced us further and further up the hill. Somewhere along the way we lost sight of Gen. I don't know what happened to him.'

Sachi was silent. She couldn't bear to tell him he was dead. 'Finally they forced us out on to the hilltop. I guess that was when ... I got hit.'

His face crumpled. 'It was a good fight,' he mumbled, choking out the words. 'A glorious fight. Many men died ... heroic deaths. But I ... I was useless. I failed my comrades and my Lord.

I'm ashamed. I should be dead like everyone else.'

Like everyone else... For a moment Sachi couldn't breathe. The heat and closeness seemed to close in on her. She tried to keep her voice from shaking. 'You mean ... Toranosuké and Shinzaemon...'

'They were there when... We were all together,' he said helplessly. 'I don't know what happened to them.'

So there was still hope. Her throat was so dry she couldn't speak.

'Didn't you see them?' he asked. 'When you found me – weren't they there too?'

'They weren't there,' Sachi whispered. She didn't know what to say – she didn't want him to think they had gone off and left him alone on the battlefield to die. But she also didn't want him to think they were dead.

'Maybe they went to get help?' she offered feebly.

'Help?' He smiled grimly. 'They thought I'd had it. It was a massacre.'

'We looked for them,' said Taki. 'We searched the whole battlefield.'

'They must be alive,' said Sachi. Her voice was shaking. She needed to persuade herself as much as him. She took a breath and continued firmly, 'I'm sure of it.'

He nodded. 'That's it,' he said quietly. 'That's what happened. They went north. We always said if we made it through we'd go north. I've got to get up there. I've got to join them.'

Sachi closed her eyes. She was back on the bridge. She felt Shinzaemon's arms around her, saw his eyes burning into her. Someone as alive as he could never be dead. And if he was alive ... she had to get a message to him. She had to tell him where she was so that when he returned...

She looked at Tatsuemon, bent down and put her mouth to his ear.

'When you find your comrades, will you...?' she whispered.

Their eyes met. He nodded.

She looked around for paper and a brush and told Taki to grind some ink for her. She thought for a moment. That poem by the poet Teika, written long before the Tokugawa era began, about being together, dreading the approach of dawn, knowing that the future most likely held only sadness – it expressed her feelings perfectly. In as beautiful and flowing a hand as she could manage she brushed the first three lines:

Hajime yori	From long ago
Au wa wakare to	Though I had heard to meet
Kikinagara	Could only mean to part

Shinzaemon would know the ending:

Akatsuki shirade	Yet I gave myself to you
Hito o koikeri	Forgetful of the coming dawn.

She added a scribbled note: 'At the Shimizu mansion ... waiting.'

She looked at it for a while, made sure she was happy with every rise and fall of the brush, blew on it, waited for it to dry. Then she rolled it up and wrote Shinzaemon's name on the outside. She slipped it into Tatsuemon's hand and closed his fingers round it.

'Don't forget,' she whispered.

III

Edwards called for tea. He was squatting uncomfortably on the floor, his great legs bent up on each side of him like a cricket's. His body was so angular, all elbows and knees. It made Sachi aware of how compact and rounded her own was. He bowed and took a cup from the tray which the maid held out. Sachi glanced at his huge pale hands with their broad square-tipped fingers, sprinkled with reddish hairs. The porcelain teacup looked even tinier and more fragile in his grasp.

As she sipped, she looked around curiously at this exotic foreigner's house. It had tatami mats and sliding doors and windows like any other but it was cluttered with strange objects – containers like chests standing on end and a table so tall only a giant could write on it. The top of it was above the level of her head as she sat on the floor.

In the alcove, instead of a hanging scroll or a piece of calligraphy, there was a picture of a woman, painted in some thick oily substance. She had plump cheeks and big round eyes like Edwards's and something shiny and metallic on her head like the crest on a samurai helmet. She was wearing a voluminous gown even fuller and more lavish than a courtesan's kimono but her arms and shoulders were naked. Sachi was about to ask if she was a courtesan when Edwards saw her eyes on it and said, 'That is the queen of my country – Queen Bikutoria.' Sachi heaved a sigh of relief that she hadn't said anything. What a strange country to be ruled by a semi-naked woman who dressed in such an undignified way.

She caught a hint of something rich and spicy, quite different from the subtle scents she was used to, and a background odour of damp. The house was full of mysterious foreign smells. It filled her with a mixture of fascination and repulsion. She felt sorry that Tatsuemon had to stay in such a place, yet she was envious too. Then there was the smell that hung about Edwards, his pungent body odour that smelt of the meat he ate. Initially Sachi had found it disgusting but now it seemed rather exciting. There was a whiff of something untamed about it, like a wild beast.

'Can I ask...?' said Haru, shifting forward on her knees. Her small slanted eyes were open wide and her round face was brimming with curiosity. Sachi prayed she wasn't going to ask something outrageous. Even at the darkest moments Haru never lost her earthy sense of humour or her liking for naughty tales. Sachi remembered that time when she was young – the very day after she had gone to His Majesty – when Haru had told her about dried lizard powder and how it was supposed to fill anyone who ate it with desire; and those jokes she always used to make about mushroom stems.

'In your country...' Haru whispered, crossing

508

one plump hand, then the other, over her mouth and keeping her eyes on the tatami, 'is it true you have iron monsters that travel faster than a horse? I heard they can go as far in a day as a man can walk in seven.'

Sachi glanced at Tatsuemon. He was lying back weakly, but she could see that he was listening. Perhaps some foolish talk might cheer him up and distract him from dark thoughts. She smiled and shook her head.

'Iron monsters indeed!' she said. 'The things you say, Big Sister!'

'But those ships we saw in the bay – they were iron monsters,' said Taki. 'Perhaps there are iron monsters that travel on land as well.'

The women looked expectantly at Edwards. He was looking at Haru, his pale eyebrows pushed together in a puzzled frown. Then he threw back his head and laughed, showing his teeth.

'It's true,' he said. 'How on earth do you know that, Lady Haruko?'

'I saw one,' said Haru. She blushed so fiercely even the backs of her hands glowed, then lowered her hands to her lap and looked around. A provocative smile hovered on her lips.

'You saw one?' Sachi and Taki stared at her in amazement. Edwards's round eyes grew even rounder and his mouth opened in a grin.

'Yes,' said Haru, nodding. She glanced round to see if Tatsuemon was listening then paused for a while, letting them all take it in, holding them in suspense.

'Tell us, Big Sister,' pleaded Sachi.

A shadow crossed Haru's face as if it caused her

pain to look back into the past. She took a breath.

'I'll never forget it,' she said quietly. 'It was the first time the foreigners came, fourteen years ago. They came to the castle. It was just after the old shogun, Lord Ieyoshi, passed away. Lord Iesada was the new shogun.'

Fourteen years ago, thought Sachi; four years after she was born, after her mother ... disappeared.

'We were all dying to see the foreigners, we women,' Haru continued. 'Of course we weren't allowed into the men's palace, but they took the foreigners to the great courtyard in the middle palace. We sat behind the lattices there to look. That was the first time I ever saw foreigners.'

She glanced at Edwards. Her plump cheeks dimpled.

'We thought they looked terrifying,' she said, smiling ruefully. 'We were glad they didn't see us though they stared in our direction. I think they guessed we were there though we sat quiet as mice. That was when we saw the iron monster. They had brought it to present to His Majesty. You've never seen anything so big. It was black and shiny, like a huge tree trunk laid on its side. It was made of iron.'

There was a rustle. Tatsuemon was sitting up on his cushions, leaning forward, his eyes shining. He was gazing at Haru as if he didn't want to miss a word.

'The noise it made! Like an old lady snoring. That was what we all said. It puffed out smoke, as much as a thousand watchfires or ... or like

510

the chimney of a potter's kiln or a swordsmith's furnace. Or those ships we saw in the bay.'

'Or a cannon?' asked Tatsuemon, butting in unexpectedly. 'As much smoke as that? And a boom like that?'

'Not smoke. Steam,' said Edwards. 'We call it a "steam engine". I heard about it. The first American delegation brought it as a gift for the shogun. Not that he would have had much use for it. We heard he was like a prisoner in that palace of yours.' He looked at them hard. Sachi looked away.

'It ran on metal rails, round and round,' said Haru. 'Some of the senior counsellors took rides. You've never seen anything like it, those grand officials in their robes flying round and round. They were clinging on for dear life, doing their best to look dignified.' She cupped her hands over her mouth and laughed.

'It was a model, like a child's toy,' said Edwards. 'Real steam engines are much bigger. You should see one. We have them everywhere in our country. They pull huge metal boxes, much bigger than palanquins or trunks, filled with goods and people, hundreds of people.'

The women gazed at him wide-eyed. It was impossible even to imagine a world so different from their own. Yet they had seen the ships, they had heard the cannons, they had ridden in the wheeled carriage. They could see that there were things in the world they'd never heard of.

'You'll get one here too very soon, I promise. Probably several. You thought my carriage went fast. They go much faster. You could travel along the entire Inner Mountain Road in a day in one of those.'

Sachi stared down at her small white hands neatly placed one on top of the other on her kimono skirts. She couldn't imagine wanting to travel so quickly, without stopping to see the famous views. Surely the whole point was the journey? That was why people travelled.

'Really?' she said, smiling at him. 'But you've forgotten all those mountains. I think you must be a fortune teller.' She couldn't help teasing him. 'You have no divining rods, you make no incantations, you haven't even looked at our faces or hands or asked us for a fee. And yet you say you can see the future.'

Edwards grinned at her. 'Maybe I can,' he said playfully. 'There's no holding back progress, it'll come no matter what. And I'll tell you another thing: an engineer has already arrived from my country to build a ... a... When you see watchfires on the hills and you know there's a fire or an army approaching. You know? It's like that. To pass a message across a long distance. But much more precise. You tap out a message here in Edo and someone – for example in Osaka – receives it immediately. At the same moment.'

'Sounds like black magic,' said Taki disapprovingly.

Sachi pursed her lips. She had heard the stories that went round about foreigners practising magic but she had never paid much attention. But what Edwards was saying really did sound sinister. An iron monster she could imagine. It had something in common with the big ships and

512

the cannon fire she had heard with her own ears. But the sending of messages that were not spoken by a voice or written on paper...

'But why?' she asked. 'We already have "flying feet". We can send a message from Edo to Kyoto in three days by messenger, one day by horse. Why would we want to get it there any faster?'

Tatsuemon piped up. 'It's like rifles and swords.' Everyone turned and looked at him. There was colour in his cheeks and a spark in his eye again. 'With swords the best man wins. But with rifles – a man can shoot you and you never see his face. You can kill a man and you don't even know it. There's no glory in it. At least when you can see their faces you know you've killed them. But people who fight with rifles win. They beat people who fight with swords. So we have to have rifles to make sure we win. Good rifles. English rifles. And if they have whatever it is Edwards-*dono* is describing – these magic messages – we must have that too. I'd like to see those things you talk about. I'd like to ride on an iron monster. I'd like that more than anything.'

'You will,' said Edwards. 'The magic messages will come next year. I don't need to summon the spirits to tell you that. And after that the iron monster. No matter what happens with the war, you'll have your iron monster.'

IV

Every day Sachi went to the parapet and gazed out at the fire-blackened landscape and the distant hill, yet she couldn't help noticing that day after day nothing changed. In the past after a fire people would have been out straight away, repairing the damage and starting to rebuild the houses. But a terrible lethargy had fallen over the city. Sachi was afraid that soon Edo would be overrun by woods and moorland until there was no sign there had ever been a city there at all.

Marooned in lonely splendour in the hilltop mansion, she felt as if the life of the whole great metropolis had drained away along with the blood of its warriors. Her own life seemed to have shrunk until there was no more than the four walls that surrounded her. She and Taki slept together, halberds at the ready. The remaining ladies-in-waiting and even the invisible attendants who always hovered in the background had all disappeared. Haru took care of the princess and the cooking. Occasionally they heard voices in distant parts of the mansion but still it felt as if it was populated by ghosts.

The old man guarded them. At night they heard the clack of his wooden clapper. It echoed sharp and cold across the silent grounds, warning off any intruder who might think of crawling under the building and stabbing a blade up through the gaps between the floor mats.

Each day she wondered what the next day would bring. Their money and supplies could not go on for ever. Whenever they could – whenever Edwards sent the carriage – they went to visit him. Edwards was full of tales of the strange countries he had visited and of his own country, where women of good family did not expect to spend their whole lives indoors. Sachi secretly dreaded the moment when Tatsuemon was fully recovered and they would have no excuse to visit any more.

A few days after their first visit Haru came padding through the empty rooms of the mansion with a message: Her Highness required the Retired Lady Shoko-in to attend on her immediately.

Ever since they had moved to the Shimizu mansion the princess had kept to her rooms. She seemed to feel that everything that had happened was her fault, as if her coldness to His Majesty had caused the whole disaster.

Sachi was yearning to see her. Of the three thousand women who had formed His Majesty's household only the four of them were left. With the princess in seclusion, all the responsibility for maintaining their household fell on Sachi's small shoulders. But she was apprehensive too. She wondered why Her Highness had summoned her now of all times.

Incense smoke wafted from the princess's rooms – sandalwood, cloves, cinnamon, ginger, ambergris and the other spices that made up the perfume burned on a Buddhist altar. It was a dark, holy, heavy scent, a fragrance wound about with mystery and awe. It conjured up the dark shadows and rich furnishings of temples, the glimmering gold of the altar, the chanting of priests, the beating of drums, the centuries-old piety of millions upon millions of worshippers and the smoke of the funeral pyre. As she breathed it in, Sachi's spirit grew calm and her thoughts turned to the world that was to come. She could hear the murmur of prayer. She waited for a while then slid open the door.

The princess had turned her room into a shrine. His Majesty's memorial tablet was on the altar with offerings in front of it and candles burning with tall yellow flames. A small figure knelt before it, telling her beads.

Sachi knelt beside her. Her eyes lit on the daguerreotype of His Majesty's gentle young face. For a moment she was back in the women's palace, in a room walled with gold screens and lit with huge golden candles, with crowds of attendants loitering in the shadows. Women's voices, chattering and laughing, floated through the gold leaf of the walls and across the painted transepts exquisitely carved with cranes and tortoises, peacocks and dragons. The quilted hems of kimonos swished as they glided across the tatami. Everything sparkled with gold – the robes on lacquered stands, the delicate tiered shelves, the cosmetics boxes, the porcelain tea sets.

She remembered the masques and plays and dancing. And the first time she had caught a glimpse of His Majesty. She had heard his laughter and peeked through the lattices and seen him, sitting on his horse with his falcon on his wrist, surrounded by courtiers. She had been just a child then, fresh to the palace, a maid of the lowest rank who still spoke with a rustic accent. She had admired him from afar, so slender, so youthful, so beautiful. Then the memory of the night they had lain together came back to her – the silken sheets, the warmth of his body, his pale chest and mischievous smile. Sachi was a great lady now and a samurai, but still she had to swallow hard to stop tears spilling down her cheeks.

But there was another memory colliding with that one, threatening to extinguish it. For a moment she was afraid that the princess might be able to read her mind and see the image of Shinzaemon burning there.

But the princess seemed no longer part of this world at all. Inside the fine silk of her summer kimono she was as frail and insubstantial as a reed. Sachi could see the blue veins and slender bones through the translucent skin of her hands, and her eyes, large and luminous, as if she was already gazing towards the world to come. No matter what blows fate might rain on her, she was of the blood. She was the sister of the late emperor. No one could take that away from her.

'Those were happy days,' murmured the princess. It was so long since Sachi had last heard that high-pitched birdlike whisper. 'Or at least when I think back on them they seem happy. It's good to see you. You are blooming like a morning glory. Me – I am fading.'

Sachi gazed at the tatami and listened respectfully.

'You heard the cannons, I'm sure,' the princess went on. 'You know that the last supporters of the Tokugawa – the militia – were destroyed or expelled from Edo. There is a new government now, ruling in the name of His Grace the emperor

– my nephew.' She gave a snort of bitter laughter.

'They have sent me notice of their intentions. Even this meagre life we lead here is to end. The Tokugawa clan is to be punished. We and our retainers are to have our stipends reduced almost to nothing and are to be expelled from Edo. We are to go to Suruga to join the retired shogun, Lord Yoshinobu, in exile.'

Sachi frowned, trying to grasp the enormity of what she was saying. Without their stipends, they would be ruined. They would have to find some way to make a living or they would die. Most fearful of all, they were to be exiled to Suruga. It felt like the end of the world.

Then she realized the full implications of this sentence. If … when … Shinzaemon came to find her, if Tatsuemon had managed to find him, he would look for her at the Shimizu mansion. Even if Tatsuemon never met up with him, Shinzaemon would know she was somewhere in Edo. But if she went to Suruga she would never see him again. Nor her father, either.

She became aware of the princess's silence. In the past she used always to announce bad news with wailing and lamentation, yet now she exuded an almost otherworldly calm. Perhaps her months of prayer and meditation had given her such inner peace that she had risen above the problems of this world.

'Twelve thousand households will have to move,' said the princess, her eyes burning with anger. 'A hundred thousand people. The government has given us a month to pack our belongings. When we have gone, the city will be empty.

This government wants to destroy Edo and everything it stands for.'

Sachi knew her duty, knew what she should say: 'I am at Your Highness's command. If it is your will I am ready to leave Edo whenever it suits Your Highness.' But she suddenly felt a fierce determination. She would stay in Edo, no matter what. Even if she had to go into hiding she didn't care. She was not going to be forced to leave, to be sent to some distant unknown place.

There was a long silence. The princess was gazing at her as if she wanted to imprint her face on her memory. Sachi wondered if there was some hint of rebellion etched there.

'You are like a sister to me,' the princess breathed. 'My little sister. I'll never forget that moment when I saw you for the first time in your country village. Usually I didn't notice country people. But you – you looked at me with your big eyes, so bright and curious and alive, and I could see that you weren't afraid at all. And that face of yours – so like mine. Like a younger, happier me.'

The princess drew herself up. Her small mouth curved into a smile.

'When I married into the Tokugawa family I swore to share their destiny,' she went on quietly. 'The world has moved on but I am not a part of it. I never can be. But you – you are different. You brought us all sunshine. Even His Majesty, in his short life: you brought him happiness. You have always done your duty. Now I release you. I erase all obligation you might ever have had to me. If you wish to disobey the edict, that is for you to decide. I am sure you can find a way to remain here in Edo. For myself, I go willingly into exile.'

Sachi was on her knees, her hands pressed to the tatami. She looked up at the princess, tears running down her face. For so long their destinies had been linked.

'We may never see each other again,' Princess Kazu said. 'Though I was forced to leave Kyoto and my family, I have had you for a sister. I will never forget you.'

12

A Visit to the Pawnbroker

I

Summer had come to an end. It was chilly and wet – the first typhoon of autumn was on its way. Sachi was in a dreadful state of restlessness, expecting every moment to hear the tramp of heavy feet as soldiers barged in with orders to evict them. But day after day passed and nothing happened. Sometimes she wondered if the princess had been mistaken, that there was no decree or, if there was, that no one was going to enforce it.

But whenever they set off on one of their regular visits to Edwards they would see that the Eastern Sea Road was clogged with refugees. They would be swept up in a vast mob of people with grey, despairing faces, stumbling along, treading on each other's heels, dragging carts laden with possessions. These, Sachi thought grimly to herself, must once have been bureaucrats, civil servants, guards, clerks, officials in charge of this department or that, undersecretaries of undersecretaries, ladies-in-waiting, maids, cooks. They must all have been in service to one branch of the Tokugawa or another. None of them had done any more or any less than loyal servants were expected to do. Now they were traitors, banished from the only home they had ever known, condemned to lifelong disgrace, exile and poverty.

Sachi knew that she and her little household could not escape the edict for ever. In the not-too-distant future they too would be reduced to the fate of these faceless refugees on the Eastern Sea Road.

Just as she was thinking things couldn't get any worse, Haru came to tell her the storeroom was almost empty. Rice, miso, salt, vegetables, firewood, lamp oil – nearly everything was finished.

All the time Sachi had been at the women's palace she had always had everything she could possibly want. Lengths of fabric, beautiful kimonos, every cosmetic or game or musical instrument that had ever been invented – if she was lacking anything she had only to clap her hands and it would appear. As for food, she had never been able to finish a meal, there had always been so much. Even in the village they had always had food; they had grown it themselves. But now...With a shock of fear she thought of the grounds smothered in weeds. The gardeners who

521

tended the vegetable gardens must have disappeared along with everyone else.

'So ... so we have no money?'

In the past she had never even had to think of money.

'We have money, my lady,' said Haru with a touch of reproof in her voice. 'You can rest easy on that score. Do you think your father would let you starve? Why do you think no one has come to attack us? He is protecting you and us along with you, and he has made sure we have money.'

Sachi looked at her in amazement. She had not seen Daisuké for months, not since they left the castle. Even after the battle, when the city was in chaos, he hadn't sought her out to reassure her or make certain she was safe. She had thought him not much of a father, for all his fine words.

All the same she had wondered why they continued to lead such a trouble-free life. At a time when all the houses of the Tokugawas and their allies were being demolished or requisitioned by the southerners, they had had no soldiers billeted on them, nor had they been ordered to leave. So he had been watching over them from afar after all.

'We must notify the rice merchants,' she said. 'Why haven't they delivered?'

Even as she was speaking it was beginning to dawn on her. They couldn't notify anyone. They had no servants.

'They don't come any more,' said Haru quietly.

Sachi looked at her sharply. Her plump face had grown thinner and there were dark shadows around her eyes. She hadn't been eating properly;

she had been saving half her food to give to Sachi. Tears came to Sachi's eyes at the thought of such devoted loyalty.

'I'd like to ask permission to go into town,' Haru added. 'I need to find a new supplier.'

Sachi narrowed her eyes. 'You'll carry money?'

'Of course.'

'But the city is in chaos. We must all go, all three of us.'

'It's too dangerous, my lady,' Haru protested. 'You stay here in the mansion. Taki and I will go. It's not proper for fine ladies to roam the streets or go to places where the common people live.'

But Sachi had had enough of hiding out. She was stifling in these grand empty spaces, these dusty silent rooms, all this sadness and solitude. She was hungry for life and people.

'Three is safer than two,' she said in tones that brooked no argument.

Sachi changed into simple townswomen's robes, with a padded *haori* jacket in an unobtrusive shade of brown. She rather liked the familiar feel of the coarse cotton on her skin. In the townsmen's districts even the humblest hint of silk would be an invitation to robbers. Haru filled a wallet with gold coins and tucked it into the bosom of her kimono, wrapping her obi tight around it. It still made a visible bulge.

In the grounds gusts of wind blew through fields of sedge. The women scrambled through tangles of knotgrass, ferns and plantain and around clumps of giant plume grass to reach the gate. Sachi noticed with foreboding that even the bridge across the moat was beginning to crumble.

To get to the townsmen's districts they had to pass through the burned-out wasteland that lay between the mansion and the hill, in the opposite direction from the route they took to go to Edwards's house. Great black ravens swooped above the deserted streets and settled on the husks of buildings, peering at the three walkers with beady yellow eyes. Their harsh caws echoed around the ruins, making the place feel even more desolate. The hill loomed still and silent on the horizon. It was the first time they had been in this part of the city since the dreadful day of the battle.

The women tucked up their kimono skirts and pattered along as quickly as they could on their wooden sandals, every sense on the alert. The last thing they needed was to be robbed.

They were pit-patting along in the silence when they saw a crowd of ragged men ahead of them, lurking in the shadows. As soon as the men saw them they rushed out and spread across the road, entirely filling it. There were ten or twenty of them, desperate, ravenous-looking characters. They were brandishing staves and sticks and chunks of wood that looked as if they had been ripped from the ruined palace of a daimyo.

Haru folded her arms tightly across her obi. This time the women were on their own. There was no Shinzaemon to defend them and no Edwards around and no likelihood of either suddenly turning up in such a desolate place.

One of the men stepped forward until his nose was pressed against Sachi's. His smell was so foul it made her retch; he clearly hadn't washed for many days. He had a thin twisted face, hair tied in a greasy knot on top of his head and a crazed look in his eyes. He grinned. Half his teeth were missing and the rest were blackened stumps.

'All by yourselves, fine ladies?' he mumbled. It seemed their townswomen's robes were not much of a disguise, but at least the men were too ignorant to realize what a prize Sachi herself was. 'Just gi's your money and we'll let you go.'

Sachi glanced around. Another fellow had grabbed Haru's arms and was trying to drag them away from her chest. Haru was standing like the well-bred gentlewoman she was, head slightly bowed, toes turned inward. Her face was impassive. The man was shaking her. He lunged forward and swung a blow at her. Her expression didn't change. She twisted out of the way, keeping her arms folded, then waited till he was off balance and made a movement so small even Sachi barely saw it. Sachi smiled in satisfaction. She had forgotten what a fine fighter Haru was. The fellow staggered past her, staring stupidly, tripped and smashed chin first on the ground. His scrawny legs quivered then he went limp.

The other men's jaws dropped. They gawped at their fallen comrade then turned fiercely on the three women.

'One time lucky,' snarled one. 'One time only.'

They closed in tighter. The stench was overpowering. 'We have nothing of value,' Sachi said quietly. 'Please let us pass. We don't want trouble.' She put her hand on the hilt of her dagger. The three women were standing back to back. Haru had both arms tightly folded across her obi.

'Think you're such fine ladies, with your airs and graces,' sneered the first man. Gobs of yellow spittle flew from his gap-toothed mouth. Sachi twisted her face away. 'All your finery won't do you any good. We'll 'ave your money and we'll 'ave you. Right, lads?'

Sachi looked at them levelly, weighing up the odds. The men had brute strength on their side, but they had no idea how to fight. If they had been less ignorant they would have known better than to attack palace women. Admittedly she and Taki and Haru did not have their halberds and the men had staves, but she could see that the men had no idea even how to stand. It would be easy to use the force of their own movements to tip them off balance. Still, there were a lot of them and they were desperate, like ravenous dogs.

The man blocked her path. She tried to step to one side of him then the other, but he stood stubbornly in her way.

Baying like a pack of wolves, the men swung their staves and began to lash out. Out of the corner of her eye Sachi saw a couple of staffs flashing through the air towards her head. She stepped out of the way of one, grabbed it and twisted it with a sharp flick of her wrist. There was a crunch as a man hit the ground. She was just in time to step out of the way of the other as the second man lost his balance. He stumbled clumsily towards her then tripped and crashed heavily to the ground.

As a third stave descended, she snatched it out of the fighter's grasp, twisting it so that he staggered into a wall and lay where he fell. It was not a halberd but it was as good as a practice stick. She swung around and around, lashing out at heads, chests and knees. Then a blow seemed to come out of nowhere. She was struck on the chest and fell, winded. She was trying to get her breath when a couple of men threw themselves on her and held her down with her arms pinioned so tight she feared her ribs would crack.

'Got this one,' yelled a voice. 'The other one's got the money! Grab her too!'

Sachi twisted and turned, trying to free herself. She managed to wriggle one arm round till her hand was on her dagger. With a single movement she wrenched her arm free, dagger in hand, and swung round. She heard Haru screech, 'Never! Get off me!' Sachi's arm moved with a momentum of its own. Before she knew what had happened the man fell back, yowling, clutching his face.

She sprang up. Haru's clothes were ripped and her face bruised. Her obi was flying loose but she still had both arms round her stomach and was lashing out with her feet and shoulders. As Sachi turned a man walloped Haru on the back. She staggered forward and for a moment lost her grasp. The man snatched the wallet and started to run. Without thinking, Sachi hurled her dagger. It curved through the air and sank up to its hilt in his back. He fell and was silent. She leaped across the fallen bodies, picked up the wallet and wrenched out her dagger. Several men were lying on the ground with their hands over their eyes and blood pouring through their fingers. Taki was

527

wiping her hairpin on her skirts.

Towards the back of the group, some of the men were still standing, blinking like terrified rabbits. Sachi turned towards them and they scuttled away like cockroaches. Panting, she gave the wallet to Haru, who tucked it back into her kimono and carefully retied her obi. In silence the three women smoothed their hair and slapped at their kimono skirts, trying to brush off the stench of the men. Sachi wiped her dagger on her handkerchief and slipped it back into her obi.

In the distance Ueno Hill looked like a peaceful tree-covered knoll. Birds circled above it, their harsh cries echoing around the pale dome of the sky. Keeping well away from it, the women headed east towards the townsfolk's districts.

II

As they neared the east end of the city, Sachi began to hear the hum of voices and catch the whiff of food cooking, wood fires burning and the pungent smell of human waste. Soon they came to a huge open space where jugglers, mountebanks, acrobats and storytellers showed off their skills. A woman was putting a monkey through its tricks. Another was selling flowers. Small stalls offered grilled octopus and omelettes cooked on the spot. People milled around, gawping and cheering. Hard-eyed women with haggard faces trawled the crowd, offering themselves for sale. Even in a city on the edge of extinction life went on. Everyone had to survive.

Scrawny men with the faces and hungry eyes of rats circled outside the crowd, homing in on the women. Haru kept her arms folded at her waist. Sachi pulled her scarf tighter around her face so that her pale skin and aristocratic features didn't draw unwanted attention. It was reassuring to see other women around. Some were geishas or prostitutes but there were ordinary women too, going about their business. It made it far easier to disappear into the crowd. Despite the urgency of their mission, Sachi was enjoying being outside, away from the stuffy rooms of the mansion, back in a part of the world where men and women rubbed shoulders.

The street was lined with shops, but many were boarded up and those that were open seemed to have few goods or customers. There was a rice merchant's sign outside one. They peeked through the slit and tried to shove open the door but it was firmly locked. The rice merchants – like everyone else who could afford to do so – all seemed to have left town.

They wandered down a lane lined with tenements, then another. The houses were jammed in right next to each other, so close together that not a shaft of sunlight pierced the shadows of the alleyways. Sachi, Haru and Taki walked in single file, backing up against the wall to let people pass in the other direction. The drainage channels ran with foul water, the place was rank with the stench of rotting food and human excrement, rats scurried about, caged birds warbled and insects shrilled. Here and there people thin as sticks sat propped against walls, holding out

529

bowls, crying plaintively for alms.

By now they were completely lost. Sachi said nothing, although she was becoming apprehensive. Then a young woman sashayed towards them, tripping along on high wooden clogs. They stepped back to let her pass. She looked at them, her jaw dropped and her eyes opened so wide it looked as if they would burst out of her head.

'*Hora!*' she gasped. 'Isn't it... Haru-*sama?* And ... Lady Oyuri!'

Lady Oyuri. Sachi had last heard that name more than three years earlier, when the shogun was still alive, when she was still His Majesty's concubine, the lady of the side chamber.

And that voice, shrill and high-pitched – she knew it immediately. Words echoed in her ears: 'Dirty peasant. I can't bear to be near you. Why aren't you in the stables with the animals?' Images swam before her of a haughty pert-nosed girl in an elaborate kimono with the whole city of Edo captured in its embroidery, flouncing along the grand corridor that led to the shogun's entrance; of practice sticks clashing and the ferocious fight they'd had in the training hall which, against all the odds, Sachi had managed to win. Then she saw a raised hand, heard a sandal hissing through the air. She felt the pain and humiliation as it hit her around the ear, heard the sniggers, saw a pretty face contorted with hatred and jealousy...

Fuyu.

Then there had been that last meeting when Fuyu had seemed half mad. She had disappeared after that and no one had ever discovered what became of her, although some of the women had said she must have been executed by her family. All that time Sachi had wondered if it had been her fault, if she had brought that terrible fate on her enemy by wishing it on her.

And now here she was, right in front of them. But could it really be her or was it a fox spirit?

Beneath the thick make-up the woman had Fuyu's pert nose and olive complexion. There was still the outline of that pretty heart-shaped face that had made her the acknowledged beauty among the junior ladies, but it had grown pinched and haggard. She looked beaten down. Her shoulders were stooped as if she often had to beg favours and her kimono hung on her like a shroud. There was a hard look in her eyes. Fuyu had had to struggle to survive.

'You here too, are you?' she grunted. Her teeth were blackened and a couple were missing. She was wearing an incongruously bright crepe kimono with long swinging sleeves like a young girl's. In the palace her Edo accent had been overlaid with the intonation of a high-ranking samurai, but now she had reverted to pure Edo. 'Would've thought with your luck you'd have made it through.' She was looking at Sachi. As she spoke there was a flash of the old venom.

Taki turned away abruptly. Sachi knew that she was trying her hardest to conceal her feelings, as was proper for a samurai, but her thin shoulders were quivering with distaste.

'You ladies,' said Fuyu. 'Y'all end up down 'ere.'

'You mean ... there are other women here?' Taki demanded. 'Other women from the palace?'

531

Sachi thought of her ladies-in-waiting, her maids and attendants, all those women who had disappeared. All this time she had assumed they were safely back with their families. Surely none of them could have ended up here?

'Sure. Some are on the streets. Some are in the brothels in the Yoshiwara. They're not so high and mighty now, that's for sure.'

'And you?' asked Haru softly.

'Don't give me any of your pity,' snapped Fuyu. Her voice was hard and brittle. 'My master's a pawnbroker. He takes care of me. I made a mistake. I was young. But then...' Her voice softened. 'Anyway, it's all fallen apart, hasn't it? Whether you become the shogun's concubine or whether you don't – makes no difference now. It's all come to nothing.'

A pawnbroker's mistress! No doubt Fuyu had brought her destiny on herself, but no matter what had happened between them, it was terrible to see her fallen so low. Much though Sachi disliked and distrusted Fuyu, she couldn't help pitying her. To have come to this – Fuyu, the star of the women's palace, the Retired One's preferred candidate to be the concubine of the shogun. Sachi too had fallen a long way since then, she knew that. But not as far as Fuyu.

'What you doin' here anyway?' Fuyu demanded. 'Somewhere to stay, is that it? Work? You want some work? Come. My master'll help you out, whatever it is you want.'

Sachi glanced at Taki and Haru and nodded slightly. They were totally lost and had little choice but to follow her. Fuyu led them deep into

532

the warren of streets and they walked behind, all their senses on the alert.

'Perhaps she's planning to sell us,' Taki muttered to Sachi, glancing around her with big eyes. 'Anything's possible these days. Fuyu knows better than anyone who you are and how much you'd be worth if she handed you over to the southerners.'

'Don't say that,' murmured Sachi, shaking her head.

'No Edo-ite would collaborate with the occupiers,' whispered Haru sternly. 'Not even poor Fuyu. We're all in this together.'

They turned a corner on to a broader stretch of road. There was a barber's shop, a public bath, a vegetable merchant's and next to that a large shop with a pawnbroker's sign displayed outside. Fuyu ducked under the curtains.

'Oi, Fuyu, is that you?' croaked a voice. 'What you doin' runnin' off when there's work to be done?'

'Oi!' snapped another voice.

A fug of smoke swirled inside. A shrivelled old woman bundled up in a shapeless brown garment, with her hair in a knot, was sitting, skinny legs folded under her, smoking a long-stemmed pipe. She turned a withered face towards the newcomers. A man was sprawled behind a railing. Beside him a notice warned sternly that pledges would be accepted for a maximum of eight months. Eight months, thought Sachi. Who could possibly know what the world would have come to by then or where they would all be?

A hunted look like that of a cornered animal

flashed across Fuyu's face. Then she drew back her painted lips in a coquettish smile.

'It's me,' she said in a girlish falsetto. 'Brought some friends. From the old days.'

The man sat up slowly when he saw the three women and tapped out his pipe. His merchant's gown was crumpled, the top of his head unshaved. He narrowed his eyes and peered at them suspiciously, then smiled slowly, all affability, flashing a few rotten stumps of teeth.

'Palace ladies, is it? Come in. Our shop is very small. Something to pawn, have you?'

'No. We're looking for a rice merchant,' said Haru.

'Run out of food, unh?' he scowled, fingering his abacus. 'Yup, times are hard. It's had it, this place. Those folk what used to make their living off the daimyos, all gone. Left town. We got our stuff packed up ready to go too. Isn't that right, Fu-*chan*?'

Fuyu put her mouth to his ear. His jaw dropped nearly to the floor. He gave an audible gasp, threw aside his abacus and scrambled to his knees, grinding his face into the straw matting.

'So sorry! So sorry!' he squawked in muffled tones, his mouth rubbing against the matting. 'Forgive me, your honourship. Your honourable concubinage. Thank you for honouring my miserable shop. Whatever I can do to help. We'll never forget... His young Majesty.'

A big tear, then another plopped on to the grimy matting. He brushed his hand across his eyes. The old woman too had scrambled to her knees.

534

'We're all loyal subjects down 'ere, your eminenceship,' she croaked. 'We 'ate those southerners much as anyone. Whatever we can do. Whatever we can do.'

Sachi wasn't sure how sincere they were, but it didn't matter as long as they could get food. Haru dipped into her obi and pulled out a single gold coin.

'We'd like to arrange to have rice delivered. We have a deposit,' she said.

The man picked up some glasses, brought the coin close to his face and peered at it. He handed it to the old woman who bit at it thoughtfully.

'Heard it was all gone,' he said in tones of wonder. A cunning smile crossed his face. 'Beggin' your pardon, your honourship. Not sure this will do down 'ere. See, it's marked with the Tokugawa stamp.'

Sachi took the coin and turned it over, bewildered. Sure enough, there was the hollyhock crest of the Tokugawas.

'Y'see, they'll think we nicked it. There's been soldiers down 'ere, southern soldiers, ransackin' people's 'ouses. Say they're lookin' for the shogun's gold. Say it's gone missin'.'

'Don't be stupid, Older Brother,' snapped Fuyu. 'It's big ingots they're lookin' for. Don't forget I used to live in the palace too. Anyway, no one really thinks it's down 'ere. Wherever it is it's been smuggled out of the city long since. Do them ladies a favour. You can 'ave it remelted.'

'Ain't you ladies got any copper?' said the man with an obsequious smile. 'Just a few *mon*. That'll do for a deposit. After all, it's for her honourable

535

concubinage. The lads will see you all right.'

Haru dug around in her obi and produced a string of copper coins.

'I'll see ya fair, m'ladies,' said the man. 'Gotta do my bit for the memory of His young Majesty.'

III

The pawnbroker was as good as his word. The next day Haru reported that enough rice, salt, miso, lamp oil, vegetables and firewood had arrived to keep the women supplied for many months.

A few days later Sachi was writing when she heard the whisper of silk. Taki appeared at the door, her fingertips pressed to the tatami, her immaculately coiffed head bowed.

'A visitor,' she announced in her most official voice.

Something was wrong. Taki's mouse-like squeak was a fraction shriller than usual. There was a note of hysteria in her voice.

'Edwards-*sama*?'

'No,' said Taki sharply. 'Your honourable father. Daisuké-*sama*.'

Sachi put down her brush in amazement.

'My father! But... But why? I know he's been taking care of us ... but I'm not sure I want to see him.'

The words came out before she could stop them.

'I know he's your father,' Taki said. Her thin face was stern. She pinched her eyebrows to-

536

gether into a frown and drew her breath through her teeth in a hiss. 'But it frightens me to think you might let him get too close to you. He's not ... the same sort of person as us. He's not of the samurai class. Remember what happened to your mother.'

'All the same I have to see him,' Sachi murmured almost to herself. 'I have to find out more about my mother.'

It wasn't that she had forgotten her mother; but she had tucked her, and the mystery of what had become of her, somewhere deep inside her mind. Like a fire that has been damped down and left to smoulder, now that yearning burst into flame again, blazing more fiercely than ever.

Taki held up a mirror. Sachi's face glimmered palely back at her from the polished bronze surface. These days she no longer wore her hair cut short like a widow but coiled into a loose twist. She remembered the days when she had had a new hairstyle every time she rose in rank and a different set of kimonos to mark the passing of each month. She smiled sadly as she thought of that innocent time, when such things had seemed so thrilling and all-important. That world was gone for ever.

She brushed her finger across her cheek. There was sadness on her face. It looked thinner, the cheekbones cut a little more sharply, and there was a faint shadow around the slant of her eyes. She had yet to reach her nineteenth year yet it was hard to imagine what future there could possibly be for her. But it was not only herself that she saw. She was getting closer and closer to

537

the age her mother had been when she met her father. It was strange – disconcerting – to be inhabited by her own mother, a mother she didn't even know. The more life touched her, the more her face was shaped by suffering, the more she must look like her mother. Daisuké would see it immediately.

While Taki scurried before her, making sure the doors were open, she glided from one shadowy room to the next. The quilted hem of her kimono swished behind her. Part of her wanted never to reach the great hall, never to see this untrustworthy charmer, this father of hers. Yet another part of her could hardly wait. She slowed her steps till she was barely moving, sliding one foot then the other across the tatami the way she had been taught to walk at the palace, the way great ladies walked. But her spirit seemed to race in front of her.

Long before she reached the great hall she smelled the woody fragrance of tobacco smoke and the distinctive foreign aroma that always clung to Daisuké's clothes. There was another scent too. She paused. Hints of musk, aloe, wormwood, frankincense – the kind of perfume a court lady would use to scent her robes. Despite herself her feet moved faster.

She caught the sound of familiar voices. Haru was there already.

'Haru.' It was Daisuké's low rumble. In the stillness Sachi could hear every word. She stopped and gestured to Taki to be silent.

'Haru, did I do wrong? Should I have waited at the temple? All these years it's preyed on me. I thought it would be best for her if I disappeared.'

For her. So he was talking about Lady Okoto, Sachi's mother. His voice was an agonized growl.

'I have to know why she never came back. Was she locked up? Sent into exile? Was she forced to kill herself? If I knew she was dead at least I could mourn. I can't bear it, not knowing. All these years I've had to carry it inside myself.' He gave a deep sigh.

'Haru, you must have some idea what became of her. Please tell me. I've paid for my misdeeds. I've suffered enough.'

Sachi hardly dared breathe. She had always told herself that her mother might still be alive somewhere, that it was just a matter of finding her.

'Not now, Older Brother.' Haru was speaking in the softest of murmurs. 'My lady is on her way. She will be here at any moment.'

He groaned. 'If she's alive, just tell me. Just one word, that's enough.'

Unable to bear it any longer, Sachi stepped forward into the great hall.

Threads of smoke coiled in the shafts of sunlight that slid through the cracks between the paper doors. Smoke drifted like mist around the huge black rafters. Daisuké and Haru sat leaning towards each other on each side of the tobacco box. Between them, glowing like a piece of the sky, was the brocade. Sachi's mother's over-kimono, neatly folded. Daisuké's large hand rested on it as lightly as a caress.

When they saw her, they started and leaped back as if they had been caught plotting some terrible crime. Daisuké snatched his hand from the brocade. His eyes opened wide and a look of shock flickered across his face. Sachi knew it was not her he saw but her mother. Then he put down his long-stemmed pipe, scrambled to his knees and bowed.

The broad shoulders and massive back, the bull-like neck and large head covered in black stubble speckled with grey, the powerful hands on the tatami – everything about him was strong, capable, honest, open. Despite the months that had gone by it was as if no time had passed at all. Sachi knew she should be wary: he had caused her mother's downfall and had fought on the side of the southerners. But she also knew that he had taken good care of her, Haru and Taki. She couldn't help feeling a surge of relief and joy that this man was her father. Quickly she knelt.

He raised his head and gazed at her with a long steady gaze, as if he was afraid that if he once stopped looking she would disappear again. He looked a little careworn, his jaw was more jowly, the crease between his eyebrows deeper, but he was still as warm and handsome as ever.

'Daughter,' he said solemnly. Then his face relaxed. He broke into a smile.

Sachi bowed. It was hard not to smile back.

'Welcome,' she replied stiffly. She knew he wanted her to address him as 'Father' but she couldn't. Not yet.

'I'm sorry,' she said. She couldn't be bothered with the usual exchange of platitudes and compliments. 'It's very rude but ... I couldn't help overhearing what you said.'

540

Haru was on her knees with her face pressed to her hands. The gleaming loops and coils of her coiffure quivered slightly.

'Haru,' Sachi said softly. 'Please tell us. I beg you. My mother...'

There was a long silence. Haru looked up. Her plump face was drained of colour and her lips were trembling.

'If she is dead,' Sachi pleaded, 'I need to know. I am her child. I need to make offerings and pray. With no one to pray for her she will be a hungry ghost. I need to be sure she is safely in the next world.'

Haru's face crumpled in anguish. She closed her eyes. When she opened them she seemed to be staring into a past she had tried her best to forget.

'My lady, I told you,' she whispered. But which 'my lady' was she speaking to? And what was it she had told her?

'You told me that after I was born my mother went back to the palace,' said Sachi. 'Then she received a summons to go home...'

She remembered Haru's tale perfectly. Her mother had been summoned home because her brother, Lord Mizuno, was desperately ill, on his deathbed. That was what Haru had said. And yet... Sachi had seen Lord Mizuno herself, with her own eyes. She could never forget that fearsome hawk-like face scarred with the marks of smallpox, or those muscular swordsman's hands. He might have been on his deathbed all those years ago but he certainly hadn't died.

'She was summoned to the family residence,'

541

said Haru slowly. 'They said that... her brother was dying. She was to go home immediately. I helped her pack. I'd never left her side before, never, but she told me I must stay behind, that I must go back to the temple and tell Daisuké-sama...'

'I waited, Haru, but you didn't come.' His voice was hoarse with pain.

'I was going to make an excuse and sneak out. But then ... then a message came.'

Haru put her sleeves over her face. There were tears running down her cheeks. She brushed them away with the back of her fist.

Daisuké leaned forward. His bushy eyebrows were jammed together. He stared at Haru as if he was trying to carve into her soul with his eyes.

Haru opened her mouth then closed it again. She shook her head violently, took a shuddering breath, then another. Sachi reached out and put her small white hand on Haru's. Haru screwed her eyes so tightly shut they nearly disappeared into her plump cheeks.

She muttered some words. Sachi shuffled closer, trying to catch what it was she was saying. Taki was just behind. Daisuké was so close she could feel the warmth emanating from his large body. She could hear his rasping breath, smell his sweat mingled with the scent of some foreign fragrance.

Haru spoke again in the faintest of whispers. This time Sachi made out the words. 'It said ... that she had passed away. She was taken ill and passed away, all of a sudden. That's what it said.'

Sachi caught her breath. For a moment she

couldn't make sense of the words. Then she realized, and felt a chill that rippled out from somewhere inside her until the tips of her fingers and toes were like ice. The sunlight had faded and the candles flickered in a sudden breeze. She shivered.

'You didn't tell me, Big Sister,' she said hoarsely.

Daisuké ground his great fist into the tatami.

'The day after?' he roared. 'That's not possible. How could she die so suddenly?'

Haru's shoulders slumped, her plump face sagged. 'Maybe she fell ill,' she said, avoiding his eyes. It was as if the words were wrenched out of her, as if she was reciting something she had told herself a million times to try to persuade herself of the truth of it, like a spell that could drive out ill fortune. 'She'd just had a baby. People die in childbirth. It's very dangerous to move around after you've had a baby. You're supposed to stay sitting up for seven days to stop the blood flowing to your head. I suppose that was it.'

Daisuké looked at her accusingly.

'Is that what you think, Haru? Is that what you think happened? We were together. I saw her after she had the baby. She was fine.'

Haru flinched. 'Anyway,' she mumbled, 'the family offered apologies to the shogun for depriving him of his concubine. They sent money, a lot of money. After all, she was a valuable possession. Lady Honju-in saw the letter and told us about it. I think we were meant to take it as a warning not to forget that ... it was a crime, what my lady did. Not to make the same mistake ourselves.'

The crease between Daisuké's eyebrows had

543

deepened into a furrow. He clenched his huge fists so tightly the veins stood out. The black hairs on his knuckles stood on end. 'So she died just like that in a single day. And you went to the family residence for the funeral?'

'There was no notice of a funeral, only a death. We women aren't allowed to leave the castle for private matters. But I did manage to sneak out. Not for the funeral. I went to the temple. But you'd gone. And taken ... your child, my lady, with you.'

'And you really believe she's dead?'

'I don't know,' said Haru. Then she opened her eyes and looked straight at Daisuké. 'Myself, I've never believed it. When women commit a crime like hers, families do very strange things. Sometimes they lock the woman up for ever. Sometimes they execute her. But often they can't bear to, so perhaps they made up the story and hid her away somewhere. Perhaps they put her in a convent. I didn't go to her funeral, I didn't see her body, I didn't take part in any religious observance. I didn't observe the seventh day and the fourteenth day and all the other ceremonial days after her death. As far as I'm concerned, she's alive.'

In the candlelight Daisuké looked tired and old. His face haggard, he stared blank-eyed at the tatami. His mouth was twisted in torment. He picked up the brocade and buried his face in it. When he put it down again the exquisite embroidery was stained with tears.

'After all, both of you were dead to me and now you're here,' said Haru quietly.

They sat in silence, not daring to meet each other's eyes, until the charcoal in the tobacco brazier began to fade from red to grey. Taki filled a pipe and tamped it. She picked up a pair of tongs, stirred the embers until she found a live coal, then lit the pipe and handed it to Daisuké. He took the delicate stem in his big fingers and slowly, as if he was very old, put it to his lips. Taki prepared a pipe for Sachi, Haru and finally for herself.

'The nightingale died,' said Sachi, staring at the dying coals. She suddenly felt like a child. Tears pricked her eyes. 'Father, I wish you'd come sooner.'

Father. She was surprised at how easily the word slipped out now and how natural it felt to say it.

Sachi could barely remember what it was like to have a father. Ever since she left the village and entered the women's palace she had been surrounded by women. Then suddenly she was out in the cold, making decisions and taking responsibility. Now she knew that someone was watching over her.

She understood so many things now – how difficult it had been for Daisuké, an official of the imperial government, to make even this one visit to their house, to be seen entering the compound of women who were not just close to the defeated Tokugawa clan but family members. How dangerous it must have been for him to make sure she was protected; to provide succour to the family of the enemy was certainly a crime. Yet he had done so for months without her ever knowing it was him, without expecting acknowledgement or gratitude. Now she knew what it was like to have a father. That was what a father did.

He nodded gravely. She could see that he had registered the word and the sentiment.

Their eyes met. There were pouches below his, and lines at the corners. They were the shape of bitter almonds, just like the eyes she saw when she looked in the mirror.

He reached forward, took her small hands and folded them in his large ones. His palms were soft like silk – the palms of an official, not a carpenter.

'Daughter,' he said, 'I hadn't intended you to hear these terrible things. I came to tell you that I'm going back to Osaka. There's talk that Osaka may become the new capital.'

She stiffened. 'Capital of what?' she wanted to say. 'Whose capital? The war isn't won yet.' But she didn't want to spoil the newly formed bond between them. It was too precious.

'I will make sure that you're protected and provided for,' he said. 'There'll be no visits from southern soldiers, no problem with looters or robbers. The mansion won't be requisitioned and no one will make you leave. I hope ... I believe that your mother is alive. As soon as I can, as soon as the fighting is over, as soon as the country is at peace, I'll find her. I promise you that.'

Part V

The Eastern Capital

13

The Coming of the Emperor

I

The rain seemed never to end. Leaves hung dripping on the trees and lay in sodden piles on the ground. Never before had a year been so sad and grim. The city sank deeper and deeper into desolation; even the banks of the castle moat were slipping and sliding into the water. Whenever Sachi saw them they had collapsed still further. No one would ever have guessed what a glorious city Edo had been only a few months earlier.

Then one day rays of sunlight came slanting through the cracks between the wooden rain doors. The air was crisp and cool. From inside the gloomy mansion Sachi heard footsteps crunching across the stones of the courtyard.

Her heart leaped. For a moment she told herself it was a messenger, one of the 'flying feet', bringing a letter from up north. She pictured him, thin and wiry, standing at the door in his black uniform and flat straw hat, panting and covered in sweat. He would bow, open his ornate lacquered box and hand her a scroll. As she unrolled it she would recognize the hand. There would be the last two lines of the poem she had sent Shinzaemon. She sighed. Everything was so chaotic there was probably not even a postal system any more.

It was a long time now since Tatsuemon had left, taking with him her poem. Now at least Shinzaemon must know where she was. Every day she told herself a letter might come from him, but each day she was disappointed.

Tatsuemon had looked so young and brave when he had said goodbye. His cheeks were plump and rosy again, flushed with the excitement of heading off along the road on his own.

'I can't wait to see Tora and Shin,' he had said.

There was no more than fuzzy down on his upper lip and the top of his head was not yet shaved. He still had a long forelock like a child. At fifteen he was old enough to kill and be killed, like any samurai. Nevertheless her heart had been heavy. Tatsuemon was not yet fully grown, not even a man.

Now she wondered with dread what might have happened to him. Then, as now, the roads were swarming with southern soldiers and the chances of his making it through were small.

And even if he managed to find Shinzaemon and Toranosuké, they were probably holed up under siege in a castle somewhere. For a moment the thought passed through her mind that he might be wounded or dead, but she pushed it away. Even to think such a thing was tempting fate.

But it was all nothing more than a daydream. The footsteps on the gravel were not those of a messenger at all. Messengers scuttled about in straw sandals or clopped around on wooden clogs. Only one person stomped along in that determined, firm way: Edwards, with his long legs and boots made of animal skin. The floorboards in the entrance hall groaned as he stepped inside.

Sachi had assumed that after Tatsuemon left they would never see Edwards again. He would stop sending the carriage and the window he had opened on to the outside world would slam shut. But it hadn't. Edwards continued to visit.

The first time they invited him in Taki had been scandalized. But he was, as Sachi reminded her, a foreigner and not really human at all, so there was no impropriety. In any case, they were hugely in his debt. He had rescued them on Ueno Hill and been endlessly kind to Tatsuemon. He was virtually family. Besides, they needed him. Working at the British Legation, he was always up to date with the news and kept them informed of the latest developments on the war front.

She hurried to the great hall. Edwards was already there, squatting on the tatami, his knees sticking out like the hairpins in a courtesan's coiffure. Sachi was aware of his big chest inside his coarse linen jacket, the way his great legs awkwardly bent up. He filled the room. He glanced up when she came in. He looked worried; she could see there was bad news. Foreigners were so strange, she thought. Here he was, a grown man, but he didn't know how to conceal his feelings. Whatever he happened to feel at the time – anger, fear, concern – was written on his face, like a child.

She hurried through the compliments and greetings, then folded her hands in her lap. The hall fell silent.

551

'You have news,' she said quietly. 'Something's happened.'

She could feel a knot of fear in her stomach. In the last month there had been nothing but bad news for everyone who yearned for the return of the shogun. The southerners were sweeping all before them. First they had stormed the city of Nagaoka. The town had been reduced to rubble, the castle destroyed and most of the defenders killed. Five weeks later Yonezawa had been lost. Now Aizu Wakamatsu was under siege. Wakamatsu was the northern citadel, the capital of the resistance, the most ancient and powerful fortress of the north. All those who remained loyal to the shogun and the northern cause had retreated there and there had been fierce fighting for the last month. Every time Edwards brought news it was that the attackers had pushed further into the city, taking moat after moat. His most recent reports had been that they had reached the outer walls of the castle. It was heavily fortified, he had said, and should be able to hold out for a while, at least.

Wakamatsu was the last line of defence. If it was taken there might be a few stubborn bands of samurai who would flee to the far north and hold out there, but basically it would all be over.

The furrow on Edwards's forehead deepened. The bristly hairs of his straw-coloured eyebrows knitted together above his prominent nose. Large though it was, it was actually rather a fine nose, Sachi thought, and delicately shaped.

Taki lit a pipe and handed it to him. He took a few puffs.

'Aizu Wakamatsu has fallen,' he said. His voice was gruff. 'I'm sorry.' Silence filled the hall.

Aizu Wakamatsu.

Sachi closed her eyes. She had steeled herself for the worst, but nevertheless the news came as a shock. She had hoped that Wakamatsu might win through, that at least the north might remain in northern hands. For Edwards it was only news and at least it would mean an end to the fighting. But for her it was personal.

Shinzaemon had surely been there, and Toranosuké, and Tatsuemon. She knew a samurai woman should feel pride that the warriors of her clan fought so bravely, dying in battle rather than coming home in defeat. She suspected Taki might be proud if they died to the last man. But ever since she had gone to the hill it had all seemed different. She pictured them huddling together around a camp fire, shivering under thin blankets as the days grew colder. Perhaps they didn't have a fire or blankets or even food. All this time she had hoped and believed the northerners would win and Shinzaemon would return. But now those prospects seemed like hollow dreams.

'I heard from Dr Willis.' Sachi knew that Dr Willis had gone north at the request of the southern high command, to tend to their wounded. 'He said the battle was very fierce. Both sides fought bravely but the imperial army had more men and better arms.'

'The imperial army!' snorted Taki, jabbing her needle into her sewing as if she was delivering a death blow. The 'imperial army' was nothing but a grand name for the southerners.

553

'The northerners don't have much of a chance. All they have is French weapons.' Edwards's lip curled sardonically as he mentioned the French. 'The imperial army have...'

He didn't need to say it. The southerners were armed by the English – by his people.

'So Dr Willis didn't see any of our men,' said Sachi.

It was a statement, not a question. He grimaced and shook his head. Sachi knew very well that there were never any northern wounded, that the southerners always beheaded them. It was very hard to keep hope alive, knowing such things.

'Your northern troops suffered terrible losses,' Edwards continued. 'And the dead will suffer the same punishment as ... the men on Ueno Hill. The imperial command ordered that they were not to be buried.'

Sachi thought of those men left to die so far from home, and their widows and mothers who would never know what had become of them. Some would wait months, some years before they accepted that their husband or lover or son was never going to return. She realized with a jolt that she might be one of them.

Supposing Shinzaemon never came back? It was half a year now since Sachi had seen him last and there had been not a word since then. Was she to spend the rest of her life in mourning, eternally waiting? She tried to picture life without him. It would be duller and greyer but it would go on all the same. It had to. Yet it was hard to imagine what the future could hold. All the bonds that anchored people in society – the bonds of family, clan, domain – seemed not to be there for her. Her father, Daisuké, was not really part of her life at all; he was in Osaka. She had even tried going back to the village and knew she didn't belong there either. She had expected to spend her life in the palace but now was reduced to a refugee, camping out in someone else's home. She would have to start all over again.

'And for those men who do come back,' said Edwards brusquely, 'there'll be no jobs, no work, no money. They'll be exiled to Suruga with the shogun, Lord Yoshinobu.'

Sachi felt weighed down by sadness, as if nothing could ever make her smile again. The war was over; they were beaten. There was nothing left but to endure. To accept, to endure, to survive. Nothing to hope for any more.

With an effort she raised her head. 'And Tatsu?' she asked.

'I've heard nothing,' he said. 'How can he send news?'

'Even you seem sad,' she said, 'and yet your people support the southerners.'

'I care about this country,' he said. 'I can't bear to see it torn apart.

She was surprised at the fervour in his voice.

'And you. I care about you,' he said. His loud tone had suddenly become soft. His eyes, big and round, flickered across her face. 'All of you,' he added hastily. But it was too late. She had seen the way he looked at her, caught the note of yearning in his voice. He was no longer a foreigner with different-coloured skin and hair and different-shaped eyes. He was a man. The awareness sent a shock quivering along her spine and tingling in her stomach. She lowered her eyes.

'At least there will be peace,' he said, breaking the silence. 'People will have a chance to rebuild their lives.'

The women nodded numbly.

'I've got other news for you. Good news.'

Good news. It was impossible to imagine that news could be good.

'The new government is going to make Edo its capital. It'll be renamed. It'll be To-kyo – the Eastern Capital.'

But Edo was Edo. It was the shogun's city. To give it a new name, and make it the southerners' capital was like ... not just occupying it but destroying it, turning it into something it was not, forcibly subduing the city and its people, beating them into submission. A new name would take away the city's soul and life and character.

'How can the country have a new capital?' demanded Sachi. 'Kyoto is the capital.'

'There'll be two capitals,' Edwards explained. 'Kyoto will be the western capital, the emperor's capital. Edo will be the eastern capital. Government and business will be in Edo, just as they used to be. Everyone will come back, more people than ever before. The city will come alive again. It'll be rebuilt. You'll have to get used to calling it Tokyo. It's great news for Edo. Everything is going to turn out all right.'

So Daisuké too would come back, Sachi thought. He sent letters from Osaka every now and then, telling her about his life there, about the weather, that he was healthy and busy, but he never wrote about the war or the huge changes that were transforming their country. She wouldn't have expected him to.

'The war isn't over yet,' snorted Taki. 'Everyone here hates the southerners. They'll never control this city.'

'No, the war isn't over. But it soon will be,' said Edwards bluntly. He shuffled awkwardly, stretching out one huge leg, then the other. His narrow-legged foreign trousers brushed the tatami, rustling loudly in the silence.

'There's no turning back the clock. But things will get better, that's for sure. The emperor is above northern or southern. He will unite the country. It won't be different provinces any more, but one country.'

'You're a foreigner,' muttered Taki. 'What do you know about our country?'

They had had this argument many times. Everyone knew the emperor was not much more than a boy, and that the men who stood behind him and manipulated him were southerners. It was they who would rule, not the emperor. Taki scowled and went back to her stitching. She was finishing the sleeve opening of a winter kimono in a fabric and colour suitable for a townswoman.

Edwards leaned forward. His blue eyes gleamed. 'I have some news that will interest you too, Lady Takiko. Shall I tell you? The emperor...'

'What about His Grace?' snapped Taki.

'...is coming to Edo.'

'His Grace? Here?' squeaked Taki. Edwards had finally succeeded in winning her attention. Her eyes were bright, her thin cheeks flushed

557

with excitement.

'He's already left Kyoto,' said Edwards. 'He'll be here soon, very soon. In a few days. I'll take you to see his grand entry if you like. It'll be a splendid procession, the most splendid you ever saw. He's to live...'

The women whispered the words in tones of stunned disbelief: 'In Edo Castle?'

A shadow fell over the hall. The shogun had been expelled along with the princess, Sachi, and all his thousands of ladies and courtiers. Now it was to be the emperor and his court – his wife, concubines, ladies, courtiers, staff, guards, cooks, servants, maids, maids of maids, maids of maids of maids – who would occupy the sumptuous chambers walled with gold leaf with their carved transepts and coffered lacquered ceilings. It was they who would enjoy plays and music and poetry competitions in the opulent halls; they who would stroll in the pleasure gardens and go boating on the lakes, admire the cherry blossom in spring and the maple leaves in autumn. They would live the life that the princess and Sachi and Haru and Taki – and even poor Fuyu – had thought would be theirs for ever. It was the bitterest blow of all.

Edwards seemed to think it was a glorious new world that was coming. But it would not be glorious for everyone.

Nevertheless, no matter how much Sachi and the other women had to suffer, they could not do other than revere the emperor. It was hard to imagine His Grace as a human being at all, let alone one who could live in a palace or walk in a

558

garden. He was the princess's nephew, Sachi knew this, so he was clearly human, in one sense at least. But he also communed with the gods. It was because of him that the country existed, the seasons revolved and the rice crop came to harvest year after year. The priests took care of people, kept them healthy, protected them from accidents and provided blessings. His Grace took care of the entire world.

'It'll be called Tokyo Castle,' Edwards said. His voice faltered as he realized the impact of what he was saying on the women. 'They've been repairing and rebuilding it.'

Taki put another plug of tobacco in Edwards's pipe, lit it and passed it to him, then lit pipes for the women.

It was hard for Sachi to accept the end of everything she had ever known and cared about. She had let herself forget that all things were transient in this floating world. Wealth, happiness, health, beauty – one day a person might have them all, the next they would be gone. Life was but the flutter of a sparrow's wings, a momentary flicker. Everything changed; all things passed away. It was a lesson she must try always to bear in mind.

Slowly a fug of smoke filled the great hall, laced with the sweet fragrance of tobacco. Edwards looked at the stony faces around him.

'I've heard these palaces and mansions used to have very beautiful gardens,' he said gently. 'Yours must be still unspoilt.'

'The gardeners left long ago,' whispered Sachi. 'It's terribly overgrown.'

'Will you show me?' said Edwards. 'It would be

good to walk.'

The three women tucked up their kimono skirts and slipped into clogs.

The leaves were changing colour and the gardens blazed in hues of copper, gold, orange and red. Edwards went first, pushing aside the dripping grass and ferns and holding them back for the women to pass through. Sachi followed, treading carefully in her high clogs from stone to stone, trying not to step in the mud or the piles of mouldering leaves. When her foot slipped on a patch of sodden moss he was ready with a hand to steady her. It was bewildering to have a man solicitous of her well-being. After all, men were masters, women servants. That was the way of the world. Men strode in front while women kept three paces behind. They certainly did not worry about whether a woman's clothes got wet or dirty. At first it made her feel awkward and embarrassed to have a man behaving in such an unmanly way, but then she began to find something comforting about Edwards's attentiveness.

After a while they came to the lake. In the middle was an island with a stone lantern, half hidden beneath trees. A heron, a splash of white, stood on a rock; a couple of turtles crouched like stones on another; ducks scooted about; there was even a jetty with some boats drawn up. For a moment Sachi was back in the women's palace, gliding across the lake in one of the red-lacquered pleasure barges, dabbling her fingers in the water while musicians sang and played. But the boats were swimming in fetid green water and the paintwork was faded and peeling.

She looked around. Taki and Haru had fallen behind. She was alone with a man, a foreign man – with Edwards. She stopped hastily, realizing the impropriety of the situation. She was about to call to the women to hurry when a mad recklessness seized her. Everything was over: the war was over, the country was ruined. Everything they had ever taken for granted had proved as insubstantial as the plume-grass down that floated in the wind. Nothing mattered any more, only the present. She was not the late shogun's concubine now. She was just herself. And Shinzaemon... Perhaps it was time to accept the brutal truth. He was almost certainly dead.

Edwards had stopped. Slowly he took off his tall, black and slightly crumpled hat. There was something endearing about its shabbiness. People of her country with their narrow, half-closed eyes kept their souls hidden inside themselves. But he with his big round eyes – you could see his soul right there. As their eyes met she couldn't help noticing the colour of his – dazzlingly blue, as blue as the sky in summer. His hair was not straw-coloured at all but gold, like fine spun gold. In the sunlight it was like a halo around his head. His big nose and chin, his eyes set in caverns in his head, his bushy eyebrows... She gazed at him, transfixed by this being from another world.

He stretched out his hand and she started as his fingers touched her palm. It made her shiver. He closed his thumb over her fingers and held them. She stared down at her small white hand resting in his big pale one. There were golden hairs on his fingers and the back of his thumb.

Before she could pull her hand back he raised it to his mouth. She stiffened, fearing he was going to bite it. Then she felt the moisture and the softness of his lips on her fingers. His moustache pricked her skin.

For a moment they stood frozen, his lips pressed to her hand. Then she tugged it away. Somewhere in the depths of her being she knew she should be shocked and horrified. But she wasn't. It was so intimate, yet so gentle. She had never before imagined that a man could behave in such a way. It was like a fresh breeze, blowing away the cobwebs, bringing her back to life.

As she returned her hand to her obi, she felt Shinzaemon's toggle there and realized with a shock that she had betrayed him. He needed her. It was her duty to wait for him, to be there if ever he got back.

She stared at the ground. Her bare feet were poised neatly side by side on a stepping stone with the toes touching, crossed with the silken thongs of the clogs. They were the delicate feet of a court lady. But they were no longer as pure and white as porcelain, but brown, stained and splashed with mud. It was like an omen. Branches swept low overhead, clouds scudded across the sky and a shower of icy drops fell like needles on her hair and shoulders.

'You are so beautiful,' said Edwards. He spoke hurriedly, under his breath, looking over his shoulder for Taki and Haru to appear. 'If you would let me... If you would accept me... I could take care of you. I know I'm a foreigner, but you could get used to me. I'll cherish you. You'll be my queen. I'll take you to my country. We'll see the world together.

'I ... I like you. I wish I knew how to say it in your language, but there isn't any word for it. It's not affection, like a man feels for his parents, or respect, like a man of your country feels for his wife, or lust, like a man feels for a courtesan. It's more than those, much more. It's the feeling that binds a man to a woman for ever. In my language we call it *rabu* – "love". That's what I feel for you.'

Sachi laughed uneasily. Men might talk like this to a courtesan, but it was not an appropriate way to speak to a decent woman, let alone one of high class. For a moment she had let down her defences, she had allowed him to touch her hand – and now he was talking as if they were to be together for the rest of their lives. Surely he'd been in her country long enough to know that matters like that were nothing to do with human feelings?

Nevertheless it made her wonder – who was she to spend her life with? She was a widow and widows usually lived with their parents. No one could marry outside their caste, but she had been a peasant and then the shogun's concubine; she didn't know what caste she belonged to any more. But a foreigner was outside all the rules and conventions that governed normal life. And she had to admit, she had become used to Edwards. She looked forward to his visits.

She peeped shyly up at him and their eyes met and lingered. She tried to frown, to show her displeasure – but she couldn't help smiling instead.

He opened his mouth to say more, but she

563

raised her hand. There were voices behind them. Taki and Haru were pattering along the path.

The following day there were footsteps in the courtyard, the scuffle of straw sandals. Taki ran to the entrance hall. When she returned she was smiling so brightly it looked as if the sun had burst out in the gloomy chamber, lighting up the darkest corners. She paused in the doorway. She was holding a scroll aloft in both hands.

Sachi unrolled it. There in his manly scrawl were the last two lines of the poem she had sent:

Akatsuki shirade   Yet I gave myself to you
Hito o koikeri   Forgetful of the coming dawn.

And a single word: *'Dounika...* Somehow...'

'Forgetful of the coming dawn...' Dawn was when lovers were forced to part, that was what the poet had meant. But 'forgetful' – it sounded so like Shinzaemon. He didn't care what anyone thought or expected. He ignored them, went his own way. Sachi was filled with joy. Dawn really was coming, the dawn of a new age. Perhaps, as Daisuké kept promising, it would be an age when people like them could be together. Maybe there would be a future for them after all. Somehow.

Sachi read his words over and over again. Shinzaemon was alive and thinking of her. Her patience had been rewarded.

But even as she thought of Shinzaemon she felt a pang of sadness, and of shame as she recalled her encounter with Edwards the previous day. For all his openness she could never know what

564

he really thought or felt or see inside his foreign soul. He was probably just playing, she told herself. She had heard that foreigners liked to play with women. Yet he had been so gentle, so considerate. No one had ever treated her in such a way before. She had been wondering whether to tell Taki what had happened, but now she realized she couldn't.

A little later she heard the crunch of animal-skin boots in the courtyard. She steeled her heart. 'Tell him I am unwell,' she said to Taki.

Dounika. Somehow. But 'somehow' could be a very long time. At first Sachi started every time she heard the tiniest noise in the courtyard and sent Taki running to see who it was. But the days went by and there was no further message, no sign of any wild-haired warrior with cat-like eyes. She realized she had forgotten what he looked like. The wild hair, the eyes – she remembered those, she had pictured them over and over again to herself – but apart from that she was not sure she would even recognize him any more. Perhaps Shinzaemon would have that blank-eyed look young Tatsuemon had had, as if he was seeing horrors, staring into the void. He had spent months fighting for what he must have known was a losing cause. He would be dog-tired, scrawny, ravenous, beaten down, miserable, maybe disillusioned and embittered.

So much time had passed. Edwards had told her about other ways of seeing the world, other ways of life...

Edwards. That was where all these misgivings

were coming from. Like the southerners taking over Edo, he had changed her, filled her with uncertainty and doubt.

She had assumed that Edwards would be so abashed at the forwardness of his behaviour that she would hear no more from him. A couple of rebuffs and that would be the end of it. The first day he visited she had sent a message that she was unwell. The second day she sent the same message. But no matter how sternly she refused to see him, she couldn't help rerunning their encounter in her head, feeling the same delicious shiver that had tingled along her spine when he put his lips to her hand. Then Taki returned, carrying a huge bunch of autumn flowers and leaves – camellias, wild chrysanthemums, branches ablaze with sparkling red, orange and yellow maple leaves. Sachi exclaimed in delight. Taki ran to get a vase and they knelt down to arrange them.

On the third day he sent her a mysterious object. It was small and round and made of metal. She turned it this way and that, then tried slipping it on her finger. It fitted perfectly. She took it off again quickly. It didn't feel right to wear it.

She had never come across such behaviour before. She told herself she should be angry but it was rather flattering. Shinzaemon had been gone for so long. When – if – he returned it would be like a stranger stepping back into her life. And Edwards was right there. It couldn't do any harm to let him visit again, if only for Taki's and Haru's sake. They enjoyed his company too.

So Edwards resumed his visits.

Meanwhile the emperor's entry into the city was approaching.

'We must have new clothes when we go to greet him,' said Taki. She was in a great state of excitement.

It was hard to know what to wear. They couldn't dress in the robes of ladies of the shogun's court, that was obvious. The shogun and his household were enemies of the state and Sachi was afraid that if the three of them were recognized, they might end up in prisoners' cages and be bundled off down to Suruga. In the end they decided to dress like well-off townsfolk. When the merchants came, Haru ordered rolls of silk in colours and designs appropriate for townswomen and she and Taki set to work with their needles.

It was equally obvious to Sachi that they couldn't go with Edwards. To parade in public with a towering huge-nosed foreigner and his troop of bodyguards would be madness. They would go on their own.

The day before the procession was due to arrive, a message came from Daisuké: he was coming back to Edo and would escort them.

II

Early the following morning Taki helped Sachi prepare. She blackened her teeth, shaved her eyebrows and dressed her hair in an ornate townswoman's style, coiling it into a lustrous knot and studding it with hairpins and combs. Then she helped her into kimonos. The new silk felt cool and crisp against her body. The top one, warmly lined, was in a fashionable shade of red with a design of maple leaves across the hem. Taki had laid it over an incense burner overnight and it gave off an elegant musky scent. Taki and Haru also had gorgeous new clothes for the occasion.

Daisuké was waiting in the courtyard. In the pale morning sunlight he exuded dignity and power. He was in formal dress, in black pleated *hakama* trousers and an over-jacket with starched shoulders jutting out like wings. He had grown heavier, Sachi noticed, and his belly swelled impressively above his obi. He had two swords tucked into his belt. He was a man of rank and influence.

He had said he had wanted to be a father she could be proud of, and he had succeeded in that. Sachi greeted him with quiet joy. She felt, as she always did whenever he looked at her, that he saw someone else as well.

'Daughter,' he said, smiling.

'Father,' she said, with a bow.

As they left the mansion, Sachi could see that everything had been tidied up. The walls of the moat had been shored up, the parts of the bridge that had tumbled down had been rebuilt. The roads had been weeded too, and swept and sprinkled with water to lay the dust. There was a smell of damp earth like the clean fresh smell after rain.

The great boulevards that ran between the daimyos' palaces were silent and empty no longer. They were full of people hurrying in a never-ending stream towards the castle. The plaza in front of the castle was already packed with men and women in their holiday best, in silk kimonos in brilliant reds and golds.

Daisuké led the way through the crush towards Wadakura Gate, the gate the emperor would pass through. Sachi followed close on his heels, edging between hard and soft bodies, tall and short bodies, rich and poor bodies, bodies that resisted and bodies that moved aside. There were men, women, old, young, children and people with babies on their backs. Her eyes flickered across the sea of faces. She half wondered if she would see a familiar face framed with wild hair, with slanting cat's eyes. Every now and then she saw someone that for a moment she thought was him, then she would look again and realize with a pang that it was not.

They had reached a line of soldiers when Sachi noticed a woman in the crowd. Her gaudy kimonos hung low at the back of her neck, revealing a suggestive expanse of unpainted skin, like a geisha or a prostitute. Everyone was peering intently in the direction the emperor was due to approach from, but she was looking the other way, chewing her underlip. She stared distractedly at the castle, gazing with a look of stony disbelief at the ramparts and turrets and towering white walls. A tear trickled down her painted face.

'Fuyu,' Sachi cried. Fuyu's face expressed everything she herself felt. She reached between the massed bodies jammed together, and grabbed her sleeve. She caught a whiff of cheap perfume as she tugged her gently out of the crowd.

'Those times were not so wonderful,' Sachi said softly. But even as she said it she knew it was a lie. Those gates were closed to her too. That fragile, beautiful world was gone for ever, like a priceless porcelain vase which has been smashed to the ground.

Daisuké had arranged a place for them near the gate, in an inner area reserved for government officials, where they would be protected from the crush. Sachi looked out at the mob before her. She had never imagined there could be so many people in the world.

'Look at them,' said Fuyu, swabbing her eyes and nose with her sleeve. 'First they're ready to die for the shogun. The next thing you know, they're bowing to the emperor. Then they'll be cheering for the shogun again when the lads come back from Wakamatsu.'

Sachi felt a lurch in her heart and her mouth was suddenly dry. The lads. Shinzaemon would surely be among them.

'They're coming back?' she whispered.

'Those that made it. Marching down. Be 'ere in a few days. We know who the real 'eroes are. We'll show 'em a good welcome.'

It was approaching the hour of the horse, when thousands of fires would usually have been burning for the midday meal. But today all fires had been banned. Far in the distance wisps and shreds of sound could be heard. Everyone fell silent, trying to catch the floating harmonies. It was music, ancient otherworldly music. Sachi shivered. It was as if the gods were coming down to earth.

Above the sea of heads, small in the distance, banners appeared, winding their way slowly through the crowd. They swayed from side to side, fluttering in the breeze. They were deep scarlet, marked with a golden roundel – the chrysanthemum crest of the emperor. Sunlight flashed from the tips of pikes and spears and halberds, shooting out dazzling shards of light. Screwing up her eyes, Sachi made out a mass of tall black shapes moving in stately procession – the towering black-lacquered hats of rank upon rank of courtiers. Flat helmets, peaked helmets, horned helmets, helmets of all different shapes and colours moved along in great blocks. In the distance the lacquered roofs of palanquins shone in the sun.

Sachi thought of the daimyo processions she used to see passing through the village and of the princess's magnificent procession that had swept her up and taken her to the castle. This was more splendid still. But there was also something different. In every procession she had ever seen there had always been guards singing out, *'Shita ni iyo! Shita ni iyo!* On your knees! On your knees!' These troops marched in silence.

The procession began to emerge from the crowd. From where Sachi stood she could see musicians banging drums and tootling flutes as they played their Shinto melodies. Behind them came pike and standard bearers, great banners flapping above their heads. Soldiers followed, regiment after regiment, dressed in foreign uniforms, as if to remind the conquered populace

571

that the old era – of the shogun and the samurai – was over, and a new one beginning. Some had rifles slung over their shoulders; others swaggered along with swords at their hips. Porters humped lacquered trunks with attendants walking alongside.

Then came lords and nobles. Some were hidden in palanquins, others on horseback or on foot, dressed in voluminous robes and high black hats such as Sachi had only ever seen in woodblock prints before – the ancient fashion of the imperial court. Marching before and behind them were ranks of courtiers and guards in brilliantly coloured court costume. There were hundreds of grooms leading hundreds of horses, bearers of parasols, bearers of shoes, bearers of the imperial bath, endless attendants of every sort. The whole court, it seemed, enough to populate the vast castle, had turned out to accompany the emperor.

Everything was strange and alien – soldiers in foreign uniforms, courtiers in ancient costume which no one in Edo could have ever seen before. Even their faces were different from Edo faces, from the craggy southern looks of the soldiers to the pale etiolated features of the aristocrats with their long noses, small mouths and high foreheads.

An army of Shinto priests followed, shuffling through the crowds, swishing mulberry-paper wands. The emperor was on his way. The people, the buildings, the trees, the ground, the air – everything had to be purified.

Approaching very slowly was an ebony and gold palanquin larger and more splendid than any

Sachi had ever seen in her life. It was hung with drapes, with red silken cords at each corner, and its roof gleamed in the sun. It was borne aloft by a great mob of bearers, all in voluminous robes of yellow silk with black hats on their heads.

On the top was a gold phoenix of the most delicate filigree work. It shimmered and sparkled as it swayed along.

As the phoenix car approached a profound hush fell over the crowd. The murmuring and movement, the hissing and whispering, the turning of heads as people tried to get a better view all stopped. No child spoke, no baby cried. The only sounds were the rustling of the sleeves and skirts of the bearers and the clack of their black-lacquered clogs.

Sachi's knees seemed to bend of their own accord. Hardly conscious of anything but an overwhelming awe, she knelt on the ground with her face to her hands. She was barely aware of the whisper of the bearers' robes, the crunch of their clogs or the creaking of the silken cords that held the palanquin steady. A fragrance filled the air, an ancient hallowed scent that spoke not of the austere creed of the Buddhas but of the nature gods of Shinto, not of darkness but of light, not of death but of life.

There was no doubt in Sachi's mind that the being within the palanquin was the child of the gods, the son of the sun goddess. With the golden phoenix glittering above him and the yellow-clad bearers like a halo of the sun's rays around him, it was as if the sun herself had descended to earth.

It was only long after the palanquin had passed that anyone dared move their heads. Sachi glanced around. Taki and Haru still had their noses in the dust, while all around them people were beginning to clamber to their feet, looking bewildered as if they were wondering what had come over them. Down-to-earth Edoites that they were, they seemed annoyed that they could be so easily seduced. The grumbling about the southern barbarians would continue, but something had changed. As Edwards had put it, there was no turning back the clock.

The palanquins, the lords, the officials, the courtiers, the horses, the grooms, the soldiers, the porters and trunks, the servants, the women, the maids and everyone else all disappeared into Edo Castle until the last person was gone. Only it was no longer Edo Castle, the seat of His Majesty the shogun, Sachi reminded herself. It was Tokyo Castle, the imperial palace, residence of His Grace the emperor.

Finally the towering cedarwood gates began to move. Sachi watched spellbound, desperate for one last glimpse of the castle. A terrible sense of doom and finality swept over her. Peering through the heads of the crowd and the lines of soldiers on guard, she fixed her gaze on the narrowing gap, but all she could see was the guardhouse inside the inner enclosure. The massive stones of the wall behind it fell into shadow as the gates rumbled on and on at the same measured pace until they thundered together. The great walls shuddered. The boom echoed across the plaza.

A cold wind whistled through the crowd, making kimono skirts flutter. It lifted the dead leaves and sent dust spinning in whorls. Sachi shivered and pulled her *haori* jacket closer around her.

Daisuké's eyes were shining. The gates were not closed to him. The southern soldiers, the pale aristocrats, the courtiers in their yellow silk robes were his people; he shared their glory. The emperor's triumph was his too.

'They can 'ave the castle,' snarled Fuyu. The white make-up on her face was blotched and runny, streaked with tears. 'The streets are ours. Call it what y' like. It's still Edo.'

People were shaking themselves as if they were coming out of a collective trance, glancing around, grinning at each other sheepishly. Voices began to speak, but quietly, as if no one dared talk about what they had seen. A child started to chatter as little by little people began to leave. Most pattered off in their clogs or straw sandals towards the east end of the city.

Fuyu too lifted up her skirts, nodded a brusque farewell and hastily, as if she was afraid of incurring their pity if she stayed longer, hurried eastwards, teetering along on her high clogs. Sachi watched her back in its garish heavily patterned kimono disappearing into the crowds. She looked small and forlorn but proud. Sachi could see herself there too, in the set of Fuyu's shoulders: that anger, that refusal to give up the past, that pride – maybe they all had it, all the palace women. Maybe they would carry it with them for the rest of their lives.

Daisuké walked Sachi, Taki and Haru from the

plaza in front of the castle, around the edge of the moat, as far as the bridge that led to the mansion. He stopped there.

'I have to go,' he said. 'I have business to attend to. I'm setting up house here in Tokyo. There'll be room for all of us and maids and servants too. I'm going to make sure you all have the life you deserve.'

Sachi bowed, suddenly feeling terribly sad and alone. When 'the lads came back from Waka-matsu', would Shinzaemon be among them? But Daisuké didn't even know he existed. It was hard to imagine how he would fit into this idyllic life her father was planning for them. And Edwards, she thought, would fit in no better.

There was no one on guard at the outer gates of the mansion. Sachi, Taki and Haru walked across the gardens in silence towards the massive inner gates, picking their way around the piles of dead leaves.

On the far side of the courtyard were two men, sitting cross-legged in a patch of sunlight on the veranda outside the great entrance hall. They were deep in conversation, their heads close together. A shaft of sunlight lit the smoke that coiled from their pipes and shone on the freshly shaved pate and oiled topknot of one. The other had a head covered in bristly black hair, cut short like a foreigner's.

The shaven-pated man looked up when the women appeared. He leaped to his feet and scurried over to them, bowing apologetically. It was the old man who guarded the outer gates.

'So sorry,' he muttered. He gestured towards

the other man. 'A visitor. Just back from Waka-matsu.'

Sachi nodded. One of their lads back from the front, bringing news. That was good enough reason for the old man to desert his post. She turned to greet the newcomer. He was stepping off the veranda, quietly slipping his feet into straw sandals. His face was turned downwards, but even before he looked up she knew.

It was Shinzaemon.

14

Back from the Dead

I

Shinzaemon was looking at Sachi with a calm steady gaze. His eyes seemed to bore into her – narrow cat-like eyes in a shapely face. He was not beautiful like a kabuki actor as Daisuké had been; his face was too fierce, too muscular, too powerful for that. She recognized his arrogance, his easy grace, that look as if he was out to conquer the world. No matter that he had fought on the losing side, he carried himself with pride.

She could see he'd been out in the sun and wind. His face was darkly tanned, his clothes worn and crumpled. The beginnings of a moustache sprouted on his upper lip.

Her spirit rushed towards him but she didn't

move. She stood poised and demure, as a woman should. She was burning to fling herself into his arms but of course she did no such thing. She lowered her eyes and bowed.

Taki was bowing too, holding her sleeve to her eyes.

'Shin,' she said. 'You must be tired. Welcome home. It's been a long time.'

Shinzaemon bowed solemnly.

'Inexcusable,' he said, 'to arrive without warning.'

His voice was a deep rumble. Sachi could smell his scent – the salty smell of sweat mingled with tobacco. She remembered all those times she had breathed that scent – walking along the Inner Mountain Road with him, standing on top of the mountain, crushed in his arms on the bridge.

She bowed, mouthed the proper phrases, but she was hardly aware of what she did. She was waiting – waiting for the moment when they could be alone.

The bowing seemed to go on for ever. Then Taki grabbed Haru's sleeve. Slowly, deliberately – or so it seemed to Sachi – they slipped out of one sandal then the other and stepped up into the shadowy entrance hall. They bowed again and went inside. She watched their retreating backs until they disappeared.

The sun was setting and the sky was streaked with red, silver and gold.

Sachi had been waiting for this moment for so long but now it had come she felt shy, like a little girl. She stared at the ground. Shinzaemon's *tabi* socks were dusty, his sandals worn and broken.

There were knots where he'd retied the straw thongs. The bottoms of his kimono skirts were stained.

He was gazing at her from under his thick brows.

'You came,' she breathed.

'*Dounika*,' he said. 'Somehow.'

When they had last met they had thought they would never see each other again. She glanced up at him timidly, remembering that encounter. He was looking at her too. His eyes were fixed on her face as if he was reminding himself of every curve, every line of it. Something about him had changed. He smiled a wry smile. His shorn head made him look like a mischievous child. Even when his hair had been tugged back in a horse's tail she'd never been able to see his face so clearly.

'What do you think?' Shinzaemon said with a grimace, putting his hand to his head.

There was a frown mark between his eyes that hadn't been there before. For a moment she caught a glimpse of the faraway look she had seen in Tatsuemon's eyes, as if he had seen things he could never tell her about. But the fighting had been half a month ago. He had survived. He had walked back since then. Perhaps it was the future he was looking at, not the past.

'You look different,' she said, smiling at him. 'It's a good disguise. No one would ever recognize you.'

'But you do.'

'Yes,' she whispered. She wanted to touch him, feel his hard body, his strong hands. But she held back. The longer she waited, the stronger the yearning grew.

He reached into his sleeve and took out a comb. Tortoiseshell edged with gold, embossed with a crest. Her mother's comb, her mother's crest. She hadn't known all that it meant when she gave it to him. Now she did, and the knowledge had made her different too.

'It kept me safe. Better than armour. Better than a thousand-stitch belt.'

There was so much she had to tell him, but she knew suddenly – joyfully – that they could talk later. They had the whole of their lives ahead of them.

'Come and see the gardens,' she said.

They pushed their way along the overgrown paths. Clumps of plume grass swayed in the breeze, sending showers of down whirling through the air like snow. Insects chirruped, the last of the season. The maples blazed with colour. She led him to the parapet.

They stood side by side, looking down at the Goji-in Field and the land that had once been daimyos' estates. There were people everywhere, working industriously. In the distance the townsmen's area bristled with bamboo scaffolding and people swarmed around like ants, busily putting up walls and roofs. The tap-tap-tap of thousands of hammers travelled clear and sharp across the empty spaces.

The hill rose, silent and dead, in the middle of all the activity. Birds circled, black dots in the darkening sky, cawing ominously.

They were so close she could feel the heat of his body.

'I used to come here,' she said, 'every day. And look at the hill and wonder if you were there. I thought I'd never see you again.'

'Tatsuemon told me what you did...'

For a moment the memory of that terrible day came rushing back. The ghastly faces, the gaping wounds and staring eyes, the flies, the stench. She had been so terrified she would find him there. And now he was beside her, so warm, so alive. Tears welled up and she put her sleeve to her eyes.

He took her hand and held it tight. She could feel the calluses that rimmed his palm, rough where he had grasped his sword.

She held her breath and he pulled her to him. She could feel the hard muscles in his arms and chest. She felt his heart beating, the rise and fall of his abdomen as he breathed. His lips brushed her hair. His touch was not fierce, as it had been before, but gentle. He nibbled her ears, the back of her neck, her cheek, her eyes. Then his mouth found hers.

She drew back and looked at him, frowning. She knew as certainly as she'd ever known anything that she wanted to spend her life with this man. *Dounika*. Somehow. She'd never wanted anything so badly in her life.

Smiling, he smoothed her forehead with his fingers. 'Your eyes,' he said. 'I could never forget those eyes. That mouth. The curve of that cheek. That smile.'

He drew a line across her cheek, around her chin, along her neck. She tingled at his touch. It was as if she'd never known before what it was to be alive.

'You,' he whispered. That word again.

They climbed down from the parapet and he pulled her into the grass. The many layers of her kimono ballooned out, making a soft cushion under her. They were enclosed in a bower of tall grasses that rustled and swayed. Down prickled her nostrils; the scents of dried stalks and wild flowers swirled around her. She let herself sink into the softness, dissolve into the fragrance. In this secret place she knew they were invisible.

His face was dark against the sky. The last rays of the dying sun touched his hair, lighting it up like a halo.

She closed her eyes as his lips moved to her throat.

II

'Look at you, Shin,' said Taki. 'You haven't been eating. We'll have to fatten you up.'

A shaft of sunlight pierced the wooden rain doors, cutting through the morning air, sparkling with motes of dust and lighting up the steam that wreathed the rice and miso soup.

Shinzaemon sat, composed and impassive, while Haru and Taki fussed around him, filling his teacup, piling rice into his rice bowl, bringing out dish after dish of grilled fish and simmered vegetables. The room was full of mouth-watering aromas.

Sachi sat quietly, playing the gracious hostess, making sure all was to his liking. Every now and

582

then their eyes met. The sweetness of the evening before still tingled. Beneath her demure façade she burned with fierce joy, as if a fire had been lit within her that could not be put out. She felt her mother's blood surging in her veins. Like her mother she would grab life. She would have what she wanted, no matter what the consequences.

But in the cold light of day she was more aware than ever of how daunting it was. She had a father now, a powerful official on the southern side. Admittedly he was not a father like Jiroemon had been. He could not expect her to obey him unquestioningly as fathers usually did. But a father was a father and she didn't want to break with him. Not now, when she'd only just found him.

Sachi knew all too well that she was not free and never could be. Women were property and belonged to their families. In finding her father she had found another set of chains to bind her. In the intoxication of seeing Shinzaemon again she had imagined things might be different. Now she remembered that they couldn't be.

She looked at Shinzaemon, wiping around his bowl with a piece of pickled radish then washing it out with tea. He was such a soldier, such a *ronin*. She tried to imagine him as a respectable member of society, performing the duties of an adopted son of a government official. The thought made her smile. It was even harder to imagine Daisuké sanctioning a union with a ragged rebel who had fought on the losing side – an enemy, a member of the despised northern army.

But Daisuké had been young himself once. He

too had been angry, idealistic, impetuous, driven by passion. Maybe when he saw Shinzaemon he would see himself.

He'd be arriving soon, and Edwards too. She shivered. It was best not to try to imagine what would happen then.

Taki was clearing away Shinzaemon's breakfast tray when there were footsteps outside. Sachi held her breath. Perhaps it was Daisuké... Then came the crunch of animal-skin boots approaching across the courtyard.

Edwards. A spasm of fear cut through her. She had been alone with him and had let him take her hand. Only he knew what had happened between them. Foreigners were so open, so easy to read. If he said a word or gave a hint of it, Shinzaemon...

Doors opened and closed, footsteps padded towards them. Sachi could hear Taki's squeaky voice, telling Edwards that Shinzaemon was back.

The two young men hadn't seen each other since they had travelled together along the Inner Mountain Road. Shinzaemon had been prickly and suspicious. Sachi had felt his eyes boring into her whenever she spoke to Edwards. As for Edwards, he must have worked out that Shinzaemon was far from a bodyguard, although he too had kept his distance.

She remembered turning to look back at Shinzaemon and Edwards before she and Taki had pushed open the Gate of the Shogun's Ladies to go into the palace grounds. She could picture them still, on the far side of the bridge – the two giant foreigners and the brawny *ronin* with his bush of hair. But things had changed since then.

Edwards had rescued them all on the hill and been kind to Tatsuemon. Shinzaemon was in his debt.

Now, when she looked at Edwards, she saw a human being, and not just a human being but a man. But to Shinzaemon he probably looked like a creature from another planet. As for Edwards, he might not even recognize Shinzaemon with his short hair.

The great hall seemed to shrink as Edwards came stomping in. As he strode through the shaft of sunlight that cut across the room, his straw-coloured hair shone like spun gold and Sachi caught a whiff of his exotic odour – meaty, pungent, smelling of foreign spices, animal hide and other unidentifiable smells. It gave her a feeling of doors opening, of wide open spaces, of fresh winds blowing and possibilities. When Edwards was around Sachi knew that there were other worlds, other ways of doing things.

She felt a pang of sadness to think that this link with the great wide world was now severed for her. And – though she hardly dared confess it to herself – she was sorry that she would no longer be able to see him. She could see now that when she had enjoyed his company, it had been to console herself. She had been flattered by his attentions and touched by his romantic talk. She had thought Shinzaemon dead, but now he was back she knew her heart belonged to him.

Edwards looked startled to see Shinzaemon, but he quickly pulled himself together and bowed politely. Sachi looked at the two bowing heads. The youths were sun and moon, two sides of the

585

same coin. One with yellow hair, one with black. The smooth diplomat and the rugged soldier. They were both part of worlds that women knew nothing of and were no doubt eager to talk men's talk, to discuss politics and the war. But there was also an unspoken suspicion. Each would be wondering exactly what the relationship of the other was with these women. With Sachi.

'So Tatsu...' asked Edwards.

'Thank you,' said Shinzaemon. He was at his gruffest and most formal. 'He is well. We were together. At Wakamatsu.'

He barked out the name with a spark in his eye, as if to make it clear that he knew very well which side the English supported.

Sachi was listening hard. She was dying to know what Shinzaemon had done, where he had been, everything that had happened since she had last seen him. She imagined tales of heroic exploits, of brave men fighting to the last, holding out against impossible odds. But his lips were pressed firmly together and she dared not ask.

'Did you come back together?' asked Edwards.

'Tatsuemon rode north,' said Shinzaemon. 'To join the Tokugawa Navy. Maybe you heard – Admiral Enomoto commandeered the best Tokugawa warships and sailed for Ezo. He's leading the resistance from there. After the castle fell a lot of men were heading over there to join up.'

Edwards nodded. 'The war hasn't been kind to the northerners,' he said.

'It isn't over yet,' Shinzaemon grunted.

'But you came back,' said Edwards pointedly. His tone was polite but there was a note of triumph in his voice, as if he'd spotted a crack in Shinzaemon's armour. As if he couldn't resist the chance to snipe.

Shinzaemon was no coward, Sachi knew that perfectly well. There must have been a good reason why he had not ridden north with his comrades but had headed back to Edo instead. She knew that it wasn't just to see her. Something had happened, something terrible.

Shinzaemon's shoulder moved a fraction, although she doubted that Edwards even noticed. At another time, in another place, Shinzaemon would have been reaching for whatever weapon was to hand. Instead he made a mighty effort and sat immobile as a rock.

There was a voice in the entrance hall. Daisuké came breezing into the great hall as casually as if it was his own home, without bothering to wait to be announced. He looked big, happy, confident, handsome, a man who had achieved everything he could possibly dream of. There was only one thing missing to make his happiness complete: Sachi's mother.

He stopped short when he saw Shinzaemon and Edwards and looked from one to the other, his heavy eyebrows rising. A frown of surprise flitted across his broad, smooth, slightly jowly face.

Sachi ran forward to greet him.

'Father,' she said, bowing.

Shinzaemon and Edwards were on their knees. Edwards introduced himself.

'So you are with the British Legation,' said Daisuké. 'I know Satow-*dono*. He has been very generous to us. The English have been very generous in supporting our cause. I am indebted to you for your kindness to my family.'

He bowed deeply. He was all politeness. Edwards was a foreigner and a guest in their country. Nevertheless Daisuké looked at him sharply as if he was wondering what on earth he was doing there.

'Shinzaemon of the Nakamura, domain of Kano,' Shinzaemon said in his most formal voice. His big swordsman's hands were pressed to the tatami, the tips of the forefingers touching, and his head with its thatch of bristly black hair was bowed. Sachi had never seen him so punctilious. She glanced at Daisuké. A foreigner was one thing – one had to treat foreigners with politeness and respect – but Shinzaemon was a *ronin*. It was written all over him. He was an outsider with no loyalties, no group, no one to whom he was beholden. Daisuké would see that straight away.

'The Nakamura of Kano...' said Daisuké slowly. 'The lord of Kano came over to the emperor's side rather recently, if I remember rightly. There was some dissent within Kano, was there not, as to which way to go?'

'I don't know much about Kano politics,' Shinzaemon said hastily. He obviously wanted to avoid being caught up in an awkward political discussion. 'My father is a samurai of middle rank and a town magistrate. I was sent to Edo when I was young. I've spent most of my life here, in the various mansions of the Kano domain.'

Sachi looked at one, then the other. Both Daisuké and Shinzaemon had tossed aside their station in society. Daisuké had started life as a low-ranking artisan but was now a leading figure in the new government. Shinzaemon had rejected the privileges of his samurai status and abandoned his clan to follow his ideals. They had both shaken off the old hierarchical restrictions to make their own way through life. If only Daisuké could see how similar they were.

'Shinzaemon took care of us on the road, Father,' she said. 'We travelled together. He is a great swordsman.'

'He is like a brother to us,' Taki added.

'In that case I am in your debt,' Daisuké said gravely to Shinzaemon. He looked at him hard. 'We need to have a talk, young man. I need to know where you stand on things – whether you're with us or against us.'

Shinzaemon nodded.

'There's so much of my daughter's life I've missed,' said Daisuké. 'I'm happy to meet you young men who have been protectors to her.'

Sachi heaved a sigh of relief. For the time being at least there would be no confrontation. Taki lit long-stemmed pipes and handed them around. Haru ran to get tea. Shinzaemon and Edwards withdrew to the side of the room and smoked quietly.

'There's something important I have to tell you,' Daisuké said. He was speaking to Sachi. 'I believe it will make you happy. As soon as I got to Edo I went to the Mizuno mansion. It was your mother's family home. I wanted to see the house where she lived and smell the air she breathed. It was a ruin. The Mizunos were close allies of the Tokugawas and had fled. They must

589

have been some of the first to go.

'Ever since I found you I've had a dream that we could live there together, all of us. Now it seems it may be possible. The estates and palaces of the lords who were enemies of the state have been taken into state control.'

Sachi shifted uneasily. She knew very well that by 'enemies of the state' he meant loyal servants of the shogun. But she said nothing. It was not for her to argue.

'They're to be government offices or accommodation for government officials,' Daisuké continued. 'I've asked for the Mizuno estate.'

Sachi felt a chill run through her. She had always known her father had huge ambitions – but to think of taking the estate of a family like the Mizuno... Even if they were her relatives, it didn't mean she was entitled to their property. She understood very well that the northern lords had fled, that officials of the new government were to be given their land. But nevertheless... It seemed inauspicious. Surely such an action would draw down bad luck on them all.

'The Mizuno family weren't particularly powerful,' Daisuké continued, 'and the estate is not particularly desirable or spacious. It's about right for someone of my rank.'

Haru's plump cheeks had turned pale at the mention of the Mizuno family.

'There are too many ghosts there,' she whispered. 'Too many memories. But maybe ... we could get to the root of what happened to my lady. Perhaps we could find her.'

'It belongs to Lord Mizuno,' said Sachi. 'Surely

590

we can't just take his land.'

Lord Mizuno. As she said the name she saw him as if he was kneeling right in front of her. She had been hiding in the shadows behind the princess. Lord Oguri, with his bland courtier's face, was speaking and Lord Mizuno raised his head. She saw the leathery dome of his shaved pate, the fierce eyes burning like coals, the nose like a hawk's beak, the pockmarked skin, the thin cruel mouth. It made her shiver. He had had a tic, she remembered. He had left his sword at the gate but his arm still kept jerking as if he was trying to wrench it out of its scabbard – as if he was expecting attack even in the women's palace.

Daisuké was frowning, looking at her with a curious questioning expression.

'What do you know of Lord Mizuno?' he asked. 'He's dead, isn't that right, Haru? He died long ago.'

'The last I heard of him he ... he was on his deathbed,' Haru whispered. Her voice trailed away uncertainly.

'He isn't dead,' said Sachi. She and Taki had kept their secret for so long. But now the shogun and the women's palace no longer existed, there was nothing to prevent them from speaking out. Sachi had to stop herself shouting the words. 'We saw Lord Mizuno, didn't we, Taki? He came to the palace with Lord Oguri to tell us His Majesty was ill.'

A sound broke the silence, the clunk of a long-stemmed pipe striking the tobacco box. At the side of the room the two youths shifted slightly.

Haru's mouth fell open. She raised her hand,

let it fall again. She made a strangled sound, halfway between a gasp and a groan, and the contours of her plump face seemed to sag and dissolve.

'He... He can't be. It's impossible.' She shook her head. 'Not ... Lord Mizuno. Lord Tadanaka Mizuno. Are you sure?'

'Lord Tadanaka Mizuno,' said Taki. 'I remember very well.'

'He was a bad man,' muttered Haru. 'An evil man. It would have been better if he had died.'

There was a long silence. Daisuké's face had creased and darkened. It was no longer as handsome as a kabuki actor's but had become a demon mask. 'So it was a lie!' he shouted. He slammed his great fist on the tatami.

'What was, Father?' Sachi whispered. 'What was a lie?'

The sun had gone in. Candles and lamps glimmered in the dark corners as a chill fell over them. The smell of tobacco smoke drifted from the far side of the room and threads of smoke wavered upwards and coiled around the dark beams of the ceiling. Edwards and Shinzaemon were like statues, their pipes in their hands.

'She said there was no one in the world she was afraid of except him.' He turned to Haru. 'Was it true what ... what she told me? That it was all his doing? That he forced her to go into service?'

'I thought he was dead.' Haru was rocking herself backwards and forwards. 'I remember them arguing. "You're a woman," Lord Mizuno said. He was shouting. "How dare you defy me! You think you can live without us, but you're nothing without us. You *have* to do it. For your family's sake."'

'You didn't want to enter the palace,' said Daisuké softly. There was a presence in the room with them. Sachi's mother. It was as if he could hear her voice, as if she was speaking to him. 'Wasn't that what you told me? It was like entering a convent, like being imprisoned. A place with three thousand women and only one man, and old ladies watching everything you did, waiting for you to make a mistake. Just sewing and fixing your hair all day – that was all you had to look forward to. "It's no life for me," that's what you said. "I'm a wild creature. I'm a bird. I'll fly away."'

'What was the lie, Father? What was the lie?' whispered Sachi.

'They had everything, the Mizunos,' said Haru. Her voice was strained as if the words were being wrenched out of her against her will. 'A castle, a huge annual stipend – but they were chamberlains. My lady's father was lord chamberlain of the Kisshu family and Lord Tadanaka, the young lord, couldn't stand it. He couldn't stand being number two. He used to stomp around shouting, lashing out at servants. Then my lady, his sister, grew up and he saw a way to get what he wanted.

'He decided she was to go into service in Edo Castle, no matter what. A woman of her status was supposed to enter as a junior lady-in-waiting of middle rank. But there were very few openings at that level and the competition was stiff. It was the old ladies who made the selection and they didn't take beauty into account. It was all to do with rank and status and how old your family was. It was much easier to get in at a lower level, so the young lord ordered my miserable family to adopt her. You can imagine what she thought about that! But what could she do? So she became my adopted sister and we were both taken on as lower-level maids.

'Lord Mizuno knew he just had to get my lady into the palace where the shogun could see her. She was so alluring, so beautiful, so bright. He knew the shogun would fall for her straight away and make her the lady of the side chamber. And she'd take the whole family with her. Her father would be made a daimyo, then Lord Mizuno after him. Firefly daimyos. They'd flit along after the fire in her tail. Only it didn't quite work out like that. The key thing was, she had to bear the shogun a son and heir. But her first son died, then her next child...'

'And then everything started going wrong,' said Daisuké. 'She told me His Majesty stopped visiting her. She met me. And then her belly began to swell.'

'People noticed,' whispered Haru. 'She had enemies. A lot of the women were jealous of her and if any of them had said anything it would have been a disaster for the entire Mizuno family. The young lord would have had to cut his belly and the family line would have been ended. He would have wanted to avoid that at all costs.'

'He must have got wind of our affair somehow,' said Daisuké. 'Maybe he summoned her home to get her out of the way before the shogun and his officers found out.'

'So that was the lie?' whispered Sachi. 'That he was on his deathbed?'

'To get her home. To cover up the scandal.'

'But what did he do then?' Sachi could hear her voice, small and forlorn. 'What did he do when my mother went home? Where is she?'

Daisuké looked at Sachi.

'If anyone knows what became of your mother, he does,' he said. 'We'll find him. No matter what it takes.'

The great hall was utterly still.

If they could only find Lord Mizuno, Sachi thought. Then she remembered that she had seen him a second time. In her mind she could hear the rushing of a river, the murmur of refugees desperate to cross, the cries of wild geese, the crunch of porters' feet, the clatter of a ferry pulling up on the bank.

'Taki and I saw him again just a few months ago,' she whispered. 'At Takasaki. We were waiting to cross the river. They were leaving Edo, he and Lord Oguri. Shin was there too.'

'The way he looked at you, my lady!' It was Taki's voice.

Sachi saw Lord Mizuno's dark face pressed up close to hers. She heard his rasping breath, felt it on her face. He had shouted, 'Get away! Leave me alone!' As if he was crazy. As if he had seen a ghost. Perhaps that was what he had seen when he looked at her – not her but her mother.

From the other side of the room Shinzaemon spoke up. His face was alight, his eyes gleaming. 'They had those strongboxes,' he said, his voice full of excitement. 'There was something odd about them. They looked very heavy. And the porters didn't look like porters – they didn't have tattoos. They were ... samurai. Samurai whose hair had grown out. I remember wondering what they were up to.'

'The southerners will be out to get them, powerful men like that,' said Edwards, his blue eyes shining too. 'I don't know about Lord Mizuno but Lord Oguri was chief minister of the shogun's government. Their chances of survival are small; we need to find them quickly. I'll come with you. You'll need all the help you can get. I can provide horses and porters. I have to conduct a survey anyway now the country is open to foreigners. We've never been able to travel freely before. It'll be an adventure for me and I could be useful to you too.'

Shinzaemon nodded.

'I can only offer my arm,' he said quietly, 'but it's a strong one. I came through Takasaki on my way back from Wakamatsu. I took the long way round to avoid the southern armies. I know the road well. And I have an idea about where they were going.'

Daisuké was thinking hard.

'We must move immediately. It's going to be winter soon and it'll be snowing already on the high passes. But if we wait for spring it'll be too late. I owe it to your mother and to you, my dear daughter. I can't rest till I know where she is.'

15

The Gold Digger of Akagi Mountain

I

After the men had gone, Sachi brought out the brocade – her mother's overkimono. It had been stored away in a drawer in a kimono chest, and the fragile fabric rustled as she lifted it out and gently unfolded it. The colours were those of a time gone by. She pressed it to her face and breathed in its subtle ancient perfume – of musk, aloe, wormwood, frankincense. She wanted to fix the scent in her mind, to know it when she next encountered it, as if she might recognize her mother by her fragrance.

'We're coming to find you,' she whispered. 'We'll be together at last.'

That night Taki made a fire in the hearth in the main room of the family section of the mansion and pulled up cushions around it. Then she, Sachi and Haru wrapped up warmly in layers of thick robes. Smoke swirled around the room, making their throats sting and their eyes water. The fire crackled and spat fiery sparks on to the polished wooden floor. The lid of the iron kettle hanging above the fire clattered, jiggling and dancing as steam puffed out. It was a homely, comforting sound.

Shinzaemon sat with them as if he was already part of the family. He lounged on his elbow, a little apart from the others, his eyes half shut, a long-stemmed pipe in his hand. Sachi glanced at him, shyly at first, then let her eyes roam more boldly across his face. The angles of it, his square chin and full mouth, were thrown into relief by the flickering light of the flames. He was so still, so contained – like a cat, she thought. He only appeared to be relaxed. In reality he was poised and alert, ready to spring at any moment.

Taki was bent over her sewing, pretending to concentrate, although Sachi could tell she was yearning to ask a thousand questions. Taki had not asked about Toranosuké. After all, if Toranosuké had given Shinzaemon a message for her, Shinzaemon would have told her. She must have decided to keep a dignified silence. Nevertheless there was a hurt, sad look in her big eyes and her pointed face was even paler and more drawn than usual.

At last Taki stretched out a thin hand and picked up the poker. She shook up the glowing embers then lifted the lid of the kettle and ladled hot water into a teapot. She filled a teacup, put it on a tray and held it out to Shinzaemon.

'Shin,' she squeaked in her most wheedling tones. 'Didn't you say you'd heard something about Lord Oguri and Lord Mizuno? Was that when you were up north?'

'On the way back,' said Shinzaemon and fell silent again.

'So Tatsu found you,' persisted Taki, her voice

trailing away.

He laughed.

'It was easy,' he said. 'He knew where the fighting was.'

'You met up ... at Wakamatsu?' asked Sachi. She too was eager to hear what he knew of Lord Mizuno's whereabouts. But more than that she wanted to know about him – where he had been, what he had done, what had happened to him in the months they had been apart – and she guessed that that was what Taki and Haru wanted too.

'You want to hear about Wakamatsu?'

The women nodded. He thought for a while, staring into the fire.

'We were at the castle there – White Crane Castle – a couple of months,' he said slowly. He took a puff on his pipe. 'We had to get there before the southern armies took the roads. Our job was to keep watch on a rise outside the main compound of the castle, me and Toranosuké. And Tatsu too, after he got there. We could see the town from there. When the enemy attacked we could see them swarming through the streets below us like a mass of black ants. Thirty thousand, we heard. Against three thousand of us. Some of the elderly and women and children from the town had taken refuge in the castle too, and had to be protected. Then the southerners set up their cannons and started bombarding us, morning to night.'

As he talked in his brusque soldier's way Sachi was no longer warming her hands at the fire, safe and cosy. She was there beside him, standing on

599

the battlements. She looked out and saw clouds of smoke rolling across the city. The streets were dark as night. Here and there were tongues of flame and the raw red of smouldering fires. She heard the whoosh of flames, the crash of tiled roofs collapsing. There were no screams, no human voices, only a dreadful silence.

'Then the enemy broke through. They came swarming across the wall of the moat. They looked like cockroaches – an invasion of cockroaches. We picked them off but they kept coming. No matter how many fell, more appeared. They broke into the third compound, then the second. We could see them clearly by then: men in black skinny-legged foreign uniforms and shiny pointed helmets, men in dog-skin capes and the Tosa men in their red bear wigs – like we'd think they were bears and run away.'

He snorted with contempt.

'It was all very well picking them off with rifles. I was just waiting for them to get close enough. I wanted to get down there, into the middle of them. I wanted to see their ugly faces, make their blood spurt and their heads fly. I'd had enough of waiting. I knew you'd want me to die a glorious death. That's what you'd expect of me – a death fit for a samurai.'

He was talking to all of them but his words were addressed to Sachi. He put his hand in his sleeve where her comb was hidden. His face was immobile, as if carved out of stone, but his jaw was clenched and a muscle in his neck twitched.

'That's how it would have been,' he muttered. 'In the old days. When men fought with swords, not rifles. When you could see the face of the man you killed or the man who killed you. When you fought man to man and the best man won.'

He scowled. The women sat mesmerized, waiting for him to carry on.

'It's finished.' He spat out the words. 'It's not just that the north lost and the south won. The old ways are over.' He shook his head. 'Honour, duty, the way of the sword, everything that means anything – finished. Over.'

'But... what happened?' Sachi whispered. He spoke with such passion she was afraid.

'By the twenty-first day of the ninth month they had us by the throat. It was a month since the beginning of the siege and we were nearly out of food and ammunition. They bombarded us all day long. We fought back, picked them off – you could see them falling. A lot of our men fell too. The place reeked of corpses; there were too many to bury. The end was coming, staring us in the face.

'We all knew what would happen next. There'd be brushwood piled inside the main citadel; we would hold the enemy off until his lordship cut his belly. Then whoever was still alive would set the castle alight and the gunpowder store would blow. Alive or dead, we'd have done our duty. We'd have lived or died with honour.'

Taki had put down her sewing. Shinzaemon was still scowling, staring into the fire as if he saw Wakamatsu burning there.

'That night anyone still on their feet partied. We made bonfires and sang and danced. Some of the men were fine performers of the Noh dances. We

were going to go out in a blaze of glory. Toranosuké did "Atsumori". He's always been a good
dancer.'

Caught up in his words again, Sachi saw the
faces glowing red in the light of the bonfires and
torches. She heard the chanting, saw the measured pace of the Noh dances, the slow waving of
the fans. Every movement was deliberate and
perfect, as it always had been through the ages:
warriors celebrating before their glorious last
stand.

So Toranosuké, with his handsome face and
noble demeanour, had performed 'Atsumori' –
the tale of a beautiful young warrior who is killed
in battle. Afterwards his slayer finds a bamboo
flute lying next to his body and realizes that this
was the young man whose music had wafted
across from the enemy camp the previous night.
It was the most poignant of dramas, expressing
the glory, romance and exquisite sadness of a
warrior's death – a perfect drama for samurai
expecting to go into battle the following day.
Sachi imagined Toranosuké, his face as immobile
as a Noh mask, sweeping his fan as he danced
and intoning in his deep voice:

'But on the night of the sixth day of the second
  month
My father Tsunemori gathered us together.
"Tomorrow," he said, "we shall fight our last
  fight.
Tonight is all that is left us."
We sang songs together and danced.'

602

She glanced at Taki. Taki's expression had not changed but there was a soft light in her big eyes. She was murmuring the same lines.

But even as Sachi pictured the scene it was beginning to fade, like a painting on gold in which the gold was beginning to tarnish. Now that she'd seen the glittering rifles and the rows of corpses and heard the roar of cannons, seen the great ships in Edo Harbour and heard about the iron monsters, the scene Shinzaemon was describing sounded no more real than a pageant. The age of the warrior had been a glorious time – but what he said was true, it was over. There was no place for a samurai in the new world that was dawning.

'We were all waiting for the order the next day. We knew what it would be. "No surrender. To the death."'

He bowed his head. 'But that wasn't the order. It was... "We've surrendered. Lay down your arms."'

So that was it. Their men, the northern warriors, had surrendered. Like weaklings, like women. As if they cared more for their skin than honour. Even if the war was over, even if it would have achieved nothing, in the past they would have fought to the death – for the samurai code, for honour. That was what the north had always stood for. The northern warriors were men who would die for their country, their liege lord or their family, without a thought for themselves. Without their honour it was hard to know what they were fighting for. Taki and Haru shifted uncomfortably, struck dumb with the shame of it.

'All the while we'd been fighting and dying, his lordship had been negotiating behind our backs. We had to shave our heads, all of us, the whole garrison.' Shinzaemon grimaced and plucked at his shorn hair. 'A retainer came out with a banner inscribed with two characters: *"Ko-fuku"*. "Surrender". His lordship followed. He'd shaved his head and was dressed in ceremonial robes. This was the man our comrades had given their lives for; this was the man we'd been prepared to kill and die for. He hadn't even been man enough to kill himself.

'Then we were told that the castle was to be handed over. We were all supposed to file out and give ourselves up. The dead were so thick on the ground we were treading on the bodies of our comrades.

'That was when I realized it had all been for nothing. Some of the men took out their swords and cut their bellies right there. The rest of us were stumbling around like we didn't know where we were. Everyone was throwing down their weapons and piling out through the main gate. We looked at each other, me and Toran-osuké and Tatsuemon. "I can't do this," I said. "Me neither," said Toranosuké. We hung on to our swords and grabbed every rifle we could lay our hands on. Then we sneaked out through a back gate. Somehow we managed to slip around the southern troops, although we met up with a couple of patrols and had a skirmish or two. Then we were out in the fields.

'Toranosuké and Tatsu wanted to head for Sendai, to try and get there before the Tokugawa fleet left. They were determined to head north, carry on the battle up there. But for me it was finished. There was nothing left to fight for. I just started walking.'

Sachi wanted to reach out and put her hand on his arm, to let him know that she understood how ashamed and betrayed he felt, but instead she sat staring into the fire. Because he had lived and she was glad of that. He had fought and fought; he had done all he could and she was proud of him. And now, instead of lying rotting in some northern field, he was back with them. Back with her.

He looked round at her and Taki and Haru and grinned as if he'd shaken off something heavy that had been resting on his shoulders.

'I kept my head covered until my hair started to grow again,' he said, 'and pretended I was a Buddhist monk. I came by back roads and got completely lost. Then one night I ended up in a village in the foothills of Mount Akagi. It was like a town of ghosts. People seemed afraid. No one would talk to me. I thought I recognized the crest outside the mansion at the end of the village, but I couldn't think what it was. Half a day later I came out at the River Toné, at the place where we crossed it in the spring. When I heard you talking to your father this morning I thought it might have been the Oguri crest. Perhaps when we saw him Lord Oguri had been fleeing Edo, heading for home.'

The women were silent. A chance sighting of Lord Oguri's crest didn't sound like much of a lead.

II

The next morning they set off along the Inner
Mountain Road as it wound grandly through the
city, passing alongside the long wall that edged
the vast estate of the Maeda lords. Ueno Hill rose
dark and silent in the distance.

Daisuké had decided they would travel in a
convoy of palanquins as far as they could. Sachi
leaned back on the cushions in her little box and
braced herself for a long journey. The wooden
walls creaked and rattled. The palanquin swung
violently as they rounded a bend and she reached
for the carrying rope to steady herself. She tossed
from side to side as the bearers jogged along,
grunting rhythmically in unison with their steps.
She could hear the crunch of their straw sandals
pounding the earthen road and the occasional
groan or curse as they toiled up a hill.

Uncomfortable though it was, it was good to be
on the move again after so many months hidden
away in the mansion, waiting and watching for
the war to end, wondering if it ever would. When
the box stopped rocking for a moment she leaned
forward and pushed aside the slats of the
bamboo blind. The city was coming back to life.
Houses had sprung up again where the fire had
swept them away. Shops were open again and the
streets were bustling with people.

By the hour of the horse, when the sun was
reaching the middle of the sky, they reached the
checkpoint at Itabashi. The last time Sachi was

606

there it had been swarming with soldiers. Now the guards waved them through without even stopping them.

Then they were out of the city, swinging along between groves of mulberry trees. Withered leaves rustled on the branches. There was the occasional whiff of animal dung and human waste spread on paddies and vegetable fields to fertilize them. From time to time they overtook slower traffic. Sachi heard the clop of hooves or the heavy tread of oxen laden with rice, silk, fish manure, salt or tobacco. Then the sounds and smells faded behind her as the bearers sped on.

She tried not to think about what was ahead. She was glad Daisuké and Shinzaemon were with her, and Edwards too. It was a relief to let them take charge. She had begun a new life; she was no longer on her own.

In the middle of the second day they reached the River Toné. The bearers' feet crunched across the gravel, then they lowered the palanquin to the ground and she climbed out stiffly, straightening her legs. Edwards had already leaped off his horse and was at the door, offering his hand to help her out. She laughed and brushed it aside, then smoothed her skirts, glad to be on solid ground. It was good to breathe the autumn air and hear the cries of birds and the whisper of water lapping the shore. The last leaves were floating down, clouds scudded across the sky and a couple of herons flapped by with a flash of white wings.

Shinzaemon was tying up the horses and instructing the porters as Taki, Haru and Daisuké clambered out of their palanquins. Edwards was ready with a hand for Taki and Haru too. Haru was the last to emerge. Her face was drawn and pale.

Sachi remembered Haru's words again. She was the only one who knew Lord Mizuno. She looked more than uneasy – she looked afraid.

Lord Oguri and Lord Mizuno had crossed the river here, heading towards the mountains, Sachi knew. But then they had disappeared as completely as if the earth had opened up and swallowed them. She shivered and pulled her kimonos closer around her.

On the far side of the river the Inner Mountain Road wound around the lea of the hill. She could see people like specks in the distance and rows of inns, then the road disappeared into a cluster of steep thatched roofs. Behind the hills the sky was the colour of an ancient indigo robe, washed and washed until there was no colour left. Paddy fields were carved into niches in the river bank. Tattered sheaves of rice stood tied into cones, their straggly stalks flapping in the wind.

Shinzaemon was frowning, staring across the river as if he was searching the recesses of his memory. His swords bristled at his side and Sachi saw that he had a pistol tucked into his belt. He turned to Daisuké.

'It was over there,' he said. 'I think that was Lord Oguri's village.'

Daisuké nodded slowly. 'I did some research of my own,' he said. 'Lord Oguri's family is from somewhere round here. You're right: if we can find his village we might be able to find him. And perhaps he can tell us where Lord Mizuno is.'

'It was six months ago,' whispered Taki. 'We could be heading in entirely the wrong direction. And Lord Oguri and Lord Mizuno were on the losing side. They'll be in hiding.'

'It's the only lead we've got,' said Daisuké sternly. He turned to Shinzaemon. 'Can you remember how to get to the village?'

'It wasn't on the Inner Mountain Road. We need to follow that track there, into the woods,' he said, pointing.

The river rolled sluggishly, as grey as the sky. A rickety ferry was zigzagging slowly towards them. They filed on board, leaving the palanquins to be stored and the horses to be stabled in the village till their return. The ancient ferryman, *happi* coat tucked around his thighs, leaned on his pole so hard he nearly fell into the water as the ferry creaked away from the bank.

Once on the other side, they climbed through shadowy forests of dark-leaved pines and towering cedars. Pine needles crackled underfoot and pale sunlight trickled through the leaves, dappling the path.

Edwards was walking ahead with Daisuké, talking in his loud voice and waving his big hands around. It sounded as if they were discussing the structure of the new government and how to win over the people of Edo. After all, Edwards was a diplomat and representative of the country that had armed the rebels, and Daisuké an official of the new government formed by those same rebels. No doubt they had a lot to talk about. Nevertheless it made Sachi apprehensive. She

609

wondered if Edwards's real aim was to impress her father; perhaps he intended to ask for her hand in marriage. After all he had said that day when he took her hand in the garden, he wouldn't easily give up his pursuit of her; and he probably didn't realize there was anything between her and Shinzaemon. Why should he? Just as she had trouble interpreting his foreign ways, no doubt he had trouble interpreting hers.

She peeped at this huge person clomping along in front of her in his animal-skin boots, beating down the weeds and long grass with his riding crop, his gold hair gleaming in the sun. How could she have encouraged his advances even for a moment? He was so outlandish! It was extra-ordinary how he treated women. For all his size he behaved not like a man but a servant, helping them as solicitously as if they were ill, and not just her but Taki and Haru too. It would be unprecedented for her father to take such an alien being as his adopted son; yet he was such a modern man that he might want to make an alliance with the English.

By the time they reached the top of the ridge they were all breathing hard. They stopped for a while to catch their breath and get their bearings. Sachi gazed at the tree-covered hills rolling into the distance. Mountains floated beyond them, pale as ghosts, wild and craggy.

Shinzaemon was behind her, so close she could feel the heat of his skin and hear his breath. She glanced around: Daisuké and Edwards were a little way away. Shinzaemon pointed to a nearby peak. His kimono sleeve fell back and she could see the hard muscles of his forearm. His skin was smooth as silk, the colour of dark gold. In her imagination she reached out shyly and ran her fingers across it.

'Mount Akagi,' he said. 'Lord Oguri's village is somewhere in the foothills there. And that high mountain way over there – it's towards Waka-matsu.' Sachi shaded her eyes with her hand. She could just make out a sinister black peak among the crests shimmering in the distance.

They followed the road back down into the woods. Shinzaemon stayed close beside her while Daisuké walked ahead with Haru. Sachi could see their backs receding down the path: the tall broad-shouldered man with a flat straw hat slung on his back and his kimono hitched up, revealing a pair of brawny calves, and the small round woman with her hair wrapped in a scarf, pattering along holding a long-stemmed pipe, taking the occasional puff. They were walking side by side, heads bent, talking intensely. Sachi looked at them in amazement: not even a peasant or a townsman would walk beside a woman. They seemed to have forgotten all the social proprieties. It was as if there was no time any longer to worry about what was acceptable and what wasn't.

She wondered what they were talking about, whether Haru was persuading Daisuké that Shinzaemon was a suitable young man to take as an adopted son, despite the fact he'd fought at Wakamatsu. Or perhaps it was more intimate than that. After all, they were getting close to finding the woman whom both of them loved. Daisuké must feel the same uncertainty, hope

611

and fear that Sachi herself had felt when she had waited and yearned for Shinzaemon. Or maybe over the years his feelings had dulled until there was nothing left except a grim determination to find the answer, no matter what it might be. Perhaps, she thought, the only certainty in life was the certainty of uncertainty. It was important never to forget the Buddha's teaching: that life was suffering.

She could hear the crunch of fallen leaves behind them. Taki and Edwards were following. No doubt Taki, at least, was a few steps behind Edwards. She heard Edwards's loud voice and Taki's high-pitched laugh. She was relieved to hear her friend laugh again; it seemed a long time since she had been happy.

It felt thoroughly wicked – excitingly so – to be walking alongside Shinzaemon. They had been apart for so long that all she wanted was to be with him, though she knew very well that he too would have to find a way to impress Daisuké if they were to have any hope of spending their lives together.

She looked down at the earth and stones of the path, the piles of mouldering leaves and the great trees soaring alongside. Between the trees the hillside fell away, covered in ferns and grass. Every now and then she caught a glimpse of rolling hills, faint in the distance. There were her small feet in their straw sandals, scuffing along, toes neatly turned in. And there were Shinzaemon's next to hers, stepping out with big strides.

Shinzaemon kicked at the leaves with his sandals.

'Wakamatsu,' he grunted. 'I thought I'd never fight again after that. But if I have to, I'm ready.'

She looked at him and smiled. They walked on in silence. He was frowning, thinking hard. After a while they caught up with Daisuké.

'There's something bothering me,' Shinzaemon said. 'Those strongboxes that Lord Oguri and Lord Mizuno had. It took four men to carry each one, and even then they were staggering. Do you think there might have been gold inside? And those porters – they didn't look like porters at all to me. They looked like prisoners, samurai who'd been locked up so long their pates had grown out. Yes. I'm sure that's what they were.'

Gold. There had been talk of gold before, Sachi remembered. She pictured herself back in Edo, in the east end, in a grubby pawnbroker's shop. There was the pawnbroker with his pointed rat-like face and sly, ingratiating smile – Fuyu's lord and master. He was looking at them through narrowed eyes, refusing the gold coin they had offered him, showing them the stamp on it: the hollyhock crest of the Tokugawas. 'Seems the shogun's gold has gone missing,' he had said with a grin.

'In those boxes...' she said softly. 'Could it have been ... the Tokugawa gold?'

Daisuké stopped suddenly and thumped his huge fist into the palm of his hand.

'Of course!' he said, so loudly that a bird fluttered from the trees. 'The Tokugawa millions. We thought when we took over the castle we'd find it. Fifteen generations' worth, accumulated ever since the Tokugawas came to power. We've been stumbling along ever since, trying to set up a government and run the country with a bankrupt treasury. Of course! Lord Oguri was the chief commissioner of the treasury. He would have wanted to make sure we didn't lay our hands on a single copper *mon* of it. He probably started shifting it out of Edo the moment it became clear the shogun was in trouble. Maybe he's planning to fund a rebellion!'

'Gold?' said Edwards, his blue eyes gleaming. 'The Tokugawa treasure? We heard rumours of that at the legation. Well, if this place we're going to really is Lord Oguri's village, then you could be right. That would be something, to find that gold, and Lord Mizuno too.'

He was scowling thoughtfully, kicking at the ground with his shiny animal-skin boots. He looked up and caught Sachi's eyes on him and gave a rueful half-smile. Then he looked away as if aware that a curtain had fallen between them.

'You know it's a criminal offence, stealing state funds,' said Daisuké grimly. 'If we find them and they do have the gold, I'll make sure their heads are well and truly off their shoulders – once they've finished answering my questions. They're traitors, that's what they are.'

Sachi could feel Shinzaemon bristling.

'Rebellion. Treachery,' he muttered with a curl of his lip. His face was stony and Sachi could see that he was making a mighty effort to keep silent. She could guess what he was thinking. If Lord Oguri and Lord Mizuno were organizing the resistance, Shinzaemon would have to make a rapid decision about which side he was on –

whether he was with Daisuké or against him. Disillusioned or not, she doubted if he was ready to betray his principles quite yet.

III

They reached the village late in the afternoon. It was huddled against the mountainside. A forest of cedars loomed behind, casting deep shadows across the wooden walls and steep thatched roofs of the inns, and strands of mountain mist trailed in the hollows.

For such a remote place it seemed strangely busy. Shifty-eyed men with stubbly faces and greasy hair pulled into knots prowled around while shrivelled maids, aprons tied over their indigo work kimonos, bustled out into the street, grabbing them and hauling them into their inns. Sachi guessed business must be bad if they had to drag in low life like that.

Out on the street some of the men had already started drinking and the air was rank with the fumes of the local brew. Sachi overheard snatches of conversation. 'Set up as a merchant, that's what I'll do.' 'Not me. I'll be down the Yoshiwara where you can't tell day from night. The most beautiful women in all two hundred and sixty provinces!' 'I'll buy a few for mistresses.' 'I'll put it on the dice. There'll be no stopping me.' She wondered what they were talking about.

Daisuké sought out the best inn in town and took a room there. It was a big wooden building with hefty smoke-blackened beams in the entrance hall that reminded Sachi of the inn where she had grown up. She slid open the rain doors. Outside there was a tiny garden with a pond with carp swimming in it and a few rocks covered in bright green moss.

After they had bathed, a bent old maid hobbled in to prepare their room for dinner. She was dressed in a kimono of coarse homespun cotton, with her hair tied in place with hemp yarn, and stared at them suspiciously out of tiny eyes sunk in her crinkled face. Sachi realized how out-landish they must look: three aristocratic-looking women, two men with hair eccentrically cropped and a huge red-headed barbarian – and all of them speaking with strong city accents. The woman peered up at Edwards then made a tutting noise and turned away as if the presence of such an alien being was too much even to think about.

'Down from Edo, are you?' she asked. She had almost no teeth, which made it even harder to understand the 'shu shu shu' of her grating northern burr. 'Used to be we didn't see no grand folks like you one year to the next. Can't imagine what you're doing here. Not on the way to nowhere. No hotspring, no famous temple.'

'I'm on my way back from Wakamatsu,' said Shinzaemon quietly. 'My friends here have come to meet me.'

'Wakamatsu, huh?' A long rumble of awe and appreciation rose in the woman's throat and her old face softened. For a moment there was a flash of the young girl she must once have been. 'Well done,' she croaked. 'Well done. Fought well, you boys. Held out. Did your best.'

She heaved herself to her feet, limped out and returned with a tray laden with tiny dishes. She folded her legs under her and placed it in front of Daisuké.

'We've had our troubles too. His lordship...' She shook her head and drew her breath through her few remaining teeth with a hiss.

'You mean...' Sachi held her breath.

'Yes, yes, Lord Oguri,' the old woman rasped impatiently. 'You must have heard of him. Important man, his lordship, up in the city. Never used to see his lordship from one year to the next. Mind you, he was a fair man. If any of us townsfolk had a complaint, he'd listen to it. My old grandfather used to be a retainer up at the big house, and I was a wet nurse for his lordship when he was a baby. Then they sent him down to the Edo estate to turn him into a warrior. I never saw him again. But we all heard what an important man he'd become. We were all proud of him.'

'So his lordship...'

She waggled her head from side to side. 'You won't believe what happened.' She sniffed. 'When was it now? Before the rice-planting season. Well before. Would have been before the flower festival, except we didn't celebrate the flower festival this year. How could we after what happened?'

She hobbled out and returned with another tray which she set before Edwards. There was silence in the room. Sachi glanced around; everyone was looking at the floor. Like her, no one dared break the spell by asking where Lord Oguri was.

617

The old woman went out a third time and returned with another tray of food. As she placed it before Shinzaemon she smiled at him.

'Bear meat,' she croaked. 'Gave you a couple of extra slices. For Wakamatsu.' Her ancient face crinkled up like a walnut. 'We had those southern soldiers here too,' she muttered. 'Right here in this village. Mean-looking characters. Bow legs. Strange clothes. Can't understand a word they're saying. They headed straight for his lordship's. We didn't even know he was back. They fan out, they're searching every house. Even here. Look. See what they did?'

The interwoven bamboo of the ceiling was in shreds. It must have been stabbed a thousand times, as if the soldiers had been sure their prey was up in the rafters somewhere, hiding.

'"He's not here," we said. "Never comes here. He's up in Edo." "He's here all right," they said. Could understand that much. Before the rice-planting season, that's when it was.'

She stopped and swabbed her rheumy old eyes with her sleeve. 'Turns out they were right. Seems his lordship and his young lordship were here. They weren't gonna run away, were they, proud men like them! They were up at the big house, waiting. Guess they knew what was coming. Soldiers arrested them, and his lordship's personal servants too, and marched them down to the river bank. Chopped their heads off right there.'

Sachi stifled a gasp. Lord Oguri's soft courtier's face, the colour of vellum, flashed before her eyes. She saw his white scholarly hands – the hands of a man who had never wielded anything

618

heavier than a writing brush.

The old woman was wiping tears from her shrivelled cheeks.

'Nailed his lordship's head to a board,' she quavered. 'Carried it through the village, as a warning, like. We belong to his lordship, they know which side we're on. I saw it myself. First time I saw his lordship's face since he was a baby. Such a noble face. Nailed it to the prison gate with a sign. "Traitor to the emperor". He was no traitor. We're his retainers. And proud of it. Proud.'

She started as if she'd suddenly realized what she'd said and glanced around nervously. Her mouth snapped shut and she hurried out of the room. She scuttled in and out with the remaining trays without another word.

Not hungry any longer, Sachi sat picking at the wild mushrooms and bean paste soup, trying to grasp what the woman had said.

It was Edwards who broke the silence.

'So what happened to Lord Mizuno?' he asked, stretching out one long leg, then the other, then folding them in front of him with a grimace.

'Well,' said Daisuké slowly, 'we know he came over on the ferry with Lord Oguri. And, if it really was the Tokugawa gold they were carrying, he knows about it.'

'He probably knows where it is, too,' said Edwards. Sachi noticed the same gleam in his eye, the same sudden look of urgency, of intense interest, that she had seen the first time gold was mentioned. 'In fact, if Lord Oguri is dead, he's the only one who does. If that was the Tokugawa gold, those porters you saw are dead. They would have been killed the moment they got the gold to wherever their lordships wanted it to be.'

If. So many 'if's, Sachi thought. Yet she couldn't help feeling a twinge of excitement.

'Surely Lord Oguri and Lord Mizuno would have separated as soon as they'd got rid of the gold,' said Shinzaemon. He leaned forward, his eyes shining. 'They would have hidden it somewhere then gone in opposite directions. Lord Oguri would have known his life was in danger. Lord Mizuno too. They would have wanted to make sure at least one of them survived, otherwise the gold would be lost for ever.'

'What makes you think they'd want to share it?' demanded Edwards. 'Maybe both of them wanted it. Maybe one of them cheated the other and went off with it. Maybe Lord Mizuno betrayed Lord Oguri and told the soldiers where to find him. Gold drives men crazy.' He was staring at the tatami. '*Rabu* too,' he muttered. 'But in the end sometimes it's better just to admit defeat.'

Shinzaemon and Daisuké looked at him. Sachi hoped no one but she understood what he was talking about.

'We don't even know there is any gold,' said Taki hastily, breaking the silence.

'Then why are all these men hanging around the village?' Shinzaemon asked. 'They're after something – I can feel it.'

'But we still have no idea where Lord Mizuno is or even whether he's alive,' Sachi objected. 'Supposing he did the same as Lord Oguri? Supposing he fled to his home village? It's at the

620

other end of the country – isn't that what you told me, Haru?'

'It's in Shingu, in the country of Kii.'

'If he's there, we've come in entirely the wrong direction,' said Taki with a sigh. 'We'll have to go back to Edo and start all over again. Or just give up.'

'I'd like to find out what's happening in this village,' said Shinzaemon. 'I'm sure there's a link somewhere to Lord Mizuno. After all, we know he came this way. Where was he when Lord Oguri was killed? What did he do then?'

They were all silent as the old woman came in to clear away their dishes. She crept over on her knees to pick up Shinzaemon's tray then stopped and twisted her neck until she was looking up at him.

'Wakamatsu, huh?' she muttered in her creaky old voice. 'Let me look at you. You did good, you boys. First time I've had the chance to see one of you boys.'

She put a withered claw on his knee and pushed her wizened face close to his. Shinzaemon cocked his head and looked at her with his slanted eyes.

'Tell me, Granny,' he said. 'All these men out on the street here, hanging round the village. You tell us there's no hotspring or famous temple, but there must be something to draw these fellows.'

'Ne'er-do-wells, the lot of them,' the old woman croaked. 'Turn up every evening, drink the place dry. Plenty of business for the geishas and prostitutes, that's for sure. But I don't like it. This used to be a quiet place, no one ever came

621

here. Just pilgrims on their way to the mountain. First those ruffians, now you – even an honourable barbarian,' she added, squinting up at Edwards. She shook her head. 'Never happened before, that's for sure.'

She knelt quietly for a while, her head bobbing. Her chin sank lower and lower till Sachi was afraid she'd fallen asleep. Then she straightened up slowly.

'It began not long after his lordship passed away,' she said. 'Around rice-planting time. They started to turn up – first one, then another, then more and more. Rowdy types – gamblers, yakuza, even outcastes, some of them. They don't come in the daytimes, just the evenings. You get fights on the street sometimes. Never used to be like that.'

'So no one knows why they're here or what they're up to?' Shinzaemon persisted.

'I don't worry about that sort of thing. Not my business. Got too much to worry about already. You should ask my old man. He's been up on the mountain a few times to take a look around. Tells me there's something going on up there. He'll take you if you want.'

IV

The old woman's husband appeared early the next morning. He looked even older than his wife, as if he had weathered several lifetimes of rain, wind and snow. He was dressed for the mountains in straw boots and a straw raincoat, with a sedge hat hanging on his back and a staff in his gnarled hand. He tramped off, chattering excitedly in his barely comprehensible dialect, while Sachi and her companions hurried to keep up with him.

He led them up the hillside into the woods, along a rough path that looked as if it had been hacked out very recently. Soon they were picking their way between densely packed trees wound about with vines and swathed in foliage. They passed a cluster of fallen branches put together to make a shelter, then another and another, propped between the trees.

'Some of these fellows live out 'ere,' said the old man in a low voice.

Then they heard the sound of shovelling. The path opened into a clearing riddled with holes and heaped with piles of earth, like the casts of a gigantic worm. Scrawny men were bent over, digging feverishly. Some were in ragged indigo work trousers like peasants, while others wore nothing but loincloths despite the icy wind that shook the branches and sent leaves spinning. They looked up as the old man approached followed by Sachi and her companions. Sachi noticed Shinzaemon and Edwards putting their hands on the hilts of their pistols.

The men's eyes swivelled as they saw Edwards. 'What's that?' muttered one. 'A *tengu?*' They shrank back, their mouths open and their gums bared.

'Nah, that's no *tengu,*' said another. 'It's one of them barbarians.' The men circled around them, staring at them with glittering eyes, like wolves.

'Oi, Granddad. What you doing bringing strangers round here?' growled a skinny man with a thin twisted face and squinting eyes. He bent down and picked up a stone. 'Keep away,' he snarled, spewing a gobbet of yellow spit on to the ground. 'Bloody samurai.'

'Find your own patch,' snarled another. 'Yeah, that's it. Clear off!'

Once they were well past, Shinzaemon muttered to the old man, 'Gold they're looking for, is it?'

The man narrowed his eyes to slits and clamped his lips together.

'So there are no fellows with gold to spend hanging around the village, then?' Shinzaemon persisted.

The old man grinned. 'Not so far,' he said, relenting. 'They've not had much luck so far – you can see that. There's more men digging further up the mountain. You might see something interesting up there.'

As they climbed on, the path disappeared altogether and the woods closed in around them. They clambered over rocks and fallen tree trunks, scrambling through bushes and piles of leaves and around great gnarled roots. They climbed in a sort of twilight, under a thick canopy of branches and leaves.

Above them the woods came to an end and light glimmered through the trees. They came out on to moorland – an endless field of pale dry miscanthus grass that swayed high above their heads, rustling in the wind. Withered fields. It made Sachi think of the haiku poet Basho's death poem:

624

Tabi ni yande   Ill on a journey
yume wa kareno o   My dreams wander on
kakemeguru   Across withered fields.

The old man was out in front, tramping along with Daisuké, Shinzaemon and Edwards right behind him. Daisuké and Shinzaemon strode along together, their broad shoulders side by side, their cropped heads – one greying, one glossy and black – close. Taki and Haru followed, their white headbands bobbing through the grass.

Sachi could hear the old man's voice: 'A lot of strange things happen on this moor. There was a story my granddad told me, about a traveller. Got lost up here one night. Was wandering around and met a woman. A real beauty.'

Sachi could guess how the story went; it was always the same. The woman lures the traveller back to her mansion, somewhere deep in the moors. The next day, enthralled by her beauty, he goes back to look for her. He searches and searches but all he can find where the mansion had been is a gravestone many hundreds of years old, covered in moss. He looks at it closely and sees her name carved on it. Sachi shivered. Ghosts – she didn't want to hear about ghosts. It was tempting fate, especially now, when they were searching for her mother, desperately hoping they would find her. She fell back a little, let the others get ahead.

She ran her fingers through the tall grass, watching the down spin off and float in the breeze. The sky was dark and gloomy and clouds

625

scudded overhead. There was snow in the air. She tugged her robes closer around her. She could hear the grass swishing as she brushed through it and the rustle of her straw sandals on the ground.

Then she heard another sound – a rhythmic thunk and a sort of tapping, like a ghost knocking from under the earth. She started, overcome with superstitious dread, then held her breath and listened. It was not a ghost at all, she realized. It was digging, the crunch of a shovel biting into hard ground followed by the rattle of earth being thrown. It was a little way away, somewhere out in the long grass. The others were not far ahead, cutting a furrow across the moor. It would just take a moment to have a look and then she could catch up with them.

She was pushing through the tall stalks, following the sound, when she suddenly found herself on the edge of a huge hole. She stopped abruptly. It was big and wide and deep, big enough for the burial of a shogun.

There was a man inside, digging feverishly, so engrossed he hadn't noticed her approach. He was panting hard, slamming a shovel into the earthen wall of the pit, hurling shovelfuls of dirt to one side. He was thin and ragged, his hair unkempt and matted. His back was burned black from the sun, and despite the chill in the air it glistened with sweat. His skinny shoulder bones jutted like wings, moving under his dirt-encrusted skin as he worked. He had a ragged towel knotted around his head and scrawny ankles protruding from grimy work trousers. There was an overpowering stench of sweat and urine and human excrement.

But what was he doing looking for gold so far from everyone else? And in this great plain of grass, why had he chosen to dig here, of all places?

He gave a groan that was more animal than human and put a blackened hand on his back. His nails were thick and long like claws. Slowly he straightened up and turned around.

It was him. There was no mistaking the hooked nose, the fierce features, the gaunt face pitted with marks of the pox. There was the same wild gleam in his eye that Sachi had seen half a year ago at the ferry.

As he saw her he gasped and staggered backwards. His eyes bulged and his jaw dropped until his mouth was a circle of horror.

'Leave me alone,' he whimpered. His voice was the faintest croak, the words whipped away on the wind.

They stood frozen, staring at each other.

Sachi had imagined what she might say to him, how she would reveal who she was, perhaps even greet him as her uncle. After all, he was her blood relation. But she couldn't move or utter a word. She was mesmerized, as helpless as a deer in a hunter's sights.

Then, as his expression changed from terror to hatred and fury, she realized she was in danger. Terrible danger. He lunged towards her, and as he flung himself half out of the pit his arms closed around her legs. She struggled wildly, then lost her balance and fell. He slithered back down, dragging her with him.

Winded and stunned, Sachi crashed into the pit. The earthen walls towered around her like the walls of a grave and for a moment the sky was full of whirling stars. Her kimono skirts had fallen open and her hair had come loose. She gasped painfully, trying to catch her breath, to move her limbs. Stiffly she pulled her kimono skirts together and groped for her dagger. She was in the clutches of a madman.

Before she could reach her dagger he shoved her face into the ground and slammed his foot on her back, pinning her down. She tasted earth and salty blood. Then he grabbed her by the hair, dragged her to her knees, then to her feet and wrenched her head back. His arm was across her face. There was something sharp at her throat.

She tried to shout but all she could manage was a dry croak. Her head was spinning. A vile stench emanated from his pores and his scaly skin scratched her face. She realized that she might die – not gloriously like a samurai but right here in this foul pit, before anyone found her.

Lord Mizuno was panting. *'Mayotta na!'* he muttered hoarsely. *'Mayotta na!* Got lost, huh!'

She suddenly understood. Got lost on your way to the next world, he meant. It was not her he saw, it was her mother, the ghost of her mother, come back to haunt him.

'Mayotta na! Mayotta na! You lost your way. You lost your way,' he muttered. It was like an exorcism, as if she would disappear if he said it enough times. 'But you're warm,' he said. For a moment he seemed to regain his senses. He sounded puzzled. 'How did you get so warm? You

were cold when I buried you. Cold as the earth. I didn't want to do it – I told you so. But I had to. It was my duty. And now you won't let me rest. Got lost, huh? Can't find y'way? Come to take me with you, have you?'

His arm was pressing on her mouth and nose. Sachi gasped, smelling the dirt and sweat, feeling the sharp hairs prickle her face. She wanted to scream to Shinzaemon and Daisuké to come and rescue her, but she had let them get so far ahead that they might not hear her even if she shouted. Perhaps no one would find her and she would rot here for ever in this hole in the long grass.

Somewhere in the distance voices were calling, 'My lady! My lady!' For a moment she felt a surge of hope. But the voices were growing fainter, moving further and further away.

She wriggled fiercely, trying to free herself, careless of what he might do.

'Gotta finish the job,' he growled. 'Once and for all. I'm going to cut you up in such small pieces you'll never come back again.'

He loosened his grasp and she took a gulp of air, choking and coughing. As she felt breath flow into her lungs her panic subsided. She had to think, concentrate. He had killed her mother – she knew that now for sure. The certainty of it made her giddy. It was the end of all their hopes, their yearning, their prayers. She never would meet her mother after all. Daisuké would never see her again, nor Haru either.

That made it all the more important for her to live, not for her own sake but for Daisuké's.

'You defy me,' shouted Lord Mizuno. 'You've

defiled our family's name. You've brought shame and ruin on our family. I'll obliterate you. I'll obliterate you so completely no one will ever know you existed.'

It was the same conversation he had had all those years ago with her mother. He must have repeated it again and again to himself ever since.

'Hiro,' he barked.

She started. Ohiro. Her mother's name when she was a girl, before she entered the palace. She felt herself dissolving. It was she, Sachi, who had committed that terrible crime, she who had disgraced the family. Her mother lived again in her. Was it all predestined? Sachi asked herself. She too had become the shogun's concubine, she too had betrayed him, and she too had allowed herself to be swept away by passion. She had forgotten that women were property, and that their only duty was to obey. She had thought she could grab life for herself, take what she wanted with impunity. Was this to be her punishment?

'Hiro,' barked a voice. She didn't know if it was her brother or her uncle who was speaking. 'Hiro. Prepare to meet your death. Do you have any last words?'

Sachi thought frantically. If only she could make him follow the proper execution procedure he would have to release her. She would kneel on the ground while he raised his sword with both hands and swung it down. There would be a fraction of a second when she had a chance to escape. It had been her mother's plan, she knew that. It hadn't worked that time – but this time it would.

630

'Do it,' she croaked, her mouth dry. 'Do ... what you have to do. But ... do it right. You're a samurai, not a murderer. Let me die like a samurai, not a common criminal.' She took a breath and spoke as clearly as she could. 'Give me the privilege of a samurai's death.'

She was ready to twist clear the moment he released her. But he gripped even tighter.

'You won't escape this time,' he hissed. 'I cut you from your neck to your belly. I saw your blood spurt. I saw you dead. But you keep coming back again and again. You're cunning like a fox. I'll do it again, a hundred times if I have to, till you're well and truly dead. Till I can have some peace. Till I can have some peace.'

Slowly, deliberately, he pulled her head back. She saw the tall white clumps of plume grass swaying at the edge of the pit. A buzzard dipped and swooped. She felt quite calm. So this was it, the last thing she would ever see. She felt the bones of Lord Mizuno's thin chest pressed into her back, his arm wrapped around her face. His hand was shaking. There was a sting as the blade scratched her skin. A drop of something warm trickled from her throat, growing cold as it ran down to her chest. She closed her eyes.

In the silence there was a rustle above them, the clatter of pebbles falling into the pit. Sachi felt Lord Mizuno stiffen. His head jerked up. His grip relaxed a little and the pressure of the blade on her throat lessened.

Sachi opened her eyes as a shadow fell across the pit. There was a figure silhouetted against the dull grey sky, a plump woman with a sweet round face and slanted eyes. Ringed with light, for a moment she seemed more like a heavenly presence than a human being – a bodhisattva come to take Sachi to the Western Paradise.

'Haru.' As Sachi breathed the name she was not her mother any more. She was herself. She felt such a surge of relief she thought she would faint.

For a moment Haru's mouth was open and her eyes round with shock. Then her face twisted into a reproving frown.

'Older Brother,' she said sharply, as if she was talking to a naughty child. 'Tadanaka. It's me, Haru. What are you doing down there?'

Sachi felt Lord Mizuno's chest heave as he gave a juddering gasp.

'Haru!' he croaked.

'Put down that knife, Older Brother,' barked Haru. 'Let go of her. Don't be so foolish. What's come over you? Do you think you've seen a ghost?'

For a moment Lord Mizuno's grasp loosened.

'But... But, Haru,' he stuttered weakly. 'What are you doing here? Why aren't you in the palace?'

Haru slithered into the pit, bringing a small avalanche of earth tumbling down with her. She tugged her kimono skirts into place, glaring at Mizuno, holding him with her eyes.

Sachi stared at her helplessly, imagining how she must look – wide terrified eyes, her face and clothes covered in dirt, blood on her throat, in the grip of this crazy black skeleton of a man. Her hair was hanging wild and loose like a ghost's – like the ghost of her mother.

Haru edged towards them, one step at a time.

She was holding out her hand, open, with the palm up.

'Give me that knife,' she said.

Sachi fixed her eyes on Haru's soft, plump hand. She felt as if she was drowning and the hand was stretched out to save her.

'Ohiro is dead. Dead,' said Haru. 'You had to punish my lady for her crime. You did your duty – for the family, for honour. You did the right thing. But it's all over now, over long ago. This is not her. Show me where she's buried and we'll pray for her together. We'll put her spirit to rest, then she won't haunt you any more.'

As Haru came closer, Lord Mizuno's arm tightened around Sachi's face like an iron band.

'Don't interfere with me,' he snarled. 'You women – you're foxes, nothing but trouble. Get back where you came from.'

'No one blames you,' said Haru quietly, persuasively. 'Let her go. Give me the dagger.'

'She disgraced the family, this mistress of yours,' rasped Mizuno in a hoarse growl, his voice shaking. 'I have to execute her now, before the palace finds out. If I don't, the shogun's police will. You want them smashing down the doors, ordering my father and my brothers to cut their bellies – all because of some worthless woman?'

'That used to be the way,' said a deep voice. Sachi recognized the Edo accent overlaid with an Osaka twang and gasped with relief. A burly, broad-shouldered figure had appeared on the rim of the pit. It was Daisuké. He jumped down, keeping his eyes fixed on Lord Mizuno as intently as if he was stalking a deer. 'But not any

633

more,' he said firmly. 'Things have changed. The shogun's gone. There is no palace, no shogun, no shogun's police. You have nothing to fear.'

He was so close Sachi could smell the scent of tobacco mixed with the faint odour of southern spices he always carried with him. She looked at his broad, handsome face, slightly saggy around the eyes and jowly around the chin. She could see the pores on his nose, the thick black hairs of his eyebrows, the hair bristling on his upper lip. If only she didn't take her eyes off this face she would be safe.

There was another scent too. Shinzaemon was there, hidden just behind Mizuno. She was so close to freedom, so close to safety.

'Who are you?' demanded Mizuno, his voice shrill with suspicion. His grip tightened and Sachi felt the blade pressing into her throat. 'Who are you, interfering with my family? This is a private matter. Who are you, poking your nose into our family business?'

'This is not Ohiro,' said Daisuké in firm, clear tones. 'This is not your sister. Your sister died a long time ago.'

'Who are you?' screeched Lord Mizuno again.

Daisuké's face hardened. 'Let her go,' he snapped. 'This is your sister's child. Your niece. You have no reason to hurt her.'

'You're lying,' shouted Lord Mizuno. 'I know my own sister.'

'It's true,' barked Daisuké. 'She's my daughter. My daughter. I'm her father.'

Lord Mizuno gave a hoarse gasp. Suddenly the arm gripping Sachi was gone. He shoved her aside and she staggered forward and fell.

She heard Lord Mizuno screech, 'You!' It was more like the savage yowl of an animal than a human voice.

Then there was a scuffling of feet. Sachi looked up, dazed. She caught a glimpse of an arm raised and a blade flashing. The dagger was descending towards Daisuké's throat when Haru lunged between them, snatching at Mizuno's arm. The blow hit her full in the chest, just below her left shoulder. As she fell back, Mizuno wrenched the dagger out. Blood spurted from the wound. Sachi felt the hot drops sting her face.

'Haru!' she shrieked.

There was a noise from above them. Shinzaemon was on the rim of the pit, directly above Mizuno. Edwards was beside him, his golden hair gleaming in the sun, Taki's thin frightened face peeking from behind. There was a click as Shinzaemon cocked his pistol.

'Shin, no!' yelled Daisuké.

Mizuno had lowered his arm. He was staring at Haru, his eyes wide and his mouth open, panting noisily, gasping for breath.

Blood was pumping from the wound in Haru's chest. Sachi sprang to her side. She had forgotten her ordeal, forgotten the mud and filth that covered her, forgotten everything except Haru. She knelt beside her, took her hands and rubbed them, cradled her head in her lap.

'Haru, Haru!' she said. Haru was wheezing painfully. Sachi could see her life draining away. 'Haru, don't die, you mustn't die. I need you.'

Mizuno fell to his knees. The wild gleam had

635

gone from his eyes. He looked bewildered, as if he'd woken from a nightmare. Then, his face to the ground, he crumpled up, his bony shoulders heaving.

'My lady,' breathed Haru. Her voice was no more than a whisper. Each word seemed to emerge painfully. 'My lady Ohiro. Tell us... Where is she? Please ... tell us, and I can die in peace.'

Lord Mizuno looked up. Tears ran down his face, cutting pale furrows across his dirt-encrusted cheeks. He swabbed at his face with his hand.

'The big old plum tree in the grounds,' he said, 'where we used to play hide-and-seek when we first went to Edo. She's there. I buried her there.'

Haru moved her lips. Her face was turning blue. Blood trickled from the corner of her mouth. There was silence, only the rustling of the grass and the cawing of the birds and Haru's wheezing as she gasped for breath.

Daisuké took Haru's hand and Sachi saw her face change. The years seemed to fall away. It was the face of a young woman, her mother's faithful and devoted maid, who had been a friend and mentor – almost a mother – to her too. Haru's eyes were fixed on Daisuké. Sachi realized with a pang how much he had meant to her all these years. He was bent over with his face close to hers, holding her hand in both of his.

'We're going back to Edo, Haru,' he whispered. 'We're going to find your mistress, Lady Ohiro – you and I.'

Sachi stroked Haru's forehead, trying to hold back her own tears. Haru looked peaceful. Her eyes flickered towards Sachi. Sachi knew that when she looked at her she saw her mother. Sachi's face was the last thing Haru saw as her eyes closed.

They all knelt, stunned into silence. Taki was on her knees weeping at the edge of the pit. Shinzaemon and Edwards were next to her. Lord Mizuno was bowed over with his face to the ground. Everyone was frozen, mourning.

Daisuké shook his head. 'She did it for me,' he muttered. 'That blow was meant for me.'

He turned to Lord Mizuno.

'Enough killing,' he said. His voice was dull. 'Let's go back to Edo and pray at your sister's grave.'

Mizuno raised his head and sat up slowly and deliberately.

'There's one job left,' he muttered. He raised his dagger. For a moment Sachi thought he was going to cut open his own belly. But he turned towards Daisuké.

'Adulterer!' he hissed. 'It was you – you that caused all the trouble. You destroyed our family. You killed my sister.'

Sachi stared at him, realizing, too late, that he had no choice. He had to do his duty. According to the laws of the old world of which Lord Mizuno was a part, Daisuké was a criminal. Adultery was a crime punishable by death.

Daisuké drew back, his eyes widening. Sachi looked at him. There was a luminous look on his face. His eyes were strangely bright. She could see that he was thinking of her mother. He had found the answer to the question which had

637

tormented him his whole life. He knew now where she was, knew she was dead. Without her, for him the world was an empty place and he was happy to join her. There was a faint smile on his lips. He didn't move or fight or try to escape, he simply waited.

The two of them watched, mesmerized, as the knife flashed down.

But before the blade could reach Daisuké's throat there was an explosion so loud that Sachi started and fell back. A cloud of choking smoke hung over the pit, permeated with a strange acrid smell. She knew the smell. Gunpowder. For a moment she was dazed by the noise. Her ears ringing, she looked around. Lord Mizuno had fallen back against the wall of the pit. His dark pockmarked face was as fearsome as ever and he seemed to be staring blankly towards her, but his head was lolling. The dagger had fallen from his hand. Blood bubbled at his lips and spurted from his scrawny sunburned chest.

'Forgive me,' said Shinzaemon. He looked like a giant, looming above them at the edge of the pit. His pistol was in his hand and smoke coiled from the barrel. 'I only meant to wound him. But he was too close to you. I couldn't risk it.'

Daisuké looked up. His broad handsome face was drained of colour.

'I thought my life was going to end. But it didn't. Not today. That wasn't my destiny. I'm indebted to you.' He bowed his head.

Sachi tried to stand up and realized she was trembling so much she couldn't. She was vaguely aware of Shinzaemon jumping into the pit, picking her up very gently and lifting her out. As she let her head rest on his shoulder, she realized she was safe at last.

Epilogue: The Last Secret

Tokyo, 14 October 1872

'Today everything has to be perfect,' said Taki, sliding open the drawers of the cosmetic box and laying out brushes, tweezers, combs and jars of make-up on a square of silk on the floor. The box was one of the few things Sachi had managed to bring with her from the palace. Even the handle of the slenderest brush was of finest lacquerware, marked with a tiny Tokugawa crest in gold. Every item was imbued with the faint but unmistakable fragrance of those far-off days.

Taki slipped out of the room with a swish of her kimono skirts and returned with the small iron kettle of tooth-dyeing liquid. The bitter smell of iron, vinegar and sumac-leaf gall suffused the room. She knelt in front of Sachi.

Sachi looked at her thin pale face, her big, rather startled eyes and pointed chin. Taki was still as sharp-boned and prickly as ever, a samurai through and through. Sometimes when she thought Sachi wasn't around the placid expression she worked so hard to maintain would fade. Sachi suspected she thought of Toranosuké.

Neither he nor Tatsuemon had ever reappeared. Just that year there had been an amnesty and all the stubborn northern warriors had been pardoned. Even Admiral Enomoto, who had fled north with the Tokugawa fleet, now had an important job in the government. If Toranosuké and Tatsuemon were going to return it would surely be now. But no one knew what had happened to them. They might have stayed in Ezo; they might have gone back to Kano; or they might have died. Sachi knew that many people had never come back from the war and no one ever discovered what had become of them.

She also knew that Shinzaemon was determined to find out. He was not going to stay in Tokyo for ever, being a bureaucrat. He would be off again soon enough in search of adventure. She would never try to quench that fiery spirit of his.

For, despite everything, they were still together. Sometimes Sachi looked back over the years and thought how fortunate they had been.

After Haru's death, they had come straight back to Tokyo. The mansions of the defeated lords were all being turned into government ministries or accommodation for leading political figures and shortly after they got back Daisuké was granted the Mizuno lands. They buried Haru next to Sachi's mother, under the great plum tree in the grounds.

They left the old man who had guided them up the mountain to bury Lord Mizuno and to carry on digging the pit in the moorland; he seemed to be sure he would find gold there. Edwards too seemed fascinated by the Tokugawa gold and stayed a few days longer on the mountain after Sachi, Daisuké and the others left. But it wasn't the gold he was interested in; it was obvious he had finally realized that Shinzaemon was far more to Sachi than a friend or a brother and that he had no chance of a liaison with her, let alone marriage. Sachi was glad. She knew very well where her heart belonged, where it had always belonged since the day she'd first seen Shinzaemon when she was fleeing from the palace.

But she also knew that as a woman she had no say over what happened in her life, no matter what her personal feelings might be. A new government had been installed and new laws were being worked out, but it made no change to something as fundamental as that. It was obvious that Daisuké needed an heir, needed to adopt a son. Sachi was afraid that once they had settled down he would call on the services of a go-between to arrange meetings for her with prospective candidates. Many ambitious young men who had fought on the southern side would be eager to be taken on as her husband and her father's successor.

One day not long after Haru's funeral Sachi was sitting with her father in the great hall. Daisuké was smoking quietly. He looked at her from under his bushy eyebrows and said suddenly, 'My dear daughter, I didn't seek you out in order to make you unhappy.' It was as if he had read her mind.

'Your mother chose me and I chose her,' he continued. 'I have no intention of forcing you to marry anyone you don't care about. It's obvious

641

to me that you care for Shinzaemon and he for you. The war is over, he is a brilliant young man and I owe my life to him. If I am right, I am happy to take him as my adopted son.'

They were married shortly afterwards. Sachi smiled as she remembered their wedding day. She had been dressed in beautiful robes and carried through the streets in a wedding palanquin, surrounded by bridesmaids and preceded by retainers carrying lanterns, boxes and a spear, before the week-long ceremonies began. Daisuké had insisted on arranging palanquins to bring Jiroemon, Otama, Yuki and the children from the village in the Kiso valley and Shinzaemon's relatives had come up from Kano for the occasion. His stern father and sweet-faced mother seemed delighted to be in an alliance with Daisuké, a powerful member of the new government, and relieved that their rebellious second son had become respectable at last. Shinzaemon had taken Daisuké's family name and he and Sachi settled down to their new life together. They adopted Yuki and kept her with them when the rest of the family went back to the village.

Taki was frowning in concentration. Both women loved this daily ritual when they could forget everything else and concentrate on this small but important task. First she tweezed out Sachi's eyebrows. Next she blacked her teeth, applied her make-up, painting her face white, and smudged in moths' wings high on her forehead. Then she combed her long black hair over and over again till it gleamed. It cascaded down her back in a luxuriant mane. Taki swept it back, not into the usual matronly *marumage* style but into a long tail, loosely bound with ribbons here and there, such as she used to wear at the palace. Finally she painted in her lips in red.

There was a scrabbling at the door and little Daisuké scampered in. Clambering on to Sachi's lap, he put his arms around her neck.

'Me too! I'm coming too!' he yelled.

'Not today, Daisuké,' said Sachi, laughing and giving him a cuddle. He started rummaging among the brushes and combs and jars of make-up. He was going to be as handsome as his grandfather, she could see that already. The same broad open face, the same big black eyes. He had the same curiosity too, the same energy and determination.

Taki had brought out some of the formal robes Sachi had had as part of the princess's retinue. It was years since she had worn them. Taki helped her into the heavy robes one after another and arranged the different-coloured layers so that they were perfectly aligned at the collar and cuffs. Then she handed her her ceremonial fan.

Sachi stared at herself in the mirror. A shiver ran down her spine. She saw a woman dressed in the archaic robes of the shogun's concubine – a woman with a pale oval face, eyes set wide apart, slanting at the corners, a small mouth with full lips and an aristocratically arched nose. It was a long time since she had looked in the mirror and seen not herself but her mother. She was twenty-two, she realized, the very age Okoto had been when she met Sachi's father.

643

Her reflection glimmered back at her. She was not sure who she saw hovering before her, whether it was the Retired Lady Shoko-in, widowed concubine of His late Majesty the fourteenth shogun, or the Lady Okoto, concubine to the twelfth shogun, Lord Ieyoshi. She had thought she had laid the past to rest, but it came to life again so easily. She had only to put on these robes.

'Shinzaemon won't recognize me,' she murmured uneasily. She had never told him about her life in the women's palace. All the women had promised on pain of death never to reveal anything about their life there. It was part of that old world of shadows and darkness, where everyone was suspicious of everyone else and everyone had secrets. Shinzaemon knew that world too and respected it and had never asked anything about her past. But today he was to meet the princess. Today the door would open a crack. Sachi wondered how he would feel, whether it would change his feelings towards her.

Shinzaemon was waiting with Daisuké at the entrance. His broad face with the shapely cheekbones and slanting cat's eyes was as dramatic as ever, but the look of untamed warrior ferocity had been replaced by a fierce intelligent determination. It reassured Sachi to see him. He didn't live in a world of ghosts and spirits, didn't live in the past. He had wholeheartedly embraced the present.

He was formally dressed in starched *hakama* trousers and *haori* jacket, nattily combined with European boots, a bowler hat and an umbrella in the modern style. With his short haircut, cropped *jangiri*-style, he was the very picture of the modern young man. There was a ditty people hummed: 'Tap a head with a topknot and you hear the sound of the past; thump a *jangiri* head and it sings out "civilization and enlightenment".' These days 'civilization and enlightenment' was what everyone talked about. Sachi wasn't at all sure what the phrase meant. But she was certain that Shinzaemon was the very embodiment of it.

Daisuké too was dressed in the modern style. He had stepped into the background a little, allowing Shinzaemon to take over some of his governmental duties. He had grown a little greyer around the temples, but he was still the fine handsome man whom Lady Okoto had risked everything to be with.

Sachi could see the two men looking at her and Taki as they came towards them in their formal court dress, moving very slowly, swishing along in their full trousers with the quilted hems of their kimonos fanning out behind them. She knew that Shinzaemon had never seen them in court dress before; they had never worn it outside the palace. He said nothing, simply nodded.

Daisuké had turned pale. He was looking at her with a haunted look she had not seen since the time they had come down from the mountain. She realized that she was dressed exactly as her mother must have been when she had met Daisuké for their assignations at the temple. It was as if Lady Okoto had come back from the grave.

Before they left they walked through the grounds to her mother's and Haru's graves. Sachi put fresh flowers in the vases and murmured a sutra. She thought of them with tears in her eyes. It was good to be living on the Mizuno estate, where her mother had lived when she was in Edo. Daisuké had made a good decision when he had asked for the house; it felt right to be there.

Shinzaemon and Daisuké set off in a carriage with Sachi and Taki following behind in another. The old man was at the gate and bowed as they drove through. The sight of his kindly weather-beaten old face, broad grin and bandy legs always made Sachi smile. He was a link with the past. He had taken care of them at the palace and at the Shimizu mansion. When the Shimizus had been forced to leave, Sachi had brought him with her to her new house. Now he took care of them here, although he was so old and frail that it was really they who took care of him.

There were rickshaws everywhere: *jin-riki-sha*, 'human-powered wheel'. They seemed to have sprung up overnight like mushrooms. Now they rattled and clattered around the streets, pulled by scrawny tattooed fellows who raced along, yelling at the tops of their voices, warning people to get out of the way. Sachi remembered how thrilled she had been the first time she had ridden in Edwards's carriage. These days she was always bowling around at breakneck speed. The streets were packed with wheeled vehicles – carriages, horse-drawn omnibuses, two-wheeled rickshaws, four-wheeled rickshaws. They could hardly move for the traffic whizzing in every direction, which, Sachi thought, was surely a sign of civilization and enlightenment. Another was the foreigners

646

who had appeared en masse and were busily changing the face of the city. They had already built a tall building with a flashing light in the harbour, called a 'lighthouse', and installed a telegraph, just as Edwards had predicted when he told them about the 'magic messages'.

Daisuké was looking around, beaming. He had seen it all coming. He loved being at the forefront of change, helping to plan and build the new Japan. Sachi felt a burst of pride in this father of hers.

Crowds of people were heading in the same direction as Sachi, Daisuké and their party. Everyone was splendidly dressed, as they had been when they had gone to see the emperor's grand entry into Tokyo. Then, everyone had looked nervous and resentful, as if they had no idea what the future held and didn't like having this new government thrust upon them. All they had been able to see was doors closing, the end of something. It had never occurred to them those doors might be about to open on to a brand-new world, more different than they could ever have imagined.

Now the crowds were cheerful and festive-looking. The women dressed as they always had but the men sported European boots or hats or overcoats as well as their usual robes and there were plenty of *jangiri* haircuts dotted among the old-fashioned shaved pates. Sachi wondered if Fuyu was out there somewhere. She hadn't seen her since the day they'd stood together watching the emperor enter the castle. Those palace

647

women – all three thousand – seemed to have vanished entirely.

Everyone was moving towards one of the wonderful gleaming new western-style buildings that Daisuké loved so much. It was actually two buildings of white stone, like the twin guard towers of a castle, decked inside and out with flags and coloured lanterns as if for a festival. Officials escorted Daisuké, Shinzaemon, Sachi and Taki inside. Sachi gazed around at the spacious, airy building, feeling rather cowed. On the far side was an open, roofed corridor, rather like the covered arcades that had led from one building to another in the palace or a huge version of the *hanamichi*, the 'flower road' on which actors walked through the audience in a kabuki theatre. It led through the middle of a perfectly smooth, perfectly flat expanse of ground.

And there, standing out in the open on the smooth iron road it would travel on, was a massive iron monster. As she looked at it, Sachi had to blink back tears as she thought of how proud and thrilled Haru would have been to see it. It was huge and black, exactly as Haru had described it all those years before. It towered above them, casting a vast shadow, like nothing they'd ever seen before, and puffed out smoke, making a lot of noise.

They walked round it, looking at the massive wheels and the great rods that connected them, then stepped back and gazed up at the mighty funnel. Timidly they went up the steps of one of the huge boxes that people were to travel in and peeped inside. Sachi had never imagined anything could be so big. It was like a small town in there, as big as a whole street of houses. Every now and then there was a loud shriek and smoke puffed from the funnel.

The dignitaries gathered there were almost entirely men. Only women of rank, with a special relationship to the emperor, had been invited. Many of the dignitaries were foreigners.

Edwards strode over to greet them. He had grown more serious since their ill-fated journey up the mountain and was no longer as carefree and boyish as he used to be. His hair no longer shone like gold, there were lines on his face and his eyes were a little faded although they were still the colour of the sky on a fine day. They smiled and bowed. Edwards enquired after Sachi's son, little Daisuké, and Sachi enquired after Dr Willis. They reminisced for a while.

'So did anyone ever find the Tokugawa gold?' Edwards asked in his direct way. In all these years it was the first time anyone had brought up that harrowing memory.

'I think we'd have heard if someone did. I expect the old man from Lord Oguri's village is still up there, digging,' said Daisuké. He smiled rather sadly.

'I could never understand why Lord Mizuno didn't know where it was,' said Shinzaemon. 'Didn't the old man tell you anything when you stayed up there with him, after we'd left?'

'Apparently Lord Oguri and Lord Mizuno had an argument,' said Edwards. 'Someone in the village heard raised voices. That was how the rumours started about the gold. The old man

649

thinks Lord Oguri tricked Lord Mizuno. He found a pretext to send him away somewhere and got rid of the gold before he returned. The old man's convinced that Lord Mizuno must have had some idea where it was buried. It must be somewhere on that moor. The trouble is, the gold was buried in spring and by summer the whole place had grown over. There's nothing to distinguish one spot from another. The grass goes on for ever.'

Sachi shivered, remembering the pit. She thought wistfully of Haru. She had been the custodian of their story, entwined with their destinies even before Sachi was born, ever since she was a child, growing up with Sachi's mother. She had guarded her secret until she could guard it no longer. And finally it had brought her face to face with Lord Mizuno. Tears came to Sachi's eyes at the thought that she was no longer there to share these wonderful new experiences with them.

Yet she also understood that her uncle, Lord Mizuno, had had to do what he did. That was how it had always been in the old days. Everyone had known what they had to do and had done it, no matter what, without stopping to think about whether they wanted to do it or whether it was even the right thing to do. They had done their duty.

That was what made Shinzaemon and Daisuké different, and Sachi too. They thought for themselves.

Sachi looked around. On the far side of the crowd, standing apart from everyone else, was a group of women. They were dressed as Sachi and Taki were, as ladies of the court. As Sachi looked, she no longer heard the metallic shrieking of the whistle or the mechanical huffing and puffing of the great engine. In the middle of the group was a small thin woman, her glossy black hair cut short like a widow or a nun. She stood so quietly no one would ever have noticed her. Her eyes were lowered and she was looking at the ground as if she had retreated so deep inside herself it was painful to have to come out. In the whole crowd Sachi could see nothing but her small pale face with its big ethereal eyes. She forgot everything but that special love she always felt for the princess.

A gentle smile crossed Kazu's face when she saw Sachi.

'Child,' she said. 'The Retired Lady Shoko-in. It's been so long. You have bloomed like a flower!'

She greeted Taki too with joy.

'I spend most of my time in prayer and contemplation,' she said when they asked her how she was. 'But my nephew the emperor begged me to come out this one time. His Majesty has been very kind to me. He begged me many times to go back to Kyoto and I did go back once for a visit. But now His Majesty has established his court in Tokyo I have moved back here. My life is very quiet. The Shimizu family take care of me still and I write poetry and think. It is a good life.'

Sachi was aware of nothing but the luminous presence of the princess. Standing there in their court robes it was as if time had stood still, as if they were still in the palace.

'And Haru?' the princess asked suddenly, looking around. When Sachi told her that Haru had passed away, she stood in silence for a long while, her head bent and her hand to her eyes.

Suddenly Sachi was aware of Shinzaemon watching with his piercing eyes and felt a tremor of fear. What would the princess think when she discovered Sachi had made an alliance with another man instead of spending the rest of her life devoting herself to the memory of the shogun, as she herself had done? Would she not think that Sachi was bound – by honour, if nothing else – to the Tokugawa clan? This was certainly the choice the princess had made.

Trembling, Sachi introduced Shinzaemon. 'My husband,' she said. 'He fought loyally for the Tokugawas to the very last.'

The princess didn't seem to hesitate.

'Welcome,' she said. 'I am very happy to meet you. Lady Shoko-in has been a devoted friend and sister to me for many years. It is a bond that can never be broken – I as the wife, she as the concubine of the shogun. Had things gone differently, she would have been one of the highest ladies in the land. We are bound for ever to the Tokugawas.

'We may be relics of a past age, but we are also survivors. We have all found a place for ourselves in this new world. I'm happy to give my blessing to your union.' The princess inclined her head formally to Shinzaemon.

It was the last secret, the last mystery. Now Shinzaemon knew that Sachi had been not just a court lady but the last concubine of the shoguns.

The last veil between them had been lifted. In the old days he, a *ronin* from Kano, and she, the shogun's concubine, could never have been together. They had succeeded where her parents had failed and had managed to grasp the life they wanted.

To Sachi's relief Shinzaemon did no more than nod quietly. He looked at her and smiled. In his eyes she read pride, admiration and affection. No, more than that. There had been a word that Edwards had taught her all those years ago when he had taken her hand in the garden. It was not affection, like a man feels for his parents, he had said, or respect, like a man feels for his wife, or even lust, like a man feels for a courtesan, but more than all those put together. She remembered the strange foreign syllables: *rabu* – 'love'. That was the only word to express it. In his eyes she saw love.

A man had arrived in an open carriage, surrounded by a huge escort. Sachi knew that it was the same person who had been inside the phoenix car which they had watched enter the castle in grand procession. At that time they had thought they would die if they so much as looked at him. Timidly Sachi glanced up just for a moment. He was in scarlet court trousers, white robes and European boots and was very young – the very age His Majesty the shogun had been when she had known him. She quickly lowered her eyes.

The princess stepped forward. They exchanged a few words, then she beckoned to Sachi. An extraordinary fragrance such as Sachi had never smelt before floated around the young man – the legendary imperial fragrance.

'The Retired Lady Shoko-in, only concubine of his Late Majesty Lord Iemochi,' said the princess, introducing her. 'She has been my devoted friend and sister, a comfort to me for many years.'

Sachi bowed low.

'Ah, Lord Iemochi,' said the emperor. He had a youthful piping voice and spoke the special language that only the emperor spoke. 'I remember him well,' he said. 'A very gentle man. So tragic that he died so young. My late father was very fond of him. We've had so much loss, so much tragedy. It's good that we now go forward together. I'm very happy to meet you, my lady.'

Then the emperor moved on. He made a speech as smoke poured from the engine, then he and a few other dignitaries got on board. Sachi, Shinzaemon, Daisuké and Taki watched as the princess disappeared inside.

The whistle shrieked, the huge wheels started to move, at first very slowly then faster and faster. The train rumbled off and disappeared into the distance.

Afterword

During my research for *The Last Concubine,* I came across a reference to the lost Tokugawa gold, in a footnote in a history of the Mitsui company. Apparently Lord. Oguri had smuggled the shogun's hoard of gold coins out of Edo when Lord Yoshinobu was still in power and buried it somewhere in the foothills of Mount Akagi. He was beheaded shortly afterwards and all trace of it disappeared. The author added that treasure hunters had been digging for it for three generations, riddling the lower slopes of Mount Akagi with tunnels and trenches.

Tantalizing though it was, that was the only reference to the gold I could find in any of the many books I researched, so in the end I concluded it was just a rumour. Nevertheless the idea of the gold and the hopeless quest for it had stirred my imagination.

When I was nearing the end of writing this book I decided to go to Mount Akagi. I didn't expect to hear anything about the gold; I just wanted to get an idea of the place and the landscape. Mount Akagi is way off the beaten track, not in any English-language guidebook, but I finally found the address of a hotspring inn. I took the bullet train to Takasaki, then drove up a long winding mountain road.

Once there I decided I might as well ask the owner of the inn about the Tokugawa gold, absurd though it seemed. To my amazement he was not remotely surprised. 'It's not here,' he said in very matter-of-fact tones. 'It's on the other side of the mountain.' He showed me a map. The next day, I set off through the rain in search of it. Thoroughly lost, I asked in a lonely store and was directed through the woods and across some allotments to a dilapidated house. Next to it was a hummocky expanse of overgrown woodland with a mechanical digger in the middle. I ended up having tea with a man whose family has indeed been digging for the gold for three generations. His account of how the gold got to Mount Akagi is different from my fictional version but nevertheless I was thrilled to discover that the Tokugawa gold might actually exist – though no one has found it yet – and so it became part of my tale.

Sachi and her story are fiction but the world in which she lived is not. I've done my best to make the historical framework as accurate as possible (though I have taken the odd liberty in the interests of telling a good story). The battles, political events and even the weather (miserably cold and wet in summer 1868) were pretty much as described. The individual shoguns (who in books on Japanese history are usually referred to only as 'the shogun') really existed and the details of their stories are largely true. Princess Kazu really was sent to marry Shogun Iemochi when she was only fifteen and took the Inner Mountain Road through the Kiso region to Edo, to live in Edo Castle.

Very little is known about life inside the women's palace. It was kept strictly secret and those who lived there were prohibited from speaking about it. After it was dismantled a few maids recorded their recollections. I have used these in imagining life there. The stories of intrigue and murder are all true, the names of the concubines – old Lady Honju-in and the others – all as they were. Princess Kazu really did insist on dressing in the imperial style, feuded with her mother-in-law, Lady Tensho-in (the Retired One), and after the women were evicted from the palace moved to the Shimizu mansion. Before the shogun set off on his last journey to Kyoto, she gave him a farewell gift: a concubine. After his death she remained a nun and died of beri-beri in 1877, at the age of thirty-one.

Lady Okoto too, Sachi's mother, really existed and the story of her liaison with the handsome carpenter is largely true. She was a member of the Mizuno family and the last and favourite concubine of the twelfth shogun, Lord Ieyoshi. We don't know the name of her lover (he was not a carpenter, in fact, but a carpenter's agent, a sort of building contractor); but we do know that he looked just like the ravishingly handsome kabuki actor Sojiro Sawamura. Her brother's machinations to get her into the shogun's palace and her sad end too are true. I made a couple of changes. The events actually happened in 1855, after Lord Ieyoshi was dead, not 1850; and there's no record that she had a child.

Japan in the 1860s was an extraordinary place. No one knew their world was about to change, not gradually, as ours did in the Victorian West, but overnight. Everyone assumed that life as they knew it would go on for ever. It was a world in which scent played a large part and wheeled vehicles were used only to transport goods; people walked or travelled by palanquin. Gunpowder was little used, samurai fought with swords and samurai women were trained in the halberd. I researched the clothes, the hairstyles, the incense, how people lived and, as far as possible, how they thought and felt. I've also kept to the Japanese calendar of the time and used the Japanese clock and Japanese distances.

Women's lives were very different from our own. High-class women seldom left the home and were expected to maintain an impassive demeanour at all times, no matter what dreadful calamity befell them. This was a society in which the concept of love and the word for it had yet to be introduced from the West. When people fell in love, the experience took them by surprise. To be so overwhelmed by brute passion that one failed to do one's duty was a disaster. Kabuki plays and Japanese novels on the subject end not with marriage but with love suicide. There was also no word for 'kiss'. The kiss was one of the geishas' esoteric sexual techniques and decent women like Sachi didn't know anything about it. It was a challenge to write a love story set in a society in which there was no concept of romantic love – and without ever using the word 'love'!

Not long after it became the Imperial Palace in Tokyo, Edo Castle was razed to the ground. Where the women's palace used to be is now the Imperial Palace East Gardens; the expanse of the gardens gives some idea of how vast the palace must have been. The Gate of the Shoguns' Ladies with its massive guardhouse – officially known as the Hirakawa Gate – is still there, as is the outer gate of the Shimizu mansion. At Himeji Castle, west of Osaka, the women's quarters still exist, though much smaller than in Edo Castle. The Tokyo National Museum on Ueno Hill is on the site of what was once Kanei-ji Temple. In Tokyo I paid my respects at Zojoji Temple where Lord Iemochi is buried alongside Princess Kazu. There is a life-size statue of Princess Kazu there. I also reacquainted myself with the Inner Mountain Road (the Nakasendo) and the villages of Tsumago and Magome, on which Sachi's village is modelled. As for Kano, that is the old name of Gifu, where I lived for the first two years I was in Japan; though the treacherous behaviour of the daimyo of Kano is pure fiction.

History is always written by the winners and never more so than in the case of the civil war that culminated in 1868 with the so-called Meiji Restoration. It is often described as a 'bloodless' revolution; as readers of this book know, it certainly wasn't bloodless. I tried to imagine how it must have been to be one of the hundreds of thousands of people on the losing side, and most especially what happened to the women of Edo Castle after the women's palace was disbanded.

The history of the time – the plots and counter-plots and secret alliances – is labyrinthine. People living through it would have had little idea of what was going on outside their own small world. I've simplified it and tried to show it as it must have seemed to Sachi. I've lumped the Satsuma, Choshu, Tosa and their burgeoning band of allies together and called them 'the southerners', which makes geographical sense and, funnily enough, is exactly as *The Japan Times' Overland Mail* and other contemporary western observers referred to them.

In the period in which this book takes place Japan had just begun to open up to the West. The Victorians who visited were well aware that they were seeing an extraordinary world – and one that was on the brink of disappearing. Many of them wrote diaries and books which I read with great envy. Some are listed below. For me, writing *The Last Concubine* has been the latest chapter in a very long love affair with Japan. Everyone who goes there wishes they could have experienced the old Japan – that magical, fragile world which has gone for ever. Writing this book has given me the chance to imagine myself there and to take my readers with me.

Acknowledgements

This book would not exist were it not for my agent, Bill Hamilton. Bill insisted I embark on the project and has been a part of it all the way through, offering wise advice and support. Huge thanks also to Sara Fisher, Corinne Chabert and everyone at A.M. Heath.

I've been very fortunate in being able to work with Selina Walker at Transworld. Selina did a great deal to shape this book and keep me pointed in the right direction. I'm much indebted to her and to all her team, including Deborah Adams and Claire Ward, who have been full of support, enthusiasm and patience when required.

Thanks to Kimiko Shiga, who deciphered the archaic Japanese of Takayanagi Kaneyoshi's *Life in the Women's Palace at Edo Castle*. Gaye Rowley and Thomas Harper were in on this project from the beginning and shared their extensive knowledge of Japan and of the Edo period, Tom's speciality. Colin Young – one of only three teachers of the Shodai Ryu school of swordsmanship outside Japan – provided much esoteric information and gave me the chance to wield a real Japanese sword, a thrilling experience. Thanks to all of these for casting a critical eye over the manuscript and making many invaluable suggestions, and also to Louise Longdin and Ian Eagles. Thanks too to the teachers and students of the London Naginata Association, where I learned how to handle a practice stick and watched competition-level *naginata* (halberd) duels. Yoko Chiba and John Maisonneuve (another swordsman) also provided information about the halberd.

The translations are my own. I have based my description of Sachi's mother's overkimono on a beautiful early-nineteenth-century *katabira* in the Tokyo National Museum, which features a landscape with a pavilion, a gate, a rope curtain and a nobleman's cart (TNM Image Archives Source: http//TNMArchives.jp).

I owe a debt to all the Japan historians whose work I've drawn on to write this book (though all mistakes, misinterpretations and liberties with the facts are my own). Some are listed below; there are many more. Professors Donald Keene and Timon Screech kindly shared their expertise. Professor Conrad Totman's wonderful books on the last years of the Tokugawa Bakufu, together with Professor M. William Steele's analyses of 1868 Edo, provided the factual underpinning of my story. I enjoyed a lengthy and entertaining email exchange with Dr Takayuki Yokota-Murakami of the University of Osaka on love and sex in old Japan. The information on dried lizard powder is from him. His book listed below, despite the daunting subtitle, is fascinating reading.

Last but most important of all is my husband, Arthur, without whose love and support I couldn't possibly have written this book. He gave me the leisure to indulge in fiction, read and commented on each draft and, as an expert on military history, made sure I got the rifles and cannons right. He has shared Sachi's world with me. We walked the Inner Mountain Road together, strolled around Edo Castle, and went to Himeji Castle and to Zojoji Temple to see Princess Kazu's tomb. At this point he is something of an expert on Edo-period Japan and can even recognize the Tokugawa crest – an ability few can claim!

This book is dedicated to him.

Select Bibliography

There are an enormous number of wonderful books on the Edo period. Below are just a few that I have found particularly inspiring.

Biographies of Edo-period samurai, novels and other books that make the period come alive:

Bolitho, Harold, *Bereavement and Consolation: Testimonies from Tokugawa Japan,* Yale University Press, 2003

Katsu Kokichi, *Musui's Story: The Autobiography of a Tokugawa Samurai,* translated with an introduction and notes by Teruko Craig, University of Arizona Press, 1988

McClellan, Edwin, *Woman in the Crested Kimono: The Life of Shibue Io and Her Family Drawn from Mori Ogai's 'Shibue Chusaki',* Yale University Press, 1985

Meech-Pekarik, Julia, *The World of the Meiji Print: Impressions of a New Civilization,* Weatherhill, 1987

Miyoshi Masao, *As We Saw Them: The First Japanese Embassy to the United States,* Kodansha International, 1994

Shiba Ryotaro, *The Last Shogun: The Life of Tokugawa Yoshinobu,* translated by Juliet Winters Carpenter, Kodansha International, 1998

Shimazaki Toson, *Before the Dawn,* translated

by William E. Naff, University of Hawaii Press, 1987

Walthall, Anne, *The Weak Body of a Useless Woman: Matsuo Taseko and the Meiji Restoration,* University of Chicago Press, 1998

Yamakawa Kikue, *Women of the Mito Domain: Recollections of Samurai Family Life,* translated with an introduction by Kate Wildman Nakai, Stanford University Press, 2001

Diaries of Victorian travellers:

Alcock, Rutherford, *The Capital of the Tycoon, volumes I and II,* Elibron Classics, 2005 (first published 1863)

Cortazzi, Hugh, *Mitford's Japan: Memories and Recollections 1866–1906,* Japan Library, 2002

Heusken, Henry, *Japan Journal: 1855–1861,* translated and edited by Jeannette C. van der Corput and Robert A. Wilson, Rutgers University Press, 1964

Notehelfer, F. G., *Japan through American Eyes: The Journal of Francis Hall,* Westview Press, 2001

Satow, Ernest, *A Diplomat in Japan: The Inner History of the Critical Years in the Evolution of Japan When the Ports were Opened and the Monarchy Restored,* Stone Bridge Press, 2006 (first published 1921)

Indispensable and well-loved works on literature and poetry:

Keene, Donald (ed.), *Anthology of Japanese Literature: to the nineteenth century,* Grove Press,

1955; Penguin Books, 1968

Miner, Earl, *An Introduction to Japanese Court Poetry,* Stanford University Press, 1968

Waley, Arthur, *The No Plays of Japan,* George Allen and Unwin, 1921; Charles E. Tuttle Company, 1976

Key academic works about the period:

Keene, Donald, *Emperor of Japan: Meiji and His World,* Columbia University Press, 2002

Roberts, John G., *Mitsui: Three Centuries of Japanese Business,* Weatherhill, 1973

Steele, M. William, 'Against the Restoration: Katsu Kaishu's Attempt to Reinstate the Tokugawa Family', in *Monumenta Nipponica,* xxxvi, 3, pp. 300–16

Steele, M. William, 'Edo in 1868: The View from Below', in *Monumenta Nipponica,* 45:2, pp. 127–55

Totman, Conrad, *Politics in the Tokugawa Bakufu, 1600–1843,* Harvard University Press, 1967

Totman, Conrad, *The Collapse of the Tokugawa Bakufu, 1862–1868,* University Press of Hawaii, 1980

Yokota-Murakami, Takayuki, *Don Juan East/West: On the Problematics of Comparative Literature,* State University of New York Press, 1998

The best book on the women's palace:

Takayanagi Kaneyoshi, *Edojo ooku no seikatsu (Life in the Women's Palace at Edo Castle),* Tokyo

Yuzankaku Shuppan, 1969

And a fantastic website on the Nakasendo, the Inner Mountain Road:
http://www.hku.hk/history/nakasendo/

The publishers hope that this book has given you enjoyable reading. Large Print Books are especially designed to be as easy to see and hold as possible. If you wish a complete list of our books please ask at your local library or write directly to:

Magna Large Print Books
Magna House, Long Preston,
Skipton, North Yorkshire.
BD23 4ND

This Large Print Book for the partially sighted, who cannot read normal print, is published under the auspices of

THE ULVERSCROFT FOUNDATION